Praise for Ed Ruggero's Previous Novels

Firefall

"*Firefall* by Ed Ruggero is REAL; it's the essence of warriors in combat; it portrays the thin line between coward and hero. *Firefall* captures a high-possibility scenario. Fiction or forecast, it's the total emotional roller coaster of WAR!"

—Richard Marcinko, coauthor of the #1 *New York Times* bestseller *Rogue Warrior*

"Ed Ruggero writes about men in combat like a soldier who's been there."

—John Harrington, *The Daily Oklahoman*

"Fast-paced. . . . memorable. . . . *Firefall* is thrilling for those who long to plunge themselves into the thick of battle."

—*Kirkus Reviews*

"Ed Ruggero takes you into the heart of the modern soldier and shows you what a hero truly is. His descriptions of the spirit of the fighting man are unsurpassed."

—Gerry Carroll, author of *North S*A*R** and *Ghostrider One*

"Ed Ruggero has a wonderful talent for rubbing two headlines together and starting a fictional bonfire. *Firefall* burns with excitement from beginning to end. . . . Ruggero gets better and better. . . . *Firefall* is a very hot read."

—Ralph Peters, *New York Times* bestselling author of *Red Army* and *The War in 2020*

Praise for
The Common Defense

"*The Common Defense* provides not only a lot of action—ambushes, raids, and a climactic running gunfight at the end—but a good look at how professional soldiers impart their skills to others, all of this against a frighteningly believable backdrop of political events that could very well constitute tomorrow's headlines.... The worst thing about *The Common Defense* is that it isn't long enough."

—Dan Cragg, *Washington Times*

"A fast-paced ... military thriller.... *The Common Defense* will be in heavy demand."

—Stanley Planton, *Library Journal*

"An engaging ... story of international suspense.... *The Common Defense* is action-packed. It raises good questions about the vulnerability of the United States to both terrorism and Mexican-based drug activity. And it offers plenty of rumination about the military's future in the new geopolitical scheme."

—Thomas J. Billiteri, *St. Petersburg Times*

"Effective.... convincing.... Ruggero demonstrates sound knowledge of the U.S. Army's inner dynamics...."

—*Publishers Weekly*

Praise for
38 North Yankee

"A dazzling first novel about men in combat."

—Tom Clancy

"A fast-paced military adventure in the modern idiom. Ruggero will keep you turning the pages."

—Stephen Coonts

"Ruggero has the heart of a real soldier; it shines through on every page. . . . He uses his fine writing talent and firsthand knowledge of life in the infantry to excellent advantage. *38 North Yankee* is an auspicious beginning. . . ."

—Dan Cragg, *Washington Times*

"The action is swift and sure. . . ."

—Bob Trimble, *The Dallas Morning News*

"Engrossing. . . . Depictions of battle—and all the confusion and horror that battle usually entails—are as skillfully written throughout as they are compelling to read."

—Steve Weingartner, *Booklist*

Other Novels by Ed Ruggero

Firefall
The Common Defense
38 North Yankee

Published by POCKET BOOKS

BREAKING RANKS

ED RUGGERO

POCKET BOOKS
New York · London · Toronto · Sydney · Tokyo · Singapore

This book is a work of fiction. Names, characters, places and incidents are products of the author's imagination or are used fictiously. Any resemblance to actual events or locales or persons, living or dead, is entirely coincidental.

POCKET BOOKS, a division of Simon & Schuster Inc.
1230 Avenue of the Americas, New York, NY 10020

ISBN: 0-671-89172-3

First Pocket Books paperback printing December 1996

10 9 8 7 6 5 4 3 2 1

POCKET and colophon are registered trademarks of
Simon & Schuster Inc.

Front cover illustration by Lee MacLeod

Printed in the U.S.A.

For Mom and Dad

I'm happy to acknowledge the help I received with this work, from the pinpoint suggestions to patient listening.

Thanks to Don and Jennifer, whose hospitality, generous aid and encouragement have been there for my asking. Thanks also to Sharan, and to Greg and Kendy, who helped me get a fresh look at a world I've left and often missed. Thanks to Howdie and Maggie, who gave me my first look at the Puzzle Palace.

And thanks to the dedicated men and women of the Eighty-second Airborne Division; America is fortunate to have such a "Guard of Honor."

My most sincere thanks goes to Paul McCarthy, who has undertaken my training with the same selflessness and patience I saw in my first platoon sergeant. As I get older, I see more clearly the debts I owe and the help I've received. I hope that, over the course of a career, I can give at least one-tenth of what I've received.

Thanks, Paul.

"All warfare is based on deception."

—*Sun Tzu*

1

THE BETTER PARTS OF MAJOR MARK ISEN—THE OFFICER-and-gentleman-by-decree part, the conservative-Protestant-by-upbringing part, the habitually circumspect part—thought it wildly inappropriate that funerals made him horny.

Well, not horny, exactly, he thought as he stepped blinking into the sunlight and the sultry heft of Washington summer outside Arlington Cemetery's Memorial Chapel.

Just glad to be alive, I guess, and one thought leads to another, and so on.

The "and so on" part in this instance, who'd been seated with the grieving family, wore a sleeveless black dress, loose enough to be appropriate for the occasion but tight enough for Isen to notice. Blond hair, pulled straight back and held with a simple gold clasp. She was up there now, milling about in quiet confusion as the family sorted itself out behind the long train of a full military funeral.

You have no life, Isen, he thought. *It's pretty bad when a funeral turns out to be the most interesting social engagement you've had in two months.*

Isen stepped aside the press of people leaving the chapel and pulled his garrison cap on a forehead already slick with perspiration. The blond woman was only a few yards away, but he couldn't get any closer unless he walked up and introduced himself. Under the circumstances, he couldn't rationalize that.

I should take out a personal ad, he thought. *"Divorced white male, thirty-five, going nowhere career-wise, seeks woman for companionship: dinner, dancing, movies, funerals."*

Isen glanced at the honor platoon from Washington's Old Guard, the Third Infantry Regiment stationed here at Fort Myer. The three ranks of soldiers in dark blue coats stood perfectly still out on the hot, black expanse of parking lot. The heat, rebounding in uncertain waves, made them shimmer. *Those guys have to be sucking wind,* he thought.

Behind the soldiers and at a distance, a young mother loaded two small children into a station wagon in the post exchange parking lot. Isen looked for his mentor, Major General Patrick Flynn, who would be somewhere behind the caisson where the flag-draped casket was being loaded.

"These things are always tough when it's a young person."

To Isen's right, a short, heavyset woman was speaking earnestly in a whisper. He nodded.

"I mean, it's sad if it's an older person, too, of course." She tucked her chin in slightly as she talked, giving little nods as if agreeing with her own pronouncements. "It's just that, well, at least the old ones have had a chance to live their lives."

"Yes, ma'am," Isen said, stepping away after a polite pause and deciding he was better off with his lascivious thoughts.

Isen saw Major General Flynn helping a younger woman who looked a great deal like him off the curb and onto the street behind the caisson. That would be Flynn's sister, the mother of the deceased.

Second Lieutenant Michael Hauck, United States Army, was about to participate in one of the most impressive and tradition-rich ceremonies the ritual-conscious Army had to offer: a full military funeral at Arlington National Cemetery. All of this—the honor guard across the road standing with rifles at rigid salute; the band in their red-piped blue coats; the team of six white horses and the corporal of the detail mounted ahead of the caisson, his black gloved hand raised in salute—all of this had been marshaled to honor a young officer who hadn't been in the Army long enough to wear out his first pair of GI socks. But Hauck, dead by his own hand a few short days ago, was going to miss the show.

This is for us, Isen thought. *The ones left behind, the ones who need to be reassured that we are all important.*

Flynn motioned to Isen, who tacked through the crowd as quietly as he could.

"Mark," Flynn said when Isen drew close, "I want you to walk with us." He was talking over his shoulder and had not let go of his sister's hand. Michael Hauck's mother stood staring at the back of the caisson, where the pallbearers, eight young soldiers who were—and she had to notice this—probably her son's age, were meticulously fastening the straps that would hold the flag in place when the caisson started moving.

"This is my niece," Flynn said, motioning to the young woman Isen had been studying. "My niece Marian. You walk with her."

"Yes, sir," Isen said.

Marian Flynn, even more attractive from this vantage point, smiled stoically at Isen as he stepped off the curb and offered his left arm.

"I'm Michael's cousin," Marian said, explaining, Isen thought, why she was in the procession.

"I'm sorry for your loss," Isen said. He tried to determine if his comment sounded canned—what everyone would say to the family today—but decided it would be just fine if he managed to keep his eyes off her shoulders and the tempting space that appeared between her arm and the front of her dress whenever she moved.

Get a grip, he told himself.

The funeral director's cars were not at hand. Apparently the family had decided to walk behind the cortege, the train made up of the platoon leader—a lieutenant in dress blues with saber—the small phalanx of an honor guard, the band, the caisson and its solemn cargo. Isen was a little surprised. He had driven through the cemetery on the way to the chapel and had noticed that the active sections, where current burials were ongoing, was at the bottom of a long slope to the northeast corner of the sprawling grounds. It would be a long walk in hot weather for the family. Isen looked down; Marian was wearing heels.

Over General Flynn's shoulder, Isen noticed that the commander of troops had finished his inspection of the caisson and all the straps and buckles meant to hold the casket firmly for its last ride. The captain, whom Isen could only see as a broad blue back, raised his hand in a slow salute, the white glove unhurried, as if he had all the time in the world to stand around in the heat and a dress uniform—jacket, tie, white shirt, black shoes, ceremonial belt, dark cap—as if time made no more difference to him than it did now to the young man in the box. Isen watched the sweat run out from below the man's cap, down the glistening sides of his shaved head and into the collar of his starched shirt. To Isen's right, the honor guard still held rifles at present arms, the perfect vertical lines of the slings punctuated by white gloves.

"ORDER . . . ARMS."

The platoon leader began to position his men for the long downhill walk to the gravesite. Isen felt, rather than saw, the ragged little procession of family members, into which he'd been drafted, shift and shudder into readiness.

"Why do they move so slowly?" Marian asked.

Isen inclined his head toward her but kept his eyes downcast.

"It's all part of the solemnity of the service," he said, wondering how he'd come up with "solemnity'" on short notice.

Her perfume is affecting my brain.

"Have you been to a lot of these?" she asked.

"No, not really," Isen said. "My dad was buried at a veteran's cemetery, and some guys from the local VFW came out, and some soldiers from Fort Benning, which was nearby. Nothing like this."

By "nothing like this" he meant none of these trappings, but there was more to it than that. There had been no family, just Isen and a few of his dad's friends. Isen, who had no brothers or sisters and who wasn't close to his small extended family, had wondered then who would come to his funeral.

The band was moving now, behind the platoon of soldiers, stepping off to the beat of a single stick on a drumhead's sharp rim. When the people in front of him moved—General Flynn, his sister, her husband—Isen automatically stepped off on his left foot.

Up ahead, the pallbearers marched alongside the caisson. Isen kept his eyes on the bright red, white and blue of the flag, watching the colors swing around against the backdrop of green, the thick trees off in the middle distance.

"Did you know my cousin?" Marian asked, a little louder now that the scraping and clopping of the horses' hooves was so distinct.

"No. I never met him," Isen said, looking at her briefly. "I used to work for your uncle. He asked me to accompany him."

"In case he needed an errand boy," she said.

Isen looked at her again to see if her expression matched her tone. It did.

"I'm sorry," she said, sounding tired. "My tolerance level for the Army is worn pretty thin right now."

"Present company excepted," Isen said.

"Yeah," she said, almost smiling. "Thanks for coming."

Isen thought she might have pressed his arm, but he wasn't sure.

As they moved past the end of the sidewalk, Isen noticed four officers in dress green uniforms, all of them wearing the maroon beret and the shoulder patch of the Eighty-second Airborne Division, the dead man's unit. A captain and two lieutenants stood just behind a big lieutenant colonel who looked vaguely familiar to Isen. The last, Isen figured, must be Hauck's battalion commander. When he was abreast of the little group of paratroopers, Isen looked over at the black name tag on the colonel's uniform. Veir.

Isen, who had been running a mental inventory of his Army acquaintances to match the face with a name, suddenly made the connection. They were past the little group now, but Isen looked back over his shoulder to catch another glimpse.

So that's the famous Colonel "Hollywood" Veir, he thought.

"You know that guy?" Marian asked.

Isen looked at her; she was following his gaze.

"Colonel Veir," Isen said. Lieutenant colonels—one rank below a full colonel—were addressed and referred to as "colonel."

Six weeks earlier "Hollywood" Veir, whose real first name was Harlan, had graced the cover of *Newsweek* magazine as part of a story about the "new" Army, the faster, leaner, more deadly force that was the descendant of the old Cold War and Desert Storm behemoth. The magazine had done a spread worthy of *Life* magazine's old days of hero-making after following the photogenic Veir around Fort Bragg, North Carolina, for three days. Veir, and by extension, the Army, had come off very well as a result of the article.

The jokes about "Hollywood" Veir came mostly from officers who, like Isen, were finding it harder and harder to distinguish themselves in a fighting force that was dwindling in terms of size and—it seemed to many on active duty—its importance to the Republic. Isen was not the only one a little bit jealous of the cachet Veir had no doubt picked up as a result of having his handsome face spread all over America.

Up ahead the procession was turning into the Memorial Chapel gate. Mark Isen had been to a dozen or so military funerals, but Arlington came to mind whenever he thought of the ceremonies that attended laying a soldier to rest. The vast grounds, on the Virginia side of the Potomac River just across from the nation's capital, had once comprised the estate of Robert E. and Mary Anna Custis Lee. When the nation began to splinter in the spring of 1861, Colonel Lee was offered command of the Federal forces. That night, his last in the uniform of the United States Army, Lee walked the boards of the house that sits atop the cemetery's hill. When he rode to Washington the next day to report that he'd chosen Virginia over the Union, he left this home and never returned. The Union Army chose the confiscated grounds as a burial site for Federal soldiers.

Up ahead the procession turned right onto McPherson Drive. Hauck's mother, on General Flynn's arm, walked head up, like her soldier brother.

"He'll be buried by my grandfather," Marian offered.

Which explained why they weren't heading to the newest

section, Isen thought. Arlington officials tried to accommodate, as best they could, a family's wish to have related service members buried near each other.

"Other family members are buried here, then?" Isen asked, risking a look down at her. Marian pushed at her hair, a few strands of which were alluringly out of place. She was about twenty-six or so, Isen judged.

"Five generations. A lot of them buried right here," she said. Then, after a pause, "Six generations now, I guess."

Isen did some quick calculations. Michael Hauck, a suicide in the first year of his service, was to be buried with forebears who might very well have fought in the Civil War.

"Lot of pressure, don't you think?" she asked. Her tone said rhetorical question, but Isen bulled ahead.

"That's a lot for a young guy to live up to, yeah. I guess." Marian pressed her lips into a tight line.

"He didn't," she said.

"What's that?"

"Live up to it. He didn't live."

They were on Grant Drive now, winding down the long hill that gentled at the bottom before stretching to the riverbank. From here, fragments of Washington's famous skyline were visible. Isen decided that, as cemeteries went, he liked Arlington.

When he'd been assigned in Europe, he'd had occasion to visit the American military cemetery in Normandy, just above the Omaha Beach landing site. There, where the whole gravesite was on a flat promontory, the white headstones lined up in arithmetic precision, an eerie order that belied the chaos of death in combat. Here, on the northernmost of Virginia's gentle hills, the markers rolled with the land, bent around the numerous trees, yielded to the folds in the ground. Here the rows were imperfect; straight lines, to be sure, but every once in a while the errant headstone leaned out of formation, like a soldier a half step out.

Ahead now, Isen could see more blue-coated soldiers, guards detailed to keep the tourists away.

Lots of manpower invested here, he thought. *I'm surprised someone hasn't taken the budget axe to this, too.*

Then the caisson pulled up, the six horses tossing their heads gently. The caisson detail corporal, riding a seventh white horse at the lead, turned to check the position of his troops. A walkie-talkie, a touch of the modern, was secured to the saddle blanket behind the soldier's leg.

The honor guard turned off the road just above the open grave, which was marked by four ranks of chairs draped in black cloth. Isen looked uphill to where a single dogwood marked the center of the slope. In spring the little hillside would be colored in pink or white blossoms. Up above, on the lip of the rise, four or five tall trees stood like an uneven skirmish line.

"I could be buried here."

"Pardon?" Marian said.

Isen hadn't meant to speak out loud. "I . . . uh . . . I could be buried here, I guess," he said.

She gave him a look that she might reserve for a morbid joke. Isen studied her profile as she watched the pallbearers loosen the straps on the casket. Clear eyes, clear skin, strong shoulders of a swimmer, perhaps, certainly an athlete. Isen figured he wasn't old enough to be her father; on the other hand, he doubted if the men she dated had many firsthand memories of the Nixon years.

The pallbearers had the casket now, and Isen stood holding a salute as the detail moved in those mincing steps that were an absolute exaggeration, but assured that there would be no caskets dropped, not ever, by Old Guard troops.

The eight soldiers moved the coffin graveside, and the family fell in behind them, stepping to the chairs. Isen led Marian to the row behind her aunt, where she held on to his hand for a moment.

"Thank you."

He nodded.

The pallbearers had stretched the new flag tight at waist level. A military chaplain from Fort Bragg, home to the Eighty-second Airborne Division, stood at the head of the grave, sweating in dress greens, his trousers tucked into gleaming jump boots, his beret stuffed under the epaulet of his blouse. Isen looked around for the others from Fort Bragg, spied them standing together a few feet behind the last row of chairs. They were Hauck's friends and comrades, but this ceremony was for family. He imagined that the unit had had some kind of memorial for the young man, with the traditional down-turned rifle, the empty paratrooper boots standing in for the absent soldier.

As the chaplain began the Rite of Protestant Burial, Isen stared off at the firing party, which stood some fifty meters away, out in the direct sunlight, eight men in dress blues, perfectly motionless in the roiling sun. Seven shooters and a corporal. Seven rifles, three rounds each.

"Now we are at the edge of autumn," the chaplain was saying. "It is difficult, in the summer's heat, to recall winter's chilly blasts. Yet we know they will come, as surely as darkness will follow this daylight. Summer gives way to autumn. All around us the leaves will change, then die. The earth will become still, silent in the winter of renewal. Then with the spring comes new birth."

He paused, surveying the seated guests.

He looks genuinely sad, Isen thought cynically. *Wonder if he knew the kid or if that's just his professional mourning face.*

"And so it is with this death," the chaplain continued. "This is the deep winter of our grief. But spring will come, and with it, rebirth in the Lord. Michael, too, will be reborn, as will each of us. Though the season of mourning is long and bleak, let us be comforted in knowing that it will pass."

The chaplain closed his book carefully, then nodded at the commander of troops. The firing party snapped half-right, angling their weapons skyward. General Flynn's sister cried softly until the rifles' reports made her jump, releasing something in her. Isen could see the woman's shoulders shaking between her brother and her husband. Leaning forward, he could also see Marian, who was composed, her face unchanged save for the tears running thickly down her cheeks.

Behind Isen, partially hidden by the low branches of a tree, the bugler stood ready. Isen and the others in uniform rendered a hand salute as the musician raised the silvery bugle. For a moment, there was no sound except the faint breath of wind through the trees. Then the first notes of "Taps" rolled over the ranks of stones:

9

Day is done
Gone the sun,
from the earth, from the sea, from the sky,
rest in peace, soldier brave,
God is nigh.

The pallbearers pulled the flag even tighter, then folded it into its neat triangle. A sergeant at the end of the casket flattened the blue-and-white package by hugging it against his chest, the closest any of those in uniform would come to a comforting gesture. As the officer in charge presented the flag to Hauck's mother, Isen swallowed hard.

Mark Isen, a combat veteran, had seen young men die before, some in ways more horrible than what had happened to Hauck. He'd loaded young men, whose lives he'd been responsible for, into body bags. And no matter what the circumstances, no matter what had been won, the common denominators were always loss and waste.

And it was those deaths, in combat and by accident, of young men who'd been full of life, that he thought of and grieved for now. Isen could not mourn Hauck, whom he'd never met, because Hauck had caused a great deal of pain for the people who loved him. More than that, suicide was absolutely antithetical to the disciplined world Isen inhabited, a world bounded by strong beliefs, by the guiding light of his sense of duty. He couldn't help it; he couldn't feel sorry for Hauck as he scanned the crowd, as he watched the grieving parents.

How could he do this to them?

Isen walked with the family back up the hill to the parking lot by Memorial Chapel. Marian Flynn surprised him by kissing him on the cheek just before she got into a car with another cousin. Isen closed her door, tapped the glass and smiled at her again as she left. When he turned around, General Flynn caught his eye. Isen walked over to the curb and waited until Flynn had said good-bye to his sister, who would be flying back to Dallas later that day.

"Can you stand by with me for a few more minutes here, Mark?" Flynn asked.

"Certainly, sir."

The two men watched the little procession of cars go by,

the whole Flynn family and a good sprinkling of Haucks, the dead man's paternal side. Because they were in Washington, or because this was a military affair, or both, General Flynn had become the master of ceremonies, shepherding his sister and her family, all of his relatives and the other visitors, going out of his way to make sure that everything went as smoothly as possible. Some people, Isen knew, handled their grief that way. Better to find something to keep busy with, even if it was just asking a sergeant who'd had the funeral detail a hundred times for yet another briefing on the sequence of events.

The contingent from Fort Bragg approached, the three junior officers a few steps behind their commander. Isen thought he noticed Flynn stiffen as the men approached. The lieutenant colonel saluted.

"Sir, I'm Lieutenant Colonel Harlan Veir, Lieutenant Hauck's battalion commander." He waited until Flynn returned his salute before he went on.

"On behalf of General Tremmore, the Division Commander, and the soldiers of our unit, I'd like to extend my sympathies to your family." He spoke precisely, a rehearsed speech.

"Thank you, Colonel," Flynn said. Then, turning to Isen, Flynn said, "This is Major Mark Isen."

Isen stepped forward and shook hands with Veir. The colonel was a head taller than Isen, which put him at about six two. Handsome in a rugged sort of way that must have attracted the *Newsweek* photographers from the start. He fixed Isen with blue eyes—dark blue, almost purple—that were untouched when he smiled. "Pleased to meet you, Major."

Veir turned back to Flynn, and Isen studied him. His uniform was impeccable, rivaling those of the Old Guard officers who spent so much of their time being ogled by the public. Veir sported a combat patch from the Eighty-second, so that his left and right shoulders both bore the red, white and blue double "A" of the "All-American" division. Isen guessed Veir had been with the unit during Desert Storm, although he could have earned his decorations on a tropical excursion in Grenada or Panama.

Veir introduced the captain, one of his staff, and the lieutenants, platoon leaders who'd come to Bragg at the same time Hauck did. None of the other three officers spoke to Flynn beyond mumbling "Sir" when they shook hands.

"Will you be staying here in Washington, Colonel?" Flynn asked.

"No, sir. We have to get back to Bragg this evening."

Flynn, who was not good at hiding his emotions, had his war face on. Isen wasn't sure what, if anything, Veir had done; but he thought the signal clear. Yet Veir was smiling as broadly as the occasion—the general's nephew had just been buried—would allow.

"Have a safe trip back to North Carolina, then," Flynn said.

The general turned away sharply, surprising the four paratroopers, who were left saluting his back.

Isen fell into step on the general's left as the older man made his way back toward the cemetery gate. Flynn, barrel-chested and short-legged, moved quickly, a green-clad block of determination gliding close to the ground. He'd been an All-American wrestler in college. Even now, almost thirty years away from the mat, he moved with intimidating physicality, an undefeated twenty-year-old athlete in the guise of a fifty-year-old man.

Isen walked quickly to keep up. He wanted to ask what Veir had done to piss Flynn off, but figured he was along to listen, as was frequently the case when he accompanied a general officer. Flynn liked to think out loud, and he liked having Isen around as a sounding board for his ideas.

Some years earlier Major General Patrick Flynn, then a colonel, had commanded the brigade in which Isen, then a captain, led a rifle company of one hundred and ten infantrymen.

Flynn's subordinates had called him, aptly, Bulldog, and Isen used to joke that Flynn had earned the handle while still in the cradle. He was courageous and determined, but like many men who'd carved successful careers in the military, the single-mindedness that had made him a success also made him difficult to live with. Once he'd made his choices, Patrick Flynn was not a man to be crossed lightly.

Their paths had intersected again when Isen was assigned to Fort Benning, Georgia, for a stint with the U.S. Army

Rangers. Isen had looked up Flynn when he'd been assigned to the Pentagon, less than six months earlier.

"Sorry I wasn't around this week to give you a hand," Isen said. He'd returned from a temporary duty assignment—ten days at Fort Drum, New York—just eighteen hours before the funeral.

Flynn raised his hand. "Don't worry about it," the general said. "I needed to keep busy . . . and you probably couldn't have gotten free anyway."

"That's true, sir," Isen said.

"So how do you like Purgatory?" Flynn asked.

The two men, predictably aware of the vast gulf of rank between them, nevertheless always spoke plainly.

"Aptly named, I'd say, sir," Isen answered.

When he last came up for reassignment, Isen had been in line for a good job with a combat unit. He had already spoken to friends at Fort Lewis, Washington, about getting to a troop unit there. Late in the assignment process, all that changed. His branch chief—one of the officers responsible for filling majors' billets around the Army—told Isen that he'd spent more than his fair share of time with troops. It was time to let someone else have a shot at the exciting jobs, which left paper pushing for Isen.

Isen suspected, but had never been able to prove, that a senior officer he'd clashed with during his time with the Rangers had seen to it that he, Isen, got shunted off to a dead end job in Washington.

"What time did you leave work last night?" Flynn asked.

"Around twenty-one hundred, sir," Isen said. Nine o'clock. Nine-thirty by the time he'd walked to his car at one of the remote parking lots that clustered around the huge office building like a moonscape of blacktop and white lines.

"And you were in at?"

"Six-thirty, most days," Isen said. "Six today."

Isen checked his whining. This was Flynn's third tour in Washington, and though he lived at Fort Myer now, in a big flag officer's house almost within sight of the Pentagon, his first tour here had also been as a major. Flynn knew the drill. But he'd also asked how Isen was doing.

"So, what do you think so far?"

"Well, it's only been six months, of course, sir. But all in all I think I'd rather take a sharp stick in the eye."

Flynn chuckled. "At least people would send you flowers in the hospital, right?"

Flynn unbuttoned and pulled off his uniform blouse, the dark green jacket heavily laden with ribbons, stars, buttons and badges. He threw it casually over one arm.

The two men retraced the steps of the funeral procession, down the sloping hill on Grant Drive, stopping a hundred meters or so above the gravesite. Cemetery workers, who must have been standing by during the service, were lowering Hauck's casket into the ground. Flynn didn't seem to want to go closer.

"Marian told you we had a bunch of relatives here, huh?" Flynn said without looking at Isen.

"She mentioned that Michael would be the sixth generation buried here."

"Well, that's not exactly right," Flynn said. "Sixth generation in uniform, not all of them represented here, though."

Flynn was in a reflective mood, and though every moment Isen lingered at the cemetery meant that he would have to stay later at the office, he felt he owed this much to his friend and mentor. It could be that Flynn wanted to see the grave closed, or maybe he wanted to commune with the dead soldiers among his forebears. Isen fidgeted, felt the perspiration soaking his shirt.

"She didn't seem ... I mean, she wasn't ..." Isen stumbled.

"She doesn't like the Army," Flynn said.

"That's what I read, sir," Isen said, relieved that he hadn't overstepped his bounds.

"I suppose all of this," Flynn said, gesturing with his hand to take in the whole cemetery, "put a lot of pressure on Michael. Hell, I know it put pressure on me, too. And Michael was already driven, more than I was. He wanted this life. Badly."

Flynn shook his head, confused, maybe a bit angry at his nephew for all the pain he'd caused.

The two men watched the work crew hoist the vault cap and lower it into the tight fit of the hole. Isen looked beyond the hill to the trees that separated the cemetery proper from the maze of highways less than a half mile away.

"Had you ever met Colonel Veir before, sir?" Isen asked.

"Not unless you count reading about him," Flynn said. "America's new breed of hero ... my ass. He waited until my sister was gone before he came up to me. If he wanted to offer condolences to the family, he should have spoken to Michael's parents."

"You think he was avoiding them, sir?" Isen asked, unsure as to why that might be.

"Ah, who the hell knows," Flynn said. "Maybe he was embarrassed because he thinks—as I do—that if he'd been a better commander, if he'd known what the hell was going on in his command, my nephew might be alive today."

They watched as the grave crew began to toss shovelfulls of dirt into the hole.

"I'm glad they don't push it in with a backhoe," Flynn commented. "Seems a little more dignified this way, I guess."

Isen was thinking about Veir, but Flynn's mind was elsewhere.

"My dad's buried right there by Michael," Flynn said after a pause. "Served in North Africa, Italy and France."

"Marian said that Michael would be buried by his grandfather," Isen said.

"I have a brother buried up at West Point, too," Flynn said. "Marian's dad. The only West Pointer in the lot."

The general stared out over the tops of the trees that marked the edge of the cemetery and the bottom of the slope.

"Lots of history," Isen offered.

"Lots of baggage," Flynn said. "You're born into a family like this, there's a lot on your shoulders."

"I got the feeling Marian felt that way," Isen said, brushing at the perspiration that was beginning to sting his eyes. "Did Michael feel that way, too?" he asked.

"I didn't think so. I thought he reveled in the family's history. Maybe I was wrong," Flynn said. "I'm afraid I didn't know Michael as well as I might have. We're like a bunch of tumbleweeds. Military families. Hell, you know that," Flynn said. He shifted his uniform blouse to his other arm,

15

turned and started up the hill to where his car was parked by Memorial Chapel.

"I visited Michael at Bragg when I was down there for a conference recently. His attitude seemed OK. Not great, just OK."

Flynn pulled off his cap and wiped his brow with the sleeve of his shirt.

"He seemed to like the Army all right, but I thought his life was a little . . . hinky."

"What's that, sir?"

"A little weird," Flynn continued. "Out of kilter, like maybe he wanted help but didn't know how to ask."

"Maybe he would have been hesitant to ask for help," Isen offered. "It would have looked like he was running to Uncle General."

Flynn nodded in response. "This morning I asked my sister if she thought Michael was unhappy. She said his letters were kind of vague. He complained a bit, but she thought it was just normal bellyaching."

The two men walked in silence the rest of the way up the hill, Isen waiting for Flynn to say more. By the time they got to the top, both of them were drenched in sweat. Flynn's shirt was plastered to his back; the sweat had begun to stain the waistband of his trousers.

"I hate DC in the summertime," Flynn said.

When they got to Flynn's car, the general threw his blouse into a heap on the back seat.

"Mark, I'm going to ask a favor of you. But before I do, I want you to promise me that you won't say yes unless you feel comfortable."

"OK, sir," Isen answered.

"I would like you to take a few days, go down to Bragg and ask a few questions about what happened to my nephew."

Get away from the Pentagon? Isen thought. *When do I leave?*

Isen waited, sensing that Flynn wanted to say more.

"I know this is out of the ordinary . . ." Flynn said, giving Isen a chance to respond.

"What about the CID report?"

Isen assumed that the Criminal Investigation Division, the

Army's own investigative service, would have questioned anyone even remotely involved with the last days and hours of Hauck's life and filed a report. Doubtless some drawer at Fort Bragg held a file folder that, if it didn't fully explain the messy end to Lieutenant Hauck's career, at least satisfied the Army's need for closure. Isen's instincts told him it wasn't a good idea to unravel those neat ends.

"I saw the preliminary report, and I don't think it's all that thorough," Flynn said. "I said as much to the CID commander who was kind enough to send it to me, and he got pretty defensive. You know how they guard their turf, how they don't like people questioning their work."

"Do you have some specific problem with the report, sir?" Isen asked.

Flynn seemed unsure of himself—which was not a characteristic of the man Isen knew.

"It's just that . . . I'm not expecting much from the final report, you know?" Flynn said. "Look, maybe this isn't such a great idea, Mark. It's OK for you to say no."

"No, that's not it, General. I'd love to get the hell out of the Pentagon for a few days—although I wish it was under more pleasant circumstances. I'm just wondering if there's something specific you have in mind."

"I just feel there are a lot of unanswered questions about why this might have happened." Flynn opened the driver's door and a blast of hot air rushed out. "I'll tell you what I have. I have a nephew who had waited and worked for years to get to this point in his life, yet something obviously didn't work out. I have a bunch of paratroopers closing ranks down there and assuring me that nothing was wrong." Flynn allowed himself a small, incredulous smile. "That's what Michael's company commander actually said when I called him. 'Nothing was wrong, sir.' Shit, it sure looks to me like something was wrong."

Flynn was struggling. He'd probably been going constantly since this thing broke at the beginning of the week. Four days of attending the details and ignoring the fundamental question had worn him down.

"I know it's a normal reaction," Flynn said, pinching the bridge of his nose. "But my sister wants to know why Michael killed himself. And out there on that hill, she took my

17

hand and asked me to find out what happened to her son. What could I say to her?"

Isen shifted his weight from one foot to the other. A score of good reasons he shouldn't go came to mind, but he wanted out of Washington. "I guess I can go take a look around, sir."

"Good," Flynn said. "Great. I'll talk to your boss; maybe I can get him to send you down there next week. I'll spot you some cash for expenses. You let me know if you need more."

"Roger that, sir," Isen said. He saluted as Flynn climbed behind the steering wheel. "I'd like to see that CID report, too, sir."

"Sure, sure," Flynn said, pulling the door shut. "I'll give you a call. Thanks, Mark."

As he walked to his own car, Isen shook his head. *I don't see how anything good can come of this,* he thought. *I'm going down to Fort Bragg, where I won't be welcome because I'm not a beany-wearing paratrooper; I'll be looking into the suicide of the youngest son of a distinguished military family; and all the while I'll be stepping on toes around the CID and the kid's chain of command. Should be fun.*

Later, as he inched along with the lunchtime traffic on his way back to his monk's cell in the Pentagon, he cheered up a little.

"What the hell?" he said aloud. "Nothing is going to bring that kid back. But a day away from this place is a day away." He began to tap his fingers on the steering wheel in time with the radio's blaring.

2

Hauck's funeral was on Thursday, the sixteenth of September. By Friday at noon, judging by the reaction of Isen's splenetic boss, General Flynn had already sprung him for the trip.

"I understand you have more important things to do next week than work here."

Lieutenant Colonel Albert Tynan had posted himself at the edge of Isen's tiny cubicle, a pseudo-office defined by a windowless wall on one side, two orange partitions and an open space that was only slightly larger than the overweight Tynan. Arms crossed, eyes narrowed petulantly behind oversized glasses, he pouted by Isen's desk.

"Yes, sir," Isen said, smiling. "I have to run down to Fort Bragg for a while." He paused; Tynan didn't move.

"Ten days, actually," he said, gloating a bit.

Chances were Tynan didn't know exactly what Isen was going to be doing at Bragg; the little weasel was just pissed off that Isen would be out of his sight, away from the fluorescent-lit cage.

"Well, I can imagine that you're eager to spend some time

19

away from here," Tynan said. "I know your heart isn't in this work."

It was only by dint of extreme self-control that Isen kept from laughing at the understatement. He hated the office, the work and Tynan, though not necessarily in that order. The real irony was that Tynan had been a successful field soldier—otherwise he wouldn't be working on the Army Staff. But after a few years of the interminable working hours and office politics of the Pentagon, he had evolved into something else. Isen wasn't interested in experiencing the same metamorphosis.

Over his thirteen years of service, Isen had built a strong performance file; efficiency reports written during his time spent with soldiers were uniformly impressive. He had done all the right things to this point in his career; he was an excellent field soldier and a decorated combat leader. Said so right in the files. But the Army's grand scheme dictated that one must also be a consummate desk jockey. For the moment, that meant kissing up to paper shufflers like Tynan, whose comment called for something contrite. Isen wasn't up to it.

"I imagine the Pentagon will manage to inch forward without me," Isen managed. "Sir."

"Yes, well ... This means you must finish that action you're working on before you leave."

Tynan didn't call projects "projects." To him, everything was an "action," as if they were liberating Kuwait.

"Sir, this wasn't due until next Wednesday," Isen protested. He was working on yet another revision of yet another Army publication, one of the training manuals that taught the Army's warfighting doctrine.

"Well, obviously things have changed, since you're not going to be here for a while," Tynan said, smiling greasily. "You didn't expect me to just drop the ball, did you? I mean, important work has to get done no matter what the other demands on your time."

The last word, Isen thought, *should be "Stick it up your ass, Colonel."*

"I understand, sir," Isen said.

* * *

Isen worked all day Saturday, along with several thousand other Pentagon drones, finally getting home at nine forty-five on Saturday evening. He thumbed through the pile of mostly unopened mail that had been accumulating during the week, marveling at how the world went on without him while he was locked up in the five-sided dungeon. He changed into jeans and a cool short-sleeved shirt for the walk down the street to his favorite local bar, an establishment with a difficult-to-find mix: good food in an atmosphere just seedy enough to prevent it from being a hangout for the legions of suits who flooded Old Town Alexandria on Saturday night.

He left his apartment on foot and made his way into the crowds. The air was still hot and close and would remain so for another month, but that didn't deter the Saturday evening strollers who patronized this lovely red-brick corner of the metro area. Isen smiled at a group of three young women walking in the opposite direction; they looked right through him.

That's bad, he thought as he entered the small bar that was his destination. *When you get to the age where you don't even come up on the female radar screen.*

Isen knew he was not a remarkable-looking man. Average height, ten pounds over his ideal weight (still below the national norm, he comforted himself) with unremarkable features—except for his eyes, which were gray and, according to his ex-wife, as expressive as most people's faces.

"Adding to your little black book, Mark?"

The bartender, Rachel, was a dark-haired, sloe-eyed beauty some ten years off her prime. She tapped a dark red fingernail against the cover of Isen's address book, which he'd set on the bar before him.

"At my age I should be thinking about cutting a few names from the team, don't you think?" Isen said, opening the cracked binding. "All those energetic ones might just kill an old man like me."

"I hope that means I get to stay on the A list," Rachel said, winking.

Isen had spent more than a few nights at this bar fantasizing about Rachel. But every time he made ready to set out on that path, he reminded himself that such an indulgence would probably end the friendship *and* require the hunt for a new watering hole. He contented himself with responding to her teasing from behind the safety of the bar, what Rachel had once referred to as the ultimate safe sex.

"Top of the list, baby. Top of the list."

Like the address books of most people he knew in the military, Isen's was done mostly in pencil, and even those entries were supplemented by dozens of notes and scraps of paper stuck in odd places, all of which chronicled the constant movements of his friends in uniform. Some of the names went all the way back to his days as a junior officer in Germany, fighting the good fight of the Cold War. The people he'd kept in contact with over the years had two or three entries. There was a break, not noticeable on the page but clear enough to Isen, that signaled the end of his marriage. Many of the friends he and his wife had had in common followed one camp or the other after the divorce.

Isen made four phone calls from the booth near the men's room after ordering his food. He caught up on some new transfers, made a couple of changes to his book, and managed to find—with the help of North Carolina directory assistance—numbers for a few friends at Bragg. He called one.

Major Sue Lynn Darlington had been assigned to Schofield Barracks, Hawaii, when Mark Isen was there and they were both captains. Isen had been married then, and although his relationship with Sue Lynn extended beyond the strictly professional to the social, they had been nothing but proper. Darlington, Isen suspected, had not much cared for his ex-wife, and Adrienne Isen had let her husband know she felt the same way about the attractive, athletic and decidedly single aviator.

There had been rumors of Darlington's promiscuity, which Adrienne Isen rehearsed for Mark whenever the couple ran into Darlington at a social event; but Isen knew that such rumors attached themselves to practically any woman in uniform who wasn't married (and to a few who were), and most often had nothing to do with reality. Besides, Isen had always considered, since Darlington was single, there was no reason she shouldn't conduct herself the way her male colleagues—especially the aviators—did, which is to say they'd screw anything that moved. The cold logic and sensitive farsightedness of this argument made Isen no points with his wife.

Out at the bar, Rachel set Isen's sandwich by his glass.

If some guy answers the phone, Isen told himself. *I'll tell them that dinner was just served.*

The coward in him was relieved to hear her answering machine. The message was characteristically direct; none of this nonsense of a number and no name, or, worse yet, something cute with music in the background.

"Hi, this is Sue Lynn Darlington. Please leave a message."

Seven little clicks, then a beep. *She has a lot of callers,* Isen thought.

"Sue Lynn, this is Mark Isen."

He paused for a moment, remembering the last time he'd seen her. It had been at Fort Benning, when he'd been stationed there with the Rangers. She'd been there for a week, only discovering him a few hours before she had to leave— enough time for them to have a beer and for Isen to realize that there was some hot spark of sexual tension there. He'd been divorced then, and, as of that meeting a year earlier, she wasn't married.

"I'm calling from DC," he continued. "I'm on my way to Bragg for a week and a half. I was hoping we could get together for dinner or something."

Isen wondered if she would think the same thing of that term—something—that he was thinking as he said it. But then he decided that that was juvenile. He left his home number and hung up. He started to dial another number at Bragg, a friend he'd known as a lieutenant in Germany, but then he closed the book.

Isen moved back to the bar and took a couple of big, hurried bites of his sandwich.

A couple of years of eating like this and I'll look like Tynan, he thought. He was a long way from the trim youngster Darlington had known in Hawaii.

Once during those years he'd been paired up with Sue Lynn during a sports festival. He held her ankles while she did as many sit-ups as she could do in two minutes, part of the standard fitness test. In spite of the physical training uniform, which was the same for men and women, and in spite of the fact that she was concentrating on doing well—

groaning and sweating inelegantly, her cheeks puffing in and out with the exertion—Isen had found the whole thing considerably more enjoyable than, for instance, holding the feet of one of his sweaty, hairy-legged infantrymen. He had tried and failed to keep his fantasies in check.

After that, there were times when Isen felt a stronger pull toward Sue Lynn. At parties, or in the Officers' Club, he always knew where in the room she stood. He always heard her voice among the others, always seemed to know, without looking, where she was. He moved in and out of the circle of her attraction with an exaggerated caution. Mark Isen was married, and he didn't fool around. But he was honest enough with himself to let Sue Lynn move in his daydreams.

Isen didn't get back to his apartment until just past midnight. As usual, the crowds in Old Town did nothing to cheer him up. He didn't care to think about how many weekend nights he'd spent alone with his books in the studio off Washington Street, a few blocks from the Potomac. It wasn't as if he felt a need to be out drinking or trying to meet women in bars; he had never been one for a lot of carousing. But the day-to-day work part of his life was empty, and the emptiness of his weekends and free time, rather than being a welcome rest from tough work he enjoyed, now only mocked the loneliness he felt throughout the week.

"Well," he said to himself as he shut the door behind him, "another thrilling Saturday night in the only life I'll ever live."

The message light on his machine was blinking.

"Mark, this is Sue Lynn. I'm so glad you called."

Her drawl was thicker than he remembered. *Ahm so glayed ...* Sue Lynn carried a lot of her Texas upbringing with her, and was as adept as any man Isen knew in playing the game of the good ol' boy: slow-talking, dumb as a fox.

"When you come down here I want you to stay at my house. I've got all sorts of room here."

She rattled off the address and told Isen to call her when he knew what time he'd arrive.

Isen looked at the machine, hit the replay button.

It seemed to him there was a hesitation between her invitation—I want you stay at *mah* house—and the explanation that it was a big place. As in plenty of extra rooms.

Watch yourself, Isen, he told himself as he pulled his kit bag down from the top of the only closet. *Just because you used to dream of her doesn't mean she returned the favor. You do stupid things when you get horny, and you could ruin a ten-year-old friendship here.*

Thus chastened, he felt better. But he packed a half-dozen condoms in his shaving kit.

Isen spent most of Sunday running the errands he hadn't attended to during the week. He went by Flynn's quarters, as instructed, and found a large manila envelope under a table on the screened porch. There were five new one-hundred-dollar bills inside—as Flynn had told him there would be—but no copy of the preliminary CID report.

I'll have the old man fax me a copy, Isen told himself as he pocketed the cash. He wrote on the envelope: "Got the $. Will call with fax # for report. Mark."

At one o'clock he dragged himself for two miles along the jogging trail that passed the Pentagon on the banks of the Potomac. Running once or twice a week wasn't going to keep him in shape, and running just before he left for Bragg wasn't going to make him any slimmer before he saw Sue Lynn, but he figured it was better than nothing. He was back in his apartment by two-thirty, showered and packed by three. He paid a few bills, took out the trash, left a note for his landlady and was soon nosing through the Beltway traffic, headed south and counting on a five-hour drive.

Between Washington and Richmond, Virginia, Isen passed the Civil War's most contested ground, some hundred miles of the bloodiest stretch of land on the continent. Isen had spent a few summer weekends visiting the battlefields in the area: Manassas, Fredericksburg, Chancellorsville. Just before Labor Day he had driven all the way down to Appomattox, where the courtly Lee, in sword and sash, the very picture of an old order already dead, had surrendered to Grant, who'd ridden up in a mud-splattered private's coat.

Isen knew that Lee had written, a few years after the war, about how much he enjoyed "the charms of civil life" and his new role as president of Washington College: "I have wasted the best years of my existence" pursuing a military career. By the time Lee acknowledged his mistake, he had only five weeks to live.

Isen, at thirty-five, was also questioning his choices. The force had shrunk tremendously since Isen had pinned on his second lieutenant's gold bars during the Cold War, and those changes had forced a lot of tough choices on people who'd dedicated their lives to the service. But Isen was philosophical about the drawdown and all the heartache that went with it for those professionals who thought the Army would always be there for them. Isen had once worked for an officer who was fond of warning his lieutenants: "You can love the Army, but the Army is never going to love you back."

South of Richmond the interstate cut through less populated areas, and here the road took on the character that made it so boring, the homogeneous view of America that obliterated differences between regions and states.

Isen turned off the radio and began to consider what he might find at Fort Bragg. The Army he'd grown up in was changing, with new, ill-defined missions and tremendous demands on the people who wanted to stick around. Many soldiers Isen knew operated—on a daily basis—out of fear for their jobs. The pressure led, in some cases, to an unhealthy competitiveness and careerism at the expense of service. But that attitude was far from rampant, and at any rate, Michael Hauck seemed too young to have succumbed to that kind of pressure. Still, with his family background, maybe he was more susceptible than most lieutenants.

It was easier to see Flynn in that context. Flynn, who was older and—with his two stars—accomplished in his profession, apparently also felt the same pressure from the family standard. Flynn's shepherding the funeral guests had been part of his duty as keeper of the family honor, an honor that had been sullied by Michael Hauck. Isen wondered how much of this fact-finding mission was to satisfy Hauck's mother and how much was for General Flynn.

Isen planned to begin his visit by making a courtesy call at Division Headquarters. General Flynn had once served with the man who now commanded the Eighty-second Airborne, and Flynn had called ahead to smooth things over for Isen. Someone at Bragg would probably call Veir, the battalion commander. Isen wondered how that meeting would go.

Isen got off the interstate and headed for Fayetteville, North Carolina, Fort Bragg's gatepost community. Ten miles off the highway, he approached Fayetteville from the south. The installation sat north and west of the town, rolling off in a huge egg shape across the steamy, flat land. Looking ahead, Isen spotted the great dark shapes of a half-dozen Air Force cargo planes, appearing and disappearing amid the pointed tops of pine trees as they traced a racetrack pattern and made ready to drop their loads of paratroopers.

Isen pulled to the side of the road to watch. It wasn't unusual for a field problem to begin on a Sunday, and most of the exercises for the units on jump status began with a drop. This one was going to be big.

There was a dual fascination for Isen as he watched, waiting for the jumpers to appear. Although he had jumped many times himself, there was still something incredible about watching hundreds of men and women delivered—in this case to a mock battlefield—by parachute. Soldiers and equipment stepped or rolled from the big green planes out into a slipstream of one hundred and ten knots. Most people who hadn't done it—and that was most of the population—were amazed at the confidence it took to leave an aircraft in flight.

Paratroopers capitalized on this mystique, playing it up to the point where many of them believed that the Army they were in differed significantly—read "was superior"—from the one that arrived by land.

And that was the second point that fascinated Isen. When the paratroopers landed, they were just like any other soldiers. In fact, the airborne units packed a lot less firepower than the units rolling in on wheels or tracks. Still, they thought of themselves—indeed, believed it with the fervor of the saved—as better than the rest of the Army.

Isen watched as the soldiers appeared, looking, from this distance, like tiny ribbons released from the sides of the aircraft. After a few seconds, the parachutes blossomed and floated, like so many mushroom caps, down to rejoin the earthbound.

Arguments abounded, in military circles as well as in Washington, that these forces were too lightly armed, too expensive to maintain, too limited in capability to be much use in the modern world. They were a holdover from another era, with no more real utility than the flashy dress uniforms of the Old Guard. Yet, for all he thought of the parachutists' bravado, Isen, like so many others in uniform and out, was fascinated. This was the Army's sacred calf, untouchable, sacrosanct.

The airborne.

The very word, accented—aggressively—on the last syllable, was an all-purpose term, a mantra. Air*borne*.

The members of this society intoned the word hundreds of times a day; it was "hello" and "good-bye"; "yes, sir" and "I'll try." It replaced the colorful regionalisms the soldiers might have brought from their homes, from "fuckin' A" to "word" and everything in between.

Isen watched the aircraft make their lumbering first pass over the drop zone.

"Airborne," he said to himself as he climbed behind the wheel again.

Just outside the town there was a great deal of the rural south evident in the businesses and the signs, mostly weathered plywood, that spoke to the occasional drive-by customer. One stand advertised "Home Growed Tomatoes." Another, set beside a fenced-in lot spotted with little concrete statues, hawked "Yard Critters."

The closer he got to town, the more garish and aggressive the businesses. Yadkin Road, connecting Fayetteville to the post, was a lot like Victory Drive near Fort Benning, and the main drag near Fort Hood, and dozens of gatepost communities at military bases all over the country. "Military Insurance," "U Can Rent," "Bragg Pawn," "EZ Used Cars," "Pussy Cat Lounge"—tacky signs announced a host of businesses designed to separate soldiers from their money. Whenever he read about how a military community "pumped" money into a town, he thought of this picture and the word *sucked,* as in "the town sucked money from the GIs." Without that industry, Fayetteville would dry up and blow away across the flat sand.

Isen found Darlington's house easily. The large two-story was in a quiet neighborhood a happy distance south of the post and north of the town center.

"Been investing that flight pay, I see," Isen said as he admired the house from the road. Darlington, an aviator, made over six hundred dollars a month more than Isen, her contemporary, for putting herself at risk in helicopters. Isen had stopped kidding her about the pay and her worth after the Gulf War, where she ferried combat troops through rain and vicious winds during the Allied ground offensive. Sue Lynn Darlington, who now mostly rode a desk in the Division's Aviation Section, had earned her flight pay and her combat decorations.

Darlington opened the front door of her house as Isen stepped onto the narrow front porch.

"Well, hello there, Mark Isen," she said exuberantly.

She stepped up to him, threw both arms around his neck and kissed him on the cheek. Isen dropped his bag and gave her a brotherly hug, his hands on the long muscles in her back.

"Let me look at you," she said, stepping back, holding his shoulders. "You look good."

"You look pretty great yourself," Isen said truthfully. He wondered if he could hold in his paunch for the whole visit.

"Well, let's get inside here," Darlington said, stepping back. "We've got some catching up to do. Just drop your bags anywhere." She talked over her shoulder as she moved toward the back of the house. "Can I get you a beer?"

"Sure," Isen said, taking notice, as he followed, of her tight jeans. She led him to the family room, where a big fireplace backed up against the rear wall of the house. Unlike his own apartment and the homes of most of his unmarried male friends, this one was not decorated in what Isen had come to think of as "Army style." Which translated to "complete lack of style."

Darlington's furniture was outsized, homey, a big couch and chair set above a braided rug before the fireplace. There were photos on the wall, including a couple of Sue Lynn with people who looked enough like her to be family. These were set in the same predictable tourist spots to which Isen had dragged visitors when he was overseas: the Berlin Wall, now a relic; German churches and castles; Hawaiian beaches.

"Here you go," she said, returning and handing him a bottle of beer and a frosted mug. "You infantry guys do know how to drink out of a glass, right?"

"I'll see if I remember," he said. "They have glasses in the bar where I mostly live now, but I wouldn't drink out of them."

Isen watched her as she poured her own beer. The young Lieutenant Darlington could cause quite a stir in the Officer's Club when she entered in her flight suit, a one-piece green overall that was designed to be anything but flattering. Her hair had been long then, light brown and worn, when she was in uniform, pulled up on the back of her head. Now she wore her hair short, and there were tiny wrinkles at the corners of her eyes and traces of laugh lines around her mouth. Although heavier now than he remembered her, she still had the athlete's body that had encouraged fantasies among her comrades.

Sue Lynn was pretty in an unconventional way; "striking" was how Isen's ex-wife had described her once. She had a long face, and not much in the way of the cheekbones that defined the pop culture standard of beauty. Thin lips and a slight gap between her front teeth did nothing to diminish her smile, which came from deep within.

"Is this your crew from Desert Storm?" Isen asked, indicating a framed photo on a small letter-writing desk.

"Yes," Sue Lynn said, moving beside him and picking up the frame. "These two guys are from the ground crew." She tapped the glass with a fingernail. "And these guys were my flight crew."

Darlington stood in the middle of a group of four men, her flight helmet tucked under her arm, one foot perched jauntily atop what looked to be an ammunition can. The men grinned widely for the camera and history; Darlington smiled at the center of her charges. Behind them, the fuselage of their aircraft had been punched through, a half-dozen nasty tears in the metal skin.

"Took some fire."

"A little bit," she said. "No biggie."

Isen looked at her. "If you'd been born twenty-five years earlier," he said, "you would have been one of those Vietnam Air Cavalry guys who wore black cowboy hats and silk scarves."

"If I'd been born a man," she corrected him, taking the frame from his hand. "And I'd hardly be interested in *that* trade-off."

In her company again, Isen remembered something he'd discovered years earlier about Sue Lynn: flying was more than just her profession, it was the perfect metaphor for her life. Calm and confident where others panicked, she seemed to move somewhere above the petty concerns that plagued life on the ground.

"Sit down, Mark," Darlington said. Her eyes, light green, fairly sparkled, and she used them the way some people use their hands in conversation. She wore a white oxford cloth shirt, open to three buttons and exposing a small gold chain with a tiny diamond. The shirt was much too big for her, and was pulled away loosely at her waist. When they were in their twenties, she was more of a girl, thinner, more angular. Now, in her mid-thirties, with softer, generous curves, she was terrifically attractive, with the pull of a bright moon. Isen tried not to stare.

"So what do they have you doing up there in the puzzle palace?" she asked.

Isen gave her a short description of his job, leaving no doubt as to how unhappy he was.

"Sounds like a real blast."

"I'll tell you how anxious I was to get out of there," he said, explaining what he was doing at Bragg.

"General Flynn sent you down here to poke around an unfinished CID investigation?" she asked.

"It's about wrapped up," Isen said. "Or at least that's the impression he gave me. It's just that he's not happy with it."

Sue Lynn opened her eyes wider still. "Already? He's complaining before it's even finished?"

"The family was left with a lot of unanswered questions. I'm just doing the old man a favor," Isen said, wondering how he got to be in the position of defending Flynn.

"Well," she said, leaning back and propping her bare feet on the coffee table. "He's not doing you any favors."

"I see you haven't lost your knack for speaking your mind," Isen said, smiling above his beer mug.

"And I hope I never do. Too many people around here these days spend all their time covering their asses when they should be speaking up."

Isen briefly considered volunteering for the job of covering Sue Lynn's ass, but he let it go, smiling at her instead.

After a pause she asked. "This kid was in Harlan Veir's battalion?"

"Yeah," Isen said. "You've met Veir?"

"Couple of times, briefly. But even before that I knew *of* him," Darlington said, standing and moving to a bookshelf, where she began to leaf through a stack of old magazines. "Even before the big spread in *Newsweek*. He's one of those guys whose reputation precedes him."

"And what is that reputation?"

"Oh, you know. The usual paratrooper BS. Superstud. Work hard, play hard. Rides his battalion like a bunch of mules. Works them half to death and then tries to drink them under the table."

She turned. "Here it is."

"You just described every battalion commander in the Army, Sue Lynn," Isen said as she walked toward him. "All the ones left standing after the purge, that is."

"Yeah, yeah," Sue Lynn said. "Everyone wants to be . . . needs to be a standout, I know. Veir, well, Veir is something else."

Isen took the magazine. The cover photo showed Harlan Veir in field gear, one thumb hooked on his belt, helmet pulled low on his face. The shot, waist up, was made outdoors, and the whole scene was suffused with the golden light of evening.

"Dashing," Isen said in his best British accent.

"Just so," Sue Lynn replied in kind. "They call him the Dark Prince."

"Why's that?"

"He has this sort of . . . I don't know . . . aura about him. Like he's always getting away with something. A sort of

James Dean bad boy image. You'll see for yourself when you meet him."

"I did meet him, actually," Isen said. "Briefly. After the funeral."

"And what did you think?"

Isen thumbed open the magazine to the article. More pictures of Veir under the banner headline "THE NEXT GENERATION OF THE AMERICAN WARRIOR."

"I hardly had time to form much of an opinion," Isen said, closing the magazine. "But I don't think General Flynn thought much of him."

"He say why?"

"He thinks Veir should have been more on the ball, should have known his officers at least well enough to see something like this coming."

"Well," Darlington said, "that might not be fair. He's got seven hundred men to worry about. Who knows how secretive Hauck was? But I can certainly see how Flynn and the family might be just generally ticked off."

"And what, may I ask, is your opinion of Veir?"

"Aside from the palaver in there?" she said, indicating the article. "Well, I've only met him a couple of times, but whatever I saw confirmed what I'd heard. He's—how shall I say this precisely?—he's a dickhead."

Isen laughed. "Don't sugarcoat your feelings, Sue Lynn. Just come out and say what's on your mind."

"He has to take off his hat to pee, OK?"

"Major Darlington," Isen said, "I'm surprised to hear you use that kind of language to describe a fellow officer."

"He's supposed to be quite a swordsman, too, I hear," Darlington continued.

"Oh?" Isen said, raising an eyebrow.

"Forget it," Darlington said. "I wouldn't know anything about that personally. His tastes run to much younger women. He dated some gal down in the Aviation battalion for a short while, and there was a rumor going around that he was boinking the Commanding General's female driver."

"My, my," Isen said. "And the journalists from *Newsweek* . . . let me guess. They left all this out, right?"

"Right. All of this is just rumor, you understand, part of the Dark Prince mystique, maybe," Darlington said, smiling.

"Since that article, the Division's golden boy can do no wrong. He brought a lot of very positive publicity to the Division and to the Army at a time when the brass thinks we need it desperately. With all the cutbacks still in the pipeline, we need to shine as much as possible."

"I can't say I disagree with that," Isen said. There were rumors—more than the usual number—around the Pentagon that the next series of budget cuts would be huge. The feeling of unease was pervasive, almost a siege mentality—unmatched, the old hands said, in the post-Vietnam era.

"When are you going to talk to this guy?" Sue Lynn asked.

"I'm supposed to stop by Division Headquarters tomorrow morning and see the boss or the Chief of Staff. Then I guess I'll call Colonel Veir to find out when I can ask him a few questions."

"Tread lightly," Darlington said.

"Why is that?"

"Two reasons," Darlington said. "Veir's Superman cape got a little wrinkled with this suicide. I mean, he's still the big man on campus, and most people probably wrote off the suicide as Hauck's problem—for which the kid should have sought help. But there is some whispering that maybe Veir's people aren't happy. Veir might be touchy. Defensive."

"The second reason," Darlington said, running her fingers through her hair. "You're down here in paratrooper land—in which all rules of behavior that govern the rest of the Army are suspended, by the way—and you were sent down here as a flunky-snoop by some Pentagon general. And not only are you digging through some unpleasant business, but you'll be doing it right in the backyard of the most famous GI to hit the public consciousness since Norman Schwarzkopf's pudgy face ruled the media. You're the bad guy here."

"Thanks for the pep talk," Isen said. "What about General Tremmore?"

"General Tremmore is a good division commander. He's only been aboard a couple of months, but I have yet to hear anyone say anything against him. He doesn't put up with any nonsense. Talks straight. The soldiers like him because he takes their side in everything. He likes to go to the field, hang out with the grunts, walk with them in training, stand around in the rain, all that hard-core stuff that you infantry types take so seriously."

"Sounds like my kind of guy," Isen said.

"Yeah," Darlington agreed. She paused, sipped her beer. "About three weeks ago a soldier got shot in one of the tire houses," she said, referring to the roofless "houses" constructed of stacks of old tires. Soldiers used them to practice room-to-room fighting with hand grenades and automatic weapons fire—live ammunition.

"The initial report said the training was screwed up— too many guys in the house, the house was too small, stuff like that."

"Could happen," Isen agreed.

"Yeah. Anyway, the next day another unit was scheduled to go through, and all the little lieutenant colonels were scared of getting someone hurt, thinking about calling off the training so as not to jeopardize their precious careers. So just before the first group is set to go through, General Tremmore shows up and asks the buck sergeant whose men are first in line if he can join them. So the general—who had someone bring him a weapon—gets in line with the privates, throws a couple of grenades, rushes around the rooms with these guys shooting all around him, the whole deal."

"No kidding."

"And at the end he tells them—get this—he tells them that the training *is* dangerous, but it would be more dangerous if they didn't know how to do these things and they got called to go fight somewhere. 'And I'm not about to risk your lives by having you unprepared,' Tremmore tells them."

"Great acting?" Isen asked.

"Great timing, great delivery," Darlington said. "But the man believes in what he's doing, and he's willing to stick his own neck out, too."

"And let me guess, word of this little exercise got around the division pretty quickly," Isen said.

"Faster than a dirty joke," Sue Lynn said. "Tremmore is the kind of guy who, if he decides to punch your lights out, walks up to you and says 'I'm going to punch your lights out.' "

"I can deal with that," Isen said.

"Veir is the kind of guy who has someone else punch your lights out while he's smiling at you," she added as counterpoint.

"Sounds like I'm going to have a good time down here," Isen said.

Darlington relaxed in her chair, tilting her head back so that Isen could see the length of her throat.

"Oh, it doesn't have to be all that bad."

Sue Lynn put Isen in the guest room, right next to the master bedroom suite, kissing him on the cheek as she said good-night.

She stretched out on the bed, tired but not yet ready for sleep, and compared the Mark Isen in the next room to her memories of him. There was no doubt he had changed; the past few years seemed to have aged him more than was fair. She blamed a lot of that on his job, which, though he'd been there only a short time, he so clearly hated. But she also saw that he wasn't wound up as tightly as he'd been, either, and he was unmistakably out from under the influence of his ex-wife.

She stood, pulled off her jeans, slipped out of her underwear and bra and stood naked before her dressing mirror. She touched her ribs below her sternum. There had been a flutter there when she kissed him. Sue Lynn didn't want for male attention, but she had often been disappointed, finding men who needed mothering or, worse, lessons in honest communication. Mark Isen was no longer the hard-bodied captain he'd been in Hawaii, but he was, as always, the genuine article.

She took her nightgown off the hook on the back of her door, then, changing her mind, dropped it to the floor and slipped into bed nude.

Darlington was up the next morning at five. Isen could hear her from the guest room as she moved about, getting ready for physical training, which was at six—zero six, in military parlance—for the division staff. Isen lay on his back, staring up at the darkness and a little rectangle of reflected streetlight carved on the ceiling.

"You should get your fat ass up and go for a run," Isen told himself. " 'Cause if you ever get to see Sue Lynn naked, she's going to think it weird when you keep your clothes on."

He sat up in bed, fumbling around in the dark until he found a small table lamp. He pulled on running shorts that barely fit him—*The irony is a little thick this morning,* he thought—and went out into the hallway to find the bathroom. Darlington had already left, but he found a pot of coffee brewing and the morning paper on the table, along with a note.

Mark,
  You might consider wearing civvies when you go to see Tremmore and Veir. The unofficial motto here is that there are two kinds of people in the world: paratroopers (identifiable by the silly hat) and people who wish they were paratroopers.
  Since you don't have a beret and you probably won't wear civvies, stick a bag over your head.
  Good luck.

  Sue Lynn
  PS. Dinner this evening?

Isen thought about Darlington's advice on civilian clothes. Paratroopers, he knew, liked to stare scornfully from under their berets at anyone who wasn't so accoutered. And he knew that a large measure of the first impression he would make would be lost because he wasn't one of *them.* But he couldn't imagine showing up at Division Headquarters to see the Chief of Staff, maybe even the commanding general, in casual slacks and a pullover shirt.

Isen fixed himself a cup of coffee and went back upstairs to take an inventory of the clothes he'd brought. He had three sets of BDUs, the camouflage-pattern battle dress uniforms that would be the duty uniform for everyone on Bragg; he had his greens, the more formal uniform he'd worn to Hauck's funeral; two pair of jeans; a pair of khakis and a couple of casual shirts.

The investigators for CID, who were all soldiers, wore civilian clothes on the job. The idea was to remove whatever problems might arise because of differences in rank; most investigators were warrant officers, who ranked, technically speaking, below commissioned officers and above soldiers and NCOs. But CID agents, with their bad suits and brown shoes, were about as inconspicuous as a soldier in camouflage would be on the streets of most American cities.

Isen opted for the camouflage BDUs.

As he drank his second cup of coffee, Isen made some notes in a small book about what kind of questions he might ask and whom he might want to talk to. He wrote "chain of command," which began with General Tremmore, the commander of the Eighty-second Airborne Division. Isen didn't think that Tremmore would have anything of substance to say about Hauck, as there was a great distance between the general and the division's many lieutenants. Isen would visit Tremmore as a courtesy—he would be snooping around this man's command—and because Flynn had directed him to stop in. Another courtesy call to the brigade commander, Veir's boss, and then Isen would go to see Veir, the battalion commander. Finally, Isen wanted to talk to Hauck's company commander, the captain who was Hauck's immediate superior and would, theoretically at least, have had the most impact on Hauck's professional life. He also wanted to talk to Hauck's NCOs, the sergeants who worked for him and, assuming that Hauck had been a smart young officer, upon whom he would have relied. Isen also made a note to track down Hauck's roommate; General Flynn's sister had supplied the name and address.

He'd talked to Flynn on the telephone twice in the last three days. Flynn had given him the barest outlines of the case and then had failed to give him the CID report.

Isen wrote at the top of the notebook page, "Get fax # to receive CID report." On the top of the page facing this list, Isen wrote "Questions."

He took a sip of coffee and stared out at Darlington's small backyard as he thought about what he might ask.

He wrote, "Any indicators of depression? Recent successes or failures on the job? Changes in habits?"

In parentheses, Isen wrote, "drugs? alcohol?"

He wrote "personal problems" on the right-hand page, then, at the bottom of the list of names, he wrote, "girlfriend? social life?"

Isen thought about the graves at Arlington, about Hauck's forebears who'd worn the uniform, and he wrote, "family pressures?"

He considered that last entry and began to wonder: was he supposed to develop a theory of what happened first, and then pursue that (*Hauck killed himself because he was afraid of failing, afraid of letting his family down*), or would developing such a theory limit his questioning, close his mind to other possibilities?

Isen drained his cup and considered how little he knew about investigative techniques. There had to be a logical way to approach this thing, and, considering that this was the Army, there was probably a manual that spelled out exactly how to ask such questions. But Isen was ignorant of all that; there'd been no time to learn, and there was none now. He was supposed to be in the Chief of Staff's office in forty-five minutes, and he didn't know what he was going to say to the man. Isen wondered why Flynn had chosen him, in his ignorance, to take on such a job.

He took his coffee into the den and found the rolled-up *Newsweek* Sue Lynn had shown him the night before. The first part of the article focused exclusively on Harlan Veir, who had been chosen, somehow, to represent the new Army the headline sang about.

The writer—or perhaps Veir—made a great deal of fuss about Veir's humble roots: born into a poor Kentucky family, he had worked his way through college with his sights set on becoming a soldier.

"I wanted to serve my country, and to make my family proud of me," Veir had told the interviewer. "And the great thing about this country is that even a poor boy from the backwoods of Kentucky can do great things if he applies himself and is willing to work hard."

"Damn, Harlan," Isen said out loud. "The only thing missing is the friggin' log cabin."

The article gave just a few details of Veir's career. He had served several tours with the Eighty-second Airborne Division, the Army's most celebrated (some would say publicity-conscious) unit. Veir was a member of the "Airborne Mafia," an unofficial but, in Isen's mind, very real group of soldiers who spent most of their careers in this one division. The unit was flashy, distinctive and proud. If the Army was a subset of American culture, the Eighty-second Airborne Division was a subset of the Army culture. Like members of any closed society, the "mafia" here held that the closed nature of the group lent it constancy and professionalism. Other people, outsiders, called the same result inbreeding.

"Of course there are a lot of pressures on the Army these days," Veir had told the interviewer. "The force is going through some tough changes, drawing down in size, adjusting to new missions that we call 'short-of-war': interventions and so forth. But the fundamental concerns for the commander remain the same. My job is twofold: train these soldiers so that they can accomplish whatever mission the President gives us, and bring these sons and daughters back safely to their families."

Isen thought the speech sounded canned, or at least doctored by sympathetic editors. But there was Harlan Veir, in the accompanying photo, earnest and fatherly as he talked to a group of fresh-faced young paratroopers. There was an echo in the composition, and it took Isen a moment to puzzle it out.

The photo mimicked a shot of Eisenhower talking to paratroopers on the eve of the D Day invasion. In that photo, the general had been in a dress uniform, the paratroopers loaded for combat, their faces blackened for the coming night's battle. In this modern and, Isen thought, shameless re-creation, Veir was dressed as the soldiers were. Just another defender of freedom.

"Gag me," Isen said out loud.

It wasn't hot yet when Isen stepped outside Sue Lynn's door, and the sharp blue sky here wouldn't dissolve into that milky haze that made Washington uncomfortable and unattractive. But Isen knew that by mid-morning the heat would be steady, smothering. The air was already thick with moisture, the grass wet as after a light rain, the car wind-shields streaked where the moisture ran off in tiny rivulets. The smell was all pine, at once sharp and sticky.

Isen joined the flow of morning traffic on the All-American Expressway (the Eighty-second, whose soldiers wore a double A on their shoulder patch, was the All-American Division). Cars belonging to the many civilians who worked at Bragg were identifiable by their green Department of Defense registration stickers. Soldiers' cars, also with DOD stickers, were identifiable in other ways.

Single young NCOs favored old luxury cars: eight-year-old BMWs and Volvos with little pine tree air fresheners (redundant in North Carolina, Isen thought) depending from the mirror. Younger soldiers drove souped-up pseudo-sports cars, economy cars with rear spoilers added almost as an afterthought. Windows in these were often tinted nearly black, the owners' fanciful nicknames air-brushed on the doors or on the rear like the elaborate markings on great sailing ships: "Dewbaby," "La Fox," "2 Steppr." Married soldiers seemed doomed to drive minivans, and if the bumper stickers were to be believed, every driver had a child who was an honor student.

Isen turned on to Gruber Road, passing a two-story sign with "82d Safety-Gram" in red. The sign's moveable plastic letters read "21 Days Since the Last Training / Traffic Fatality. Safety Starts With You."

Apparently, Isen thought, Michael Hauck's death fit some other category.

Isen found the Division Headquarters amid the clusters of block construction and parked in the lot across from the main entrance. The first soldier he encountered gave him a sharp salute with the unit's standard greeting, "Airborne, sir," to which Isen replied, as prescribed, "All the way."

Isen wore the fatigue cap, a small pillbox shape with a visor, that matched the camouflage pattern of his BDUs. Paratroopers, and that included nearly every military person on Fort Bragg, wore the distinctive beret of airborne soldiers throughout the world. The universe here, as Sue Lynn had reminded him, was divided into two camps: those with, and those without.

Isen had worn the black beret of the U.S. Army Rangers

when he was assigned to that unit, and he could remember how the young Rangers would swagger beneath it as they moved around other parts of post, into "leg land" as they called it, where lesser, earthbound beings—legs—dwelt under the brims of their puny BDU caps. Isen had seen nineteen-year-old privates, buoyed by the aura they felt they projected, swagger by much senior NCOs. All soldiers here, maroon berets or not, would salute him—his major's gold oak leaf was clearly visible on the front of his cap—but most of them would let him know that they saluted his rank from a position somewhat higher in the food chain.

Isen stuck the offending cap into the cargo pocket of his trousers as he entered the building. The main entrance, two stories of glass centered on a low brick building, was protected by a canopy that bore an enlarged version of the unit patch. Two more representations of the big red, white and blue flash decorated the front of the second story.

A bit overdone, Isen thought as he walked into a glass-enclosed lobby.

"Can I help you, sir?"

The window to his left, he now saw, was a two-way mirror. There were holes cut there; one for speaking, one for passing things across a small counter, like the ticket booth at a theater. The voice came from behind the glass; Isen could see a mouth through the hole.

"Major Mark Isen to see the Chief of Staff."

"Airborne, sir. May I have your ID card, please."

Isen put his green Army identification card on the tray and received, in return, a clip-on badge.

"That'll open the door in front of you."

Isen slipped the badge into a slot. There was an electronic buzz, and a soldier on the opposite side pulled the door open for him.

"Right this way, sir."

Isen followed the man along a narrow passageway. The cheap paneling was all but covered with scores of photographs; a visitor who did not know that this was a unit steeped in and proud of its history could learn a great deal in this corridor. One entire wall was covered with portraits of the division's commanders. Isen recognized World War II's "Jumpin' Jim" Gavin, who took command at thirty-seven and who carried a rifle into battle. Gavin was the only general wearing a helmet in his photo.

Isen's guide took the stairs two at a time, leading Isen to a small landing. Four or five tiny offices were crammed around a small reception area; more bad paneling, shoddy carpet, dim lighting. Isen thought the message here was clear enough: this was a division that spent its time in the field, not decorating its offices. As if to reinforce that, all of the offices—including the one marked "C of S"—were empty.

The Chief of Staff, one of the most powerful men on Fort Bragg, was responsible for coordinating the work of the entire Division Staff, which in turn administered the fifteen thousand people who wore the "All-American" patch. A handful of lieutenant colonels and a couple of dozen majors answered directly to the Chief, but his real power lay in the control he exercised over the Commanding General's calendar and office visits. Every ambitious officer on post wanted face time with the general; the Chief of Staff held the keys to the palace.

The tiny landing held a single beat-up desk and a clerk, a tall private first class who stood as Isen entered. "Can I help you, sir?"

"Good morning, Coates," Isen said, looking at the name tape on the woman's uniform. "I'm Major Isen, and I'm supposed to see either the Chief or the CG this morning."

"Very well, sir," Coates said, glancing down earnestly at the appointment book on her desk. "Won't you have a seat?"

Isen recognized the polite crispness that many women in uniform, especially the young and good-looking, used to signal "That's Private First Class Coates to you, bubba."

Coates was tall, about five nine or ten, he guessed, with a fine-boned face and a healthful vitality that would have made her remarkable even if she were not beautiful. A young male soldier, who looked just old enough for high school football, sat in a chair beside Coates's desk, trying his best to stay visible to her as Coates checked her boss's schedule. The young men who worked in the building doubtless manufactured excuses to come by this office, even though, with all the rank around, it was pretty close to the fire. Isen wondered how many of Coates's fan club were forty-five-year-old lieutenant colonels.

On the wall above Coates was a famous photo of a World War II paratrooper on his way to help stop the German advance at Bastogne, in the fight that became known as the Battle of the Bulge.

"I'm the Eighty-second Airborne," the poster proclaimed in inch-high black letters. "And this is as far as the bastards are going." The man was filthy, his checks drawn in by the cold; his rifle hung over one shoulder, and a wicked-looking fighting knife was strapped to his leg. The soldier in the photograph scowled at the camera. Or, more correctly, Isen guessed, at the photographer, who had probably jumped out of a warm jeep to snap pictures of the grunts as they walked by.

On a bookshelf just below the poster was a white, candy-filled mug decorated with a big red heart. A small teddy bear, holding a pennant that said "I love you," clung to the lip of the cup. Isen looked down at the lovely Private Coates and wondered what the World War II GI would think of the modern United States Army.

Suddenly a voice too big for the room asked, "You Mark Isen?"

Isen, distracted from his daydreams about Private Coates, jumped to his feet.

"I'm Rich Kent."

Kent moved toward Isen from the stairway, his hand thrust forward.

"Good morning, sir," Isen said, taking the proffered hand. "Thanks for seeing me this morning."

Colonel Richard Kent was a little taller than Isen, maybe five eleven, with a handsome face lined around the eyes. His uniform blouse was tight across the shoulders, loose around his waist, which suggested that Kent, like a lot of officers, did some of his networking in the post gym. He smiled as he took Isen's hand, showing off even rows of white teeth.

"Well, you didn't actually get in the door, Major," Kent said, still smiling. "As a matter of fact, the CG and I are both pretty busy this morning, so I thought I'd send you right down to talk to Colonel Veir. I understand you've met him?"

"Briefly, sir, at Lieutenant Hauck's funeral at Arlington."

Kent scowled, shook his head slightly. "What a shame, huh?"

"Yessir," Isen agreed. "General Flynn told me to thank General Tremmore personally for allowing me to visit on behalf of the family."

"I'll be sure to pass the comment along," Kent said earnestly.

But no one can see the Wizard, Isen thought.

"I'm about to drive out to a training site," Kent continued. "And I'll be going right by where Colonel Veir is located this morning. How about we ride together so you and I can talk?"

Isen didn't particularly like the idea of surrendering his mobility to Kent's whims, but he couldn't think of a graceful exit.

"Sounds great, sir," Isen said.

"Coates, how about bringing my vehicle around front?" Kent said, smiling at the young woman behind the desk.

Kent held the smile—*Notice me*—too long. The vying for attention that had been understandable in Coates's young admirer—the soldier who'd been at her desk but had since disappeared—was pathetic in Kent. Coates either didn't notice or didn't let on that she noticed.

"Airborne, sir," she said. The phrase came as easily as breathing around paratroopers. "Right away."

Coates, apparently, was the Chief's driver as well as his clerk. The prospect of riding with Kent suddenly brightened.

Isen and Kent watched as the pretty young soldier grabbed her beret and ducked out the door.

"A fine young American, right there," Kent said.

"Yessir," Isen agreed. "It's a great country."

On the road, with Isen cramped in the back of Kent's humvee, the two men had to shout to be heard.

"Are you the guy who was with the Rangers in that shootout?" Kent asked bluntly.

"Yes, sir," Isen answered. Isen, always careful about talking about his combat experiences, didn't go into detail. He'd found that if he met ten people who knew more than what the media had told them about the incident, he'd find ten different versions of what had happened.

"Word is, you did a hell of a job," Kent said without looking back.

And the word is that I screwed up, too, Isen thought. *Depends on who's talking at the moment.* "Thank you, sir," he said out loud.

Kent let a few minutes of silence go by. Isen braced himself as the vehicle turned off the hardtop and onto a bumpy dirt road. Private Coates was silent. Isen tried not to stare at the line of her throat.

"You get a chance to see the write-up in *Newsweek?*" Kent asked.

"Yes, sir."

"Great stuff," Kent said, slapping his leg for emphasis. "Some great stuff in there about the division, about the soldiers."

Kent pronounced the word "sojers," but Isen thought it was an affectation, as if some PR people told him to *roll* the word out.

"I spoke to Colonel Veir a short while ago," Kent said enthusiastically, as if such a contact were cause for celebration. Isen decided that Kent would have been a politician in civilian life.

"He said we could find him out here checking on some training. I'll drop you off, then have Coates take me to where I need to go, which is just down the road a ways. She can come back for you shortly and I'll catch a ride back to headquarters. Sound OK?"

"Sounds good to me, sir," Isen said.

"OK with you, Coates?"

Kent was smiling as he asked, but it wasn't as if the soldier had a choice.

Private Coates barely nodded. "OK, sir," she said. "Sure."

Coates turned the vehicle into a small gravel parking area. There were several more humvees and a truck lined up neatly against the tree line. Kent and Isen climbed out of the vehicle and walked toward a group of men some hundred meters away. Isen thought he recognized Lieutenant Colonel Veir, who stood at the center of the small group, one hand on his hip, one hand chopping the air importantly as he talked.

"Harlan Veir is one of the best commanders in this division," Kent said. "No, let me rephrase that: he *is* the best battalion commander in this division, maybe the best I've ever seen. His unit is consistently the top performer. They win everything they try to win, everything Veir wants to win. Colonel Veir was pretty upset by all of this—the suicide and everything. I know he'll do everything to help you find whatever it is you're looking for."

Kent turned to Isen, nodding as if agreeing with himself.

"The family just wants some more details about Lieutenant Hauck's personal life, sir. They're trying to figure out why he would do such a thing instead of asking for help," Isen said.

"I'm sure," Kent said. "You know, Isen," he continued, "whenever we have a kid killed in a training accident or a car crash, we have his NCOs go through his personal stuff before we ship it back to his family. You know, empty the footlocker, the pockets on the uniforms, that kind of stuff."

Isen wondered what Kent was getting at. He certainly knew the procedure for shipping a soldier's belongings, but he wanted Kent to continue.

"We make sure we don't send any cock books back home to some kid's mom." Kent grinned.

He's nervous, Isen thought.

Kent's comment, meant to be disingenuous, failed. He wasn't talking about looking for dirty books—no doubt some officer from Veir's command had already inventoried Hauck's belongings. He was talking about using discretion, about keeping secrets.

And he was talking about these things out of earshot of Harlan Veir.

Turning away from Isen, Kent called out. "Colonel Veir."

Veir and the officers and NCOs with him looked up, and Kent stopped walking. If he got any closer, military courtesy would have called for Veir to interrupt everyone, bring the whole group to attention and salute. Veir wrapped up what he was saying with a few more jabs, then jogged over to where Kent and Isen waited.

Veir saluted Kent, who was a full colonel, and Isen threw

in a salute—Veir outranked him—as the other man approached, just to be on the safe side. The ragged effect looked like the start of a bad comedy routine.

"How goes it out here?" Kent asked. He seemed to stiffen a bit in Veir's presence.

"Just great, sir," Veir said, practically shouting. Isen had apparently missed the training, early in his career, that said you had to be loud to be a successful officer.

"You've met Major Isen?" Kent said, half turning.

"Yessir," Veir said, his grin fading quickly into a serious look that fit the subject. "Up at Arlington, unfortunately. How are you . . . is it Mike?"

"It's Mark, sir," Isen said, taking Veir's offered hand. Veir squeezed just beyond the point of discomfort.

"As we discussed," Kent began, "Major Isen was asked by Lieutenant Hauck's family to see if he couldn't tell them something about Hauck's life here that would explain why he killed himself."

"This must be tough on the family," Veir said, frowning. "I know it was tough on us."

"I'll send my driver back for him in a little while," Kent said.

"I'd like to have your driver from the back for a little while," Veir said.

Kent, already uncomfortable, cringed. Isen decided that Veir fit Sue Lynn's description of him.

What a dickhead.

The two junior men saluted, and Kent returned to his vehicle, where Coates leaned against the hood, waiting for her boss. Veir gave Coates a little wave, which she did not return.

"Good-looking young woman, there," Veir said.

Isen kept quiet.

"Surprised she's not in the Air Force."

Isen's curiosity won out. "Why's that, sir?"

"Oh, call it Veir's Theory of Military Poontang," Veir said. "The best-looking stuff goes into the Air Force, after that the Navy. You know, they've got all those clean uniforms and air bases and stuff."

Veir turned a straight face to Isen, as serious as if he were holding forth on some great social theory.

"Call it the condo and sailboat image," Veir continued. "What's the Army got? A bunch of smelly guys in green face-paint. So even for an average-looking woman in the Army, the competition just isn't there. Presto, she becomes a beauty."

Isen had no idea what he was supposed to say. It wasn't so much that he was shocked—he'd heard cruder comments. It was just that most people were a little more circumspect in a first meeting.

Isen concentrated instead on keeping his reaction—*this guy is fucking incredible*—from showing on his face.

There was a moment of awkward silence; Isen changed the subject.

"I understand you'll be running a live-fire here tomorrow," Isen said. He was tempted to ask if Veir planned to go through the exercise with a few of the platoons to show them how safe it was—in imitation of General Tremmore.

"Platoon sized," Veir answered. "Take me three days to run the whole battalion through."

As he spoke his eyes wandered over Isen's uniform, a common rite when soldiers met each other. The U.S. Army uniform was really a walking display case of accomplishments, with badges and tags and tabs awarded for various proficiency tests and—the ultimate test—combat. It wasn't unusual for two soldiers, meeting for the first time, to check out each other's personal military history by comparing badges, a juvenile ritual of preening Isen called "measuring dicks."

Veir faced Isen squarely, leaning toward him.

"So what can I do for you, Mark?" He wore a thin smile that mostly said, *I'm busy. Let's get this shit over with.*

Isen, who didn't want to be close enough to smell Veir's breath, took a step backward.

"I was hoping to talk to Hauck's company commander and maybe some of the other lieutenants, sir," Isen said. "Naturally, I don't want to interfere with training."

"We can do that. Sure," Veir thundered. "But why don't you start by asking me whatever questions you want to pose. We're a pretty busy unit—got a thousand things going on all the time. If I can save my people, and you, some time, I'd be happy to do so."

"Did you know Lieutenant Hauck very well, sir?"

"Well, I didn't work with him as closely as his company commander, of course, but I make it a point to get to know my junior officers. And I think it's important for them to know me, too. The more they understand about the way I do things, the better they're going to be able to execute my orders when we go to the field."

Isen waited for Veir to get back to the question.

"Hauck hadn't been here that long, as I'm sure you know," Veir said. "I'm sure you checked his personnel file."

Isen hesitated, For a moment he thought about telling Veir about the hours he'd had to work in order to get away from the Pentagon. He let it slide.

"No, sir, I haven't had a chance to do that yet."

Veir looked at Isen, lifting his chin almost imperceptibly. *Strike one,* Isen thought.

"Well, you might have missed your chance. I think all of his paperwork got sent away to wherever they keep records after someone dies. I don't think they keep that stuff around."

"Of course," Isen said. He made a mental note to check anyway.

And I need to get on the old man about that CID report.

"Hauck got here around February, I think," Veir continued. "So what's that make it? Six, seven months? He went right to a rifle platoon and was doing a good job."

"Was his company commander satisfied with his performance?"

"I only heard good things about Hauck," Veir said. He spoke slowly now, a measured, precise cadence.

Cautious, Isen thought, watching Veir. *He's worried about his ass.*

"Of course he experienced some of the difficulties that all new lieutenants face," Veir continued. "These young guys have a lot to learn and almost no time to learn it when they get here. If I'm not mistaken, I think we went right to a rather vigorous training exercise when Hauck arrived. He got to know his men while we were in the field."

As they spoke, two trucks pulled up and discharged thirty or so soldiers dressed in combat gear. The soldiers climbed over the tailgate, assembling, adjusting equipment, talking among themselves. Old rhythms.

Veir and Isen watched as the NCOs moved the men onto the beginning of the course.

"Dry run," Veir said.

"I miss it," Isen admitted.

"Not much fun driving a desk, huh?"

For the briefest moment, the guards they'd already managed to put in place wavered, and they were two soldiers, talking about what they loved.

"I don't know much about Hauck's personal life," Veir said, allowing a small smile. "But then again, we work so many hours that it's quite possible he didn't really have a social life. You know what they say about second lieutenants."

Isen turned. He'd no doubt heard the joke before, but he was prepared to be polite.

"Work 'em twenty-three hours a day and they still have an hour to screw off and get into trouble."

Across the road, the soldiers moved into place. Isen thought he saw a couple of the junior officers glance nervously in Veir's direction.

"We do a lot of things together, off-duty that is, in this unit," Veir went on. "I think that kind of stuff's important for cohesion." He paused as if waiting for Isen to agree.

"I understand Hauck's roommate was from some other unit on post," Isen said.

Veir looked at Isen slowly, as if testing the visitor's knowledge. "I wouldn't know," he said.

He raised his hand and signaled to someone over by the beginning of the training lane. A figure there broke away and jogged over to Veir and Isen. When the soldier drew closer, Isen saw the two black bars of a captain on the man's collar.

"Sir?" the junior officer said even before he stopped moving.

"Some of those soldiers don't have magazines in their ammo pouches," Veir said. His tone was perfectly even; he was a stating a fact. But the captain, whose name tag read Pesce, was unpleasantly surprised. He glanced nervously over his shoulder at the soldiers.

"I'm not sure we issued the empty magazines, sir," Pesce said.

Isen was surprised Veir could see that far. Each soldier carried two pouches on the front of his belt, meant to hold the big aluminum magazines into which would be loaded the rifle ammunition. Most soldiers, when they weren't actually carrying ammo, loaded the handy pouches with candy, gum, flashlights, insect repellent and even little bottles of hot sauce to doctor up the bland field rations.

"You're not sure?" Veir said acidly.

Bad move, Pesce, Isen thought.

"We didn't issue them, sir," Pesce said. "We'll issue them tomorrow."

"I see," Veir said, a comment that could mean nothing, or could mean a great deal. "But now, if you take a look at your soldiers over there, you'll see that some of them have full pouches—no doubt stuffed with candy bars and dirty pictures—some have deflated pouches. It's not uniform."

It seemed to Isen that there was an unnecessary malevolence in Veir's tone. The situation needed correcting, but it wasn't as if a soldier's life was in danger.

"I'll straighten that out, sir," Captain Pesce said.

"See that you do," Veir answered.

As the luckless Captain Pesce hurried away, another vehicle drove up and stopped nearby. An enormous major emerged from the passenger side and approached Veir, saluting as he drew close.

"Morning, sir," the man said without smiling.

"Good morning, Len," Veir said enthusiastically. "I'd like you to meet Major Mark Isen, the visitor from the Pentagon we've been expecting."

Few introductions in the military could create a colder reception than the one Veir had just used. Visitors from the Pentagon were snoops looking to catch people wasting resources or doing things that weren't by the book. Visitors from the Pentagon did not carry good news, did not come to make life easier.

"This is Len Foote, Major Leonard Foote, my executive officer and the man who keeps things running smoothly around here," Veir said.

Isen extended his hand. Foote was even taller than Veir, about six four, Isen guessed, with an enormous upper body and sinewed arms that hung away from his torso. His uniform was achingly crisp, and his head, or what Isen could see of it, was shaved smooth, so that his beret looked like a tiny decoration on top of a black marble column.

Foote took Isen's hand.

"The CID already did a preliminary report on Lieutenant Hauck's suicide," Foote said, as if Isen might not have considered the possibility. "The whole thing is pretty straightforward; there probably won't be any big differences between that and the final version."

"That may be so," Isen answered. "But the family is looking for a little more in the way of 'why.'"

Foote didn't answer, except to narrow his eyes.

"I told Major Isen that we'd do everything we could to help him," Veir said. He appeared amused at Foote's hostility. "But frankly, I'm not sure what else we can do."

Turning to face Isen, he asked, "Did you ask about the psychological autopsy?"

"Sir?"

"The psychological autopsy," Veir repeated slowly. Isen didn't answer. Foote snorted and Isen considered that the count had jumped to two strikes.

"The final CID report for a suicide will include a psychological autopsy," Veir said. "One of the docs from the hospital will write something up, based on interviews or notes from the investigator's interviews, about the mental state of the deceased."

Veir smiled. "You should try to get a look at it, when it's finished. It might answer all your questions."

Across the road, the platoon of soldiers began to move through the assault course. Veir watched them but continued to address Isen.

"Sometimes problems come up, and we can help a man. Sometimes we never know," Veir said. "This is an infantry battalion, Major. My main responsibility is to get these men ready for combat. Lately I've had to train them to act as police officers, diplomats, translators, all that peace-keeping bullshit ... just about any goddamn mission the whiz kids at the White House dream up for us."

"Naturally I'm concerned about the welfare of all my men, but there are over seven hundred soldiers in this command, with another fifteen hundred or so wives and children to think about."

He paused for a moment, as if all of this were news to Isen.

"I am terribly saddened that this young man took his own life," Veir said crisply. He stood with his hands behind his back, staring off into the middle distance. Isen got the distinct impression that Veir had given this speech before, even if only to himself.

"I have examined my conscience to see if there was something I could have done differently to prevent that death. I found nothing; maybe you will find something. If you do, I want to be the first to know so that we can avoid tragedies like this in the future." He turned to Isen, leaning toward him, weight forward. "But you aren't going to find anything."

Veir walked away, leaving Isen alone with the hulking, silent Major Foote, who'd been watching Isen all along.

"Let's be straight with each other, Isen," Foote said as soon as Veir was out of earshot. "Just what the fuck are you doing here? Are you an investigator?"

"No, I'm not an investigator, at least not an official investigator," Isen said. "I came down here as a favor to Hauck's uncle—"

"The general," Foote interrupted.

"Yes," Isen said.

"So this is just an exercise in ass-kissing for you, right? I mean, what's your personal stake in this? Did you even know Hauck? Ever hear of him before he blew his brains out?"

Isen paused before answering. Foote had moved closer, put his hands on his hips, adopting a stance that probably scared the bejesus out of second lieutenants and eighteen-year-old privates. Apparently Foote was one of those big men—and there were a lot of them in the Army—stuck in the playground mentality that said size always intimidates.

Isen smiled. "What's your problem?"

"My problem is this," Foote said, looking around furtively to see who else might hear. "Some lieutenant decides his life is too fucked up to go on and eats his pistol. It's not pleasant, but it happens. So now the top battalion in this division looks bad. The whole thing stinks and it reflects on everybody in this organization." He tapped on his chest as he mentioned the unit. Clearly they were one and the same to Major Foote.

"But the CID comes in and does the report—by the book. The bottom line: nobody here is to blame for what Michael Hauck did to himself," Foote said. "So I don't see why some nosy bootlick from the Pentagon has to come down here and look for stuff that isn't there."

"I just came down to find out a couple of things about his personal life—"

"It doesn't matter," Foote interrupted. "You're here. As far as the other people on post are concerned, if someone has to dig around and ask questions—then we must have done something wrong. And we didn't. The only person who knows why Hauck killed himself was Hauck. And he ain't talking."

Isen heard gravel crunching behind him. He turned around to see Private Coates, Kent's driver, approaching. The young woman saluted. "Airborne, sir," she said. "Ready when you are."

"Thanks, Coates. I'll be there in a second." He turned back to Foote, frustrated that the perfect witty reply eluded him.

"I'll be around the battalion area this afternoon," Isen said. "I'm going to talk to Hauck's company commander."

"Not today," Foote said.

"Look, Major," Isen said, his control beginning to fray. "Colonel Veir gave me permission to talk to—"

Foote brought his hand up sharply.

"I'm not saying you can't talk to him. You can't see him *today* because he's not working *today*," Foote said in a sing-song, as if talking to a child. "His wife had a baby this morning. He'll be on leave for a few days, if that's OK with you."

"Thank you, Major Foote," Isen said evenly. "You've been most helpful."

"Fuck you, ass-wipe," Foote said.

3

"**H**E SAID THAT? HE SAID 'FUCK YOU, ASS-WIPE'?"

Sue Lynn Darlington was leaning toward Isen in the booth they shared at Fayetteville's "only"—Sue Lynn's description—Italian restaurant. Isen had given her a rundown of his morning as a guest of the Eighty-second Airborne Division.

"Yeah. I thought Veir was hostile. Next to Foote he was loving."

"I told you they'd be pissed off that you're here," Darlington said.

"You didn't tell me I'd need a goddamn bulletproof vest."

"Did you wear your uniform?"

"Of course I wore my uniform," Isen said.

"I still think you should wear civvies," Darlington countered.

"Then it would look like I really was a CID agent."

"Maybe people would talk to you then," she said.

"But I'm not a CID agent." He paused. That was the crux of the problem, of course. No jurisdiction, no power, no experience. And he was finding out, as he went along, that there was some basic information he needed, information Flynn probably had access to: Hauck's personnel file, the preliminary CID report, whatever part of the psychological autopsy that had been completed. Isen wondered if there might be a reason Flynn would send him out uninformed, with just a half-baked mission to "see what you can find out."

"Hell, I don't even know what kind of questions to ask," Isen complained.

"If you were a *real* investigator," Sue Lynn said, swirling red wine in her glass. "You'd probably move Foote way up on your list of suspicious characters."

"I don't have a list, Sue Lynn. Michael Hauck wasn't murdered; he shot himself."

She placed her glass on the table, wrapped long fingers around the stem and announced, "I think something's screwy in that unit."

"Look," Isen said. "The Army is looking for reasons to show people the door. Having one of your lieutenants commit suicide can't look very good to a promotion board, right?"

"Right," Sue Lynn allowed.

"So they don't want any more attention," Isen said. "They just want the case closed."

Sue Lynn shook her head. "I don't know. If they're circling the wagons, maybe there's something more, something that hasn't been uncovered yet."

"Well, there was something else," Isen said.

He told Sue Lynn what Kent said about going through a soldier's belongings.

"But he wasn't talking about taking out porno magazines."

"He's thinks you're going to find something and he wants you to keep quiet," Sue Lynn said.

"Or . . . and this is a bit strange . . . he was dropping a hint. Like he wants me to find something. Otherwise, why be careful to say all this before Veir was with us."

Sue Lynn gave Isen a skeptical look.

"What's that mean?" he asked.

"You ever hear, 'When you hear hoofbeats, think horses, not zebras'?"

"OK, OK," Isen said. "You're probably right."

"So what about Veir?" Sue Lynn asked.

"He's a character, all right. He made a lewd and totally

uncalled for comment about Kent's driver right in front of Kent, his superior, and me, a complete stranger. Then he rambled on about women in the military; finally he chewed out some captain because the troops didn't have their ammo pouches all stuffed the same way.

"I don't know about this Dark Prince stuff," Isen continued. "Looks to me like he's just a run-of-the-mill douchebag."

"He was probably showing off."

"I think he's a control freak," Isen offered.

Sue Lynn laughed. "We're all control freaks," she said. "That's why we're in the Army."

"Not me," Isen said. "I'm a free spirit."

"Right," Darlington said. "Mr. Goody Two Shoes."

"What?"

Sue Lynn leaned forward, serious now.

"That's why Flynn sent you here, I think."

"Why?"

"Because, even in this screwed-up situation—hell, he knew these guys would eat you alive—he knew that you'd do whatever is right."

"I don't know about that," Isen said.

"Hey, there's nothing wrong with going out and looking for windmills if tilting at windmills makes you happy," she said, smiling.

"Is that all I'm doing?" he asked. "Tilting at windmills?"

"Don't get all sensitive on me," she said, leaning over to touch the back of his hand. "You're a good man. I've known that for a long time."

Isen, all lost in sweet confusion, wasn't sure how to respond.

Sue Lynn straightened up. "So what's next on your agenda?"

A bit embarrassed, Isen spoke rapidly. "I'm meeting Savin, Lieutenant Greg Savin, tonight. He's—he was—Hauck's roommate. I'm hoping he can shed a little light on things for me. General Flynn thinks there was some friction there—something. And Veir gave me an odd look when I asked about the roommate. I found out the brigade commander took over only three weeks ago. He probably won't have much to add; I may skip him. I'm supposed to talk to the lieutenants in Veir's battalion tomorrow."

"You think they'll talk to you?" Darlington asked.

"A fair question, I suppose, given Foote's hostility. Let's see, I know they'll at least show up where Veir tells them to."

"And they'll probably say what Veir wants them to say."

Isen considered the point as the appetizers arrived and the waiter poured more chianti into their glasses.

"We didn't toast," Darlington said.

Isen raised his glass, studied the dark wine against the candlelight. "Here's to keeping friendships alive," he said.

Darlington touched her glass to his. "Here's to getting to know one another better."

She held his eyes over the rim of her glass for one beat, two. Isen felt warm.

"Boy, this looks good, doesn't it?" he said, setting down his wine.

There were four delicate manicotti arranged on the plate, with a thick, creamy sauce traced across the centers.

"Italian food is very sensual," Darlington offered. Her delivery was matter-of-fact, an observation, but her eyes were softer now. The candlelight played sunset colors across her face. Isen used his fork to break off a tiny piece, offering it to her across the table. Sue Lynn leaned toward him, parted her lips, blew on the hot food, then took it delicately from the fork.

Isen watched, holding the fork in midair like a wand.

"You have a roommate?" she asked.

"No," Isen said, recovering clumsily. "I've got a tiny apartment in Old Town Alexandria, really a great neighborhood." He studied the presentation of the food before him. "But I spend so little time there I hardly notice that I'm alone."

When he looked up, Darlington was watching him intently.

"I think that's bullshit," she said. Sue Lynn pronounced "bullshit" as precisely as she might say *pâté de foie gras*.

Isen smiled an agreement. Sue Lynn had him fixed with those green eyes. She wore a black silk shirt, deeply scooped at the neck, and when she leaned forward Isen could see a tiny slash of lace arcing over the curve of one breast.

"Do you miss being married?"

"Big-league questions now, huh?" He put down his fork, watched his glass as he lifted it to his mouth.

"I miss *being* married, yes. But Adrienne and I weren't right for each other."

"She hated the Army, didn't she?" Darlington said.

"Yes, she did. And after a while, I guess, some of that hostility was directed at me. It was inevitable, I suppose, since I was in uniform. I *looked* like the enemy."

"Messy?"

"The divorce? No, not as these things go. I guess we parted amicably. Friends."

"You still have contact with her?"

"Not in a year," Isen said, surprised at how long it had been.

Darlington sipped her wine. Isen noticed that he was drinking a lot faster than she was.

"She didn't like me much, back when we met in Hawaii," Darlington commented.

Isen didn't know what to say. Whenever Adrienne, his ex-wife, had made an observation like that, she wasn't passing information; she had another agenda. Isen had been conditioned to tread lightly.

It was true that the ex-Mrs. Isen didn't much like Sue Lynn. Darlington had once made a comment at a party, something to the effect that she found Mark attractive. Adrienne Isen, far from being flattered that other women found her husband interesting, not only became angry, but decided to direct that anger at her husband, although he'd done nothing but show up.

"I suppose you're right," Isen said.

"She got angry that night I paid you a compliment, I think," Darlington said.

"Oh?"

"Don't play dumb," Darlington said, smirking. When she smiled she tilted her head back just a tiny bit, the yellow light warm on the column of her throat. "I'm sure she told you about it."

"Actually, I believe the way she phrased it was 'What the hell is going on between you two?' "

"To which you said?"

" 'Sue Lynn who?' "

"Very funny. I thought, at the time, that she'd take it as a compliment. I guess I didn't know her very well."

"I've often considered that myself," Isen said. "What exactly did you say that ticked her off?"

Darlington clenched her jaw and, in mock highbrow tones, offered. "I believe I said you had a nice rear end."

Isen shook his head, imagining one of Adrienne's icy looks.

"Of course," Sue Lynn said, lifting her glass and reverting to her familiar accent, "I might have gone too far when I said I wouldn't mind looking at that butt around the house all day."

"I guess she wasn't as big a sport as you thought."

Isen took another mouthful of wine. He'd had a handful of dates over the past year, none of them this engaging.

"What about you?" Isen asked. "I can't believe someone hasn't grabbed you up yet."

That question again, Sue Lynn thought. Her family and most of her friends thought Sue Lynn needed a husband, as if getting married were the only possible outcome for an adult woman. She used to struggle against such assumptions, sometimes to the point of questioning her own judgment, until she decided that her way of looking at things was just that . . . her way of looking at things.

As a captain, she'd lived for a while in a tiny apartment in Pearl City, Hawaii. The apartment had a small balcony overlooking Pearl Harbor, a microscopic kitchen and no furniture besides a futon in the bedroom and a secondhand kitchen table with mismatched chairs. Her friends were perplexed; her father, when he visited, was apoplectic.

"Why don't you have furniture? Don't they pay you for that job?"

"It's just not important to me, Daddy," she'd told him. She wanted to say that her paradigm—her way of judging what was important to her—differed from the "norm." Instead, she told him, "You know how some people don't care

61

if they drive an old, beat-up car? Well, that's how I feel about furniture."

Lately, that was how she felt about men, as well. She wasn't averse to taking a lover, but she didn't feel as if she needed someone beside her every night. It wasn't a popular notion among her friends, or even very prevalent. But it was hers for the time being.

"I lived with a guy for a short while when I first moved here two years ago," Sue Lynn said.

"Is that over?" Isen asked.

"You don't see him around, do you?" Darlington answered, turning out her palms and smiling. She put her hands flat on the table, lowered her voice to something more serious. "I kicked him out. He was catting around with somebody's wife."

"Some guys just don't know how good they have it."

It occurred to him that the comment might sound a little lame to Sue Lynn, who hadn't been drinking as much as he had. But she reached over and touched the back of his hand, parting her lips in a smile as she did so.

"Why thank you, Mark," Sue Lynn said.

Isen cleared his throat, returned her fixed stare.

"Did you ever notice how many different signals we send with our eyes?" Darlington said softly. She had not looked away.

"What do you mean?"

"Well, I could sit here all night and hold eye contact while you talked about Veir and that other fellow ... what was his name?"

"Foote."

"I could watch you all night and not telegraph anything other than interest," Darlington said. "Good listening skills."

"Mmm-hmm."

"But then I can ... I don't know ... change just a little bit." She tilted her head the merest fraction of an inch, opened her eyes a tiny bit wider, almost imperceptible changes. She was smiling.

Isen felt as if he'd just become aware of some lovely background music. Very soft.

"And is there a message here, Sue Lynn?" Isen asked as

the waiter appeared, wheeling a small cart loaded with steaming, fragrant food.

Isen's hand was flat on the table, fingers splayed. Sue Lynn reached down, rested thumb and forefinger on the back of his hand, then traced a long, slow line, a light stroke along both sides of his middle finger.

The waiter, balancing hot plates, was about to speak. Isen raised his hand to interrupt.

"Check, please."

Mark Isen was forty-five minutes late getting to the apartment Michael Hauck had shared with Lieutenant Greg Savin. He ran up the three flights from the parking lot, found two doors at the top of the landing, one decorated with an autumn wreath. The number on the other door matched the note in his hand. Music coming from behind the door became louder when it swung open in answer to Isen's knock.

"Greg Savin?"

Backlit, the figure in the doorway was difficult to see.

"Yes."

"I'm Mark Isen. I apologize for being late; I hope I didn't throw off any plans you had for the evening."

"Not yet, sir. Come in."

Once he was inside, Isen's eyes adjusted to the light. Savin looked to be about twenty-three, Hauck's age. A thin five nine or so, with light blond hair cut a little longer than most of the "high and tight" paratrooper haircuts Isen had seen around Bragg.

"You can have a seat in here, sir. I'll be back in a minute."

Savin went back to the galley kitchen and picked up the phone. Isen, who had apparently interrupted a conversation, heard a few mumbled sentences, then, clearly, "He's finally here; I'll call you back later. I love you, too."

Isen stood by the couch and pressed his hand to his stomach, where three glasses of wine, stirred by the run upstairs, sloshed around unimpeded by food.

Just hang on to your lunch, Isen thought.

The apartment had the temporarily inhabited look that most lieutenants' apartments had. There were footlockers in the corner; a few pictures clung to the walls with no logic as to their placement, as if they'd had to find a place for these things and nailing them up was just as convenient as shoving them behind a chair.

A cheap pressboard bookcase lined one wall, with what looked to be a half-dozen or so college texts on accounting principles and management. There were big gaps along the shelves, and Isen could see, from the line of dust, that books had been removed from those spaces. On the bottom shelf several anthologies of British and American poetry lay flat, with scores of yellow notes, like tabs, sticking out of them. There were a couple of snapshots in small frames: Savin and a young woman, a younger Savin with much longer hair behind the wheel of a convertible. From one corner of the shelf hung six or seven medals dangling at the ends of ribbons. Isen fingered one of the medals; it was a running trophy.

"Please don't touch those, sir."

Isen turned around to see Savin watching him, holding a bottle of water.

"They get stained when people put their fingers on them. Cheap metal, I guess."

He wasn't fully facing Isen, but watched the older man out of the corner of his eye, as one might half turn from a dog that could attack at any moment.

"You're the runner?"

"Was in college," Savin said. "I haven't had the time to do much serious training since I got here. Here all I have time for is unit PT. Gotta run with the group, no matter how slow it is. All for one and all that jazz."

Savin was testy. *I did keep him waiting forty-five minutes,* Isen thought.

Isen pushed some magazines aside to clear a seat on the small couch. As he sat, he found that he could see into the open door of one of the bedrooms. An overhead light was on in the other room, and there were large cardboard shipping boxes open and lined up against the wall. Savin followed his gaze.

"Captain Dennison, Mike's CO, came out and inventoried most of the personal stuff, although he left it for me to seal the boxes.

"Mike's family called and said I could keep any furniture

or common stuff like that," he said, nodding toward the open door. "They want me to send back his papers, books, photos—personal stuff. They're nice folks." He looked back over his shoulder at the boxes. "Amazing how someone can live twenty-three years and accumulate just enough stuff to fill three cardboard boxes."

"Any journals, diaries, letters?" Isen asked.

"There were some bundles of letters from his mom and his college buddies. I sent those to his family already. No journal or diary that I know of."

Isen opened his notebook, wrote "Call Hauck's Mom. Ask to see letters."

"Did you meet them at the funeral?" Isen asked. "The Haucks, I mean." He couldn't remember seeing Savin there.

"No. My leave request was disapproved. Actually, I think Mike's uncle had something to do with that."

Isen must have looked surprised.

Savin shrugged. "I'm not sure, I just got the feeling he didn't like me much." He paused, unsmiling, his face half turned. "I understand he's the one who sent you down here."

"Actually, General Flynn asked me to do him a favor."

"I didn't know you could turn down general officers," Savin said. He took a sip of water from the bottle.

Isen's buzz was wearing off, as was his patience with Savin's attitude.

"May I have some water?"

"Certainly, sir," Savin said, jumping up, a little too eager.

When Savin left the room, Isen stepped toward Hauck's bedroom.

There was a single bed, stripped; a matching desk and nightstand holding two military manuals whose owner didn't need them anymore. Below the desk, papers overflowed a small plastic trash can. Isen knelt down; there were stubs from bills, some junk mail, a couple of news magazines— minor records, testimonials. *I participate in life, in the mundane.*

Isen stood up. The little chamber reminded him of some cadet rooms he'd seen at West Point: spartan, sterile, unsigned. He looked in vain for touches of the individual, trying to get to know the dead boy.

Two unsealed cartons stood in a corner. Isen pulled back the flap of one: sweatshirts, jeans, rolled-up socks. The other held books, papers, small boxes.

"Can I take a look at some of this stuff?" Isen asked, sticking his hands in.

Savin started to say no, then saw that Isen had gone ahead.

"Uh ... I guess so." He stood in the doorway holding a glass of tap water. No ice.

Isen lifted some paperback books, turning the spines outward so he could read the titles: a couple of lightweight mysteries, some military fiction. There was a baseball glove shoved down beside a college yearbook. Texas A&M, Hauck's alma mater. Isen remembered Flynn saying that his nephew had received an ROTC commission out of A&M's Corps of Cadets.

Isen tugged at the glove, upsetting a cigar box. He pinched the lid closed as he righted it and lifted it out.

"All his uniform stuff," Savin said as Isen opened the box. There was an incomplete set of buttons for a dress blouse and a couple of what the soldiers called "thanks-for-coming" ribbons, the awards given for graduating a basic training course. The collection looked forlorn, like flotsam.

"Except for what he was buried in, of course," Savin said.

Isen found a photo album with the seal of Texas A&M on the cover. Inside were a few dozen pages of Hauck and his college buddies hamming for the camera in their Aggie uniforms, another of Hauck standing tall at some sort of ceremony.

"How did you two become roommates?" Isen asked.

"I had the apartment first, and my roommate got engaged and moved out. I needed someone to share the rent, so I just asked around."

There was a wallet-sized copy of Hauck's graduation photo. He looked like his mother, Isen decided. Light brown hair, delicate chin that suggested a vulnerability. If others got that impression, Hauck tried to make up for it, straining to look older, more military. He did not smile, did not even look directly at the camera's lens, but stared off to the photographer's side. Isen had not seen a picture of Hauck before—something else Flynn might have provided—and he stared now at the fresh face, hoping to get some sense of this young man whose actions had caused so much pain.

"Did Michael have any hobbies?" Isen asked.

"He liked to go down to the gym. He'd work out, then hang around where the soldiers were shooting hoops."

"He played basketball with the soldiers?" Isen asked.

"No. I think he mostly wanted to shoot the breeze with them. That's what he liked. Just being around the troops."

"Uh-huh," Isen said. *He got one thing right, anyway.*

There were more photos in envelopes, in the book and in the box at Isen's feet, all of fellow cadets. The only framed photograph, still on the desk, showed Hauck in his cadet uniform, probably at graduation. His father stood on one side, his mother on the other. All three of them had their arms at their sides.

Isen closed the flaps of the carton. Hauck's name and unit address at Bragg were written on the lid, probably in Hauck's handwriting. The box, shipped from Fort Benning when he'd finished his training there, had preceded Michael Hauck to his new life.

"As I was saying," Isen continued, "General Flynn asked me to come down here and see what I could find out about the life Mike had here. General Flynn's sister is . . . was Michael's mother."

Isen led the way back to the living room, where Savin sat stiffly, not quite on the edge of the chair. He looked like a man readying for a fight.

"What do you expect to find, sir?"

Isen moved to the bookshelf on the other side of the room—only a few feet from where Savin sat. He pressed his fingers to his temples. *Running into all these brick walls,* he thought, *is giving me a headache.*

"I don't have any expectations," Isen said. *I don't even have a freaking plan.* "Tell me something about Michael Hauck that I won't get from reading his personnel file," Isen said.

Isen could feel Savin staring at him, and he wondered what smart-ass response the young man was considering.

"Mike loved the Army," Savin said simply.

"He was happy here?"

"I didn't say that," Savin said curtly. "I said—"

"I heard what you said," Isen interrupted, barely biting off the sarcastic *lieutenant.*

Savin looked at Isen evenly.

Good job, Mark, Isen thought. *A little more of that and he'll just flip you the bird when you talk to him. Like everyone else here.*

Savin measured his words. "No," he continued. "I don't think he was happy."

Isen practiced his patient listener routine while the inside of his head threatened to explode. "Go on."

"This place just sucks all the life out of you," Savin said. "I mean, the hours we work are only the beginning. Nights, weekends. Hell, it was almost a break for him to go to the field. At least out there you *expect* twenty-four-hour operations."

"So Mike complained a lot about the hours? About the demands?" Isen asked.

"No, that was part of his problem, I think," Savin said. "He never wanted to complain, to say anything bad about the Army, about the people he worked with. Mike was a peacemaker, wanted everyone to get along. He was kind of naive, I guess. He wanted so much to believe that everyone was trying to do a good job that he was continuously disappointed."

Savin had been staring at his feet, old running shoes propped up on the spindly coffee table. He looked up, shot Isen a glance from the suspicious corner of his eye. "Are you an infantryman, Major?"

"Yes," Isen said.

Savin didn't respond.

"Does that make a difference?"

"It did to Mike, sir," Savin said, shutting down again.

Isen was suddenly hot again, nauseous to boot. Savin wasn't talking, and Isen had the distinct impression that only his rank kept Savin from throwing him out.

"How's that?" Isen persisted.

"Well, I don't know if I should even be saying this," Savin said. Some of his brassiness was gone. "It's all just speculation—amateur psychology."

"That's OK," Isen said. "I'm an amateur investigator, so we're even."

He walked back to the couch and sat gingerly, hands on knees, eyes wide open, fighting the urge to lie down. "I came down here to find out why Michael Hauck killed himself. It's that simple."

Savin stood, then sat down abruptly.

"I think Michael was unhappy because this precious brotherhood of infantrymen that he wanted so badly to join wasn't what he thought it would be. Or at least the officer corps didn't measure up."

Savin stood again, took two steps across the tiny apartment, then two steps back to the chair. Isen continued to sit, determined to draw out, by his silence, whatever was eating away at Lieutenant Savin.

"I'll give you my view. In a lot of ways this place is like some sort of bloated high school," Savin said quickly. "A bunch of little clubs and cliques. You've got civilians—so far removed from the honorable profession of arms as to be almost beneath contempt.

"Then, even if you're in the Army," Savin continued, his anger now on display, "that's not enough. You have to be a paratrooper, complete with that ridiculous hat. Because, God forbid, if you're not ... well hell, you might as well be a civilian."

Isen nodded and gave Savin a look he hoped signaled concern, although he'd heard all of these complaints before.

"So I get here to Fort Bragg, and everyone's been telling me how lucky I am to get this assignment. And I have my little beret, and I'm in the Army, and I can run faster and farther than ninety-nine percent of the people here on post, and I work hard at my job. But one weekend we go to a barbecue, and a bunch of guys from Mike's unit are there. When Mike introduces me to his infantry buddies, a couple of them treat me like, I don't know, like ..."

"Like some puke from the Pentagon," Isen said.

"Yeah," Savin said, almost managing a smile. "Something like that."

"So what do you do here?" Isen asked.

Savin paused to take a breath and a drink of water. "I'm a Finance Officer."

Isen saw the problem. In the hybrid world of the military, Savin was a nonentity. He might be responsible for on-time paydays and getting money to families when their soldiers were deployed; he might be an absolute whiz at wading through red tape on behalf of some poor private who's trying to support a couple of kids; but to the infantry lieutenant, who looked at the world through a tunnel that had one end firmly planted in a foxhole, Savin was a nonperson, a "remf," for "rear echelon motherfucker."

" 'Oh, you're a Finance Officer?' That's what one guy said to me," Savin said. "Like he wanted to ask if I squat to pee."

Savin was whining, but Isen still hoped there was a point to all this. "What was Mike's reaction?" he asked.

"He said the guy was an asshole, and I think Mike really saw all of that, how ridiculous all that posturing was. So he was spending all his energy trying to fit into a group that wasn't what he'd hoped it would be, what he'd been led to believe. And if that wasn't bad enough, he beat himself up whenever he made a mistake, and he practically had a nervous breakdown if Colonel Veir said anything critical."

"Do you like your job, Greg?" Isen asked.

The sudden shift threw Savin off for a moment, which was what Isen intended.

"I like my job all right, but I'm doing my time and getting out."

"What about Colonel Veir?"

Savin, who had been on something of a roll, stopped speaking. Isen didn't know if he'd hit a nerve or if Savin was just leery of talking to a major about a colonel.

"What about him?" Savin asked.

"What did Michael think of him?"

"At first Mike thought about Veir what almost everyone else around here thinks of him: the man is a fucking god."

"That's what Mike said?" Isen asked.

"His very words," Savin said. " 'The man's a god,' small *g*, I think."

"And what exactly did that mean?"

"Mike bought into this whole mystique that Colonel Veir has built up around himself," Savin said. He measured Isen from the corner of his eye, apparently trying to decide whether or not to continue.

"You probably know better than I do, Major, what commanders do to get their troops to follow them. All the hocus-pocus, mirrors and smoke. It's all an act, seems to me. All posturing."

Isen bit back his first response, which was along the lines of *You little snot.*

"That may be true in some cases, Greg," Isen said. "But not all commanders work that way. Most are good people. Soldiers follow commanders who care for them."

'That's what I used to think, too, Major Isen. Until I ran across Colonel Harlan Veir."

"Anything specific?"

"Well, for one thing, Veir was always making Mike and the other guys go to these parties, drunk fests, really, that more often than not featured strippers . . . or worse."

Isen thought Savin sounded genuinely offended.

"Did Mike go willingly?" Isen asked.

"Not really," Savin said. He put his feet up on the table and reached out, straight-legged, to touch his toes.

"He went because it was expected of him, you know? But Mike wasn't a big drinker. Besides that, the goings-on with the strippers, that stuff was kind of sophomoric."

Savin drew the corner of his mouth up in a disapproving smirk as he made this last pronouncement. Isen wondered who had found the strippers more offensive, Savin or Hauck.

"Besides all that," Savin continued, "going to the parties meant more time with Veir. At the end, Mike didn't like this any more than I would have."

"You don't like him very much," Isen said.

"The feeling is mutual, too."

"How's that?"

Savin leaned back in his chair. "Once we were at the O Club, Happy Hour, I guess. Mike introduced me to Colonel Veir."

"And?"

"And I was already plowed. Brave drunk, you know? Anyway, I saw Veir shoot a glance at the branch insignia on my collar. Then he asks, in this bullshit patronizing tone, 'So what do you do, Lieutenant?' And he fucking well knows what I do. So I say, 'I'm a Finance Officer, sir. But I'm thinking of transferring out—maybe become an interior designer or an infantry officer.' "

Loose cannon, Isen thought. Still, he was impressed; Savin had *cojones.*

"So what did he do?" Isen asked.

"He read my name tag. 'Savin,' he says. Then he gives me this weird smile and walks away."

"Repercussions?"

"Not as of tonight," Savin said.

"Well, I'll say one thing for you," Isen said, standing. "When you want to piss 'em off, you do a good job."

"Thank you, sir," Savin said with mock sincerity.

"Were you questioned by the CID or by a psychologist?"

"Yes, sir. Both."

"Why do you think Michael killed himself?"

Savin, who had been on something of a tirade, wilted a bit, his face giving in to sadness.

"I wish I knew the answer to that, I really do. He was bothered by the fact that the Army wasn't what he expected. You know the old cliché, all the brothers valiant, all the sisters virtuous. Well, Mike expected to find that. But even after he saw the real thing, he was awfully worried about being successful. Living up to his family's standards or something. And Colonel Veir . . . well, I think it's probably pretty tough to live up to Veir's expectations, or maybe I should say his legend."

"Which was?"

"Veir is charmed. Nothing can touch him or the people around him. At least, that's the story some of these lieutenants bought."

"Did Mike talk to you about this business of not wanting to let his family down?"

"Obliquely, I guess. He mentioned a couple of times, when he was down on himself for some mistake he'd made, that he never wanted to disappoint his family."

"You said you met General Flynn when he was down here?"

"Sure did, sir. And after that I could see why Mike was so worried. His uncle came in here and acted like it was a full dress inspection."

The old man can be tough, Isen thought.

"Anything between them? How did they seem together?"

"Mike was nervous, that's all. It's not like he had anything

72

to hide, he was just nervous. General Flynn asked him a bunch of questions about his personal life; he was kind of a busybody."

"Was there anything you told the CID or the psychologist that you didn't tell me ... that I forgot to ask?"

"I don't think so. No, sir. I probably told you more than I told them. I was kind of still in shock when they came around."

"Can you think of anyone else who might be able to shed some light on Michael's state of mind?"

"You might try talking to this guy Bennett. He's the one who gave me a hard time about being a Finance Officer. He's a loudmouth; he and Mike didn't get along too well. I'm not saying he knew Mike well, but you might find out something of what was up in that unit."

Savin paused.

"What does that mean?" Isen asked.

"I just got the feeling things went on in Veir's unit that don't go on in other battalions."

"Like what?" Isen pressed.

Savin retreated. "I'm not sure I have a clear picture, sir. Most of what I know is secondhand."

"So I need to talk to Mike's peers?" Isen said.

"Yeah, but I'd be surprised if the lieutenants or the captains talked much," he said. "They're all pretty much afraid of Veir."

Isen grunted in agreement, then looked at his watch. "I appreciate your helping me out tonight, Greg," he said. "If you don't mind, I might call you again if I come across any good questions in the next few days."

"Fine, sir," Savin said without enthusiasm.

Isen hesitated, studying the bookshelf again, wondering about the things that might be missing from the empty spaces.

"Do you mind if I borrow this photo album?" Isen asked, walking to the boxes and helping himself to the photo album and the yearbook.

Savin hesitated.

"I'll bring them back in a day or two, just like they are now."

"OK, sir," Savin said.

"If you think of anything else you want to tell me," Isen said, writing on a pad by the phone, "you can reach me at this number."

They shook hands, and Savin followed Isen out onto the landing.

"Major," Savin said as Isen started down the stairs.

Isen turned back.

"Good hunting."

4

MARK ISEN, DISTRACTED BUT STONE SOBER, TOOK TWO wrong turns on the drive back to Sue Lynn's home.

"You almost managed to add Savin to the list of people who don't want you around," he told his reflection in the rearview mirror. "And God knows that list is long enough already."

Veir's attitude was easy to understand. His command had been sullied by Hauck's sudden penchant for drama, and that kind of attention wasn't healthy, even for supermen, in an Army that was looking for imaginative ways to cut back on the officer corps.

Foote was something else; Veir's executive officer couldn't have been any more hostile had Isen shown up wearing a white hood and robe. It could be that he hated people from the Pentagon; it could be that he was trying to protect Veir and the unit, although he was expending an awful lot of energy before he even knew what Isen was up to. Or, considering the obvious, it could be that Foote had something to hide.

Then there was Kent, the Division Chief of Staff with the beautiful young driver. There seemed to be some tension between Kent and Veir, but that could be caused by a hundred different things. Kent had been, on the face of it, polite enough; but Isen was fairly certain that Kent wanted no unflattering light to shine on the division. By extension, that meant no unflattering light on Veir.

Finally, there was Savin, who was mourning a friend and who was angry at the Army, Veir, and infantrymen (including Isen), with plenty of bile to spare. Yet Savin, Isen had decided, had proved most helpful. He wondered if it were possible that Flynn hadn't wanted Savin at the funeral. He wondered, too, if Flynn were the source of a lot of Hauck's anxiety over meeting the family standard.

But that's only half of it, Isen told himself. *Savin said that Hauck was disenchanted with the real Army he found.*

Night failed to hide the basic tawdriness of Yadkin Road. Fayetteville, Isen found, depressed him, its seediness and decrepitude like unrealized dreams. He wondered if Hauck had stumbled upon something analogous in Veir's battalion. Perhaps Hauck, raised on tales of familial glory, hadn't been ready for the shock of the real world, especially the real world according to Harlan Veir.

Isen had suffered at the hands of such a man, a Colonel—now Brigadier General—Schauffert, whom Isen had tangled with. But because there was no defensible reason to torpedo Isen's career, Schauffert had poisoned Isen's reputation with back-channel whispering. Isen loathed that kind of underhandedness; it sickened him to see people sneak around like snitches, spreading vile gossip.

Isen wasn't ready to paint Harlan Veir in the colors of evil; but it was possible that Hauck had run across his own Colonel Schauffert. If so, it was up to Isen to set things straight.

Isen found the wide street that served as an entry to Sue Lynn's development. As he turned, his imagination was assaulted by a whole new set of images.

Darlington had caught him completely by surprise when she responded to his timorous advances. Isen had dated only a few women since his separation, and only a few of those pairings had become sexual. Here, with an old friend, he'd found a woman who obviously enjoyed sex, the playful encounter, the pleasure and abandon, without all the mind

games that Isen—whose experiences thus far hadn't set anything on fire—had come to believe were a standard part of
what went on between a man and a woman. He wondered
how much he'd missed to this point in his life; and he wondered too, what the second inning with Sue Lynn was going
to be like.

Sue Lynn Darlington's thing, Isen had found in the hurried lovemaking that made him late for the meeting with
Savin, was place. Against the wall; on a heavy-legged oak
library table in the foyer, with stacks of mail and papers and
even the phone spilling onto the floor as she swept the surface with her hand, backing up and pulling him to her, one
foot hooked behind his thigh. They had started there, just
inside the door, and there was nothing gentle about the release. They moved upstairs, kneeling on the steps in places,
to the first door, Sue Lynn's office, where a swivel chair
backed up against the desk. Stumbling in the dark, pants at
his knees, Isen found the chair and Sue Lynn found him.
Straddling him, muscles tense along her legs, she balanced
gingerly on the balls of her feet while she rocked forward
and backward, forward and backward, and his hand traced
the line of her thigh and her flexed calf. Up together and
down, breathing in sharp spikes, throaty calls and rising as
over a wave, crashing finally together in hot embrace.

Sex at the end of his marriage had been what Isen called
"marital sex," with *marital* as a pejorative adjective. Sue
Lynn was fun, and determined to have fun.

Yes, there definitely is an upside to this trip, he thought as
he shifted uncomfortably in his seat, his tumescence beckoning him to stand even as he drove.

He pulled into the driveway, was disappointed to see the
house darkened. But when he cut the car's headlights, he
saw that there was a lamp somewhere deep inside, with a
faint light coming through the sheer curtains of the dining
room, and a pale crescent of window above the entryway.

Isen got out of his car and, in his haste, almost locked the
keys inside. He walked up, carrying his sexual excitement
heavy inside him, like a loaded pistol. He knocked; she had
given him a key but the scene called for him to ask permission to enter.

The door opened a bit, swinging on one creaky hinge, and

in the light—brighter now—he could see the side of her face and the long fingers of one hand.

He stepped inside. Somewhere in the house Natalie Cole was singing "Mona Lisa." Sue Lynn pushed the door closed. From behind Isen a gentle light played on her as she propped one foot on the door behind her; her long gown shone.

"I thought you'd never get back."

Isen stepped forward, took her in his arms, one hand behind her head. She had bathed while he was out, and she was a riot of wonderful smells and softness. Her hair was still slightly damp as he pulled her mouth to his. She responded, deeply, mouth and tongue, pressing back at him where their curves complemented each other. Sue Lynn moaned softly as he found her throat, pressing his tongue just beneath the line of her jaw, tracing down her neck. Her hands grasped the back of his arms, down his sides, across the front of his trousers; she made a noise deep in her throat in pleasure and appreciation as she found him swollen there.

She stepped back suddenly, pulled the gown off her shoulders, let it slip to the floor. She wore a black bustier that reached down to just above her navel. There was a strip there of delicate white above the top of her panties, which interrupted only briefly the curves of her hips, the wonderful crescent fullness that plunged down to the tops of her stockings. The final touch, spike heels.

"My God," Isen managed.

"Having a religious experience, Mark?" she asked, hands on hips.

"I believe I am," he said, pulling her to his face. "I do believe I am."

They finished on the floor beside Sue Lynn's bed, then lay entwined until their panting had subsided and they began to breathe in time with each other. She pulled a comforter off the bed and onto their bodies as they lay side by side. Isen watched a light move across the ceiling as a car drove by outside. Sue Lynn nestled closer, head on his chest; he traced long circles on her back with the tips of his fingers as he drifted along the edge of a sleepy shore.

Then she sat up.

"How did it go with Savin?" she asked, her voice clear as morning.

"Huh?"

"Savin, Hauck's roommate. How did it go? What did you find out?" She tugged her knees up to her chest now; the black stockings were still pulled up tightly to mid-thigh.

"Can't we talk about this in the morning?" Isen protested. He opened one eye and looked at the bed above him, wondering if he felt like going to the trouble of climbing up there. He tried rolling away from her.

"Get back here," Sue Lynn said, hooking one heel—minus the deadly stilletto—on his side and rolling him onto his back again. "I have to go to PT in a couple of hours."

"So what?" Isen said.

She reached down, dug her fingernails lightly into his stomach, tickling him. "So you'd better take advantage of this opportunity to consult the finest mind on Fort Bragg, if not in the whole state of North Carolina," she said. "Besides, I want to hear your plan."

"And if I don't have a plan?"

"Then we'll make one up."

"OK," he said, sitting up and leaning against the bed beside her. She draped one leg over his as he talked, and he ran his finger just under the lace top of her stocking.

"I sure do like these," he said, indicating the black hose.

"Talk, Isen."

"Yes, ma'am." He snapped the elastic. "Actually, I made some progress tonight—at Savin's, I mean."

"Good. You didn't make any more enemies?"

"I didn't say that," Isen said. "Although I don't think Savin hates me as much as Foote does. Anyway, Savin told me a little story about his meeting Colonel Veir at the O Club once. Savin said something to piss him off, and Veir made note of the kid's name."

"And?"

"Yesterday Veir told me he didn't know Hauck's roommate, but Savin said that Hauck introduced him that way. 'This is my roommate.'"

"Could be that Veir made a mistake when you were talking to him," Darlington said.

Isen looked at her. "I'm surprised to hear you taking up for Veir," he said.

She waved her hand in dismissal.

"I'm having a tough time getting a feel for what this kid was like," Isen said. "All of his stuff was cleaned up. Savin did say one of the things Hauck liked best was being around the troops."

"Sounds like someone I know," Sue Lynn said, poking Isen with a fingernail.

"I did get a chance to look through some of Hauck's personal stuff, a photo album in particular."

"What did you find?"

"Well, it was what I didn't find that interested me, and I didn't even notice what was missing until I had a chance to look at Savin's pictures, which were on his bookshelf."

"So what was missing?"

"There were no pictures of women," Isen said.

"So what?"

"Well, I just thought it a little strange, that's all. I mean, Savin has a couple of photos of him with a girlfriend—"

"He told you she was his girlfriend?" Sue Lynn interrupted.

"Well, not exactly," Isen admitted.

"Go on."

"I just thought that in an entire photo album, including a couple of envelopes of pictures, I'd find one picture of Hauck with a young woman. But there was nothing. Not a dance, not a football game, not a party. Just all shots of him and his buddies in uniform."

"And your gay-dar went on?"

"My what?" Isen asked.

"Your gay-dar," she repeated. "Like radar that picks up on who's gay and who isn't," she explained.

"I didn't say that," Isen said, backing off.

"But that's what you implied," she said. "Every homophobe in the Army thinks he can pick out gays. It's sort of a new requisite skill, like being able to disassemble your weapon and put it back together."

"Very funny," Isen said.

"But you thought it, didn't you?"

Sue Lynn leaned into Isen, and even in the half dark of

a room lit only by a hallway light, he was made uncomfortable by her direct stare.

"Yeah, I did. So what?"

"So nothing," she said. She leaned back against the bed. "But I'm not sure it's the kind of news that General Flynn and the Haucks are looking for."

"I'll have to consider it as a theory, I suppose," Isen said.

"Did you consider asking Savin?"

"Just ask him outright, you mean? 'By the way, was your roommate a homosexual?' Or better yet, 'Were you two lovers?' I don't think so, not yet, anyway. I need him; he may have known Hauck best. Besides, Savin was too pissed off tonight."

"At you?"

"At me, at Veir, at the Army, at the infantry, all of the above."

Sue Lynn paused. "Why was he pissed off at the infantry?" she asked.

"I guess some of the infantry guys in Hauck's unit must have thought he was less than a soldier because he's not in some macho job."

"What does he do?" she asked.

"He's a Finance Officer."

"Oh, the old my-dick-is-bigger-than-your-dick syndrome," she said. "I've run into that myself."

"I can imagine," Isen said. "Hell, I was going into Division Headquarters today and some private passed me, and it was all he could do to salute me because, I assume, I wasn't wearing a beret."

"Oh, my God," Sue Lynn said, hands to cheeks. "You mean I put on my best lingerie show for a . . . for a *leg?*"

Isen laughed. "I'm afraid so," he said.

"Well, at least I found a leg who can throw a leg," she said, stroking the inside of his elbow with her fingernails. She kissed him on the shoulder.

"Speaking of women," Isen said. "Have you ever noticed, in your travels around headquarters, that Colonel Kent's driver—Coates—looks like a professional model?"

"Colonel Kent is a dirty old man," Darlington said. "He's a standing joke among the enlisted women at headquarters. They refer to his office as 'a quickie way to get promoted.'"

"He's boinking his clerk?" Isen pictured Coates in civilian clothes, her hair down. A pleasant image.

"I didn't say he always gets what he wants. He gets shot down a lot. But he always manages to embarrass himself."

"So why doesn't the CG hammer him?"

"I'm not sure the CG knows everything that's going on. For one thing, he's new. Besides that, headquarters is kind of insular. Word is that Kent keeps a lot of stuff from him," Sue Lynn said. "Kent, Veir and some of the other men here treat sex like it's the only battleground available to them. You know, the chase, the conquering, all that nonsense. It's not as good as stomping the Iraqis, but it's all we've got."

"OK, Dr. Freud. So what does all of this cogent analysis have to do with the fact that Lieutenant Michael Hauck decided to eat his pistol one night?"

"Do you know where he shot himself?" Sue Lynn asked.

"In the mouth?"

"No. I mean, where his car was parked."

"Nope," Isen admitted.

"You haven't talked to CID, have you?"

"No, but that's on my list."

"Hauck was parked out back of a club called Jiggles."

"Jingles?" Isen asked.

"Jiggles," Darlington corrected. "As in jiggling breasts. It's a strip club."

"Wonderfully original name," Isen said. "Must have taken them *seconds* to come up with that. Go on."

"I don't know anything else," Darlington said. "I only know that because I heard one of the MP's talking about it."

"Wasn't that on the news?"

"No. On the news they reported that he was parked in a lot off of a county highway, which is technically true. The lot belongs to a metal shop that backs up to this strip club. But he wasn't there to pick up steel rods."

"I'll leave that pun alone," Isen said, kicking the comforter off his legs. "Then there's General Flynn."

"What about him?"

"Well, he hasn't exactly come through with all the info I might have used."

"Such as?"

"The preliminary CID report, for starters. And Veir mentioned a psychological autopsy—a term I'd never heard before. Also, it didn't occur to me until I looked in this photo album that I hadn't even seen a picture of Hauck."

"Flynn was pretty busy."

"That's true," Isen said. "But it did put a thought in my head: why would Flynn send me down here without the complete picture?"

"You think he's trying to point you in a particular direction?"

"Or away from something particular."

Could Flynn be holding back? Did he have an agenda he wasn't sharing with Isen? If so, that would mean the general was manipulating Isen, who'd undertaken this mission primarily out of friendship. All the hostility he'd encountered at Bragg hadn't affected him as much as this one unsettling thought.

He pushed his suspicions away for the moment.

"Savin also said that Flynn might have interfered with his leave request. Kept him from attending the funeral."

Sue Lynn twisted her lips in concentration. "That's odd—if it's true."

"According to Savin, Hauck was pretty nervous when his uncle was around."

"You said that Hauck was concerned about letting his family down," Sue Lynn said. "Maybe Flynn represented all that for him. I mean, if you're already nervous, having your uncle the two-star general hanging around isn't likely to make you relax."

"I'd like to get a clearer picture of how he was around his subordinates."

"From his NCOs?" Sue Lynn asked.

"And his soldiers."

"You think that'll make you like him any better?"

"What?"

"When you talk about him," Sue Lynn explained, "you're very detached. I just wondered if you felt sorry for him."

Isen considered the question for a moment.

"No. I guess I don't. Or I didn't. I'm not sure."

"Just thought I'd ask," Sue Lynn said.

"Near the end, Hauck was disillusioned with Veir and the Army, according to Savin. At least part of that was because of the parties Veir has. Strippers, lots of drinking, the whole deal. Savin called them sophomoric."

"Hardly seems like a reason to commit suicide," Sue Lynn said.

"There aren't any good reasons to commit suicide," Isen countered.

"Apparently Michael Hauck disagreed."

The call that Colonel Richard Kent had been expecting since the previous afternoon came at seven-thirty on Tuesday morning.

"Colonel Veir is on line one for you, sir," Private Coates reported from her desk just outside his office.

"Thanks," Kent said. He got up and closed the door, then returned to his desk, where he stood with a hand on the phone. He took a deep breath before he picked it up.

"Kent here."

"Good morning, sir."

"Hello, Harlan," Kent said unenthusiastically. "How did it go yesterday with that guy from the Pentagon?"

"About like I expected," Veir said. "He asked a bunch of questions about Hauck."

"Anything the CID didn't already cover?" Kent asked.

"No. As a matter of fact," Veir said, "I don't think he was all that well prepared when he came down here. He hadn't had a look at the kid's personnel file, nor had he seen the preliminary CID report."

"Should he have?"

"I'll bet this General Flynn has seen at least the CID work, if not more."

Veir had an annoying habit of giving out information in tiny doses; he enjoyed the suspense of holding on to something other people wanted.

"So why wouldn't he show those things to Isen?"

Veir chuckled on the other end, a condescending little snort. Kent rubbed one hand over the tiny stubbles of hair on the back of his neck.

"Could be that the general knows there isn't anything else to find out about Hauck," Veir said. "Maybe he's pissed off, and sent this guy down here to make some noise, cast me and the division in a bad light."

Kent had been entertaining that exact same thought a few hours earlier as he lay awake, watching the clock move toward three. One of his most important duties, something reiterated for him by Major General Tremmore, the new Division Commander, was to protect the division from bad publicity and to safeguard all the good publicity the unit had garnered recently.

Specifically, that meant Harlan Veir.

"Veir's celebrity will do the division and the Army a lot of good," Tremmore had told Kent in one of their first meetings.

The irony of the situation struck Kent then; apparently he was to be reminded of it almost daily. For it was Kent who had spearheaded a concerted, secret effort to make Veir into exactly what he had become: the nationally recognized poster boy for the "new" Army.

Kent, acting on unwritten but very specific orders from the previous Division Commander, had overseen the whirlwind VIP tour of Fort Bragg for the *Newsweek* journalists who made Veir a hero. It was Kent who made sure the civilians were treated to all kinds of demonstrations, from helicopter rides to the chance to fire some of the unit's big artillery pieces. It was Kent who wooed them and, in a fairly sophisticated piece of spin control, made the journalists think *they* had decided to lionize Veir. Kent wasn't sure who, up the chain of command, had hatched this plan. He did know that it had worked with a vengeance.

The lead writer, charmed by Veir, had made him representative of the Army; that was bad enough. But since that time, Veir's legend, in Army circles and particularly on Fort Bragg, had grown. He went from representative to symbol; Kent had no doubt that when Veir looked in the mirror, he saw the embodiment of all that was strong and powerful about the Eighty-second, the Army's self-proclaimed "Guard of Honor."

More than that, other people now treated Veir like minor royalty. He was the first battalion commander the new general asked to meet, he had been a luncheon guest of the Joint Chiefs in Washington, he had even been featured on the national news and two nationally syndicated morning talk shows.

Kent knew that Veir added to his own mystique whenever and however he could, from the way he carried himself and wore his uniform to the way he talked to the wives of soldiers and other officers. He was a local celebrity, the closest thing Fort Bragg had to a movie star. Hollywood Veir.

Kent, who knew there were more facets to Veir than Tremmore or the reading public saw, nevertheless shouldered his burden like a good soldier. His motives were not purely altruistic. The better the unit looked, both to the Division Commander and to the rest of the Army, the better his chances of pinning a general's star on his collar within the next two years. And even considering Veir's obnoxious behavior, Kent didn't see the harm in letting the public believe he was a hero.

And for now he wasn't about to alarm Veir by agreeing with his theory that some general had it in for him. There was no telling what Veir might do.

"Come on, Harlan. Aren't you getting a little paranoid?"

"If Flynn wanted an investigation," Veir said, "more than the one he got, don't you think he would have at least sent an investigator? This Isen, paper pusher that he is, has obviously spent some time in the infantry. Maybe Flynn thought Isen would know his way around a division well enough to rock the boat."

Veir's voice was rising. Kent outranked him, of course, and Veir wasn't about to start shouting at Kent, but life was a lot easier if Harlan Veir—the division's golden boy—wasn't so upset.

"Well, I don't see how there's much we can do except to cooperate with him."

Veir was silent on the other end.

"Of course there are things we can do," Veir said slowly.

Kent didn't reply. If Veir wanted him to do something, to use the position power he had to keep Isen from raising some dust around Veir's reputation—which seemed to have a life of its own—Veir was going to have to ask outright.

Kent studied the lighted button on the phone.

"But maybe you're right," Veir said after a moment. "Maybe I'm just being paranoid. Isen may go away by himself."

"Absolutely," Kent said, allowing himself a tiny bit of

relief. Then, still fishing, "After all, there's nothing he can learn that the CID hasn't already been over, right?"

"Roger that, Colonel," Veir said. "I know we both have the best interests of the division in mind, so if I need you, I'll call you. OK?"

"Right. Call me," Kent said. *You bastard.*

"Thank you, sir," Veir said, exuberant again. "It's good to know that the Division Staff is willing to back me up. By the way, you balling that driver yet?"

Kent didn't answer. He wondered what the chances were that Coates might be listening.

"'Cause if you're not, I might take a crack at it," Veir said. A second later he burst into loud laughter. "Did you hear that, 'I'll take a *crack.*' Pretty funny, huh? Jesus, I just kill myself sometimes."

Veir hung up.

Kent just shook his head as he placed the phone back in its cradle. *What a prick,* he thought.

Kent sat down, opened the bottom drawer of his desk and propped his big paratrooper boots there. On the desk, facing him, sat a framed portrait of Kent and his family: his wife, Donna, and three teenage daughters. There had been plenty of evenings he'd spent at work, looking at the family photo instead of sharing dinner with them.

He was still rising. Though the pyramid was coming to a sharper point, and more and more of his peers were deciding it wasn't worth the strain—Kent had stayed the course. He would survive all the cuts and drawdowns; like some uniquely adaptable species, he would adjust to the new pressures, evolving for the new Army.

All along, he'd told himself that he was doing it for his family. He'd made a good life for them. Not without cost, but he'd accomplished things they could be proud of.

That had been true up to a point.

Up to Harlan Veir.

The Army's Criminal Investigation Division, unlike most other agencies on Fort Bragg, is not subordinate to any local commander. The CID commander answers to a regional office, which in turn answers to CID Headquarters in Falls Church, Virginia. The intent of this arrangement is to free the service's investigating arm from command influence in those cases where the powers that be—such as a commanding general—have any interest in the outcome of some particular case.

In fact, the CID commander and his agents live and work in close proximity with their fellow soldiers. In the self-contained community that is an Army post, they share the same housing areas, shopping centers, medical and sports facilities. And in the clusters of densely packed houses, everyone is sure to notice the one neighbor who leaves for work in civilian clothes, the duty uniform for investigators.

So when Mark Isen asked the CID command for permission to review the report on Hauck's death and talk to the investigating agent, he knew that word would get back to Kent, Veir, and any other interested parties in the division.

Fort Bragg's CID Headquarters occupies one of the most modern buildings on post, a brick-and-smoked-glass cube on Randolph Street, close to the center of the original fort.

Isen entered the lobby, another sterile area bounded by glass, and spoke through a small window, identifying himself to a woman in civilian clothes who picked at a Danish with one hand as she fingered an intercom with the sticky fingers of the other.

"There's a Major Isen here to see Special Agent McCall," she said, her mouth full of food. She pronounced the name "Izzen."

"It's 'Ice-en,' actually," Isen said when the woman replaced the receiver.

"Whatever," she said. She nodded without smiling and went back to chewing and staring at the little green screen of her computer.

The power I have over women, he thought, *is downright scary sometimes.*

Isen sat in a vinyl chair beneath a poster that showed a horribly mangled car with the legend "Ever get a friend smashed?"

The room was brightly lit by fluorescent lights too big for the small waiting area. There were no magazines on the table between the chairs, no television, no radio. Nothing, Isen thought, to distract a citizen from thoughts about the weighty matters of law and order discussed within these very walls. Isen watched the receptionist break the pastry into little chunks and toss them in her mouth.

He had been there almost fifteen minutes—much of the time daydreaming about Sue Lynn—when someone opened one of the glass doors.

"Major Isen?"

Isen looked up at a small black woman, about twenty-four or twenty-five, dressed in beltless navy blue pants and a light blue button-down shirt. She had the look of an earnest college student.

"I'm Special Agent McCall," the woman said as Isen stood.

"How do you do," Isen said. He was five or six inches taller than she, which made her about five four. She was slightly built, but with a good firm handshake, which Isen liked. She wore her hair in an unflattering cut, short and close to her head; and she regarded Isen coldly from dark eyes set a bit too wide. Special Agent McCall looked all of seventeen, an image she fought with dowdy clothes and a serious expression that, he guessed, was also meant to make up for her small size.

"I understand you're here on behalf of the family and that you want to talk about the report on the suicide of Lieutenant Michael Hauck," McCall said crisply. She held a large file folder under her arm, but didn't offer the folder or even look at it.

"Yes," he said. He paused a second, waiting for her expression to change. "That would be a big help," he added after a beat.

McCall turned on her heel and zoomed down the hall in the direction she'd come from. Isen followed.

"We can sit in here," McCall said, opening a door to what must have been an interrogation room. She hit a switch just inside the door, lighting a sign in the hallway that said "IN-TERVIEW IN PROGRESS, DO NOT DISTURB."

Isen was surprised; the small space was thick with the smell of stale cigarettes.

"I guess the new Army hasn't made every room smoke-free," Isen said, trying to make conversation. "Or maybe people who've done something that lands them here are allowed a little destructive behavior." He smiled at McCall.

"You're here," she said.

Another friend for life, Isen thought.

"You understand that this report isn't finished and that I can't let you take it from the building," McCall said, pulling out a chair at a stained wooden table that, like the cigarette smoke, must have been a relic from CID past.

Isen pulled a chair from the opposite side. "Are you going to sit here while I go through it?"

"I'm responsible for this report," McCall said.

"You wrote it?" Isen asked.

"I'm writing it." She was sitting now, the big folder pressed to the table under both hands. "But what I mean is that I'm responsible for seeing that all the pages that are in here now are in here when you leave."

The preliminary report was taking on more significance than it probably warranted simply because it was so hard to get hold of. Isen had called Flynn's office in Washington twice already that morning, asking for a copy. Nothing. Now this woman across from him apparently wanted to draw a little blood before showing him the elusive prize.

Isen sat down, leaned on his elbows. "Ms. McCall, did I give you some reason to be pissed off at me?" he asked.

"Not that I can think of," she said, "Major."

"Then why would you imply that I might want to steal your paperwork?"

McCall breathed deeply, her nostrils flaring a tiny bit.

"If you inferred that, Major Isen, that's your problem. I was merely stating a fact: I will turn in a complete report when I'm finished with this."

"Nice to get off to such a good start," Isen said. "I guess you're just not a morning person."

McCall slid the package across the table with all the enthusiasm one might see in a child forced to share a favorite toy. "I'll answer any questions you have about the report."

Isen pulled the folder in front of him and opened the cover. "Why did Michael Hauck kill himself?"

"Major Severin—Dr. Severin—is in the process of finishing the psychological autopsy," McCall said.

Isen was tempted to say, *You didn't answer the question.*

"Do you have a copy of his findings?"

"Not yet."

McCall clearly wasn't giving anything up.

"Do you know what his report will say?"

"Dr. Severin found that Michael Hauck killed himself because he recently failed to get his EIB."

Isen looked up, felt his mouth open. The EIB, the Expert Infantryman Badge, was one of those awards infantry soldiers, especially infantry lieutenants, sought to demonstrate their proficiency. It was a merit badge that required some skill in shooting, land navigation and other elements of the craft. It was not something to commit suicide over.

"He blew his brains out because of that?"

"That's what the doctor thinks," McCall said. "More importantly, that's what the doctor is going to say."

"Did he—what's his name? Severin?—did he conduct his own interviews?"

"A few. Mostly he relied on mine."

Isen studied McCall, whose face betrayed nothing.

"Play a lot of poker?" he said out loud.

"What?"

"Nothing," Isen said. "What do you think? Do you think that's the case?"

McCall straightened the already neat papers arrayed before her.

"Last year a young NCO shot himself because he finished second in a training course here. Six months ago a seventeen-year-old kid—some officer's son—hanged himself because his girlfriend dumped him. A few days before Hauck killed himself, an NCO's wife with a history of mental problems did herself in with a bottle of sleeping pills after her boss criticized her at work."

"Messy post," Isen said.

"Yes, it is. And that's not counting the homicides and the assaults. My point is that people kill themselves over stupid things."

"Do you think that Hauck killed himself over a badge?"

"That's not the question I was charged with answering. My job was to determine whether or not this was a suicide."

"Which it was?" Isen said.

"Clearly," McCall said with finality.

"What was Michael Hauck like?" Isen asked.

"What do you mean?"

"Did you get to know him, even a little bit, from talking to all these people?"

McCall was hesitant. She reached up and pinched the open collar of her shirt with one hand, pulling it closed.

"That's hard to say. Everyone here has an act; it's all about facade. The officers have one face for the soldiers, another for superiors, another at home. The ones I get to talk to have another face; they're not about to open up completely to me."

Isen leafed through a bunch of forms that detailed the scene of the suicide. Since Hauck had killed himself off-post, there were a few sheets of notes from the Cumberland County Sheriff's Department. The rest of the half-inch-thick file was made up of Defense Department forms and a set of photographs.

"Did the Fayetteville police investigate?" Isen asked.

"The suicide was outside the city limits, so the Sheriff's Department got the call. They contacted the duty officer here at Bragg."

"And you got the nod."

"I was the special agent on call."

Which is different from being handpicked, Isen thought.

Isen flipped over the papers to the first picture, a grisly color glossy of Hauck in the front seat of his truck. He immediately regretted the comment he'd just made about Hauck blowing his brains out. As the photo showed, that is exactly what Michael Hauck had done.

The door to the pickup truck was wide open, showing Hauck at full length and sitting almost straight up in the driver's seat, head thrown back, mouth open as if to scream. There was a dark blotch, almost black in the flash, that reached from his shoulders all the way to the seat. From the side, it looked as if Hauck's hair was hanging past his collar. But Hauck, like all of his peers, would not have had hair long enough to hang even to his ears. The back of the boy's head had been split open, shredded, so that what looked like tendrils of hair was actually flesh and parts of his skull.

"He used a nine millimeter—his own pistol," McCall said coolly. "Stuck it into his mouth all the way past his front teeth, which weren't damaged."

Isen flipped to the next picture, this one taken from behind the truck. The safety glass was shattered, thousands of tiny lines obscuring what was inside. There was a single large hole just behind the driver's seat. Isen looked up at McCall.

"There was no note," McCall said. "Not in the truck, not in his apartment. He had not gone to any lengths to straighten out his personal affairs. As a matter of fact, there was some mail in the cab of the truck, stuff he apparently intended to drop in a mailbox. A couple of bills and a magazine subscription."

"Doesn't sound like he was planning to check out," Isen said. "Why was he carrying the weapon around in his truck?"

"According to his roommate, their apartment had been burglarized once. Hauck kept moving the gun around from place to place. Sometimes he kept it in the apartment, sometimes in the truck, sometimes he turned it in to the unit arms room for storage."

"Had he been drinking?"

"Yes," McCall said. "Quite a bit. He had a blood alcohol level of point two one, twice the legal limit for driving."

Her answers came easier now, not because she was any more accommodating to Isen but because she was focusing on the report and Hauck's death. Her comments dealt with fact, and someone had apparently once told her that it was better to be clinical than emotional.

"He was hanging out that night in Jiggles?"

"Yes, he and some of the other lieutenants in his battalion. They'd been drinking, and everything seemed fine to the others. Then Hauck went outside, and the next they saw him he was . . . like you see him in that picture."

Isen flipped to another photo, this one the long, rectangular full-length photo of Hauck in uniform that would have been part of his personnel file. He wore the same expression here as in the Texas A&M graduation photo: strained seriousness.

"Who found him?" Isen asked.

"Another customer, a civilian who was parked nearby heard the shot as he was coming out of the club. He called the police right away."

Isen pictured the parking lot, with intoxicated men coming

outside to urinate against the tires of cars before they tried to navigate homeward.

"Did he see anyone else out there?"

McCall hesitated just long enough for Isen to notice.

"He thinks he may have heard voices," she said. "When he heard the shot, his first thought was murder, so he ducked right back inside and called. The police were the first ones to find Hauck."

"But it's possible that someone else was out there?" Isen said.

"Hauck's prints were all over the weapon," McCall said. "There were contact burns at the entry wound; the trajectory of the wound was consistent with self-inflicted. He shot himself."

"You said the guy heard voices. Maybe someone else saw something."

"The guy was pretty loaded," McCall said. "And he wasn't all that sure about the voices."

"But . . ."

"If there was another witness to the suicide," McCall said, "he or she hasn't come forward."

Isen closed the folder, which would, in all likelihood, disappear into some file cabinet and be mercifully hidden from the world. Hauck's legacy.

"When will the final report be finished?"

"A few days, maybe. A week. Depends on what else comes across my desk," McCall said. Isen got the feeling she didn't want to be pinned down to a specific date.

"Will the final vary much from this? I mean, do you see any new material coming up?"

"I doubt it," McCall said.

"Can I get a copy of this?" Isen asked.

"No, sir. I'm only showing it to you as a courtesy."

"Thanks," Isen said sarcastically.

"A courtesy, I might add, extended by *my boss* to you." *Getting nowhere fast,* Isen thought.

"Did you know he came from a military family?" Isen asked.

"Yes. Several generations, I understand, including an uncle who's a two-star."

"Right. Could be a lot of pressure there, don't you think?"

"It can add up," McCall said.

"General Flynn thinks Hauck's personal life was kind of hinky."

"Hinky?"

"His word," Isen said. "Unusual, messed up, weird, stressed out."

"Did he say why?"

"No. Do you have any ideas?"

Isen had a sudden mental image—clean, sharp as a photograph—that he and McCall were circling each other, each of them looking to gain information without giving anything up.

That might be a function of her personality, he thought. *Or it might be her normal operating mode. Or it might mean that McCall hasn't finished with this case.*

"Michael Hauck had some friends here who were—who are—homosexuals," McCall said.

Isen didn't respond.

"It could be that someone threatened to make an issue out of that."

"Expose him," Isen said. "What's the term? 'Out' him."

"I didn't say Hauck was gay," McCall corrected him. "I have no evidence of that."

"But that wouldn't make much difference to your average homophobe or gossip monger."

"Right."

"Did any of the officers in his unit mention this to you?"

"No."

"Who were these friends?"

"I'd rather not say."

Isen spent a few moments considering how he might tell all of this to General Flynn.

"Can I have a list of the lieutenants you spoke to?" Isen asked. "The ones who were at the club that night?"

"Sure," McCall said, pulling the folder toward him. "But it's not going to do you any good."

"And why is that?" Isen asked.

She was bent over the pages now, writing with a pencil on a legal pad as she pulled names from the report.

"Two reasons, really. These guys don't know why Hauck killed himself."

"How do you know that?" Isen asked.

McCall looked up at him, studying him as an alert student might study a professor whose mind was slipping.

"Tell me something, Major," she said. "Are you a professional investigator?"

"No," Isen said. "I'm an infantry officer."

"So what do you know about questioning people or conducting an investigation?"

"Look, Miss McCall," Isen said, "I didn't come in here posing as an investigator. I'm sure you learned all kinds of great sleuthing techniques in your professional schooling, and I could probably use some of those right about now, as this little job is turning out to be a lot bigger than I thought. But I didn't come into the Army on the last bus, either. I've been dealing with soldiers for a few years now, and that's all these lieutenants are—young soldiers with just enough college time to make them dangerous. I doubt if they could pull any tricks I haven't seen before."

"I'm sure I'm impressed," McCall said.

Isen stood. McCall tore a page off the yellow legal pad.

"Thank you," he said. "You've been most helpful."

"Oh, Major," McCall said as he moved toward the door, "there's another reason why it won't do you any good to talk to these lieutenants." She paused, waited for Isen to turn around.

"I'm all ears," he said.

"I was considering letting you find this out on your own, since you're such an accomplished reader of men and all."

"Let's cut the crap, OK? I came here for some information. We don't have to end up being soulmates, but there's no reason to treat me like you just hauled me in for peeking into the little boys' room."

"I don't think there's any danger of us becoming fast friends, sir," McCall said coolly. "The point I was going to make was this: those lieutenants closed ranks."

"Meaning?"

"They rehearsed their story. They couldn't have been more in agreement about what happened if they were reading from a script."

"And they did this there, at the club?"

"No, I didn't talk to them until the next morning. No, noon the next day."

"They left the club after one of their buddies committed suicide?"

"No," she said. "Major Foote came and picked them up before I got there. A judgment error on his part that the CID commander brought up to Foote's superiors."

"Did you question Foote on that?"

"Yes. He said that he got a call from Colonel Veir, who told him that some of the lieutenants were in trouble down at Jiggles and that he should go down there. When Foote started to catch a lot of heat for removing the lieutenants, he claimed that it was his idea. Veir had simply told him to go down there."

Isen chewed the inside of his lip. He had a hard time believing that someone with Foote's experience wouldn't see the mistake inherent in removing the lieutenants, possibly the last people to talk to Hauck.

"How did Veir know there was trouble? Was he there?"

"Veir said he left before Hauck shot himself. Apparently Veir got a call from one of the lieutenants," McCall finished.

"Which one?"

"I'm not sure," she said, hesitant for the first time. "I won't have time to check. I'm supposed to wrap this up quickly."

Supposed to, Isen thought, watching her eyes for some other sign. *But I don't think you're ready to give it up just yet.*

"Is that standard practice?" Isen asked. "To do it that quickly?"

"We have a lot of investigations going on right now— there was another shooting last night, as a matter of fact— and some of our agents are attending schools. We're shorthanded."

"I see," Isen said. It sounded to him like young Special Agent McCall was being leaned on.

"Tell me, how long have you been here? I mean, how long have you been an investigator?"

McCall looked up, as if this were the question she'd been expecting all along. "A month, five weeks, something like that."

"Thanks for your help," Isen said after a pause, managing a little sincerity this time. He was halfway out the door when he turned around again.

"You said your job was to determine if this was a suicide, right?" he asked. "I mean, you weren't supposed to try to figure out why he committed suicide."

McCall nodded.

"Did you want to know why he killed himself?"

"Sure," she said. "I mean, just out of simple human compassion."

"You find an answer to that?"

McCall shook her head. "Not one I'm satisfied with."

Within a half hour of talking to Mark Isen, Special Agent Terry McCall was standing in the office of Lieutenant Colonel Ray Berry, the CID commander. Colonel Berry, McCall thought, was paying an inordinate amount of attention to the Hauck case. The fact that there was a death involved would have validated Berry's concern, but it was the fact that he had twice used the term "open-and-shut case" in McCall's hearing that made her take notice.

Isen's question about how long she'd been on the job was right on target. She had, in fact, been the agent on call. But once she saw the situation, she expected to be pulled from the case and replaced with a more senior investigator. That hadn't happened—a fact she'd taken as a compliment at first. But as the case developed and Berry continued to meddle, she began to have her doubts.

If Berry had wanted to assign an agent he could lean on, it made sense to go with his most inexperienced investigator.

"Wrap up the Hauck suicide report in a couple of days," Berry said.

"Sir, I was wondering if I could have some more time—"

"No, you can't," Berry interrupted. Then, as if surprised at how sharply he'd spoken, he smiled insincerely. "We've got other things that need your attention."

And this is an open-and-shut case, right?

Her tendency, which she recognized and struggled against, was to think of such things as conspiracies. Berry and Isen were both white males, functioning in an arena dominated by white males. McCall, who spent a lot of her time pushing against the pyramid base of that power structure, tended to lump such men together.

She resented Isen's intrusion, and she resented Berry's demands that she wrap it up quickly, before she was completely satisfied. Berry had been accommodating to Isen, and so she'd assumed—wrongly—that the two men were on the same side. Only now, standing in front of the boss's desk, did she see that Berry and Isen were at odds with one another.

"I was wondering why the Pentagon was so interested," McCall said, referring to Isen's visit.

"Major Isen is not here in any official capacity representing the Pentagon," Berry said. "He's doing a favor for Hauck's family."

McCall knew this, of course. Her mind was racing ahead. The powers at the Pentagon might or might not be involved; but it was starting to look like the powers at Bragg, beginning with Berry, were interested in this, *her* case. And they wanted it closed.

McCall had listed, in neat schoolgirl script, five lieutenants from Veir's command whom she'd questioned about Hauck's suicide. Isen called Veir's adjutant, the personnel officer, from a phone at CID Headquarters. The lieutenant, who had never heard of Isen, was a little unsure as to why he should bother trying to round up these officers.

"Can you hold for just a moment, please, sir?" he asked, switching lines before Isen could answer.

Isen drew little rectangles on the yellow sheet while he waited.

"This is Major Foote," the executive officer yelled into the phone.

"Hello, Foote," Isen said. "This is your old pal Mark Isen. I'd like to talk to the lieutenants who were with Hauck on the night he killed himself. I have a list here that the CID investigator provided me."

"Oh, you do, huh?" Foote sneered. "Let me guess, you didn't find the CID report tidy enough?"

"The CID investigator did a fine job, I'm sure," Isen said. "But her report is not complete, and neither is the psychological autopsy."

"Yet you think you'll find something they didn't that will tell you why Hauck killed himself," Foote said.

"That's why I'm here," Isen said. *You moron.*

"Yeah, well, we're trying to run an infantry battalion here, Isen. Our lieutenants have better things to do than sit around and talk to some dipshit paper shuffler from the Pentagon."

"Tell me something, Foote," Isen said. "Do you have to practice being such a jerk-off, or does it just come naturally?"

"Fuck you, Isen," Foote said.

"Clever retort," Isen said. "Very original." He felt himself being pulled into another playground exchange, and he knew it was unproductive. But Foote just pissed him off.

"I'll be there at thirteen hundred today. You know who the five are? I could read the list to you, but maybe you should give the phone to someone who knows how to write."

"Thirteen hundred," Foote said, and hung up.

"Nice talking to you," Isen said into the receiver.

Isen met Sue Lynn for lunch at the Officer's Club, a vaguely Spanish-looking building with arches, iron grillwork and a barrel tile roof. Inside, the lobby was dark in spite of the violent clash of furniture and carpeting. The nicer touches—framed prints of European scenes (Isen recognized the Pont D'Avignon)—were offset by vinyl chairs and dim lighting. The building wasn't quite as haphazard as Division Headquarters, but it clearly belonged on the same installation.

There was a big lunch crowd, and Isen, watching the officers enter in two's and three's, allowed himself a bit of nostalgia. Most of the men and women wore the shoulder patch of the Eighty-second Airborne Division, one of the few remaining combat units of its size in the U.S. Army. There was a sense of camaraderie in line units such as this one that was absent from other parts of the service. And it was that sense of togetherness, of being a part of a team, that Mark Isen missed the most as he toiled in the Pentagon.

Isen stood in the lobby just outside the restaurant and watched a young captain trailed by three fresh-faced lieutenants. The four men, all of them wearing the crossed rifles of the infantry on their collar points, joked their way through the serving line. The captain looked no more than twenty-five or twenty-six.

It had been almost seven years since Isen had commanded a rifle company, and in many ways that had been the highlight of his career so far. He'd spent seven years waiting for something to rival that experience. And there were times, if he let his guard down, that he knew he was waiting for something that wasn't coming.

It could be, he'd told himself more than once in the small, dark hours of morning, *that the best stuff is past.*

Isen pulled McCall's yellow sheet from his pocket and unfolded it, smoothing out the wrinkles. Five names, and Isen wasn't hopeful that any one of these men could tell him more about Hauck's death than he already knew. He wasn't even sure, he realized, whether these were the only men from Veir's command who had been at the club that night.

What had started out as a holiday was quickly turning sour. Isen had been happy to get away from the Pentagon. It wasn't as if he didn't feel for the family over the death, but, given that Hauck was already dead, he thought elation at leaving Washington behind was not indecent. He had been pleasantly surprised when Flynn had managed to get him ten days of temporary duty. Now it looked as if ten days might not be enough time.

Sue Lynn came through the front door with three other men who waved good-bye as she spotted Isen.

"Keeping the troops enthralled, I see," he said, approaching her.

"They all want what you're getting," she whispered, putting a hand on his arm.

She wore the same camouflage uniform that he and everyone else was wearing. There was not a trace of makeup, no perfume, no jewelry even, though the regulations allowed a little of each. But even her severe interpretation of the uniform regulation did nothing to quiet Isen's imagination.

"Shall we go in for lunch?" she asked.

"I'd rather go on a search for your dog tags," he said,

glancing at the point where the ID tag chain disappeared into her shirt.

"Later, *mon soldat.*"

She stepped toward the dining room, Isen walking beside her. "Well," she said, "I'm glad to see you survived your interviews so far today."

"The real fun starts in about an hour, when I get to cross paths with Major Foote."

"Ah, yes, your good friend. Going armed?"

"Just the flak jacket for afternoon wear, I think," he said. They made their way through a serving line, picking up salads and bowls of soup. Normally Isen would have gone for the full meal of beef and potatoes; but standing naked in front of Sue Lynn's dressing mirror (another of her likes) had made him conscious of the peculiar pear shape his body seemed to be adopting.

"Funny thing, everyone I talk to says that Foote is a great guy," Darlington said as they took a table at one end of the sunny, cafeteria-style room. "Hard but fair and pretty easy to get along with."

"Well, if that's the case," Isen said, "that must mean that I'm an asshole who just brings out the worst in people."

"Except, of course, for my response," she said, turning her head coyly.

"You, Major Darlington," Isen said, leaning toward her and lowering his voice, "have been most hospitable."

Sue Lynn growled deep in her throat.

"Hold *that* thought till tonight," Isen said.

Sue Lynn looked around the room, acknowledging a couple of friends.

"I miss this, you know," Isen said.

"What?"

"The soldiers, the camaraderie, the goofing around."

"Sleeping on the ground?"

"Yeah, well, you tend to forget about the bad parts when you're locked up like a lab rat," he said. "I miss feeling like I'm part of something bigger than just me."

"The Pentagon isn't big enough?" Sue Lynn asked.

"Hell," Isen said. "People are always talking about the Pentagon as if it were an entity. But there's no sense of that when you're there. The Pentagon is an office building whose tenants happen to wear uniforms, and we're so far removed from the field that sometimes I wonder if it's the same Army."

"Speaking of field soldiers," Darlington said, "there's Veir."

Isen turned around in time to meet Colonel Veir's eyes. The colonel waved at them from across the room.

"What do you think of him now?" Darlington asked.

"I don't know," Isen said, turning back. He chewed for a moment, pushing hard wedges of tomato around on his plate.

"It could be that Veir is a little slippery. Foote is the real pain in the ass, and McCall hasn't been very encouraging either."

"Who's McCall?"

"The CID investigator who handled the Hauck case," Isen said. "She's supposed to wrap it up in a few days."

"They figure out why he did it?"

"No. And I don't have much hope, either. She's only been on the job a month or so," Isen said.

Darlington made a face. "She's a probee?"

"A what?"

"A probationary special agent. If she's been out of school less than a year, she's still on probation. They work that way for a year, supposedly under the guidance of someone more experienced."

"She said they're pretty shorthanded over there," Isen said. "She was on call when it happened."

"Well, it does look like a straightforward case," Darlington said.

"Maybe, but in hindsight assigning her doesn't look like a good decision," Isen said. "A woman who may be the most junior investigator in the service is given this messy job, complete with the public spectacle of a U.S. Army officer committing suicide behind a titty bar."

"Nice expression," Darlington said. "You may work in the Pentagon, but you *talk* like a grunt."

"Sorry," Isen said. "Funny thing, though. I got the feeling she wasn't ready to wrap this up, like she thinks there's more out there. I think she's pursuing a few other things."

Isen told Sue Lynn about the psychologist's theory—that Hauck killed himself over his failure to win the EIB.

"But don't they retest for that?" Sue Lynn asked.

"Every six months or so," Isen said. "It took me three tries to get mine." He paused. "Another wrinkle. McCall said Hauck had friends who were gay."

"*That's* an interesting development," Darlington said. "Maybe your gay-dar was right. You going to tell General Flynn?"

"Not until I snoop around a bit more. McCall said she had no evidence that Hauck was gay. One more thing: McCall said that the guy who called the cops may have heard voices in the parking lot. He was drunk; he's not sure."

"So you think someone else may have found him first?"

"Could be. Could be that someone was out there with him, even," Isen said. "Maybe someone who knew about Hauck's gay friends was threatening to talk."

"Who were these friends?"

"McCall wasn't telling."

"Does she know?"

"When I asked, she told me she'd rather not say."

"Could be GIs," Darlington speculated. "I mean, if they were civilians, what difference would it make if she told you?"

"Good point," Isen said, nodding slowly. "You're pretty good at this."

"Elementary, my dear stud-muffin."

There was a lot to digest, a patchwork of rumors and animosities and half-truths. Isen felt as he did when he flew into a familiar city at night. Looking out the window, trying to piece together evidence of landmarks you think you recognize, trying to make all the little things that are so decidedly visible into some larger whole that made sense. The danger was in trying to force the mental map onto the real landscape—assuming that a brightly lit strip below is such and such a road only to see it veer off in some wildly impossible direction. Theories applied from above—or in hindsight—can't change the facts on the ground.

"I hope I can keep track of all this stuff," Isen said.

"It's a mess, all right," Darlington said. "What's next?"

"I'm going to call General Flynn again. Then I'm supposed to go over to Veir's headquarters and talk to the lieutenants who were with Hauck at the club that night. But I'm not very optimistic about finding out anything."

"Why's that?" Darlington asked.

"McCall said it sounded to her like they had rehearsed their answers."

"If they concocted a story after a few hours of drinking, there's bound to be some holes in it," Darlington offered.

"McCall didn't speak to the lieutenants until the next day. Foote came and picked them up after Veir called him."

"Not a real smart move," Sue Lynn said.

"Foote told McCall that Veir had simply said the lieutenants needed help. Foote says he decided on his own to take them home. He took a lot of heat for it, apparently. But he protected his boss."

"You believe Foote?"

"I'm not sure," Isen said. "I plan on asking him myself."

"That will go over well. He already likes you so much," Darlington said. "How did Veir know what happened?"

"Somebody called him," Isen said. "According to McCall, Veir just stopped in and was already gone when Hauck shot himself."

Darlington was studying Veir, chewing her lip in her bottom teeth in concentration. "I wouldn't be surprised if McCall questioned those lieutenants at Veir's headquarters," she said.

"That might be so," Isen said. "That's where they work."

"That's also the place where someone could keep an eye on them," Darlington said. "Have some sort of control over what they told McCall."

Isen looked at Veir across the room, then back at Darlington.

"Foote took them from the club to keep them from getting interviewed until they had time to be coached on what to say. Then Veir kept tabs on them when they talked to the investigator, making sure they gave McCall the right version of the story. Pretty wild," Isen said. "That would imply that Veir, or one or more of his officers, had something to hide."

"Maybe so," Darlington said, going back to her soup.

"But you'll be able to see better when you talk to those guys this afternoon."

The digital clock on the phone said thirteen-oh-one when Flynn's secretary buzzed him.

"Yes, Donna?"

"There's a Colin Riley on one for you, sir. And Major Isen called again."

"Thank you," Flynn said, punching the button.

"You're a minute late, Riley," Flynn barked. "You're getting soft in your old age."

"All this fucking golf is turning my brain to mush, General."

Colin Riley, retired sergeant major, was calling from Ruskin, Florida, where he divided his time between golf and fishing, with equally poor performance in each endeavor. He and Flynn had a twenty-seven-year-old friendship which had begun when Flynn, dodging some well-placed automatic weapons fire, had jumped into what he thought was an unoccupied shell crater at the edge of a foul-smelling Vietnamese rice paddy. It wasn't until he heard a voice, which seemed to come from the muck but in fact came from a mud-covered body, that Flynn realized he wasn't alone.

"You want to get your feet off my fucking back, buddy?" the voice said in a tone that seemed much too calm for the moment.

"Sorry," Flynn had said, unfolding himself without raising his head above the lip of the slimy depression. "The bastard almost got me."

"Yeah," the creature at the bottom agreed as he elbowed his way from the ooze. "The little fuck almost shot me, too." Then after a pause, "And I didn't do *shit* to him."

Flynn had told that story hundreds of times in the years since, and had brought it up at the beginning of the call he'd made a week earlier. Riley knew right away the old man wanted a favor, but he was happy to have something to break the boredom.

"I found out some interesting stuff about your boy Harlan Veir," Riley said.

"Can you hang on a second?" Flynn said. He put the

phone down on his desk and crossed the thick carpet to close his office door.

"Go ahead," he said, picking up the phone again.

"I talked to a buddy of mine, a young guy who's still at Bragg, as a matter of fact. Seems he and Veir were in the same brigade a few years back. Anyway, the word was that Veir was screwing this staff sergeant's wife. They weren't all that discreet about it either, from what I understand."

"And Veir was married at the time?" Flynn asked.

"Yes, sir. And I got a name and address for his old lady, too. Friend-of-a-friend kinda thing. You want it?"

"Yeah," Flynn said, pulling a tablet toward him. "Shoot."

Riley, proud of his detective work, gave Flynn the information, then continued with his story.

"So one day Veir gets a call from some guy who says he has information on some theft that's been going on in Veir's unit. Bunch of stuff got ripped off, CID had no clue, everybody's pissed. So I guess Veir figures this would be a good way to score some major points. But the guy on the phone says he's scared, so Veir suggests they meet, and the guy says OK."

"Uh-huh," Flynn said, wondering if the ending could be as obvious as he expected.

"So Veir goes out to some deserted spot on Bragg, and guess who shows up?"

"The unhappy husband."

"Bingo. And he brought the old lady along just for fun. Veir sees the hose-bag in the car, but before he could do anything, her old man whips out a twenty-two, points it at Veir's face and pulls the trigger."

Riley paused. He was enjoying this.

"Yeah?" Flynn said.

"The friggin' gun doesn't go off."

"Get the fuck out of here," Flynn said. When he was talking to one of the guys, he enjoyed talking like one of the guys.

"So Veir beats the shit out of the guy."

"Unbelievable."

"There are different versions of what happened next. Some people say Veir just left, others say he poked the wife one more time right in her husband's car. Either way, the ass-whupping goes unreported. After he got out of the hospital, the husband got a transfer."

Flynn leaned back in his chair and whistled out a long breath.

"The most amazing thing," Riley went on, "is this guy Veir survived all this shit."

"Not only survived," Flynn said. "He survived, his career survived—but he came off as even more of a bad-ass. It *added* to his reputation."

"Absolutely," Riley agreed. "According to people who know him, he likes living on the edge. I can't believe he's still around."

"Still around and larger than life," Flynn said. "How the hell did that happen?"

Flynn was left with that question after he thanked Riley and promised to visit when he got down to Florida. He swiveled his big chair around and looked out the window of his office to vast parking lots outside.

He had had no clear picture of what Veir was like, and he wasn't sure he had one now. But the pieces he had were unsettling. He wondered what kind of danger Isen was facing in the name of doing him a favor.

Isen knew well how important geography was when it came to questioning people. Whenever he had to counsel soldiers who had stepped out of line, he always had them come into his office, where he sat behind the big desk and they stood in front of it. Turf gives an immediate psychological advantage. As he sat in the conference room of Veir's headquarters—the only room Foote had made available to him—Isen wished he had an office.

He glanced at his watch. The lieutenants were to be outside the conference room door, according to the adjutant, at exactly thirteen thirty—which gave them three minutes. Isen studied the room, which, like almost every other military conference room he'd ever been in, was decorated with various prints showing the history of the U.S. Army. There were a few photographs on one wall that showed soldiers of the battalion during Desert Storm.

The Eighty-second Airborne Division, whose stock-in-trade was rapid deployment, was the first large ground combat unit deployed to Saudi Arabia after the Iraqi invasion of Kuwait. "When President Bush drew a line in the sand," Isen had heard some general officer say, "he drew it with the bayonet of an Eighty-second Airborne Division paratrooper."

Isen heard shuffling outside the open door, then two sharp raps. *We even have a military way to knock on a door,* he thought.

Isen had already decided that he would be direct and businesslike. He would not explain to these lieutenants that he was doing a personal favor for a general officer; he would ask them specific questions about what had happened on Hauck's last night, including whether or not any of them had gone outside with Hauck. Isen had no more time to waste arguing.

"Come in," he said.

A slightly built second lieutenant came through the doorway, walked to the edge of the table across from where Isen sat, and brought his hand up in a sharp salute, all without ever looking directly at Isen.

"Sir, Lieutenant Pendleton reporting as ordered."

Isen returned the salute from his seat. He thought about leaving Pendleton standing, but he knew the youngster would stare at an imaginary spot above Isen's head—as the manual prescribed for the positions of attention and parade rest—and Isen had no patience for such nonsense.

"Have a seat, Lieutenant," Isen said. He'd didn't offer his hand.

"I'm Major Isen, and I'd like to ask you a few questions about the night that Lieutenant Michael Hauck died."

"Airborne, sir," Pendleton said.

He sat rigidly on the forwardmost three inches of his chair, shoulders square, hands on his knees, feet flat on the floor, relaxed as a statue. Isen took one look at the nervousness and the exaggerated brace and thought, *West Point.*

"I've already read the CID report, Lieutenant, so I won't waste your time asking you those same questions."

Pendleton didn't even nod, but kept his eyes fixed on Isen's, as if watching for some clue that Isen was about to lunge at him.

If you were any more nervous, kid, Isen thought, *I'd be practicing CPR.*

"How well did you know Michael Hauck?"

"Sir," Pendleton said sharply. "Lieutenant Hauck and I knew each other for just over three months, from the time I arrived here at Fort Bragg. We were platoon leaders in the same rifle company, sir."

"Did Lieutenant Hauck say anything to you, on the night he died or at any time prior to that, to make you think he was unhappy . . ." Isen almost said *in this unit,* but caught himself in time to say, "at Fort Bragg?"

"No, sir," Pendleton said quickly. When Isen didn't respond, the lieutenant repeated himself, as if perhaps Isen hadn't heard him. "He didn't say anything that would make me think he was unhappy, sir."

Isen decided that Pendleton was a good candidate for some rattling. *Let's shake the tree and see what falls out,* he thought.

"What were you doing in the club, Pendleton?" Isen asked.

Pendleton swiped at a few beads of sweat that appeared on his upper lip. "I just, I mean, we just go there sometimes, you know, sir, to, uh . . ."

"Look at naked women," Isen said, raising one eyebrow.

Pendleton was a kid—he still had the acne to prove it—and it was shameless of Isen to try to embarrass him. But Isen had decided to take the offensive. Pendleton was probably scared of Veir; it wouldn't hurt for him to be a little nervous about Isen.

"Where you from, Pendleton?"

"Michigan, sir."

"You hang out in places like this in your hometown?"

"Er, no, sir," Pendleton said. He shifted his weight in the chair, moving even farther toward the front edge. Isen thought he might fall off.

"What did Hauck say when he left to go outside?"

"Sir?"

"What did he say when he got up to go outside to shoot himself? Did he say, 'Excuse me'? Did he say, 'I'll be right back'? Did he say, 'Fuck you guys'? Or did he just get up and walk out all of a sudden?"

"I'm not sure, sir. I mean, we were there a long time, you know, and we'd been drinking beer, and so guys had to get up and go to the bathroom quite a lot."

"I see," Isen said. He held a small spiral ring notebook in front of him, and he flipped it open and pretended to read something there. The pages were blank, but Pendleton couldn't see that. When Isen looked up, Pendleton was studying the back of the notebook. Isen wondered how Pendleton would handle things the first time a soldier told him to fuck off.

"Did you go outside with Hauck before he shot himself?"

"No, sir."

"Were you surprised?"

"Surprised, sir?"

"Were you surprised when you went outside later and found out that Hauck had killed himself?"

Pendleton seemed to regain a tiny bit of composure.

"Yes, sir," he chirped. "I was surprised and saddened."

Isen wrinkled his brow. "Right," he said. "Of course you were."

By the time the second junior officer was standing before him, Isen had decided on the tactics he would use from this point. He would shift the questions back and forth from the mundane things he knew to the things he wanted to learn in hopes of keeping the men off balance; and he would listen for the telltale phrases that sounded rehearsed, such as Pendleton's "surprised and saddened."

Isen wanted to know if Hauck was gay, but he walked a fine line here; there was no way to ask such a question without its being spread throughout the battalion. And the point at which it became hot gossip was the point at which concern for the truth died.

The next two officers Isen spoke with were considerably more composed than Pendleton had been, right up to the point where Isen started asking about Veir. Lieutenant Colonel Veir was very upset by all this, the men assured Isen. Very upset.

"He had us all in the next day," one of the lieutenants told Isen. "All the officers. He told us it was tough, and that we might not ever know the circumstances of Hauck's death.

But we did know how he lived, and that was the important thing. We each want to be remembered for how we live, which is why we have to soldier hard."

Blah, blah, blah, Isen thought.

The next-to-last lieutenant to come in was John Carroll, a Texan, judging by his accent, who appeared in muddy boots and rumpled uniform.

"Lieutenant Carroll reporting, sir," he said, touching his eyebrow with extended fingers. There was a tiny trace of tobacco on his lip, as if he had just removed a dip of snuff. He'd washed his face, but there was green camouflage paint on his neck, in his ears, at his hairline.

"Have a seat, Carroll," Isen said. "Just come in from the field?"

"Yessir," Carroll said, leaning back, hooking one elbow over the back of the chair. He was sunburned, and his nose was peeling in vicious swatches. Compact, with an athlete's easy grace, he was at his ease; Isen got the distinct impression that, given half a chance, Carroll would have put his feet up on Colonel Veir's conference table.

"I understand you were with Michael Hauck on the night he shot himself," Isen said.

"Uh-huh, yessir," Carroll said.

"Did Hauck say anything that night—or at any other time—that would make you think he was that despondent?"

Isen was prepared for the curt answer the others had given him, but Carroll considered the question a moment.

"Not really, sir," Carroll answered, drawing out his vowels as Sue Lynn did. "But he was kind of . . . out of character."

Isen looked up from his still-blank notebook page. "How's that?" he asked.

"Well, Mike didn't drink much, most times, but he seemed hell-bent on getting drunk that night."

"How much did he have to drink?" Isen asked.

"Hard to say, I reckon." Carroll pinched his bottom lip between thumb and forefinger, tugging away the tobacco and spittle there. "Like I said, he didn't generally drink much, so it wouldn't take a whole lot for him to really feel it, you know?"

"How much did you have to drink, Lieutenant?"

"Oh, I guess about eight or ten beers over three, three and a half hours."

Although he already knew the answer, Isen asked, "Did you drive yourself home?"

"No, sir, I didn't."

"How'd you get home, then?" Isen asked.

"Major Foote gave us a lift," Carroll said, knuckling his scalp. His hair had been matted into odd shapes by the helmet he'd just removed. "One of the guys must have called him. That's SOP—we get in trouble, we call for help."

"Do you know who called Major Foote?"

"No, sir. Could have been any one of the other guys."

"Did Hauck like the Army? Was he happy in his work?"

"Those are two separate questions, sir," Carroll said. "No disrespect."

"So they are," Isen allowed. He watched the lieutenant's eyes, but Carroll was as relaxed as if they were talking about a movie they'd both seen. Isen decided that he liked this kid; more than that, he trusted him.

"All in all, I'd say Mike liked the Army—or the soldiers, at least—just fine," Carroll said. "He came from some big Army family or something."

"Did he talk about that?" Isen asked.

"He didn't bring it up to me. But I heard about it from someone he went to college with, and I asked him about it. Said he had ancestors fought in both World Wars."

"And the Civil War, too," Isen said.

"Anyways, I guess he wanted to do well by all those people, you know?"

"Mm-hmm," Isen said. "Was he happy in the unit here? In this battalion?"

"Mike was pretty hard on himself when he screwed something up."

"Did that happen a lot?" Isen asked. "Was he prone to mistakes?"

"There were a couple of boners, I guess," Carrroll said. He studied his fingers, as if weighing some further comment.

"Nothing that other guys didn't pull from time to time. You know, we all make the same kind of mistakes, I mean, new lieutenants and everything. Mike just couldn't accept that fact, seems to me."

"He dwelled on his shortcomings?"

"Something like that," Carroll said. He was looking at the historical prints around the conference room. "My old man went to Vietnam," Carroll said.

Isen looked up at the closest print, which showed United States infantry attacking through waist-high grass in Cuba during the Spanish-American War.

"Mine, too," Isen said.

"It's weird," Carroll said, casually pulling out his own pocket notebook and scribbling something in it. "Dad was proud of me going into the Army and all, but he didn't want me to be an officer."

"No? Why not?"

Carroll fixed Isen with a grim look.

"Oh, I guess in Vietnam he ran across some officers who'd fuck people over to get promoted. Guys who cared more about their careers than their men."

Carroll tore a page from his notebook, then pocketed the book and the pen. He looked behind him, out the empty doorway, then turned and placed the piece of paper on the table.

"Is that all, sir?"

"Did you go outside with Hauck before he killed himself?"

"No, sir."

"OK, Lieutenant," Isen said. "Thank you for your time."

"If there's anything I can do, sir—"

"Yeah, yeah, I know," Isen interrupted. "All I have to do is ask."

Carroll stood and saluted. Out in the hall, chairs scraped across the floor as men came to their feet; when Isen looked up, he saw Veir pass by in the hall. There were muffled voices—orders, judging by the tone—but Veir did not even glance into the room.

Isen reached across the table and pulled the paper toward him. Grimy in the corner from Carroll's dirty hands, it bore a phone number. Isen shoved it into his notebook.

Isen saw, from the corner of his eye, Major Foote's large form pass by the open door.

"You're still here?" he bellowed. Then he was in the

doorway. Isen was amazed at how much of the space he filled.

"You're taking too long," Foote said. "I'm going to send these men away; they have work to do."

"I talked to almost all of them," Isen said, checking his list. "Except Bennett."

"Yeah, well," Foote said, entering the room and putting his fists on the table. He leaned toward Isen and lowered his voice to a threatening whisper. "Bennett and these others are busy little boys. You want to talk to Bennett, you'll have to come back another time."

"No problem," Isen said. "I'm glad of the opportunity to hang around here. Give us a chance to get to know one another."

Foote snorted, then turned toward the door.

"One question for you, though, if I may."

Foote leaned back into the room, scowling magnificently.

"Did you ever meet a Lieutenant Greg Savin? Hauck's roommate?"

Foote stared straight into Isen's eyes, giving Isen the impression he was weighing his response.

"Yeah, a real smart-ass. I met him once at the O Club. Division Officer's Call."

"Hauck just brought him up to you?"

"No, I went up to them."

"Why?"

Foote moved into the center of the doorway and removed a small knife from his pocket. He unfolded the blade and began to cut away some dead skin around his fingernails. After a few seconds of this entertainment, he continued.

"The kid mouthed off to Colonel Veir, and I tracked him and Hauck down to jerk knots in their tails." He closed the knife and dropped it back into his pocket. "Why do you ask?"

"Just curious," Isen said. "You picked the lieutenants up from that club after Hauck killed himself?"

"Yes," Foote said. "I've been through all this with the CID. Colonel Veir called me and asked me to go down there. I was the one who decided to take them home."

"How did Colonel Veir know what happened?"

"I suppose one of the lieutenants called him."

"Did you think that the CID would want to talk to them?"

"I told you I've already been chewed out about this thing."

Foote paused. "I knew the CID wouldn't have any trouble tracking down these guys, so I didn't see the harm. Besides, they were all shit-faced drunk and wouldn't have been any help to anyone."

Isen nodded. "Might have been a good idea to get their statements right away though, don't you think?"

The two men stared at each other, measuring for an uncomfortable moment.

Foote shrugged. "I guess we'll never know, right?"

When he returned to Sue Lynn's house, Isen found a long message from Flynn. The general recapped the Riley story and left the name and number for the ex-Mrs. Veir. Once again—to Isen's surprise—he didn't mention the CID report.

Just after seven that evening Isen called the number Carroll had given him and left a message on the lieutenant's machine. Carroll returned the call at eleven-thirty, startling Isen awake.

"Major Darlington," Sue Lynn mumbled into the receiver.

Off in the distance, Isen could hear the distinctive *crump* of exploding artillery as some unit trained through the night. In that way, living near an Army post was a little like living inside a Hemingway novel.

Sue Lynn listened for a moment, then handed Isen the phone as she buried her head in the pillow.

"Isen here."

"I'm sorry to be calling so late, sir."

The *suh* gave it away. "Hello, Carroll," Isen said.

"Did you find out anything new?" Carroll asked.

Isen pulled himself into a sitting position. Sue Lynn inched toward him, resting her hand on his leg.

"You called me at . . ." Isen looked at the clock. "At twenty-three thirty to ask me how my day went?"

"Uh, no, sir. I guess I didn't."

Isen was fully awake now; Carroll had something to tell him. But the other end of the phone was silent.

"No, I didn't learn much today, I'm afraid," Isen said,

hoping to draw Carroll out. "There was one guy I didn't get to talk to."

"Bennett," Carroll said.

"Right."

"Make sure you get back to him," Carroll said.

"OK."

Carroll, who'd been so relaxed in his interview, was struggling.

"Carroll," Isen said. "John. I figure you gave me your home number because you wanted to talk to me about something you didn't want to discuss right there in battalion headquarters. Am I right?"

"Yessir," Carroll said. "Although now I'm not so sure it's a good idea."

"Whatever you tell me," Isen said, "I'll hold in confidence."

"One of the reasons I'm calling so late is that I just got back from headquarters," Carroll said.

"Kind of a late night, isn't it?"

"Major Foote had us all there, all the guys you talked to today."

"Why?"

"He had us—I'm sure it was Colonel Veir's idea—Major Foote had us all write out reports about our conversations with you. What exactly you asked, what we said, all that crap."

"So Colonel Veir wanted to know what you guys told me," Isen said. "Why didn't he just ask you? I mean, the details couldn't have been that hard to remember. I was only in there a few minutes with each of you."

"Well, first of all, we had to write the reports a couple of times. Colonel Veir likes things perfect. Then I think he wanted it on paper, with our signatures. So if it turns out we told you something and then forgot to mention it to him, he'll have us. At least, that's what I think."

"Did he say that to you? That he would use it against you?"

"No, but the message seemed clear enough. Major Foote kept reminding us to be absolutely accurate. Kept talking about how details can get men killed in combat, all that kind of stuff."

"Was Colonel Veir there?"

"He was in his office; we were in the conference room again. But he came in a couple of times. Major Foote sat there the whole time."

"Uh-huh."

Carroll was silent.

"Anything else?" Isen asked.

"Yeah. Yes, sir. I think he kept us there to make a point about who's in charge. One time Colonel Veir even said, 'Major Isen will be gone in a few days, but I'm still going to be around.' In other words, we shouldn't count on you to help us out if we step out of line."

"Step out of line how?"

"By being disloyal. By saying something about Colonel Veir or the unit, I guess. Just anything."

"So why did you call me?"

Carroll chuckled unhappily. "That's a good question. Maybe I'm just stupid." He paused again, and Isen thought he heard Carroll sipping a drink.

"Mike Hauck wasn't happy here, sir. I know I told you earlier that he didn't make any unusual mistakes. That's true, but Mike held himself to a higher, maybe unreasonable standard. And he attracted Colonel Veir's attention a couple of times."

"He was taking heat from Colonel Veir?" Isen asked.

"Yes. See, Colonel Veir wants stuff to be perfect. And Mike wanted stuff to be perfect, too. Maybe on account of his family. So when things weren't going great, Mike had a harder time than most. You know that guy Pendleton? The first one you talked to today?"

Isen thought about the jumpy little lieutenant who had been embarrassed about being in a strip joint. "Yeah."

"Mike was even more nervous than that, sometimes, especially around Veir. Except Mike did a better job of hiding it than Pendleton does."

"Any specific incident stand out in your mind?"

"No," Carroll said. "But he seemed to be worse lately. He was pretty agitated the other night, the night he shot himself."

"Do you know what triggered that?"

"Not really. I know that Bennett kept following him

around, kind of hounding him. We were at this big table, all of us. And every time Mike would sit down, Bennett would move over next to him, start giving him shit about something or other."

"Do you know what it was about?"

"No. I asked Mike, but he said it was nothing. Bennett didn't like Hauck very much, and it seemed like they were always going on about something."

"Do you remember any specifics?" Isen wanted to know.

"Not really," Carroll said. "I do know that Mike's bullshit detector was pretty sensitive—a lot like the troops. Anyway, Bennett would set off *anyone's* bullshit detector."

"Any idea who might know what was between them? Did Mike have any especially close friends?"

"Not that I know of, sir."

Isen decided to take a chance with Carroll. The young man had the guts to call; Isen hoped he could be trusted.

"Did you ever hear any rumors to the effect that Mike was gay?"

Carroll didn't hesitate.

"No, sir. Bennett called him a 'faggot' a few times, but Bennett was always motherfuckin' somebody."

"Did Mike ever talk about a girlfriend? Did he date any women that you know of?"

"Not that I know of," Carroll said.

"OK. I'd appreciate it if you kept these questions to yourself."

"Don't worry, sir," Carroll said, belching. "I won't be telling anyone that we talked."

"Are you drinking beer?" Isen asked.

"Yessir."

"Is that normal for you, at almost midnight when you have to be at PT the next morning? In a few hours, really."

"No, sir. I'm just a little nervous, that's all."

"Because of what you told me?"

"Yes," Carroll said, leaving his sentence hanging.

"And?" Isen asked.

"Colonel Veir was there that night, sir. At the club."

The two men were quiet for a moment. Isen knew this fact—McCall had told him. But Carroll, with this late-night phone call, saw something more than coincidence.

Isen was preternaturally aware of his surroundings: the streetlight filtering in the window, the weight of Sue Lynn's hand on his thigh and her measured breathing, the slight crackle of static over the telephone line.

"Did he and Hauck talk?"

"Colonel Veir sat with us a while. He talked to all of us, I guess." Carroll swallowed hard. "But he also talked to Mike off to the side, over near the men's room."

"Did you get the impression that talking to Colonel Veir upset Mike?"

"Yes, sir, I did."

"Did Veir follow Mike outside?"

"No, Colonel Veir left before Mike did, I think."

"Is there anything else, John?"

"Yes. Yes, sir. Bennett followed Mike out. That last time, I mean."

Bennett had tried to talk to Veir at headquarters, but the colonel had waved him away with the others. When he got home, he sat by the phone, nodding in and out of uneasy sleep.

The phone jolted him after midnight.

"You talk to him?" It was Veir.

Bennett was having a little trouble focusing. "Who?"

"Isen. Who the fuck do you think I'm talking about?"

"No, sir," Bennett said. "I didn't talk to him."

"Don't. He's just trying to cause problems down here, make life difficult for us."

"You can count on me, Colonel," Bennett said.

Veir hung up without another word.

"I can count on *me,*" Veir said out loud. "And that's about it."

5

THE EXPRESS PACKAGE FROM DIANE HAUCK ARRIVED AT
Sue Lynn's house on Wednesday morning before Isen finished his second cup of coffee. Inside were two bundles of
letters in thick rubber bands. One set bore Hauck's Fayetteville address in Diane Hauck's handwriting, the others, in
the cramped printing that Isen would find belonged to Michael Hauck, were addressed to his parents' home with
"Hauck" written above the Dallas address.

A long, business-sized envelope with "Mark Isen" on the
front came out of the package last. Inside was a letter from
Diane Hauck.

> I read some of these letters over again, but could not
> get through the whole stack. I guess I was trying to
> anticipate what you might be looking for. I'm still not
> sure what that might be; however, if you're looking for
> Michael, for some idea of who he was—I thought I
> might help.
>
> Michael was a good-hearted and fairly serious young
> man. He was most happy when he could help other
> people. As a teenager he did a great deal of volunteer

work with our church's youth group. I think you'll see, in these letters, that the part he liked best about the Army was the chance to serve others.

Michael wanted to be a soldier from the time he was a little boy. Of course, he was steeped in our family's history, and he loved to visit with his Uncle Patrick.

Here Diane Hauck had crossed out something; almost half a line was obliterated with dark scratching.

"He wanted to be a success. Maybe he wanted that too much," she wrote.

Isen arranged the letters by date and began reading the litany of the commonplace life Hauck had found. He wrote about his training, about parachuting, the field exercises, the characters in his platoon. The writing was vivid, if humorless, and the effect was a portrait of exactly what Michael Hauck—and Mark Isen—liked about the Army: the chance to associate with other soldiers.

Near the end of the packet the letters became somewhat bland, the sentences choppy, the writing uncertain. Isen wasn't sure if the change meant that Hauck's attitude had changed, or that he simply did not have as much time to write.

Just after the visit from General Flynn, Hauck wrote to his parents that "the senior officers here are not all like Uncle Pat." He did not say if he considered this an asset or a liability.

In his next-to-last letter home, Hauck wrote that although most of the other lieutenants were "pretty cool," there were times when he was "embarrassed to be around them. They do stupid things, weird stuff that I just didn't expect to find here, I guess."

The remarks were cryptic, and might have been enough to give his mother pause had she been looking for some evidence that her son was troubled. In the context of a young man's letters home from a new life, they were not especially alarming. The clues were visible after the fact; they were not much of a warning.

Isen took the letters to a copy center in town where he made duplicates; he then packed the originals to ship back to Diane Hauck. He stood for a few minutes at the post office counter, his pen over a sheet of blank paper he wanted to include in the return parcel. He wanted to write something reassuring; he wanted to tell her that he would do his best to help her and her family come to some understanding of what had happened to her son. The truth was that he had nothing to say to this woman, whose suffering he could only imagine.

Finally, he wrote, "Thank you for your help. My sympathy to you in your loss."

He sealed the package, gave it to the clerk and left the post office hoping that his feelings of inadequacy would pass.

Isen spent the next few hours of the day trying to arrange meetings with Hauck's company commander and the elusive Lieutenant Bennett. Foote put him off with promises of co-operation later in the week.

"What the fuck you in such a hurry for, Isen? Afraid somebody will steal the pencil box off your desk in the Pentagon if you don't hurry back?"

Isen also placed a call to General Flynn's office, but the old man was out for the day. Just as well. Isen hadn't quite figured out how he was going to ask Flynn about Savin's not being able to attend the funeral. Flynn was a general officer first and Isen's mentor second; it wouldn't do to piss him off by taking Savin's suppositions at face value.

The afternoon didn't go much better. Isen spent a few more hours in a fruitless paper chase. Second Lieutenant Michael Hauck had already been erased from the memory banks of records at Fort Bragg. Hauck had been buried only five days earlier, and two of those days were a weekend. Isen was a bit surprised at how quickly a man's board could be wiped clean. Hauck's personnel file, medical history, pay statements, even his training records, which showed such innocuous information as how he fired the last time out to the rifle range, had been culled from their various resting places in the bureaucracy and shipped off to a central records storage site. A personnel clerk told Isen that yes, it did seem fast, but not to worry. Isen could have the records in a few weeks, if the Special Agent investigating submitted a written request.

Isen called Veir's headquarters to arrange a meeting with the colonel. He spent a good deal of time on hold before being told the colonel would see him after physical training the following morning. Frustrated, he killed some time at the post library, reading newspaper accounts of Hauck's suicide.

Isen was supposed to meet Sue Lynn at six o'clock that evening at the Officers' Club, where the dinners were just passable but which was the only place one could go without having to change out of the camouflage duty uniform. Patrons of Fayetteville restaurants, who regularly ate in poorly lit places with names like Kountry Kitchen and Hank's Pit BBQ, were nevertheless picky enough to want to avoid sharing their dining experiences with people disguised as trees.

At six-ten, Isen decided to wait in the bar. He left a message for Sue Lynn with the hostess and made his way to the basement of the building, where, with some foresight, the management had hidden the eyesore that bore the misleading sign "Cocktail Lounge."

Isen paused inside the door to give his eyes a chance to adjust to the darkness. The room was dominated by a long, narrow bar that jutted from the wall facing the door. Off to the right, a raised landing held a half-dozen round tables and an empty buffet. To the left, a worn dance floor, flooded in unflattering yellow light, was surrounded by a counter and some stools, creating the sort of arena effect that made the term "meat market" spring to mind. The prevailing smells were spilled beer and cigarettes, and the sound system could have been devised by the psychological warfare unit, located just down the road, to test human endurance. Still, the pull of cheap beer was enough to half fill the room early on a Wednesday evening. Isen sat on a bar stool next to a hand-lettered sign that said "Join Us for Hump-Day Happy Hour."

"Lots of folks dance here?" Isen asked when the bartender delivered his draft. In Isen's experience, Army officers were too concerned with looking macho to be good dancers.

"Nah." The bartender, sixty-ish, bald head shiny as glass, nodded toward the front of the room. "Everybody used to sit up there, as close as possible to the stage. Used to be we had half-naked gals dancing up there."

He pronounced the word "nekked," which was, Isen had learned in Georgia, naked with sinful intent.

"That was a few years ago, wasn't it?" Isen said, recalling his experiences in Officers' Clubs before the Army was over-run with sensitivity, correctness and an aversion to undraped body parts.

"Those guys would just get wild. Stomping all around, getting up and dancing."

"Pretty calm now?"

"In here?" the old man said. "Nah. These young guys still carry on; they just have to go downtown if they want to carry on with naked women."

Isen, his eyes adjusted, looked around as his new confi-dante answered a waitress's call. There were forty or fifty people in the room, about a quarter of them women and every one in uniform. Presumably, spouses met in the more civil dining room. This room, devoid of decoration, was more like a cell in a jail that allowed drinking.

Two more uniforms entered and walked by Isen, who sat with his back to the door. Though he couldn't see their faces at first, he thought that the young woman was Special Agent McCall, decked out for this occasion in battle dress uniform. McCall did not see him until she had walked to the far end of the room and sat down at a table in the corner farthest from the stage. Isen thought she nodded at him, and he was debating the decorum of going over to greet her—they hadn't parted friends—when Sue Lynn tapped him on the shoulder.

"You take me to the nicest places," she said.

"This is how I win all my women," Isen answered, indicat-ing the dingy room with a grand gesture all out of proportion to the surroundings. "Which goes a long way to explaining why I'm alone." He stood and they walked to a table.

"I was just trying to decide whether or not to go over and say hello to Special Agent McCall, one of the many friends I've made here at the home of the Airborne," Isen said, nodding to the far corner of the room.

"Who's the guy with her?"

"Let's see," Isen said. "Tall, skinny white guy too ugly to be her boyfriend. Even in uniform, without the black shoes and white socks that those guys think pass as civilian clothes, I'd say he's another CID type."

"They following you?"

Isen paused; the thought hadn't occurred to him. "Why would they do that?"

"I don't know," Sue Lynn said. "I just asked. So?"

"I doubt it. Maybe they came in for a drink."

Sue Lynn leaned forward in her chair for a better look at McCall and her partner.

Sue Lynn was clearly enjoying her role as an amateur sleuth.

"I can hear the wheels turning," Isen said.

"If they wanted to have a drink, there are lots of places nicer than this. And besides, they're in uniform instead of the normal civvies; that's almost a disguise for them," Sue Lynn said, standing.

"Come on," she said, starting across the floor without giving Isen a chance to respond. "I want you to introduce me."

A lieutenant at one of the tables stood up abruptly and bumped into Darlington, but not before announcing loudly, "I gotta go drain the dragon."

"Dragons only live in fairy tales," Darlington said, smiling sweetly. "You know, like in your imagination."

Isen smiled as he passed the dumbfounded lieutenant, whose friends laughed loudly.

McCall, recognizing Isen, stood. In uniform, he thought as he approached, she apparently felt compelled to extend the minimum courtesy his rank called for, something she hadn't done at CID Headquarters. When he got close, Isen saw that she wore the simple black chevrons of a buck sergeant.

Well, I'll be dipped in shit, he thought. *I thought she was a warrant officer, at least. She talked to me like she's a goddamned general.*

"Special Agent McCall," Isen said, coming up beside Sue Lynn. "Nice to see you again."

McCall didn't smile and limited her response to "Sir."

"I'd like you to meet Major Sue Lynn Darlington."

"Pleasure, ma'am," McCall said, taking Sue Lynn's proffered hand. Turning to her partner, who had also stood, McCall said, "This is Special Agent Harrigan."

Special Agent Harrigan, who wore the rank insignia of a Chief Warrant Officer Third, or CW3, was even homelier than Isen had surmised from across the room. His hair was unruly, barely combed, and his face ended with a tiny, pointed chin that looked all out of place on his long frame. He didn't make a sound as he nodded at the two majors.

The four of them stood for a few seconds of awkward silence until McCall asked, "So, Major Isen, were those lieutenants any help to you?"

"Not really," Isen said. "Sounded like they closed ranks, just like you said. "But . . ."

Isen paused, glancing at Harrigan.

"Chief Harrigan can hear anything you want to say to me, sir," McCall said.

"No offense," Isen said to Harrigan. Then, to McCall, "I found out who may have been out in the parking lot with Hauck when he killed himself," Isen said, a little smugly.

"Oh?" McCall did not seem at all surprised.

"There's a Lieutenant Bennett in the battalion, and one of the guys thinks Bennett followed Hauck outside that last time."

McCall held Isen's eyes steadily, and the four of them were suddenly quiet. Isen had a sinking feeling, wondering if he had just said too much. Behind him, the table full of lieutenants was singing along, loudly and badly, with a country song scratching from the jukebox.

"And your point is?" McCall said.

"I didn't know if you knew that or not," Isen said.

"Did you talk to Bennett?" McCall asked.

"Not yet."

"But you know that Bennett went all the way out to the parking lot? Followed Hauck right to his truck? Didn't stop off at the rest room or go to his own car or leave the area before Hauck did? You know all that, sir?"

"Well . . . no. No, I don't know that. As I said, one of the lieutenants told me he thought Bennett went outside."

"And what makes you believe this particular lieutenant, sir?"

McCall's patronizing tone was getting old. Isen had put up with it at the CID Headquarters, allowing her some slack because he had more or less dropped in on her. But now she was borderline insubordinate. The sergeant stripes on her collar points didn't help his mood.

"Because, Sergeant McCall," Isen said, leaning toward her, his hands on the table, "the lieutenant who told me that went to some lengths to make sure he was out of earshot of everyone in the headquarters. He slipped me his number and had me call him at home."

McCall, unfazed, mirrored Isen's stance, leaning toward him across the same table. She was close enough for him to catch the clean, soapy scent of her.

"And that by itself tells you absolutely nothing," McCall said, measuring her words. "Sir."

She straightened up. "Did this guy have as much to drink that night as the others?"

"I suppose." Isen didn't like the feeling that he was on the defensive.

"Did it occur to you that he might just have it in for Bennett?"

"No," Isen said. "But I don't think that's the case."

"Well, I'll tell you what, Major," McCall said. "There's an awful lot more to an investigation than jumping to conclusions from one or two facts and some unsubstantiated gossip."

McCall, angry now, pulled her folded uniform cap from the cargo pocket alongside her leg and slapped it against her thigh.

"It's not like you gave me a lot to work with," Isen said.

"You're right," McCall said. "I didn't. Look, you asked good questions, but they weren't questions I didn't think of. I didn't get many answers the first time around, that's all."

"Are you still investigating?" Isen wanted to know.

"Look, Major," McCall said. "The last time I looked, you weren't anywhere in my supervisory chain. I'm not about to start briefing you on what I'm doing or not doing."

McCall turned, nodded to Darlington, and pushed past Harrigan, who followed her without saying a word.

"Pissy little bitch, isn't she?" Isen said as he watched her back.

"She's pretty ticked off, but I wouldn't bet that that's her normal mode."

"Irate feminist agenda, I'd say." Isen turned to speak directly to Darlington, who appraised him with hooded eyes. Something clicked deep in his consciousness, like the beep a fighter pilot hears when an enemy missile has locked on. But Isen, his sensitivity to such warnings dulled by the bachelor life, plunged ahead.

"I suppose you're going to tell me that has something to do with being a woman in a man's world," he said.

"You have no idea what she has to contend with," Darlington lectured. "Not only is she a woman in a man's world, she's a black woman in a white woman's world. People are just waiting for her to screw up ... hell, they *expect* her to screw up. You can't imagine what that feels like.

"Besides that, you're down here going over stuff that she's already covered. That's not exactly a vote of confidence. In fact, it's professionally insulting."

She's probably right, Isen told himself, stopping before admitting out loud that he would never be able to cross that gulf. Sue Lynn sidestepped for him.

"But let's put that aside for the moment, shall we? Let's try to figure out what's going on with the Hauck case."

"Interesting choice of words," Isen said. "Case, that is."

"I think she's still digging."

"So do I. Which means she was not satisfied with the work she did the first time, or someone is making her do it over."

Isen sat down at the table vacated by McCall and Harrigan.

"So which is the more logical sequence?" he asked Darlington, who sat down next to him. "She draws the case because she's on call and is left on for the training opportunity, and then when she screws up she has to do it over again. Or she's left on because she's inexperienced and won't see the complications."

"But she did see them," Sue Lynn said. "Which is why she's dragging her feet about getting the report done."

"Right. Either way, she's not going to admit to me that something's wrong. And my coming along to remind her that some kid is dead and she doesn't know why is just going to piss her off—even if she is still working on it."

Sue Lynn nodded in agreement.

"All I can do is see how it plays out."

"Which leaves us with why she was here."

"She came to get a drink with her companion, Joe Personality," Isen said.

"Nope."

"She came to spy on me."

"Possibly."

"But why the uniform? Those people don't wear uniforms unless it's part of an investigation. She had to *plan* on the uniform, and she couldn't have done that without knowing where I was going ahead of time. I didn't know I was going to wind up in the bar until I saw you weren't here yet."

"Could be that she left without accomplishing what she wanted to do," Sue Lynn said.

"I think she left because she was angry at us."

"Us? What do you mean us?"

"OK, Miss Priss, angry at me," Isen said. "Let's go get something to eat."

They were climbing the strairs that led to the front of the club and the dining room when they were passed by six or seven loud junior officers, mostly lieutenants with a sprinkling of captains, all on their way to the bar. Isen recognized three of the men who were from Veir's battalion.

Darlington and Isen left the club at seven-thirty. At ten-thirty, Isen, dressed in civilian clothes, drove back, hoping for a chance to talk to some of the junior officers. On the way into the building he held the door for some retirees, older couples in cheap PX clothes who'd settled in Fayetteville and for whom the Officers' Club—mediocre food at good prices—was a big night out.

Isen tried not to think about what his retirement might look like as he made his way back to the bar, where he slipped onto the same bar stool he had occupied earlier. The jukebox had been turned up even louder, so that he merely signed to the bartender for a draft beer.

All but four or five of the tables were empty, and these had been pushed together just off the dance floor, where they clustered like life rafts. The junior officers from Veir's battalion were still there. Two men sang along loudly with the music, swinging heavy beer mugs out of time. A few others sat with their feet propped up on the tables. One man appeared to be asleep, his head nestled on his arm; his sleeve, where it met the table, was dark with spilled beer.

You're wasting your time, Isen, he thought. *You can't get much out of a bunch of drunks.*

There was some movement at one table where a man sat, back to Isen, uniform blouse off, arm-wrestling a much smaller man. Isen watched as the bigger contestant, who obviously had a flair for the dramatic, stood a lighted cigarette on the table, then twisted his arm so that the back of his hand was just above the ember. His challenger had only to push the hand down a few inches to the tabletop to win, less than an inch to force the back of the big man's hand onto the burning cigarette.

Yet in spite of all the liquid courage that had been flowing, there were no comers. The T-shirt, incensed, climbed a chair and began flexing like a bodybuilder, twisting arms and torso in unnatural poses. The lieutenants around the tables looked distracted, as if they'd all suddenly and simultaneously remembered other, more important places they had to be.

The T-shirt drew himself up, hands on hips. "Come on, Pendleton, you goddamned puke."

By leaning to one side, Isen could see the slight lieutenant he'd interviewed the day before, even as Pendleton tried to make himself invisible by sinking into his chair.

A couple of Pendleton's peers, happy to finger someone, pushed Pendleton out of his slump.

"Go on, man. Do it."

"C'mon, Pendleton."

"Go, go, go. . . ."

Pendleton smiled unhappily as the T-shirt jumped off the chair and said something Isen couldn't hear.

Asshole, Isen thought.

Pendleton moved from his chair to the one across from his tormentor without ever standing fully upright. After a few stylized puffs, T-shirt put the cigarette, lighted end up, on the table. He placed his elbow inches away, then bent his arm back so that the back of his hand touched the ember. The crowd, animated now that the sacrifice had been chosen, responded with grunts and cheers.

Pendleton made a show of positioning his arm, curling his lips in concentration as someone said "Go." But there was hardly time for the smaller man to get red in the face. The pair of clenched hands traveled the long arc away from the cigarette and down to the tabletop, and the crash rattled the glasses scattered there.

The victor jumped up, clenched arms describing a circle in front of him. "Hooah!"

Several in the group answered with their own versions of the all-purpose grunt, an exclamation that had gone a long way to replace speech in the infantry.

"That's quite a group there," Isen shouted at the bartender.

The old man shrugged, checked his watch, then leaned forward and shouted, "Last call." There was no reaction until he rang a large brass bell suspended above the bar.

Only one man roused himself at the signal. The arm-wrestling champ stood as if challenged, turned to the bartender and rendered an epic belch commensurate with his status as victor.

The T-shirt swaggered over to the bar, just a few feet from where Isen sat. He was much shorter than Isen expected. His green shirt stretched tight across an overdeveloped upper torso, and he carried his arms away from his body, a simian stance. He had a heavy forehead just above a single, continuous eyebrow that spanned the width of his face. When he saw Isen looking at him, he nodded, still scowling as if in concentration. In another time and place, men like him guarded harem doors.

"Bennett," someone yelled from the clustered tables where the rest of the group was falling back into a collective stupor.

The T-shirt turned around.

"Nobody wants any more beer. Save your money."

Bennett turned back to the bar, slapped his hand flat on the surface. "Let me have it," he told the bartender. He grabbed the pitcher by the handle, turned back to the group.

"You all pussed out on me, huh?"

An anonymous somebody answered with a raspberry. Bennett raised both hands, holding high the full pitcher in one and extending the middle finger of the other. Then, swinging his arms slightly from side to side so that there would be no mistaking that the gesture was meant for everyone equally, he brought the beer to his lips and began to drain the pitcher.

A couple of the lieutenants began to chant, then to pound the table. "Bennett ... Bennett ... *Bennett*." Other men, coherent but glassy-eyed, looked up, and they too began to hammer the tables, slapping the wood with flattened palms. "BEN-NETT, BEN-NETT, BEN-NETT!"

A few seconds later and the star was more than halfway through the pitcher, snorting mightily and spraying beer, which ran in generous rivers down his shirt front. Isen glanced back at the spectators, several of whom were struggling up through a watery haze to focus on the man by the bar.

By the time Bennett was three-quarters through, Isen—a late believer—had become convinced that he would finish. Isen also believed that Bennett would hurl the contents of his stomach in a majestic parabola back toward his table of supporters.

Then it was done. Finished, still standing, Bennett slammed the pitcher down on the bar, breaking it into shards.

"FUCKIN' AIRBORNE!" he shouted, holding up the severed handle like a scalp.

The group at the tables stumbled forward drunkenly, pounding the hero mightily on the back.

Isen, more convinced than ever that he needed to interview Bennett, left the room without looking back. He walked to the parking lot and started his car, considering what he'd say to Veir in the morning. He did not see Special Agent McCall, seated in her own car not thirty feet away and watching the door to the club, waiting for Isen and the others to emerge.

Early on weekday mornings, traffic in the division area— the southwest corner of Fort Bragg—slows to a specialized, military version of gridlock as thousands of men and women, all wearing identical, achingly plain gray physical training uniforms, take to the roads to run. Soldiers move in unit formations, little phalanxes of puffing men and women, some groups as small as ten people, some great snaking chains of gray rectangles that encompass hundreds. The distance between any two of these formations is supposed to be a constant. Says so right in the book. But following one of these units reminded Isen of driving on Washington's highways, where the traffic will suddenly slow, then crawl for miles. Then, when things start to thin out and move again, and one expects to see some accident along the road, some obvious cause for the bottleneck, there is nothing but highway.

Isen threaded his way along the path of least resistance, responding to the signals of the road guards that flanked each formation. These young soldiers, picked for speed, wore yellow reflective vests atop their PT gear. Their job was to keep an eye on encroaching traffic and signal drivers to stop. Isen watched one young man, who didn't look a day over seventeen, sprint to the head of a column of troops and take up position directly in front of Isen's car. The soldier signaled stiffly, arm straight, palm flat, a serious look in his eyes, as if Isen might try to gun the engine and spin into the crowd of bodies heaving by.

Isen made it to Veir's headquarters before the battalion returned from its run. The duty NCO, who'd spent the night in the headquarters, stood on the tiny front step smoking a cigarette as Isen came up the walk.

"Airborne, sir."

"All the way," Isen answered, returning the man's salute. "Good morning."

"I'm Staff Sergeant Gerome; I had the duty last night. The Sergeant Major told me to keep an eye out for you."

Isen wasn't sure if that was significant or not. He did wonder how much Veir's Sergeant Major—the senior enlisted soldier in the unit and a powerful influence—could tell him about the junior officers of this battalion.

"What's the Sergeant Major's name?"

"Hendrix. Sergeant Major Hendrix. Have you met him?"

"No. Maybe this morning. Point him out to me if he comes in. OK?"

"Oh, you'll know who he is," Gerome said. "Even in PT gear. He's the guy who *looks* like he's in charge."

The two men walked around the corner of the building, where some soldiers were conducting "police call," scouring the ground for any tiny bit of trash that might interfere with good order and discipline.

"The Army hardly lets us smoke anymore," Sergeant Gerome said. "Can't smoke anywhere indoors. But we're still policing up cigarette butts."

The headquarters building shared a block with three long, three-story barracks of cinder block construction. The buildings were featureless, sand-colored, with all the aesthetic appeal of a shoebox. Isen could see corners of bunk beds and lockers through the windows. Just ahead, at the end of the first building, exhaust fans pulled the smell of breakfast from the dining facility. When Isen was a new lieutenant, soldiers ate in mess halls, where Army cooks—GIs—served something called chow. Many of those facilities had been small, almost friendly, like clubs with limited membership, bad decor and cheap food.

Now the work was done by civilians on contract. And if soldiers came in late from a field problem, tired and hungry, there were no Army cooks to roust from the barracks. The civilians went home at quitting time, and sometimes hard-working soldiers went hungry. Isen figured that some bean counter, probably in the Pentagon, had figured out that the Army saved money this way. Isen had a tough time seeing it as progress.

"So how long have you been in this outfit, Sergeant Gerome?"

"About ten months, sir." Gerome was young. Isen figured, not for the first time, that when the NCOs started to look as young as the privates, it was time for him to retire.

Sergeant Gerome had taken a small cloth from his trousers pocket and was using it to wipe a nearly invisible layer of dust from his gleaming jump boots.

"And I hope I get to stay here the whole time I'm at Bragg. This is a great outfit."

"How so?" Isen turned to fully face Gerome.

"Starts with Colonel Veir and the Sergeant Major," Gerome said. "They tell these soldiers, 'We can do anything.' And the soldiers believe them. And so we can. Do anything, that is. I've seen guys hump here like I haven't seen anywhere else."

"What company are you in?"

"Charlie Company, sir."

Bennett's company, Isen thought.

"You know Lieutenant Hauck?"

"The one who killed himself? Seen him around the area, of course, but I can't really say I knew him," Gerome said. He had not moved, but Isen got the impression that the sergeant had backed off somewhat.

"Shame about that."

"Yeah," Isen said. He didn't know what the word around the battalion was about him. Chances were the NCOs knew about his visit, about his probing into the Hauck mess. Nothing happened without the NCOs knowing about it.

And a good investigator will take advantage of that, Isen thought.

"Is Lieutenant Bennett in your company?" Isen asked.

"Yes, sir."

Now, I'm getting name, rank and serial number, Isen thought.

Gerome, who'd started out talking freely, had retreated behind the formal relationship that their ranks imposed.

"I'll take you inside, sir," Gerome said.

Isen followed the sergeant into the headquarters area, which was deserted except for Gerome's runner, a private who was just finishing mopping the hallway near Veir's office.

"This is the colonel's office," Gerome said stiffly. "Sergeant Major told me I should have you wait in here. I got some stuff to do outside."

"Thank you," Isen said.

Gerome walked away. The private outside the door came back to mop—again—the section of the floor just outside the office door. Isen sat down on the couch.

No mistaking that this office belongs to the man in charge, Isen thought.

The desk was massive, dark wood and big as a boat, with a thick sheet of polished glass on the surface. There was a wooden In-box with a neat stack of file folders, all of them facing the same direction. The Out-box was empty. Isen checked the hall—empty—stood and walked to the wall opposite the windows. Like most career soldiers, Veir had an "I Love Me" wall where he displayed the photos, diplomas, citations, plaques and gag gifts he'd collected and dragged with him over nearly twenty years in uniform.

Isen had no such display in his cubicle in the Pentagon. Instead, he had a photocopied sheet that showed a cartoon hand holding a severed pair of bloody testicles. Underneath, the legend "To err is human, to forgive is not Army policy." Now, considering the impressive collection before him, Isen supposed some might think him cynical.

Centered on the wall before Isen was a large color photograph of Veir at the change-of-command ceremony that had marked the beginning of his tenure as battalion commander. Veir, his hands on the staff of the unit's colors, smiled tightly. Below that, an Iraqi bayonet hung from a small wooden plaque, with the time and date of capture. Nearby, another bayonet, this one with Cuban markings, similarly mounted, next to a photograph of then-Captain Veir in Grenada.

There were other photographs of Veir, all of them posed, many of them in the company of other officers and soldiers. One that caught Isen's eye showed Veir and two other men dressed in desert uniforms and standing before a huge portrait of Saddam Hussein, one of the many ten-foot wall-poster icons plastered all over Iraq. Some GI wag had drawn thick sideburns on Hussein's face and added misshapen glasses. The likeness was surprising. "Elvis Lives" was painted across the top of the poster.

A small bookcase displayed, in full view of any visitor, copies of Sun Tzu, Clausewitz, S. L. A. Marshall, philosophers of the military art. Isen did not approach the desk, but he could see, on the credenza that held the telephone and Veir's helmet, a framed portrait of a woman, a glamour shot. Her hair was backlit, her mouth pouting, beckoning. The woman—stunningly beautiful—looked about twenty-five.

Not young enough to be his daughter, Isen thought. *But not off by much.*

"See anything interesting, Major Isen?"

Isen spun around. Veir was in the office, walking quickly across the carpeted floor to his desk, smiling at Isen.

"Good morning, sir. Sergeant Gerome showed me in and asked me to wait here for you."

"Yes, I put the word out that you were coming," Veir said. "Why don't you have a seat here?"

Veir gestured to one of the two wingback chairs that stood before his desk. It was obvious that the furniture belonged to Veir: much nicer than Army issue, but not expensive enough to break the bank. Just enough to impress visitors.

"So what can I do for you this morning, Major Isen?" Veir said.

As he talked, he pulled a file folder from his In-box and made a few notations on some correspondence. Isen waited quietly until Veir looked up. The colonel closed the file and folded his hands on top of it. "I'm listening."

"I have a couple of sensitive questions to ask, sir. And I wanted to put them to you because I feel that the best way to preserve this confidence is to keep this in a small circle."

"Go on," Veir said. He opened a desk drawer and pulled out a grip strengthener, a little A-shaped spring with handles that some athletes use to develop a powerful grip. Veir began squeezing the thing, which made little stretching noises as he talked to Isen.

Squeak, *squeak,* squeak.

"Was Michael Hauck a homosexual?"

Harlan Veir, the very picture of control, was startled enough to blink twice. He moved the grip to the other hand. Squeak, *squeak,* squeak.

"Why do you ask?" Veir said.

Buying time to figure out his answer, Isen thought immediately.

"I have a theory, not much more than a hunch," Isen said. "But the pieces seem to fit."

Veir swiveled his chair to look out the window near his desk, still squeezing the grip tightener. Isen thought of Humphrey Bogart as Captain Queeg, rolling steel balls in his hand.

Army policy on homosexuals was muddled at best. Commanders received written guidance from the Pentagon as to what they could ask their soldiers about sexual orientation. But the Army didn't function inside a neat book of regulations, and Isen knew that there was another set of rules out here on the ground. The infantry still didn't like homosexuals, and most infantrymen would be rabid in defense of the status quo. The new rules, written to give commanders the latitude to avoid investigating, turned out to make investigations—and witch-hunts—easier.

Veir chose his words carefully.

"You think that maybe Hauck was gay, and that was why he killed himself?" Veir asked.

Isen almost said no before remembering that he was asking the questions.

"Someone from Hauck's background, sir ... it might be tough. Lots of pressure to perform, to conform. There was lots of pressure from somewhere."

"No, Major, I don't think Hauck was gay. But as I told you the other day, I'm not privy to all aspects of my soldiers' private lives."

"OK, sir," Isen said, unsure how far he wanted to push this thing.

"I understand you were in the club, Jiggles, the night that Michael shot himself."

"That's correct," Veir said. "As I told the CID agent ... what's her name?"

"McCall."

"McCall, yes. Homely little thing; she should try smiling. Anyway, as I told McCall, I left before Hauck went outside."

"Did he seem upset to you?"

"Not that I noticed."

"Did you speak to him?"

"I believe I spoke to all of my officers."

"Did you get a chance to talk to Michael alone?"

"Not that I remember," Veir said.

Isen wanted to say that Carroll remembered it differently, but he couldn't hang Carroll out there yet.

"Major Foote said that he figured one of the lieutenants called you from Jiggles that night to tell you there was trouble. Which one called you?"

"Lieutenant Bennett."

"I see. I wonder if I could speak with Bennett today."

"Certainly. As I said, we'll do whatever we can to make this job easier for you, as long as it doesn't interfere with the primary mission, of course."

"Of course."

"Did you get a chance to talk to Bennett the other day when you spoke to the other lieutenants?"

Veir knew, of course, that Isen didn't speak to Bennett, since the junior officers had given him written reports about what was said. Isen was intrigued by Veir's need to act dumb.

"No, sir. I believe we ran out of time."

"I see."

"I did see him last night, though."

"You spoke to Bennett last night?" Veir said, leaning forward slightly, interest rising.

"Didn't speak to him. Saw him. A bunch of your guys were in the O Club bar and I happened to be there as well. Bennett likes to have a good time."

"All work and no play ..." Veir said.

"I was wondering how these lieutenants fare in the morning after a night like that," Isen said. "They all seemed to have had a good bit to drink, and they had to be up for PT this morning."

Isen made the comment lightly. He knew most of the answer already; the lieutenants were in their early to mid-twenties and could pull stunts like that. He'd done it a few times himself. Still, the question was only half rhetorical.

But Veir stiffened, his eyes going smoothly cool.

He's either riding herd on his temper, Isen thought, *or coiling for a strike.*

"Major, these young men are preparing for war. They need to have a chance to let off steam every once in a while. There are people who deride the ways young men choose to have fun, but I'm not one of those people. I remember what it was like to be a young stud, full of piss and vinegar and eager to see what adventures the world had to offer me. Do you remember those days?" Veir asked. "Were you ever like that?"

Veir leaned back in his chair and steepled his fingers. "Don't get all preachy on me, OK, Major? These men could get called this morning to get on a plane that will take them in harm's way. By this time tomorrow they could be leading other men into combat, going on missions that could get them killed. Surely you haven't forgotten how heavy that burden rests, have you? You haven't forgotten where you come from?"

Sometimes I'm not so sure, Isen thought.

"I seem to remember having a good time," Isen said. "But I'm not sure I ever did PT with a hangover."

"Listen, I know what might be fun," Veir said, showing his cold smile again. "Why don't you join us for a PT run tomorrow morning? It'll do you some good to get out there with the troops again, stretch your legs, get some fresh air and get some of that stale Pentagon air out of your lungs."

Isen looked at Veir, trim in his sweat-soaked gray shirt, his legs hard from daily runs. Although Isen wasn't sure what he'd look like in a PT uniform, he knew it wouldn't be like that. But this was a world predicated on the physical, where thirty-five-year-old majors and forty-year-old colonels were supposed to keep pace with nineteen-year-old privates. Real soldiers do not plead football injuries, or war wounds, or old age. You just did it. There was no graceful exit; Veir had challenged him. More than that, Veir knew that Isen had no recourse.

"I'd like that very much, sir."

"Good, good," Veir said, showing Isen the door. "We'll see you in the morning, then, zero six, right outside."

When Isen left, Veir walked to the window of his office, from which he could see Isen moving toward his car.

A mild threat, Veir told himself. *You probably think you're shaking me up. Truth is, I like the challenge; and I've dodged bigger bullets than this.*

Veir sat at his desk and made two calls. The first was to his executive officer, Major Foote. Veir told him to send Bennett out to do a reconnaissance of a field training site at the far end of Fort Bragg's massive sprawl.

"And keep him out there until dark," Veir said. "No radio."

Got to get him off the radar screen until I figure out what to do with him, Veir thought.

The second call was to the commander of the military police at Fort Bragg, who owed Veir a favor. Veir passed along a description of Isen's personal vehicle, including the license plate number, which had been gathered from the parking lot by the dutiful and unquestioning Sergeant Gerome.

"OK, Major Isen," he said out loud after he'd hung up. "Just a little light sparring to start off with. Let's see what you're made of."

"I met an aviator today who might know a few things about Colonel Veir that his soldiers won't know," Sue Lynn said when Isen met her for lunch.

"Who's that?"

"Her name is Jenny Milan, Captain Jenny Milan. She's a pilot down in one of the lift companies. Seems she used to date Colonel Veir."

Isen thought about the woman's photograph on Veir's credenza.

"I told her I'd give her a call this afternoon and arrange to meet her tomorrow."

"You have any time to get your own work done?" Isen asked.

Sue Lynn looked at him sharply.

"I know you're smart enough to know that you need help," she said.

"You've got a point there. So you're setting up dates for me with other women?" Isen asked. "And I still get to share your bed? Hell, it doesn't get much better than this."

"I've got news for you, honey. You'll never have it better than this."

"You got that right." Isen laughed.

"Listen," Sue Lynn said, "Greg Savin called to talk to you. I told him to meet us here. OK?"

"OK with me," Isen said.

"Are you going to ask him about Hauck's gay friends?"

Isen's reply was hesitant. "I've been thinking about it."

"Why wouldn't you?"

"Well, I'm not sure I want to go starting a bunch of rumors about Hauck's sexual orientation."

Sue Lynn tilted her head to the side and looked at Isen as if he were missing something obvious.

"Look, Mark, adult human beings all have sexual orientations. Some are attracted to the opposite sex, some to the same sex."

"Yeah, that's all nice, Sue Lynn, but we don't live in an enlightened or very liberal segment of society here," Isen said, turning out his hands to indicate the uniformed crowd in the room.

Sue Lynn leaned across the table.

"And it's not going to get any better as long as people hang on to those attitudes."

"What does that mean?"

"You're projecting your prejudice onto other people. Has it occurred to you that maybe Savin wouldn't care one way or the other if Hauck was gay? Besides, who would have a better idea than his roommate?"

Isen was about to respond when Savin walked up to the table carrying a sandwich on a plate.

"Hello, sir," Savin said.

"Hello, Greg." Isen wiped his mouth with his napkin. "This is Major Darlington. Have a seat."

Savin set his plate down, then shook Sue Lynn's hand, ignoring Isen. "I'm very happy to meet you, Major," Savin said. He smiled nervously, as if he'd been knocked momentarily off balance.

"Have a seat, Greg," Isen said again.

"Thanks," he said, still watching Sue Lynn. Then, noticing Isen again. "There are some things I wanted to tell you about these parties that Colonel Veir's officers have."

"I saw some of them in the club last night."

"I was talking about the parties they have downtown," Savin said. "Like the one Michael was at that last night."

"Do they have parties downtown regularly?"

"Yes, sir. Pretty regularly."

Savin took a bite from his sandwich, then continued. "Twice a month, sometimes more. They don't need an occasion, really. For a while they kept the prop blasts here, but even those have moved to Fayetteville."

"Jiggles?" Darlington asked.

"Yes, ma'am. Jiggles was the only one they used, far as I know."

Isen was thinking about his own prop blast, an initiation that every soldier, no matter what rank, went through on joining an airborne unit. Aside from a good dose of unit history the soldier had to master, the ceremony mostly consisted of push-ups and pranks that only college fraternities could admire.

"Why'd they do that?" Darlington asked. "Move the prop blasts, I mean?"

"Well, the prop blasts are pretty wild, I guess," Savin said. "You know the drill, swim through garbage, run two miles while keeping a cigar lit, drink, push-ups, all the usual stuff. After a while, they kind of maxed out on what they could get away with here in the club. But Colonel Veir left the competition behind when he moved his parties to a private room downtown."

"He must have gotten heat for that," Darlington said to Isen.

Isen thought for a moment. "Maybe that's why he did it. The competition went from 'Who can do more outrageous things here in the club' to 'Who has the balls to do outrageous things out in town.' Someone gets hurt here, it wouldn't be pretty. Someone gets hurt out in Fayetteville, right under the noses of the taxpayers, then it's time for a career change," Isen said. "The competition becomes 'Who's willing to bet his silver oak leaf.' "

"I think that was it," Savin said. "None of the other commanders on post was willing to take that chance, so Veir won." He was nodding quickly, excited that Isen and Darlington were beginning to see that Veir was central to this drama.

"Or maybe the gods really do watch out for the Dark Prince," Sue Lynn said.

"What do you know about a lieutenant named Bennett, Brian Bennett?"

"The Anti-Christ."

"What?"

"That's what Mike called him. 'The Anti-Christ.' Mike didn't think too much of Bennett."

"Why was that?" Darlington asked.

"Overbearing, obnoxious, self-centered, rude ... let me see, what have I left out? Oh, yeah, he's a sycophant, too."

"Sounds like a charmer."

"And Bennett hated Mike."

"Any particular reason?" Isen wanted to know.

"Two, I guess," Savin said. "For one thing, Mike didn't

put up with his bullshit. When Bennett acted like an asshole, Mike would tell him, 'You're acting like an asshole.' But it was mostly the competition."

"Were they competing for the same job?"

"Not really." Savin was looking down at the table now, choosing his words carefully. He pushed his plate away, folded his hands in front of him, then unfolded them and began to pick at a loose piece of skin alongside a nail.

"Colonel Veir used to promote this competition between the junior officers. He liked to see them get all riled up." He looked up at Isen and Darlington. "At first Mike said that it was good, that it kept people from stagnating. It was supposed to be fair competition. You know, whose platoon ran fastest, shot better, all that stuff. Mostly for bragging rights."

Savin shook his head. "But Bennett thought it was about survival. He used to do things, underhanded things, to get an edge, even in silly competitions."

"Like what?"

"Well, like one time they were having a sports day, a bunch of games and stuff. And Mike swears he saw Bennett trip one of the other lieutenants in a race."

"What did Michael do?"

"He told Bennett that he was a worthless piece of garbage who had no business in uniform. Bennett said something ridiculous, like, 'This is about war. All of this is about war.' Bennett wanted to fight him—got in his face all puffed up. Mike walked away."

"Was Colonel Veir aware of what Bennett was doing?"

"That's when Mike started to get depressed," Savin said. "He told me that one of the captains said that Veir had an inner circle, officers who acted like he wanted them to act, carried on, all that stuff. Bennett was in the circle. And if you weren't in that circle, you weren't anywhere."

Isen leaned forward. "So Mike believed that Colonel Veir knew the kind of competition that was being fostered?"

"Absolutely. But then he stopped talking about it, at least to me."

"Why?"

"At first I think he confused Veir's approval with living up to his family's expectations. But he sort of drifted away from that after a while. Maybe he was a little ashamed. But then ... well, I think his CO, Captain Dennison, told him to keep his complaints to himself, and that he shouldn't talk about what went on in the battalion. Mike was under a lot of pressure to succeed, and he couldn't do that by making waves, by trying to fight Fort Bragg's big-shot commander."

"Captain Dennison told Michael to be quiet?"

"He did it as a favor," Savin said. "But I can't help this ... feeling that there's more going on here, stuff that we haven't figured out yet, stuff that might have had a bearing on Mike's death." He paused, looked into Isen's eyes. "I want to help you find out."

Isen sat back in his chair, trying to gauge Savin's sincerity. He hadn't started out being this cooperative, and Isen wondered what was behind the change. It was easy for Isen to see why Veir and Foote were resisting him; he wasn't so sure why Savin was suddenly willing to help.

"Greg," Isen said, deciding to take the plunge, "do you know of any friends Michael had who are homosexuals?"

"Is that what the other lieutenants told you?"

"No," Isen said.

Savin was calm for a moment, quiet. On the other side of the room, someone dropped a plate. Isen tensed at the noise of shattering.

"Mike wasn't gay, sir," Savin said.

Isen, embarrassed—maybe Sue Lynn was right about his prejudices—moved on.

"What goes on at these parties downtown?" Isen asked.

"I've heard stories," Savin said. "Some from Mike, some rumors that float around. But I think that this is one of those things you'd have to see for yourself."

Isen leaned back in his chair. "So when do we go?"

Savin smiled. "Tomorrow night."

"Kent here."

"Hey, sir. Harlan Veir."

Kent drew a long, uncomfortable breath. Veir was beginning to think he had a direct line to the Division Chief of Staff. "Yes?"

"I need a little help, sir, and I was wondering if you could spare me a few minutes."

"Go ahead."

"I just talked to the G3 about getting a school slot for one of my lieutenants. I think it would be a good idea if he spent some time away from Bragg."

Kent had been afraid of this—the slow, inexorable pull toward Harlan Veir. Kent wanted to resist. He was tired of giving in, and he understood that the more he did so, the more likely it would be that Veir would ask more of him, would continue to make his "requests." On its surface, Veir had simply asked for a little help; but Kent felt as if he were watching a small fire grow, with all the promise of destruction.

"What's his name?"

"Bennett."

"Where do you want to send him? What school?"

"Where isn't important; *when* is. I'd like him out of here on the next thing smoking."

A dozen questions leaped into Kent's mind, most of them about the propriety of what he was being asked to do. But there was always that leverage Veir had that made it essential that he push those questions aside.

"I'll see what I can do for you."

6

AT FIVE FORTY-FIVE THE NEXT MORNING, ISEN STOOD IN THE shadows near Battalion Headquarters as Veir's soldiers walked from the parking lot or found their way down from the barracks to the company street. Most of them, like Isen, were all but sleepwalking. The weather was fine, warm enough to be comfortable, yet with no trace of the oppressive heat and humidity that marked Indian summers in North Carolina.

Colonel Veir came up behind Isen, his voice already on full daytime volume.

"Good morning, Major Isen. Glad to see you didn't change your mind."

Isen turned and saluted. "Good morning sir. Wouldn't miss it."

He regarded Veir as the colonel looked out over his gathering troops. The man looked as if he'd been awake for hours: clean-shaven, bright-eyed, intent. His PT uniform looked brand-new, or maybe just pressed. Isen wiped sleep from the corner of his eye.

"I love this stuff," Veir said.

"PT, sir?"

"PT, the troops coming out for the day. Hell, I just like being up and about in the morning, up before anyone else." He turned to Isen. "I drive in here and it looks like the world is still asleep—except these guys, of course. It's like being alive when everyone else is dead."

Isen offered no comment. Just before six Veir took him along the company street and introduced him, it seemed to Isen, to nearly every officer and senior NCO in the battalion.

"This is Major Mark Isen," Veir repeated. The first few times Isen cringed, waiting for the deadly "Pentagon visitor" label, but Veir spared him that. "He's here to do PT with us."

Most of the men simply nodded at Isen, who was just another distraction. Some of the officers, who knew the purpose of Isen's visit, studied him as if expecting to find some clue as to what he'd uncovered about Hauck and their unit.

In the Charlie Company area, Isen asked the company commander if he could see Bennett.

"I think he's inside taking a shit," the captain said.

"I'd like to talk to him this morning," Isen said. He wanted to look at Veir but kept his eyes on the younger officer.

"I'll give him a heads-up, sir," the captain said unenthusiastically.

"Thanks."

Down in the Alpha Company area, Isen was introduced to Captain Leon Dennison, Hauck's company commander. Dennison, thin and round-shouldered, with professorial glasses and a filmy mustache, was the genetic opposite of the big, brash Colonel Veir.

"Captain Dennison has been on leave," Veir said by way of introduction. "His wife had a baby girl."

"Congratulations," Isen said.

Dennison nodded and seemed about to speak when Veir interrupted. "Did you get a chance to work on your book?"

Before Dennison had a chance to answer, Veir interrupted again. "Captain Dennison is writing a book."

Isen, who could muster no interest at this hour, couldn't think of anything more clever than, "Is that right?"

Dennison didn't try to speak again.

"A novel, right, Dennison?" Veir continued. It seemed

clear from Veir's tone that he didn't approve of Dennison's avocation.

"Yes, sir. A novel about the military."

There was an uncomfortable silence—just a few seconds, but long enough for Isen to notice.

"I'd like to talk to you later," Isen said to Dennison. "OK if I stop by?"

Dennison's eyes shifted to Veir for a moment. Out of the corner of his eye Isen saw Veir nod.

"Uh ... I guess so," Dennison said. "Sure."

"Carry on," Veir said, turning away.

When he and Isen were a few steps beyond hearing, Veir said, "I swear to God, every goddamned puke former English major in the Army is writing some sort of book."

Veir seemed angry. Isen wondered if Dennison was a threat to Veir's celebrity status.

"I noticed you had some books by soldiers on your shelf," Isen said.

"Clausewitz, Sun Tzu? Yeah, they were soldiers. But they were writing good stuff, not all this bullshit fiction. Dennison should concentrate on being a soldier. If he ever learns that, he can take the time to write about it."

"Did you forbid him to work on it, sir?"

Veir gave Isen a sideways look, dropped the staccato remarks. "Of course not, Major. That would be unethical. What Captain Dennison does on his spare time is his business."

He turned his eyes straight ahead as he walked. " 'Course, I did tell him what I thought about these fuckers who were making money on the side when they should be concentrating on being the best officers they can be."

"Absolutely, sir."

Isen didn't join in the calisthenics portion of physical training, but spent the time stretching on the side of the grass field while the soldiers worked their way through pushups, sit-ups, and partner-resisted exercises. There were one or two NCOs, school-trained fitness experts, who wandered among the company formations to give spot advice to commanders and first sergeants. The Army had come a long way from the days when Lieutenant Isen and his men had been subjected to the whims of a tyrannical platoon sergeant whose physical training expertise had been gleaned from Alabama high school football programs.

Isen, reaching over one white leg stretched before him in the grass, noticed that his stomach rolled over the top of his PT shorts when he bent over, so he straightened up and loosened his shirt to hide the roll. He had become used to gaining weight in seasonal cycles over the last few years: he was heavier in the winter, lighter in the summer as he did more running. The problem was that he was already winter-heavy, and it was only September.

At six-thirty Isen saw the battalion Sergeant Major signal the company first sergeants to move their men out to the road for the run. Isen got up, brushed himself off and took up a position just behind and beside a platoon in the trail company, Charlie Company.

"Mind if I run along here?" Isen asked one of the NCOs he'd met in the company street.

"Not at all, sir."

Isen looked around for Bennett, but didn't see him. Sergeant Gerome, the duty NCO from the previous day, nodded politely to him but did not smile.

The run started off at an easy pace, everyone warming up. They shuffled out onto Ardennes Road, named for the forest where American units, including the Eighty-second, broke the back of the last great German offensive of World War II in what became known as the Battle of the Bulge.

Some NCOs took up positions alongside the formations and began to sing "jody calls," the songs that hadn't changed since Isen was a boy, when he listened to the soldiers running by the quarters at Fort Benning, at Fort Hood, at half a dozen other posts.

> *Momma told Sally not to go downtown,*
> *Too many paratroopers hangin' around,*
> *Sally got the ass and she went on down,*
> *She came back with a belly round.*

Isen amused himself by clicking off the street names, which rang with the combat history of this famous division: Eindhoven, Bastogne, Carentan. They homed in on the big radio antenna that thrust above the pine trees, then turned right onto Longstreet Avenue.

Now there was a guy who got into trouble for telling the truth, Isen thought. *Or at least what he thought of as the truth.*

Longstreet—like Braxton Bragg, for whom the post was named, a Confederate general—was one of Lee's most trusted subordinates. Longstreet made the mistake, after the war and after Lee's death, of blaming Lee for the defeat suffered by the Army of Northern Virginia at a little Pennsylvania crossroads town called Gettysburg. Lee did bear responsibility, of course, because he was the commander and because he insisted, over Longstreet's objections, on the disastrous charge on the battle's third day. But Lee had become a saint-like figure in the South, and Longstreet was reviled by his former comrades and by the people he served, almost until his death.

The lesson Isen had always drawn from the story was simple: the truth isn't always welcome. It was right there in the history, the testimony right there in the street name.

After about a mile Isen lost his initial nervousness. He had always been a strong runner, and though he hadn't trained for a while, he imagined he could still hang through one little PT run. His feet hit the pavement with a comforting beat, his breathing came easily; it felt good to sweat. Colonel Veir had been right, he needed to push the stale Pentagon air out of his lungs. Meanwhile, the troops sang lustily, responding to the NCO leading the cadences in a throaty harmony, repeating the singer's words line by line.

> *Hey, First Sergeant, cain't you see?*
> *This little run ain't nothin' to me.*

Up ahead, the gray column flexed as the ranks crossed an intersection, climbed a small hill and adjusted to the pace, which seemed faster now. Isen looked at his watch. In his nervousness, he'd forgotten to ask Colonel Veir how far they'd run.

> *Saw an old lady walking down the street,*
> *She had a 'chute on her back, she had boots on her feet.*

Isen tried to remember what time the unit had finished yesterday, when he and Sergeant Gerome had been waiting together outside headquarters.

I said, "Hey, old lady, where you goin' to?"
She said, "U.S. Army Airborne School."

But that was on a Thursday, which might be an off day. Isen used to run his company harder on Monday, Wednesday and Friday than on the other days, just to keep things interesting.

Must have been seven when they finished, he told himself. But he wasn't convinced. Daydreaming, he'd fallen out of step. He shuffled to regain the rhythm. Left, right, left.

I said, "Hey, old lady, ain't you been told?
You'd better save that stuff for the young and the bold."

We're running about an eight-minute pace, Isen figured, *so we're talking three or four miles.*

She said, "Hey, young punk, who you talking to?
I'm an instructor at the Airborne School."

But if we run farther, Isen thought, *could be five miles.* He tried to remember the last time he'd run five miles.

He looked up ahead, but couldn't see Colonel Veir, who had positioned himself in front of the column of companies and was no doubt glaring at the units coming at them on the opposite side of the road.

Isen's foot began to hurt where he'd taken a piece of shrapnel some years back, a deep pain that felt as if someone were squeezing his heel in a vise. His shoulders and hands were tense, his breathing out of sync with his running. He took a few deep breaths to get it under control.

In for two steps, out for two steps.

The soldiers beside him shifted forward, and Isen lifted his head to see that the formation had again picked up speed. Veir's soldiers, disciplined and no doubt used to the changes in pace, did a good job of keeping the ranks closed tight. Isen fell behind.

Catch up, he told himself, stretching his stride. But the extra pounding on his heel began to hurt him more. He blinked the sweat from his eyes, wiped his brow with the sleeve of his shirt.

Up ahead, the soldiers began singing a familiar taunt. Shouting, pausing, shouting.

> *On the left,*
> *sick-call,*
> *cain't run,*
> *cain't be,*
> *like me,*
> *Airborne,*
> *Infantry*

The NCOs weren't leading this one; the men in the ranks had picked it up as the formation passed two or three soldiers from some other unit who had fallen out of their own formation and were now being passed by five hundred men happy to abuse them.

Isen remembered his first command, when his men had done the same thing. The first few times he'd let it ride; then one day his first sergeant told the young company commander it was unprofessional.

"They want to scream and yell," the older NCO had told him, "let them yell encouragement. Any fool can yell insults."

Now, huffing and puffing and feeling all the extra weight he carried with him, Isen felt, as if for the first time, how cruel such taunts could be.

Someone blazed past him, an orange rectangle. Road guards on either side raced ahead to take over the next intersection as they leapfrogged from back to front. Isen looked at the youngster, who wasn't even breathing hard.

I used to be able to do that, he thought.

Isen watched as the private tapped the other guard on the shoulder. The man so relieved raced ahead to find the next danger area, while his replacement jogged in place and watched the formation go by, his back to the oncoming traffic.

Isen didn't see the car come up, too fast, on one of the

side streets that fed traffic from a housing area to the main road. But he heard the engine at the same time the road guard did. The youngster spun around, his orange vest flapping, arm shooting up.

"Stop!" he yelled.

It was big, a black muscle car, traveling too fast, coming on broadside to the column of troops. The driver moved, sitting upright, and Isen thought, *He was bent over the radio, and he didn't see us.*

At the squeal of the tires, the formation did a little hop, as if startled. The road guard leaped out of the way as the car fishtailed to a stop where the youngster had been standing. The ranks closest to the car faltered, stepped aside, but, remarkably, kept their formation.

"Jesus Christ!"

An NCO behind Isen bolted past to help the road guard up from the ground. The running formation began to come apart as some soldiers stopped and the ones behind kept going. Out in front, some men ran on unknowing while others turned to gawk.

The guard was unhurt, though shaken up. Isen could see the driver—another young kid in PT gear—as he sat wide-eyed in the car, hands clenched on the steering wheel, too scared to move, waiting for the hammer to fall.

He didn't have to wait long.

Veir sprinted from the van of the formation. With a wave of his arm he signaled that the column was to keep moving, and instantly the NCOs were shuffling the men back into order, getting the unit going again.

Veir, his face an angry mask, first approached the road guard, who snapped to attention and braced himself as if he were going to get chewed out.

"You OK, son?" Veir said.

"Yes, sir. I don't know what happened. I—"

Veir cut him off, patted him on the arm, turned to the car.

In full view of the hundred plus men in the trail company, Colonel Veir yanked open the car door, stuck one big arm inside and jerked the driver out of his seat, shaking him like a child. Veir spun the frightened man around and pushed him back up against the hood, crowding him, his face inches from the soldier's.

"You almost ran this fucking car into my soldiers, you piece of shit!" he screamed. *"Do you know what would have happened? Do you?"*

Veir was unhinged, and his screams immediately silenced the yammering in ranks. Isen saw the big black shape of Major Foote move up beside his commander, ready to stop Veir somewhere short of violence.

"I oughta kill you right here, *you miserable fucking worm!"*

Isen was only a few feet away, close enough to see the spittle fly from Veir's mouth, close enough to see the young driver's arm turning red where Veir clenched it, twisted it.

Veir drew his fist back; the soldier recoiled, arching for safety over the hood of his car. Isen made ready to step forward, not sure how he would avoid being hit himself.

Foote spoke first. "Sir, let me take care of this."

The big major stepped up to Veir and took the driver by the arm. Veir, panting, loosed his grip and watched Foote lead the soldier around to the other side of the automobile. He stood like that for what seemed a long time, the only sounds the scuffle of running shoes and the deliberate silence of his embarrassed soldiers. One of the NCOs began quietly to count cadence. "One, two, three, four."

Veir looked around as if waking up.

"All right," he said. "OK. Let's get back on the road," he directed the few who'd gathered around him. "The show's over here."

Veir ran silently alongside Isen for a quarter mile or so as they closed with the rest of the battalion, which had slowed but kept on running.

Isen chanced a couple of looks at Veir. The bigger man's jaw was tightly clenched, his fists closed. He pounded his feet into the pavement as if trying to punish the street. Isen guessed that *Newsweek* hadn't seen this side of Veir.

"Who's setting this fucking pace?" Veir said to no one in particular. "Somebody's grandmother?"

Veir shifted gears, lengthened his stride, and was soon on his way back to the front of the running formation. In less than a minute, the pace increased dramatically. When the unit turned a corner, Isen could see Veir in the lead, running hard, his face still washed in rage.

Isen figured they were running better than seven minutes per mile now, maybe faster. He wasn't sure how long he could keep it up.

The first soldiers began to falter after about a mile of the blistering pace. At first there was nothing more than a disturbance in ranks as men tried not to trip up their buddies when they couldn't stay in step. Then a man dropped out of the platoon beside Isen. He fell dramatically to the pavement, and there was a rush of volunteers willing to stop running and stay with him.

"Get back in there," the platoon sergeant snapped. "The medics will police him up."

There was no singing now, no sound except for the encouragement offered by the hardy few to the majority, who were sucking wind.

Isen began to fall back.

The lead elements reached the bottom of a long, gentle slope. Veir picked up speed again. Isen leaned into the hill, heard Veir shouting from somewhere up ahead, "Come on, heroes."

If this had happened before the incident at the intersection, Isen would have figured that Veir was showing off, maybe even for Isen's benefit. But now it was too much like misplaced anger. Veir didn't get to beat the daylights out of the driver, so he was beating the daylights out of his unit.

Two more soldiers appeared on the side of the road, casualties from one of the lead companies. Isen was afraid to look at them.

Now Veir was turning the formation around, heading back on the opposite side of the road. Isen, who'd switched to the left side of the formation, would be in between the two halves of the column as they passed each other.

Suddenly Veir was closing in on him from the front.

"Major Isen! How they hanging?" he yelled.

Isen looked up, tried a smile, but nothing came.

"Come on over here with me," Veir said.

Isen crossed to the other lane and turned around so that he was beside Veir. He concentrated on his breathing, trying to time inhalation and exhalation with his footstrikes. The pain in his heel was a tragedy, snot and sweat ran down his face, and his sides were split as if he'd been stabbed.

"Hope you saved some for a kick at the end," Veir said over his shoulder.

One of the battalion staff officers, running beside Isen, belched and said, "I wouldn't have had all that coffee if I knew the old man was going to cut loose."

With that, he turned his head and vomited a thin stream over his shoulder. He never missed a step.

Incredibly, Isen hung on, just barely keeping pace, all thought of pride and looking good abandoned. They passed some of the soldiers who'd dropped out. The men behind Isen didn't taunt them, but ran silently now, using all their energy to keep up with the madman in the lead.

Isen faltered. His foot hurt more than at any time since it had been sliced by hot steel, and he couldn't get enough fiery air into his lungs.

I'm not going to make it.

Veir looked back over his shoulder at Isen, smiling grimly.

The curved road finally gave up sight of Veir's headquarters. It was no more than a half mile away.

I've got to do this, or I won't be able to stand up to him again, Isen told himself.

But that was his mind. Every muscle, every blood vessel, every cell of his tortured body screamed for him to stop, to roll over onto the grass, to die—anything but continue the run.

Isen focused on the end point, imagined the distance closing up. He watched his feet as they skimmed the road, eating up the yardage.

A quarter mile now.

Isen felt his stomach lurch, along with surfacing traces of last night's dinner. He realized he was praying. *Please, God, let me get through this.*

Isen could see the lettering on the sign outside Veir's headquarters, could see the blue guidons stirring out in front of the barracks. Just two blocks more and he'd stop to watch the soldiers pull up in the company street.

Less than a block now. Veir would slow down at any second.

Then they were there, pulling up even with the little headquarters building and its brown sign. Isen began to ease up.

Then Veir went past the sign.

He hadn't slowed down at all. They were going to continue.

Twenty-five yards past the sign, Isen knew he'd psyched himself out by assuming they'd stop at the headquarters. He managed to stumble out of the way of the onrushing horde of gray before he started walking, hands on hips, gulping big chunks of air and trying to keep from vomiting on the grass.

The companies slid by, and all the officers and NCOs he'd met that morning managed to get a look at him. Isen suddenly realized why Veir had taken the time to introduce him to everyone.

Veir stopped running about a hundred and fifty yards beyond the headquarters building.

Isen couldn't believe it. He'd fallen for a trick he'd seen used a hundred times. He stopped, put his hands on his knees, bent over and closed his eyes. He coughed some spittle and a string of phlegm onto his running shoes, then stood and began walking to his car.

As Veir and his men doubled back, they began singing again.

On the drive to headquarters and Sue Lynn's office, Isen was thinking about Harlan Veir when he should have been watching the speedometer. The red lights of a traffic patrol car came up behind him on Gruber Road.

"License and registration, please," the MP said.

Isen handed over the paperwork. He was still angry at what had happened with Veir that morning, and so was sure that if he opened his mouth he'd make things worse.

The MP walked to his patrol car. Isen watched in his rearview mirror as the soldier made a radio call, then walked back and held out Isen's cards and a citation.

"You need to take it easy here, Major Isen," the soldier said.

Isen grunted in agreement—*What a morning*—and put the ticket on the seat beside him. When he turned back to the front, he was surprised to see the MP leaning on the car, his hands resting just inside the open window.

He gave Isen a lopsided grin, which, Isen thought, was probably meant to be intimidating. Traces of some sort of food—eggs, maybe—clung to his mustache.

"Fort Bragg is big place," the soldier said. "But it's pretty tightly run. We know everything that goes on around here."

Isen thought about biting his lip—really biting it, to keep from saying something he'd regret. But he didn't move quickly enough.

"Get your hands off my fucking car."

The MP stood and Isen pulled away. When he checked the mirror, he could see the soldier beside the patrol car, radio mouthpiece in his hand again.

When Mark Isen walked into Sue Lynn's crowded office in the Aviation Section of Division Headquarters just after nine o'clock, he found Sue Lynn sitting on the front of her desk. A woman sat in the chair just in front of Darlington, and when Sue Lynn looked up at Mark and smiled, the woman turned around.

"Mark, I'd like you to meet Captain Jenny Milan."

Jenny Milan, Isen realized when the captain turned to him, was the woman in the glamour photo that sat behind Veir's desk; and her picture, arresting though it was, did not do justice to the woman before him.

"Major Isen," Milan said, standing and extending her hand.

"Hello," Isen managed, trying not to stare.

"Jenny and I were just talking about one of our favorite lieutenant colonels," Darlington said, rescuing Isen.

"I understand you've been spending some time with Harlan Veir," Milan said. She stood until Isen dropped into the other chair in front of Sue Lynn's desk, sitting after he did. In the photograph, her hair had been down; in uniform, as she was now, it was pinned to the back of her head. Dark, dark brown, almost black, and lustrous as polished wood. Her eyes, just as dark, were inviting pools. She had the kind of full lips, with a pronounced Cupid's bow, that made Isen think of a certain intimate act.

"Yes. I got to spend some time with Colonel Veir this morning, as a matter of fact." Isen stretched his legs in the limited space between the chair and the desk. Already, the muscles in his thighs were beginning to pull into sharp knots.

"Jenny used to date Veir," Sue Lynn said.

"Yes, I know." Isen looked up from kneading his thigh. "I mean, he has your picture behind his desk, on the credenza."

"He *still* has that there?" She spoke with a slight accent. Isen couldn't pin it down, but he knew it was no small part of her allure.

"Let me guess: he has it facing whoever might be standing in front of his desk, right?"

"Right."

Milan smiled condescendingly, shook her head. "He's so predictable," she said. "When I met him, he had some other woman's picture there, facing the same way."

Sue Lynn nodded as if agreeing. Isen felt a little lost, and Sue Lynn noticed. Rather than address his ignorance directly, she said to Milan, "Is that his trophy case?"

"Exactly. At least, that's how he thinks of it. I asked him, when I saw where he had the frame, why he didn't put it on his desk so he could look at it, the way most people do with desk pictures. Do you know what he said?"

Isen was following again, but the women already seemed to know what was coming—where he didn't—so he kept his mouth 'shut.

"He said, 'What sense does it make to have a beautiful girlfriend and not show her off?' " Milan smiled again. *"That* made him a lot of points."

"Did he treat you well?" Sue Lynn asked.

Isen knew that Darlington didn't like Veir, and he imagined she was having a tough time in this conversation, pretending she was talking about a man who didn't prickle her skin.

"For the most part, yes. Yes, he did. He can be very romantic, but he didn't want other men to see that side of him. At first that didn't bother me, then I got sick of it. He'd treat me one way in private, then another when his buddies were around."

Milan wasn't complaining, she was merely reporting what she'd found to be true.

"Of course, the sex was great."

Milan offered this in the same fashion she might comment on Veir's driving ability, or his golf handicap.

Darlington looked at Isen, who began to study a few scratches on the toes of his boots.

"I'm sorry," Milan said, teasing a bit. "I didn't mean to embarrass you, sir."

"We're trying to bring Mark out of his shell," Sue Lynn said, nudging him with her foot.

Isen looked up at Milan and tried to think of a few good questions he could ask about other aspects of her relationship with Veir. But all he could do was picture her with eyes half-closed, hair splayed on a pillow. . . .

"But eventually, sex with him was about control," Milan said. "Everything with him was about control."

Milan sat back in her chair, brought both hands up to help her illustrate her points. The accent was recognizable now. *She's Italian,* Isen thought.

"He liked to control . . ." She glanced at Isen. "He liked to control who did what to whom and when and where," she said. "He was that way in bed, he was that way in social settings, and I'm pretty sure he's that way at work, too."

Isen thought about how Veir had run him out of the PT formation, how he'd taken the time to make sure all of his officers and NCOs would recognize Isen on the side of the road. All a set-up.

"Did you ever attend any of his parties downtown?" Isen asked.

"No, those were strictly stag. Not that I would have wanted to anyway. Harlan and his men, especially the young guys, could act like complete jerks sometimes. I'm sure they were really heroic when they were downtown by themselves."

"So you went to parties at his house?"

"Two," she said. "No, one and a half would be more correct. I left the second one early. That was the last time we were together."

Isen moved to the edge of his chair. "Did something happen there?"

"Yeah. His lieutenants were having a little trouble remembering their manners. They couldn't figure out how to keep straight when they were with women who were getting paid to hang all over them, like downtown, and when they were around women who didn't want to be treated like that."

"So you left?" Sue Lynn asked.

"No, there was more to it than that," Milan said. She paused, and Isen got the impression that not many people had heard this story.

"There was this one lieutenant, in particular, who kept coming on to me. Kept following me around, putting his hands on my arms, my shoulders, that kind of stuff. Told me how he and I should go work out together. 'You've got a great body,' he said. 'I could help you get into even better shape.' He went to put his hands on me again, and I wound up shoving him out of my face."

"Because he said he wanted to work out with you?" Isen said.

As soon as the comment was out of his mouth, he knew he'd made a mistake. Sue Lynn shot him a look that could have blistered paint.

"That funny taste in your mouth," Darlington said.

"Yeah?"

"That would be your foot."

"Sorry," Isen said.

"No, Major Isen," Milan said coolly. "I didn't shove him until he leaned into me, pressing his chest against my breasts, and asked me if I wore the kind of workout gear ... let me see if I can remember exactly how he said this ... 'the kind of gear that rides up the crack of your cute little ass.'"

She nodded, as if watching a replay on some screen. "Yes, I'm pretty sure that's when I pushed him off of me."

"Did you tell Veir about it?" Darlington asked. Isen had decided to let Sue Lynn ask the questions.

"Yes," Milan said, leaning forward, her body tensed. "That's when I lost it. I went to him and told him and all he did was laugh."

"He laughed?"

"Yeah. He laughed and said that he'd put this guy up to it. 'I said I'd give him fifty bucks if he could get in your pants.' He told me that to my face."

Darlington was quiet, though Isen was pretty sure she wasn't waiting for him to ask the next question. After a moment, Milan sat back in her chair, regaining her composure almost immediately.

"He liked playing by rules he made up. Rules that only

applied when he wanted them to apply. This stupid Bennett kid couldn't even see that Veir was just using him, testing to see how much control he really had.

"Anyway, I walked out. Never looked back, never returned his calls."

Milan didn't look as if she'd been traumatized. She looked pissed off. Isen wouldn't have been surprised if Milan had told them she'd cold-cocked Veir.

"Wow," Sue Lynn said.

"Yeah, he's a real catch."

"Did Veir ever say anything around you about fostering competition among his lieutenants?" Isen asked.

"Sure. He used to talk about how he'd pit this one against that one. He'd have them competing for the good jobs. I told him he was destroying unit cohesion."

"What did he say to that?" Sue Lynn asked.

"He'd just smile. He was the division's fair-haired boy. To him, success justified whatever he wanted to do. He was a master at rationalization. And he thinks he's untouchable."

"What do you mean?"

"Well, I used to think that the *Newsweek* article convinced him that the Army would protect him. The poster boy, right? But after being around him for a while . . . I think it started before that."

Milan crossed her legs, locked her hands across her knees.

"He likes pushing the limit, trying to get away with stuff other people wouldn't even attempt. He used to tell me that he saw the same opportunities to get ahead that everyone else saw; it's just that he had the guts to go for it. So he does outrageous stuff and thinks he's just as moral as the next guy."

"Did you ever meet Michael Hauck at one of these functions?" Isen asked.

"Yes. I met him at the first party. He was shy, kind of awkward in a cute way."

"How do you mean, awkward?"

"Around women, I think. He seemed uncomfortable with the carousing, like he was embarrassed, you know? Like he couldn't believe he was in such juvenile company."

The three of them sat quietly for a moment, then Milan looked at her watch.

"We should let you go," Isen said. "If you think of anything else, would you give me a call?"

"Certainly, sir." Milan stood, tugged her beret from her pocket. She turned it over in her hand as if studying it. "Listen, I'll help in any way I can, but you have to keep a couple of things in mind."

"What's that?"

"First is that I don't much like Harlan Veir, and that's bound to color whatever I have to say about him."

"I appreciate your honesty," Isen said.

"And second is that I really didn't know him all that well. The first time I got a glimpse of something besides the superficial was at that party, I think. I didn't like what I saw, so I got out."

"So who knows him well?"

Milan shrugged. "He probably doesn't even know himself well."

Milan shook hands and moved toward the door.

"Oh, by the way," Isen said. "Who was the lieutenant who was coming on to you at the party?"

"Bennett," Milan said. "Brian Bennett."

Isen opened his mouth to speak, but just at that moment Harlan Veir appeared in the hallway just outside Darlington's door.

"Well, well," he said jovially. "The gang's all here."

Milan's face registered surprise for just an instant. "Good morning, sir," she said to Veir. Turning back to Darlington, Milan said, "Thank you for your time, ma'am. I'll get that request in before the end of the day."

Milan turned and walked past Veir without looking at him again. After she passed, Veir put both hands on the door jamb.

"How are you feeling, Major Isen?" he asked, smiling.

"I'll make it, sir."

Veir stepped inside Darlington's office.

"I don't believe we've met," Veir said to Darlington. He showed all of his teeth when he grinned; they were as straight and white as tombstones.

"Actually, we have, sir. Several times. I coordinated air support for your unit on at least three occasions."

"My apologies, then."

"Is there something I can help you with, Colonel?" Sue Lynn asked in a tone that was anything but helpful.

Veir, still smiling, clasped his hands behind his back and made a show of looking at the organizational charts posted on Darlington's wall, drawing out the silence for a few seconds. When he turned to face them, his shallow smile was gone.

"Actually, Major, you two can help yourselves. It isn't a good idea for officers to go around talking out of class, as it were. And you should be aware that the mere fact that you ask certain questions implies things to some people. So you should be circumspect about your little investigation. Do you understand what I'm saying, Major Isen?"

"Yes, sir," Isen said slowly. "I believe I do."

"Good," Veir said. "I'm so glad I happened by." He drew himself up, tilting his head back slightly and surveying the tiny office.

"Well, I'm sure that there's a lot of important work that gets done in here," he said. "So I'll leave you alone. Good day."

When Veir had gone, Darlington walked calmly around her desk and shut the door.

"Just in case Milan didn't convince you he's a prick," Darlington said, "that little display should have removed all doubt."

"I'm starting to hate that man."

Darlington seemed amused.

"What about all this stuff about objectivity, about fairness? Where did all that go this morning?"

Sue Lynn was smiling, but Isen remained stone-faced. He knew exactly where all of his objectivity had gone: he'd vomited it up—along with last night's dinner—in the parking lot after the PT debacle.

"A little while ago I watched him almost rip some soldier's head off. He completely lost it."

"What happened?"

Isen told Sue Lynn about the driver who almost ran into Veir's formation.

"The famed Veir temper," Sue Lynn said. She smiled as if pleased that Veir was turning out to be just what she'd said he was all along.

Isen, who wanted to remain objective, was afraid of getting pulled into this trap. He stood up quickly, pacing in the tiny space between her desk and the chairs, trying to forget how Veir had set him up by introducing him to all those other officers and NCOs.

"OK, so he's a prick," Isen said. "We've established that much. Let's not focus on how many different ways he tries to prove that to us."

He paused, nodding. Sue Lynn just watched him.

"All of this," Isen said, "can still be explained in terms of his covering his ass. He can't like having me come down here and stir things up with his old girlfriend, with his junior officers. Maybe he's worried that word will get out about the parties off post, or about his other behavior."

"I think his problems go deeper than that, than fear of reprimand," Sue Lynn said. "It's like he's trying, with all of this bad boy stuff, to prove something to himself. That he's—what?—successful, one-of-a-kind, a leader, lover, all of that? Handsome, desirable, fit, tough. And with the traffic incident—protective of his men.

"He's trying to fill this big hole. Call it insecurity, lack of self-esteem, whatever."

Sue Lynn held her counsel for a moment.

"The trick is, with guys like that the hole never gets filled."

"So that leaves him ... where?" Isen asked. "He's not going to quit the game. That's not his pattern, his style. So he either continues the same way or he tries new tricks, going from woman to woman to woman. Or he ups the ante. Maybe Hauck knew something more. That's certainly what Savin implied."

"If Veir is doing things that could get him into trouble, someone else must know about it. He keeps Foote and the lieutenants around like retainers, for God's sake," Darlington said. "Maybe this guy Bennett is more involved than anyone has suspected."

"Bennett didn't pull the trigger," Isen said.

"But Bennett may have been the last one out there with him, the last one to see him alive. Right?"

"Yes," Isen said. "But just remember what Milan said. When you don't like someone, that colors everything you have to say about that person."

"So?"

"Well, you don't like Veir, so you're ready to involve him in every kind of conspiracy."

"I'm telling you, Mark, that guy is dirty."

"Maybe he is," Isen said. "What about Milan?"

"What about her?"

"That little business in the doorway there. 'I'll get that request in before the end of the day.' What was that?"

"She obviously didn't like the idea that Veir knew she was here, and she tried to cover it up. It is plausible that she would be in here. She's an aviator. This is the Aviation Section."

"But if she already told him to kiss off, what difference would it make that she was talking to us?"

"Well, maybe she doesn't want to get on his bad side."

"She didn't seem like the wilting flower type. Maybe he has something on her."

"Maybe she's afraid of him," Darlington said. "Maybe Michael Hauck was afraid of him, too."

Isen considered this a moment, filed it away as a possibility. "She's quite an attractive woman," he said.

"They call her Jenny the Fever."

"Why?"

"She makes men shiver and shake."

Isen laughed. "That's good. What about that accent?"

"She's Italian," Darlington said. "Her parents came over when she was twelve. Her given name is Giovanna Milano." Sue Lynn rolled the name off her tongue.

"Ooo, I like the way you say that," Isen said. "Do you know any Italian you could whisper in my ear?"

Sue Lynn snorted. "After that comment you made?"

She exaggerated her accent, skewering Isen's ignorance. " 'And you shoved him away just because he made a little old comment about your workout gear and how it pinched the cute little cheeks of your ass?' If I whisper any Italian to you, buddy boy, it'll be 'Sleep on the couch, you sexist pig.' "

"OK, perhaps my comment was ill conceived."

The phone rang. "Saved by the bell," Isen said.

"Major Darlington," Sue Lynn said.

Isen checked to see that the door was still closed. It was. He moved next to Sue Lynn, licked the tip of his finger and traced the crease inside one of her elbows. She made a face, slapped him away.

"Yes, as a matter of fact, he's right here." She pushed the receiver at him.

"Major Isen."

"Sir, this is Special Agent McCall."

"Good morning," Isen said, feigning enthusiasm. Something about McCall's abruptness made him want to mock her.

"Yes. Listen, sir, when you were over there at Veir's headquarters to interview those lieutenants, did you tell them you were an investigator, a CID type?"

"No. As a matter of fact, I had my uniform on, crossed rifles, all that jazz. They would have known I wasn't a cop."

"So you didn't tell them you were an investigator from the Pentagon? You didn't imply that you had some sort of official mandate?"

Isen didn't like the feeling he was getting, like unexpected footsteps inside friendly lines. He searched his memory for something he might have done to give the wrong impression.

"No, I didn't mention why I was here, except to say that I was looking into Hauck's suicide. Why?"

"Some people have been asking questions about your ... techniques," McCall said.

"I don't have any techniques," Isen said, trying to lighten things up.

"That's what I told them," McCall said, businesslike. "You have to understand, first of all, that it would be a serious breach of regulations if you tried to gain information of any sort by impersonating a CID or Military Police investigator. Or even if you passed yourself off as an investigating officer when you're just doing a favor for a general officer."

"I understand that."

"Well, maybe you said something to give someone that impression. Or maybe that's just what people assume when someone shows up with a bunch of questions," she said.

After a pause of a few seconds, she added. "Or maybe someone wants to make a case that you're impersonating an investigator."

Isen saw what was happening. "To frame me, you mean."

"To get you off this case. To get you in a lot of trouble," McCall said.

"So what do I do?"

"Be absolutely circumspect about how you present yourself. Tell people what's going on. I'll keep my ear to the ground over here, and I'll try to warn you if anything is about to break. But you've got to be straight with me, Major."

"Right."

" 'Cause if you're not straight with me, I'll haul you in myself."

"Right," Isen said again. Then, quickly, "So you *are* still investigating."

"I'll talk to you later." McCall hung up.

"What was that all about?" Darlington wanted to know.

"Someone is going around asking if I've been posing as an investigator, which is a big no-no."

"Have you been?"

"No. But I haven't always announced that I have no official reason for being here, either."

"Sounds like you better start announcing it."

Isen was lost in thought.

"What is it?"

"Two things," he said. "Someone obviously wants me off this post bad enough to set me up like that," he said.

"That's easy. Everyone you've met so far has it in for you."

"Not exactly," he said. "Not anymore. Which is my second point. Why is McCall suddenly trying to help me?"

7

IN FACT, TERRY McCALL'S FIRST REACTION WHEN SHE HEARD that there were inquiries being made about Isen's tactics had been, "I hope the bastard gets arrested."

She expressed this sentiment within earshot of Special Agent Harrigan, her assigned mentor and the agent responsible for her training while she was on probationary status.

Harrigan was quite busy with his own investigations, but one of his jobs was to provide advice to McCall. He asked, "What do you have against this guy, other than the fact that he showed up at the club when you wanted to watch those lieutenants?"

McCall sized up the older man. He was an outstanding field agent whose appearance—a forty-year-old man who had never grown out of his adolescent awkwardness—and slow-talking manner put listeners at ease and gave people with something to hide a false sense of security.

"I guess he just pissed me off, coming in here and throwing his rank around like he was some big shot. He's an errand boy for some general."

In point of fact, Isen had been unfailingly polite at their first meeting, and he had tried to be just as polite whenever they spoke after that. McCall knew that any antagonism started with her; she had been more than obnoxious enough for both of them.

"Is that right?" Harrigan asked.

McCall turned her chair around so that she could see her office partner. Harrigan, his oversized feet propped up on his desk, was cleaning his nails with a straightened paper clip. For a man of so few words, he managed to be pretty incisive.

"Well ..." McCall said. "I guess maybe I was a little ticked off that so many doors opened for him."

"And those same doors are closed to you," Harrigan said.

"Yes," she said, feeling the familiar anger.

Special Agent McCall, who hailed from a family of eleven children in rural Alabama, had climbed a great mountain to get to this small desk in the Criminal Investigation Division of the United States Army. Immensely proud of her badge and her status, she was not prepared for the reaction she still saw in so many places when she talked to witnesses.

She began to speak quickly.

"When I went down to ask ..." Guard down and temper up, the word came out "ax." She paused, took a breath and corrected herself.

"When I went down to *ask* some questions of those lieutenants in Veir's command, I saw it in the eyes of some of them. I wasn't Special Agent McCall to them. I was a token, a make-pretend investigator at best, a nigger-chick with a badge at worst.

"Then Major Isen comes along, with his whitebread background and his old-boy network connections, and people talk to him as if he was ..." Pause, breath. "As if he *were* the primary investigator," she said. "I swear it makes me want to shoot someone."

Harrigan didn't look up from his fingernails when he said, "I wish you had an easier time than you do. But the fact is you don't."

He was speaking in that maddeningly slow voice that, McCall figured, probably made suspects eager to give up incriminating evidence just so they wouldn't have to listen to him any longer.

"But I suggest you do something with all this misplaced

anger. Isen didn't do anything to hurt you or your investigation," Harrigan said. "In fact, you're the one who lost it in the club when he showed up with that other major. Why not use him to help you? Let him stir the water up in his own way; something might come to the surface."

It was Harrigan's suggestion—that Isen could help her—that had led to the phone call warning Isen about people questioning his technique. Isen could take the heat for a while while she continued to investigate what was going on in Veir's battalion. McCall saw all the possibilities that Isen did—that Foote was in this up to his neck, that Bennett had more to do with Hauck's death than she understood so far, that Veir had panicked because he had something to hide. But, with her boss calling daily for the final report, McCall didn't have time to run down all of those possibilities.

It was all too soon, too quick. CID wanted it closed; McCall thought there was more. But she believed in the system and wanted to believe that her superiors occupied their positions because they knew what was going on. She was young and ambitious, but she was also inexperienced. She found it easier to think herself wrong than to think her superiors wrong, because she wanted to be right when she held those positions.

"Anything else?" Harrigan asked.

"About what?"

"Anything else bothering you about this?"

"No," she said, believing for a moment that it was true. Then, taking her cue from the question—Harrigan wasn't one for idle chatter about feelings—she found something.

"Yeah," she said at last. "I'm beginning to wonder why I drew this case."

"Your being on call isn't enough?"

"I was given the case because I was on call. I was left on the case because I'm inexperienced."

"What does that have to do with it?" Harrigan asked.

He still had the tone of the rhetorical question, and McCall wondered how much he suspected.

"They're all over me to finish this thing up." She stood up and, placing her hands on his desk, leaned toward him. "And I think there's more stuff out there."

"Maybe Major Isen will help you find it," Harrigan said, seemingly satisfied.

"Well, he'd better move fast."

The distance between Division Headquarters and Veir's battalion area was less than a mile; yet Isen managed to get stopped again by a traffic patrol in that distance.

The MP, a woman, did not call him by name, as had happened earlier. She gave him a citation for rolling through a stop sign without saying anything beyond asking for his paperwork. Isen kept his mouth shut, but wrote down the MP's name, making sure that she saw him taking notes.

He drove slowly the rest of the way to Veir's battalion area, parked his car and walked into the Charlie Company orderly room. The first sergeant didn't know where Bennett was, and he reported that fact to Isen in a tone that said, "It's not my job to keep track of officers."

A dozen soldiers and NCOs were moving in and out of the orderly room, dropping off papers, making reports. The first sergeant was a busy man; Isen was an intrusion.

"How about the CO?" Isen asked.

"He's on his way out to recon a training site," he said curtly. "No telling when he'll be back."

So fuck off, right? Isen thought.

"Thanks," he said.

He fared somewhat better in Alpha Company, where Isen found Captain Dennison, Hauck's commander, in his tiny office. Dennison knelt on the floor amid the scattered contents of his rucksack; he seemed to be repacking.

"Don't get up," Isen said as Dennison started to shift the ruck off his legs.

Isen dropped into a chair. There was a big wall locker across from him; through the open door Isen could see loose field equipment, stacks of military manuals, a couple of bagged rations and a basketball-sized wad of dirty uniforms. "Getting ready for the field?" he asked.

"Always, sir. There's no such thing as unpacking. You just trade your dirty stuff for clean stuff and move out again."

"I just stopped by Charlie Company to see if I could find Lieutenant Bennett. You haven't seen him around the battalion area this morning, have you?"

Dennison said, "No, sir," while keeping his eyes on the little bundles he was pushing into his ruck.

Isen waited for some elaboration; Dennison kept quiet.

"You do know why I'm here, don't you?" Isen asked, leaning forward.

Dennison stopped what he was doing. He reached up with both hands and, in a very deliberate gesture, adjusted his glasses. He rose slowly, crossed the stained carpet and closed the door to his office. Passing in front of Isen again, he made his way behind his desk, and sat down.

When he was settled in, he said, "Go ahead, sir."

"Michael Hauck's roommate—a Lieutenant Savin—believes that Hauck saw some things in this unit that made him uneasy, unhappy, even. Savin also says that you told Hauck not to make things difficult for himself. Not to complain too loudly."

"You make it sound like a cover-up," Dennison said.

"Was it?" Isen asked.

Dennison drummed his fingers on the desk in front of him, first one hand, then the other.

"Lieutenant Hauck was disillusioned by what he saw in the officer ranks here. He loved the soldiers, but he didn't have much time for his peers."

"Why?"

"I think he came here expecting everyone to be a sort of plaster saint. He expected everyone to be as motivated as he was . . . no, it was more than that, he expected everyone to be motivated by the same things he was."

"Uh-huh."

"He would roll his eyes, making disparaging comments about the other lieutenants, even some of the captains."

"And you told him to keep his mouth shut?"

"I told him that it wasn't a good idea for a second lieutenant to *try* to piss people off."

"I got the impression that most people liked him," Isen said.

Dennison dropped his eyes, studied his fingernails.

"Did he piss everyone off?"

"No," Dennison said.

"You want to fill me in?"

Dennison fairly squirmed in his seat.

"Look, I don't exactly know what every other officer in the battalion thought about him," Dennison said. He picked at a loose piece of skin by his fingernail until Isen thought it might bleed. "I did tell him to keep his mouth shut, to stop talking about how this one and that one were assholes, to stop referring to our get-togethers as frat parties."

Isen was thinking about what Sue Lynn had said about Milan being afraid of Harlan Veir. Maybe that was the case with Dennison; he decided to test the hypothesis.

"Colonel Veir doesn't much like the idea that you're writing a book, does he?"

Dennison pulled himself up straight in his chair, as if the mention of Veir's name had caused all of his muscles to contract.

"No. He doesn't."

"How long have you been working on it?"

Dennison looked at Isen suspiciously, curious as to where these questions were going. "About a year," he said.

"Maybe you figured you were taking enough heat for that; you didn't need one of your lieutenants attracting any unwanted attention on top of the book thing."

Dennison put both elbows on his desk and pressed his hands to his temples.

Isen was conducting the equivalent of a recon by fire: shooting into the dark to see who shot back. He leaned back, his forearms resting on the armrests, his feet flat on the floor. Open. Nonthreatening. He didn't want Dennison to shut down, which might happen if he tried to push the captain into a corner, tried to get him to say something damaging about Veir.

"What do you think of these parties? The strippers, all that stuff?" Isen asked.

"It's not in great taste," Dennison said. "On the other hand, it's not going to lose the war for the Allies or anything. It's not something I would do on my own, I guess. But it doesn't shock me."

"Me either," Isen said.

Dennison looked up, hope in his eyes. Perhaps he was thinking that Isen was backing off, that Isen understood that he just couldn't keep talking about Veir without consequences. That all of the complaints about the parties were just so much whining.

Isen almost felt sorry for him.

"I mean, it's all in fun. No one gets hurt," Dennison continued.

"I've seen a lot worse," Isen said.

Dennison almost smiled.

Isen leaned forward, his upper body almost touching the captain's desk. He dropped his voice to a whisper.

"All of that stuff was probably not enough to get Michael Hauck to kill himself."

Dennison nodded quickly just before he saw where the question was going.

"Which means something else was going on, something bigger than a lot of college boy pranks with naked women."

Isen stood, looking down on Dennison.

"Not only that, I think you know what was happening. You know what was really bothering Michael Hauck."

Dennison sat still, breathing through his mouth.

"Maybe you're too afraid of Colonel Veir to say anything. Maybe you're too concerned with covering your own ass."

Isen paused for a few seconds. Outside, he could hear men laughing. Dennison did not move, did not speak.

"OK," Isen said, turning toward the door. "You can bet your ass I'm going to find out what drove Michael Hauck over the edge."

Isen left the office, pulling the door shut quietly behind him. He stopped at the first sergeant's desk and asked for a piece of paper.

"If Captain Dennison needs to reach me, First Sergeant," Isen said as he wrote Sue Lynn's name and number on the message page, "he can call me or leave a message here."

"Got it, sir."

Jiggles, the club frequented by Veir's men and, on the Army's twice monthly paydays, by hundreds of other Fort Bragg soldiers, could well have served as a business textbook definition of low overhead.

The club was housed in a dilapidated cinder block building set only a few feet off an industrial road outside the city limits. The only other retail establishment in the immediate vicinity was a sleazy motel with a roll-away lighted sign that advertised "Special Siesta Rates."

The club's front wall had been whitewashed, and the owners had apparently retained the services of a mildly talented graffiti artist who'd spray-painted "Jiggles" in letters six feet high. There was a loose interpretation of a reclining figure, female, along the bottom of the wall. Another figure, with outsized eyes and hair that could best be described as electrified, peered over the top of the club name as if from behind a signboard. This second figure's breasts peeked out from the two circles that formed the lowercase *g*'s in the club name.

Isen, driving up with Savin, figured that the sign was identification; it wouldn't serve to attract anyone who didn't already know what was going on inside. There was a dirt parking lot off to the right, and Savin pulled in and parked his car in the back, near an entrance that led to the street that ran behind the club.

"It was over here," Savin said, getting out of the car. He pointed to another parking area, this one blacktop, that abutted the dirt lot. A small, dark building, surrounded by cyclone fence, crouched at the far side of the smaller lot.

"That's the metal company, and this lot over here is where Mike ... where Mike's truck was parked."

Isen stepped over some curbing onto the hardtop. There were no cars parked there, but he could see that once the club's lot was full, patrons would use these spaces, which were just as close and which weren't used at night by the metal shop customers.

"Did you come by?" Isen asked.

"A couple of hours later," Savin said. "They were getting ready to tow the truck by the time I got here. The police were already done and 'most everyone had left the club."

Isen turned and scanned the back wall of Jiggles. There was a single, windowless door, lit by a solitary unshielded bulb. As they watched, a car drove up and a young woman got out of the passenger side. She pulled a small bag, like a gym bag, from the back seat, kissed the driver and walked around to the other side. There she opened the rear door. Isen could see, by the dim courtesy light, that there was a baby seat in the back; the woman leaned in and kissed a child strapped in there. A moment later, someone answered her knock on the back door and she scooted inside. The car drove away.

"Just another day at the office," Savin said.

The two men walked around to the entrance, where an obese bearded man, a good eighty pounds past his prime as a bouncer, took their money and buzzed them through a door.

· Isen squinted into the darkness, waiting for his eyesight to adjust. Some sort of music banged through a sound system that did everything for the volume and nothing for the tune.

"Check this out," Savin said, pointing.

Tacked to the wall by the entrance was the same poster of the World War II paratrooper Isen had seen above Coates's desk. "82D AIRBORNE: DESERT STORM" had been printed in block letters above the soldier's head, and there were creases where the poster had been folded and—Isen imagined—mailed from the desert. Autographs peppered the illustration: "If you thought we were horny before, WATCH OUT"; "We miss the girls at Jiggles"; "Wish you were here—and we were there"; and one poor speller's attempt at poetics, "Dreaming of beaver under a dessert sky."

There was a long, dim bar along the entire length of the wall facing them; several customers and a few dancers held down stools there. These couples were deep in conversation, with lots of touching and forced laughter. The scene would not have differed from what one could see in any nightclub except that the customers, all men, were fully dressed, while the women wore an eclectic mix of lingerie, ranging from red and lacy to imitation leopard skin trimmed in black fur. Isen and Savin navigated through the darkness, sidestepping small cocktail tables that formed three concentric horseshoes around a railed stage that dominated the wall facing the bar.

When Isen reached a stool, he turned to the room. There were chairs pulled up to a narrow counter at the edge of the stage, and a half dozen men sat there, close to the show. A substantial brass rail separated the dancers from their nearest admirers, and other brass fittings formed a kind of jungle gym onstage: four posts bolted at floor and ceiling, with connecting bars at a height of about six feet. Even at this early hour—it was only seven-thirty—there were two women on stage, two separate shows. One stood on her head, leaning against one of the upright poles, scissoring her legs slowly, her red high-heeled shoes moving in half circles in the dim light. The other woman moved gracelessly, her mind so clearly someplace else that she might have forgotten she was all but naked. Both women wore tiny G-strings and pasties, and so were as fully clothed as the letter, if not the spirit of the law required.

"Obviously an athlete," Savin said, indicating the one standing on her head. "Probably working her way through medical school."

"Kind of slow, isn't it?" Isen asked.

"It'll pick up in a little while."

In the first ten minutes they stood at the bar, nursing the most expensive beer Isen had purchased in quite a while, two of the dancers approached them. One, carrying a little stool, offered a private dance; Isen declined. The second woman, wearing a wide leather bandolier over a bikini, offered something she called a Texas Shooter.

"What's that?" Isen asked.

"Glad you asked," she said. She was about twenty, Isen thought, with thin blond hair, wide hips and large breasts that were in clear defiance of gravitational law.

"You know how to drink tequila, right?" she asked, pulling a shotglass from the leather bandolier. She opened a little leather pouch on the belt to reveal some lime slices and a salt shaker.

"You mean with the salt and lime and all that?"

"Right." She moved forward until her breasts pushed Isen up against the bar.

"Except that with a Texas Shooter you lick my boob...." She ran her finger over one breast, just above the line of her top. "Put a little salt there on the wet spot, and a lime here...." She tucked a slice of lime into her cleavage, where it rested securely.

"Then you lick the salt, do the shot and grab the lime with your teeth."

"Fascinating," Savin offered dryly.

"You want to try it?" she asked, touching Isen's cheek.

"Maybe some other time," Isen said.

"OK. Let me know; my name is Ginger."

As Ginger swung away on ball-bearing hips, Savin said, "That's an alternative to dancing. They buy the bottle from the manager for forty bucks, then they don't have to dance on stage and they keep the money from the drinks."

"That right?" Isen said, wondering how Savin knew the details.

"Mike told me all this," Savin said. "He used to talk to some of the dancers, but then I think he got a bunch of shit for it from the other guys. You know, treating them like people and all that."

"Did you ever come here with Mike?"

"A couple of times. For moral support."

Isen thought Savin was trying to be ironic, but he made the comment with a straight face.

"Did Mike come here to be with his buddies, to have fun, or did he come here because he more or less had to."

"He wanted to fit in. Or at least he thought he should try," Savin said.

A man in a striped referee shirt led a dancer by the hand through the maze of tiny cocktail tables that circled the stage. The couple stopped when a customer held up what looked to Isen like a single dollar bill. The referee caught up the bill, and the dancer placed her hands on the customer's shoulders and pressed her breasts to his face, prying his legs apart with her knees. The move was artless, and the dancer wore the same bored expression as her compatriot on stage, until she saw Isen looking at her from a few feet away. She smiled at him, her lips pressed together.

It was over in less than a minute. The woman thanked the man in the chair, who sat with his glasses askew, arms dangling at his sides, grinning vacantly.

The place had begun to fill and Isen had spent almost thirty dollars on the overpriced beers before the first knot of Veir's lieutenants began to appear. Isen recognized Pendleton among the group, and he noticed that the dancers had changed—a younger, prettier lot.

The first string, he thought.

"There's Bennett," Savin said.

Bennett was already seated at a table with three other

men, the foursome working its way quickly through a pitcher of beer.

"You gonna talk to him?" Savin asked.

"I'd rather get him alone," Isen said, "and when he's sober. But he's so friggin' hard to catch up with I might not get another chance."

Isen left the bar and walked toward the table, which was close to the dance floor.

"Lieutenant Bennett, I'm Major Isen."

Bennett stood, holding one overmuscled arm in front of him, hand extended. Isen shook the offered hand.

"Hey, sir," Bennett said, his speech a bit slurred. "Sorry I missed you today. They got me running around like my fuckin' hair is on fire."

Isen thought he saw one of the men at the table nudge the man beside him with an elbow.

"I'd like to ask you a few questions," Isen said, businesslike.

"Here?" Bennett asked, clearly put out. "I mean, wouldn't it be better to wait until we could do this someplace else? Besides, I've had couple of beers, Major ... I'm sorry."

"Isen. How many beers have you had?"

"Is that our second pitcher, Bart?" Bennett asked one of the men grinning up at them from the table; he was playing for the crowd.

"I had a couple before I left home, too," he said, looking at Isen again. " 'Course, I didn't drive myself."

The men at the table were smiling openly now. Isen ignored Bennett's fans and decided to be blunt. "Did you go outside with Michael Hauck just before he shot himself?"

Bennett wavered a bit, but Isen thought his eyes were clear; he wasn't as drunk as he pretended to be.

"I think so, yeah. It's a little hazy. I mean, the timing and all."

"Did you speak to him outside?"

"I don't remember exactly," Bennett said.

"Did you have a fight?"

"Not that I remember."

"Were you drunk that night?" Isen asked.

Bennett smiled, but his eyes were narrowing to pinpricks.

"I guess I was pretty loaded. I think I went over all this with that black chick," he said.

One of the men at the table sputtered as he tried to contain his laughter. Bennett had squared off with Isen, and was now facing him full front. He seemed to be flexing his neck muscles in some odd way that filled the space between shoulder and earlobe with tightened flesh.

Isen knew how to handle this; he'd learned as a young officer that when a subordinate is performing for the group, you take the group away. He could ask Bennett to step to another part of the club, away from the table. The trouble with that option was that they would still be on the wrong turf. Isen wanted Bennett in uniform, wearing rank. Figuring that Bennett would just continue to play the dumb drunk, Isen opted for the delay.

"Guess I'll catch you later, then," Isen said.

Isen went back to the bar, where Savin asked him, "Well?"

Isen, frustrated at this turn, too, just waved his hand.

Veir's men staked out their turf at one corner of the stage. They were quiet for a while, ordering beers, getting settled in, but they were brought to their feet when the bouncer, who doubled as a master of ceremonies, Isen thought, dragged a child's wading pool onto the stage. Two women, wearing T-shirts and bathing suit bottoms, appeared carrying plastic pitchers of water. The disc jockey turned the music down.

"It's *pool party* time," he said enthusiastically.

There was a general shuffling and a flurry of dollar bills. One of Veir's men climbed over the railing when the bouncer, standing by the tiny pool, signaled to him. The lieutenant, whom Isen didn't recognize, handed his money over in exchange for one of the pitchers. The dancer faced him, and he began to pour water, in a slow stream, across her chest. Her breasts were immediately visible, as if she wore no top at all, and Isen imagined that the ultrathin layer of cotton was barely enough to satisfy the town's ordinance against total nudity in an establishment that served alcoholic beverages. Isen doubted that this was what the town council had in mind when they specified that the women had to be covered.

The dancer was moving now, bent over at the waist as the soldier, to the shouts of his peers at the edge of the floor, directed a stream of water onto the small of her back. The water slid over her, a shiny tracing of her buttocks. The woman, hands on hips, smiled and blew a kiss at the other young men, who were whipping themselves into a frenzy that produced more tip money and at least one more round of overpriced beer.

"They think that she's doing what they want," Savin said. "But she's doing a little cash-ectomy on them. They might as well just lay all their money on the table. A couple of wiggles of that rear end, a little bit of water on the old tomatoes, and she'd got them eating out of her hand."

Isen studied his companion. A couple of beers had loosened Savin's tongue quite a bit.

Isen figured that the pool party had depleted the finances of this group by about sixty or seventy bucks, by the time one totaled the beer and the tips they lavished on the dripping dancer. She obliged their shouted requests by planting a kiss on each cheek of the pitcher bearer, who held up the empty vessel like a hard-won loving cup.

"Now things can really start," Savin said, nudging Isen's elbow and indicating the door.

Harlan Veir and Leonard Foote made their way through the door. Veir, dressed in tight jeans, a rodeo-sized belt buckle and red cowboy boots, raised his hand as the lieutenants shouted their boisterous greetings. Foote looked as if he wanted to kill someone.

"Major Foote looks as friendly as ever," Isen said.

"He hates this," Savin said.

"What?"

"Mike told me that Major Foote hates this shit. His dad is a minister, if you can believe that. He just comes here because Veir wants him to keep an eye on the lieutenants."

Foote, seeing Isen at the bar, tapped Veir on the shoulder. Veir spoke to Foote, who homed in on Isen like a blunt missile.

"What the fuck are you doing here?" Foote said as he approached Isen.

"It's a public place, isn't it?" Isen said.

"If you're spying on us, you little pissant, you should at least have the guts to say so."

"OK," Isen said, "I'm spying on you. Now run along."

When Foote backed away, Savin whispered, "He could kill you. One punch."

"He could probably kill both of us with one punch."

Foote returned to Veir's side and whispered into the colonel's ear. Veir glanced in Isen's direction and nodded.

Isen lifted his beer bottle in small salute. "Fuck you," he said under his breath.

There were lots of soldiers in the place by this time. Shaved heads stood two deep at the bar and clustered in a score of small groups at the tiny tables before the stage— Veir was probably the oldest and highest ranking of any of the patrons. If that fact bothered him in any way, he didn't show it. Veir took an offered chair at the middle of his rowdy entourage and sat down to watch the goings-on.

Foote sat at the bar close to the door, opposite where Isen sat. The women working the bar for dollar dances avoided the big man with the frightening scowl.

There were, it seemed to Isen as he looked about the room, two types of patrons. The first group had been in the bar in the late afternoon and was already filtering out by the time Isen and Savin showed up: the businessmen and the regulars who came here to hide out or to indulge in a few fantasies. When one of these men approached a dancer with a folded bill in his hand, he looked neither left nor right, but kept his eyes down until he was next to the woman. When she thrust her gartered leg out toward him, propping her foot on the railing so that he could lodge the tip there, the poor fool usually broke out in a wide smile that said, *You and I have some special connection,* or *I admire your talents,* or *I value you as a person.*

Inevitably, the woman's answering smile faded as soon as the bill was in place and the man turned away.

Veir's lieutenants made up the second type of customer: loud, obnoxious, with all the reserve of a college fraternity keg party. They screamed, yelled, hooted, hollered, waved their pitiful collection of bills, feigned swoons as the dancers flashed close. They knew that this was *quid pro quo,* money for flesh and fantasy, and they were perfectly content with that arrangement.

Veir was in the former group, Isen thought, a little on the sleazy side. He had the look of a man who wants something more, something intimate, something promised but not delivered. That, of course, was the whole idea behind an enterprise such as this. Things promised. Nothing delivered. Veir's lieutenants took delight in what it was—a sexy smile and a glimpse of skin. *All I want to do is see your body. You and I both know that I would love to possess you. You and I both know that that isn't about to happen.*

Isen switched to club soda and began counting the rounds that Veir and his men bought. Veir was pounding back mixed drinks as he held court at the small table, prodding this or that lieutenant to dance beside the stage, to offer money.

Isen watched Bennett.

Bennett became more visible when Veir appeared, cavorting around the tables, the center of attention. He removed his shirt, dancing beside the stage in a parody—even more lewd than the original—of what the woman onstage was doing. The dancer smiled at Bennett; perhaps she was used to this, Isen thought.

"Watch this," Savin said. "Seems the fat guy isn't supposed to allow people to take their clothes off. But he won't say anything directly to Bennett."

The bouncer, who apparently had played this scene out before, didn't even look at Bennett, who was shirtless and beginning to unbutton his pants. Instead, the big man approached Veir, leaned over and whispered something in the colonel's ear. Veir signaled to Bennett, who put his shirt back on, though he continued to swivel his hips and grind at the back of a chair before him.

"Don Harlan," Savin said.

Isen had to admit that Veir did look a bit regal, gesturing to his minions, sending them hither and thither to fetch drinks or carry on with women. Isen also noticed that none of the dancers, who'd found a gold mine in the lieutenants, approached Veir to see if he wanted a private dance.

"Hard to say if they've given more money to the dancers

or the bartenders," Isen shouted at Savin. "They're going through the cash at a pretty good clip."

"Hey, why don't you sit down so the rest of us can see the show." This to Bennett, directed at him from one of the cocktail tables, where some bikers had their own little group, an island of black leather in a sea of T-shirts and short hair. The source of the remark was a man Isen guessed to be in his mid-twenties, with the kind of overdeveloped muscles one sees in muscle magazines and prisons.

Bennett turned around and fixed the biker with a bleary-eyed stare. He pulled his shoulders back, and Isen could see his nostrils flare.

"Sit down, Lieutenant Bennett," Veir said clearly, his voice surprisingly audible above the pounding of the over-sized speakers.

Bennett glanced at Veir, who had not turned to look at the bikers. The lieutenant sat down as instructed, but a few seconds later, Isen noticed, he turned to his hecklers, raised his middle finger and mouthed, *Fuck you.*

By now the rest of the GIs were watching another lieutenant whom Isen did not recognize. This one had slithered onto the stage on his back, crawling under the low brass railing as the Army taught recruits to crawl under barbed wire.

"*Muff*-dive, *muff*-dive, *muff*-dive," his supporters chanted.

The lieutenant produced a rolled dollar bill, which he pretended to pull from his belt, imitating, Isen supposed, a man about to throw a hand grenade. He clutched the bill in his teeth and raised both arms, beckoning to a petite dancer who shuffled nervously a few feet away. The dancer at the other end of the stage, a bottle-dyed redhead whose right breast was larger than the left, moved closer. Alerted by the shouts and catcalls of the crowd around the banister and apparently more experienced with this ritual than was her partner, she walked over and squatted above the prone soldier's face. Moving her hips back and forth lasciviously, she drove the noise higher and higher, letting the men scream themselves hoarse for half a minute before plucking the bill from the clenched teeth below her with the red-nailed fingers of one hand. She slapped her admirer playfully on the cheek, then stood and placed one spiked heel squarely in the center of the man's chest, a gladiator celebrating a victory.

The house was on its feet now, with men stomping on the floor, pounding on tables. Bennett, Isen saw, was lifting a chair and smashing it to the deck repeatedly, baying at the ceiling and the noise all around him. What Bennett did not see, but Isen did, was that the bikers had moved closer to where the soldiers stood.

Isen saw what was going to happen but was powerless to stop it. He didn't even manage to get out a warning when a man visible to Isen only as a leather jacket and dark pony-tail landed a vicious kidney punch to Bennett's back. Bennett lost his balance, and the biker brought one of his ugly black boots up and quickly down, a piston blow on the back of Bennett's knee.

Bennett crumpled.

The other lieutenants, their reactions slowed by alcohol, were just turning around when the biker started to move toward the door behind his companions. Isen reached for the bar with his glass, missed; the glass smashed at his feet. He moved for the door, but the crowd had already begun to surge toward the disturbance.

"Hey!" Isen yelled. "Stop that guy!"

Veir was on his feet now, but he, like his lieutenants, was looking at Bennett. The leather jackets were slipping out. The biker who'd kicked Bennett had his hand on the door when a thickly muscled black arm crossed him like a tollgate.

Leonard Foote blocked the doorway, and in two quick moves at the door he turned the deadbolt lock so that the men who'd left couldn't re-enter. The biker who faced him was frightened now, as much by Foote's scowl as by his size. The leather jacket backpedaled, losing his balance when he ran into Bennett, who had come up behind him.

In the space of a few lightning seconds, Bennett punched the man hard in the lower back and on the side of the head. Right uppercut, left cross. The biker tried to face his attacker, but Bennett, moving with surprising quickness for a man who'd consumed as much alcohol as he had, stepped neatly to the side, staying just out of reach. The leather jacket swung wildly, poorly. Bennett stepped inside again. Two jabs in the head and the biker went to his knees.

Foote unlocked the door and held it open as the man with the ponytail stumbled out without standing upright.

All of this happened so quickly that Isen still had not managed to push through the crowd. Bennett stepped back to a cluster of backslapping; Foote moved back to his solitary post at the bar, and Veir settled in his seat, raising his hand to order another round of drinks brought to a table already covered in glasses only half empty.

"Bennett's a fucking nut case," Savin said to Isen as the two men repositioned themselves at the bar.

"He's not the only one," Isen said.

He'd seen a few bar fights between soldiers and civilians; such things were practically a local sport in some post-side towns. But usually the GIs over twenty or so—and this included most officers and NCOs—knew that brawling wasn't such a great idea, especially in the armed camp that America had become in the late twentieth century.

"He could get killed that way," Isen said. "These days, you don't know what lunatic will pull a gun and blow you away for something like that."

"Mike said that Bennett is always packing. If he doesn't have a weapon on him, he's got one handy. In his jacket, in his truck." Savin paused, pulled on his beer. "They call him 'Free-fire Zone.' "

Isen scowled. In combat, the military used fire-control measures to determine which units could fire in certain areas, the idea being that such controls would reduce fratricide. A free-fire zone, as the name implied, meant that anyone could shoot at any enemy target. Isen wondered if the handle for Bennett meant he liked to shoot or, given his personality, people liked to shoot at him.

The quick fight with the bikers was over by eleven. At eleven-thirty Isen and Savin left the bar and went out to the parking lot, where they sat in Savin's car and watched as a steady stream of the drunk and near drunk dribbled out in small groups. Isen noticed that, among Veir's men at least, each car had a sober driver.

They had been sitting for fifteen minutes, and Savin had begun to doze off, when Veir and Foote left the club together. Foote, as far as Isen had been able to see, hadn't had a single drink. Veir, who'd had at least six, walked just as straight as his taller subordinate. The two men did not speak, except for a perfunctory good-night as Foote climbed into his car.

Savin snored lightly. Isen shifted in his seat to watch Veir, who walked toward his pickup, then turned away as soon as Foote's car cleared the parking lot. Veir looked about once, then went over to the back door of the club. He knocked once, twice, a third time impatiently. Finally a woman came outside to join him. Isen recognized her as the petite dancer who'd been unsure of what to do when the soldier climbed onstage with money sticking out of his clenched teeth.

Veir bent over and said something to the woman, then took her gently by the arm and led her toward his truck. She wore a short skirt, high heels that made negotiating the uneven lot difficult, and a shirt she held closed across her chest. Veir continued to talk, while the woman kept her head lowered, even when Veir threw back his head to laugh at his own jokes.

Isen looked around. Except for the lights at the front of the building and the solitary bulb above the rear door the lot was dark. If he hadn't seen Veir in the light by the front entrance, he would not have been able to identify him in the gloom. There were fewer than twenty cars in the lot, and Savin's car, though not close to Veir's truck, stood off by itself. He figured that if Veir looked hard enough, he would be able to see that someone was inside the car and watching. Isen, always the infantryman, knew that if he kept still there was less of a chance that Veir would spot him. He decided not to wake Savin, who now slept deeply.

Veir brought the woman to the door of the cab and reached inside the open window, then handed something to her, which she shoved into the breast pocket of her over-sized shirt. Veir bent over—he was almost a foot taller than the woman—and said something to her, pointing at the side of the truck. The woman hesitated, still shuffling nervously. Veir spoke again, lifting his head, patting her on the arm. The woman tossed her hair over her shoulder, placed both her hands on the side panel and spread her legs. Veir stepped behind her, unbuttoning his pants.

Isen felt his mouth drop open. He looked around again quickly—there was no one else in the lot. When he turned back, he saw what he expected to see. Veir had his hands on the woman's hips; her skirt was pushed up around her waist, and he rocked back and forth, all but lifting the tiny woman off the ground with each thrust.

Isen punched Savin in the shoulder, but the lieutenant, who'd had too much to drink, rolled toward the door.

"Wake up," Isen said, shaking Savin.

Savin didn't respond immediately, but apparently Veir did.

It was over quickly. While Veir leaned against the truck, the woman stepped out from in front of him, where he'd had her pushed up against the fender. She adjusted her skirt, checked the shirt pocket to make sure whatever he'd given her was still there, then hurried to the club door.

Veir buttoned his pants without turning around.

Isen was still shaking his head when Veir climbed into the truck, started it and backed up. He could have used the rear driveway, but instead he drove right past Isen and the still-groggy Savin. When the big red truck passed in front of Isen, Veir turned to him, smiled and waved.

8

"HE'S SICK."

Isen and Sue Lynn lay side by side in her bedroom, watching the weekend dawn.

"I haven't told you the best part yet," Isen said.

Sue Lynn propped herself up on one elbow.

"He drove right past me on his way out. He looked at me, smiled and waved."

"He saw you?"

"More than that, I think he knew I was there the whole time. I think the whole thing was put on for my benefit."

"Well, if it only lasted as long as you said, it certainly wasn't for her benefit."

"I think he likes being on the edge," Isen said. "The whole thing with the parties downtown is the fact that those kinds of things are just completely outrageous. Veir likes flaunting that, daring someone to reprimand him. Same thing with banging the dancer in the parking lot, knowing I was there. It's like he's shoving it in my face."

"He certainly acts as if he's protected," Sue Lynn said, rolling over onto her stomach. "So back that . . . what would you call it? flamboyance? . . . back that up to Hauck's suicide. What does that tendency look like back there? What's the connection?"

"I'm not sure." Isen rolled toward her, pushed the covers away and began to stroke her back. "Maybe Hauck saw some things he couldn't live with."

"Something he wanted to report, you mean?"

Isen paused. "If I accept the theory that there was some conflict between Hauck and Veir, it could be that Veir wanted Hauck dead."

There was a pause in the conversation, a crisp silence.

"Hauck shot himself," Sue Lynn said.

"Yeah, yeah. But suppose they were more involved—Bennett might have been out there; Veir talked to Hauck just before he went outside. Suppose they thought that Hauck might do something like that. Maybe they tried to stop him, maybe they let him go on, even pushed him. Maybe that's the ultimate challenge for a control freak like Veir, someone who gets his kicks pushing the rules."

"I think they're all a bunch of sickos," Sue Lynn said. "Starting with Veir, down through Foote and the rest of those . . . children."

When Isen didn't respond, Sue Lynn turned her head toward him, appraising him with one eye.

"But following Veir around isn't going to be enough," she said.

"I can't follow Hauck around," Isen said testily. "He's dead."

"Don't get flip. There has to be more information out there. You still haven't talked to Bennett."

"And I'm beginning to think I never will. And then there's General Flynn."

"He called last night," Sue Lynn said. "Still no CID report. It's kind of a moot point now, isn't it?"

"Probably. I've still got to call him later."

"And Savin?"

"Savin has it in for Veir. But as far as I can tell, he has no more reason than personal animosity. Veir is a pig, but so far that's all."

Isen told Major General Flynn about the incident with the PT run in the first three minutes of their phone conversation.

"You getting a little paranoid down there, Mark?"

"Hell, sir, I wouldn't be paranoid if everyone wasn't after me."

"So you haven't made any friends at all, huh?"

Isen thought about Sue Lynn. "I wouldn't go that far, sir."

"At least not Colonel Veir, though, right?"

"No. I don't think Veir would be unhappy if I left. He has an interesting little world down here. He pretty much does whatever he wants while he thumbs his nose at propriety, at any sort of code of behavior."

Isen told Flynn what he'd seen at Jiggles, including the tryst in the parking lot.

"Damn," Flynn said. "Well, that certainly gives his subordinates wide parameters for behavior. Whatever happens, don't let this turn into a private pissing contest between you and Veir. He's still enough of the fair-haired boy that you could get crushed."

"The thought has occurred to me, sir," Isen said. "I was wondering if you still had a copy of the preliminary CID report you mentioned when I was in DC."

"Didn't McCall show you a copy?" Flynn wanted to know.

"Yes, sir, but ... I was wondering if her version was different from the one you had."

Flynn paused. "Maybe you were wondering why I didn't show it to you," he said.

"That, too."

"I didn't want you to be influenced ahead of time. I wanted your impressions. I asked you, Mark, because you're a smart guy. You know a lot about human nature, and I trust you."

"Thank you, sir."

"What did you find out about Michael's life?"

Isen thought about the photographs, and about the conversation he'd had with Sue Lynn about Hauck's sexual orientation. He wondered if Flynn knew something and had just sent Isen to confirm it.

"Special Agent McCall said that Michael had some friends who were gay."

Nothing from the other end.

"Sir?"

"Is that the same as saying that Michael was gay?"

"No, sir. In fact, she made a point of stating that she had no evidence of that."

More quiet.

"If someone threatened to make an issue of that, sir . . ." Isen began.

"I can imagine," Flynn said. "Did he have enemies?"

"There's one lieutenant in the battalion, a kid named Bennett, who didn't like Michael very much. From what I've been able to see, this guy's a certifiable asshole."

"So maybe he was leaning on Michael?"

"Well, there's at least one of the other lieutenants who says that this guy Bennett might have been the last one to see Michael alive."

There was a weighty silence on the line, background noise like the sighing of an electronic wind.

"Did you talk to him?"

"No, sir, I haven't been able to get to him. They keep finding more important stuff for him to do."

"Uh-huh."

"Did you meet Michael's roommate when you visited Bragg, sir?"

"Yes. I visited Michael's apartment and met . . . what's his name. Greg. I met Greg. The three of us had dinner together."

"Lieutenant Savin put in a leave request to attend the funeral in DC, but the request was denied," Isen said. "Do you know anything about that, sir?"

Flynn wanted to lie, and for the simplest reason: he wanted to cover something he was ashamed of. But he couldn't.

"Yes," Flynn said. "I made a couple of calls to make sure Savin wouldn't be here."

"Why?"

"I thought Savin was turning Michael away from the Army, encouraging his cynicism. I know it sounds pretty lame now, but I thought Savin was a bad influence, and I didn't want him around."

So I abused my power and rank, Flynn thought. *And I leaned on my nephew—my own flesh and blood—without ever trying to find out what was wrong with that unit, with his boss. I gave Michael the whole line about the family name, and doing a good job. Set him up for a fall, maybe.*

"OK, sir," Isen said. "I have some ideas about where to go from here."

"Except you have to be back at work in the Pentagon on Monday."

"I thought I had a few more days down here."

"So did I, but I got a call from my boss; he didn't think your little junket was such a great idea. And something else has come up that will probably make this whole thing a bit harder."

Flynn paused, and Isen could hear papers shuffling on the other end.

"We just got word that the Secretary of Defense will be visiting Bragg in a couple of weeks. The Army is going to put on a big show for him. Mobility, firepower, lots of razzamatazz. And Veir's been tapped to be in the center ring."

"So he's going to be busy," Isen said.

"It's a little more than that," Flynn said. "Seems that the President has told the Pentagon to come up with a better plan for the budget. He wants to know which service he should invest in to get the most worldwide responsiveness for his defense bucks. The Marines are going ape-shit over this thing. They're putting on a demo out at Camp Pendleton, and the word is that they think this is going to decide who's left standing when the dust clears. Only one service is going to be picked to be the nation's quick reaction force. The service that isn't picked is going to see the budget dollars dry up. If the Army gets it, the Marines will go back to guarding ships. If the Marines get it, the Army will lose all but its heaviest units. All the airborne, all the light units, all the Rangers will go away. Thousands, literally thousands of people will see their careers disappear."

Isen, who was sitting at the kitchen table doodling on a legal pad, drew an outsized dollar sign on the paper.

"How long has this been in the works, sir?"

"The visit?"

"The visit and the fact that Veir is going to do the show."

"My guess is the visit and demo have been in the works for a couple of months, although it's very hush-hush. Obviously the service chiefs have been in on it. But the individual services have been kept in the dark. There's even a rumor that a Marine brigadier got shipped out of here because he tried to get some advance word on the President's and the Secretary's selection criteria. There are people here who would kill to get a leg up in this thing."

Isen traced over the dollar sign, making it bigger and bigger.

"As for Veir," Flynn continued, "he probably got the nod after the *Newsweek* piece."

Flynn paused, and Isen could hear him drinking something. Isen checked his watch; it was after four o'clock on a Saturday. Chances were good that Flynn was drinking something Irish and neat.

"I think it's asinine, myself," Flynn said. "No one is saying 'We've got to give the taxpayers their money's worth.' They're all worried about beating the Marines; like it's some big popularity contest. I swear, sometimes I think that nutcase Hackworth is right."

"You mean that guy up in Montana who says we should do away with the services because we waste all our time in interservice rivalry?"

"He's the one. The stuff you see in the next few weeks is going to verify everything he says. He'll look like a goddamned prophet by the time we're finished. The point is that I doubt if you'd be able to get close to Veir, even if you could stay down there."

Isen was surprised at the change in Flynn; the urgency was gone. Isen had not only taken over the investigation, he seemed to be on his own.

"I think it would be worth another trip for me, sir," Isen said.

"I'll see what I can do," Flynn said.

Isen noticed the pickup parked across the street when he passed through the front hall to go upstairs. There was a man in the driver's seat, and he appeared, from a distance, to be watching Sue Lynn's house. When Isen came back downstairs a few minutes later, the truck was still there, so he walked outside and across the street. As he approached the vehicle, the driver—a young black man with the "high and tight" haircut of a paratrooper—rolled down his window.

"Major Isen?"

"Are you looking for me?" Isen asked. He stopped some four to five feet from the truck, not quite knowing what to expect. Centered on the truck's windshield was a Department of Defense vehicle registration sticker with the red markings of an enlisted man and "FT BRAGG NC" in bold letters.

"Yes, sir. Well, yes and no, I guess. I mean . . ." Stumbling badly, the man put both hands on the steering wheel and took a deep breath.

"Who are you?"

"My name's Sergeant Gabriel, Mitchell Gabriel." He paused. "I was in Lieutenant Hauck's platoon."

Isen, who wasn't quite ready to let his guard down completely, stepped closer and opened the door. "So you came to talk to me."

When Gabriel nodded, Isen said, "Let's go inside."

"I don't know if that's a good idea, sir," Gabriel said. "The First Sergeant said I shouldn't spend a lot of time here."

"Your First Sergeant knows you're here?"

"You left Major Darlington's name and phone number on his desk yesterday after you talked to Captain Dennison. Everybody in the battalion knows why you're here."

Gabriel got out of the truck. He was shorter than Isen, maybe five seven, with the thin build of a runner. Neatly turned out in black pants and an expensive-looking linen shirt. He was clearly uncomfortable; he folded his arms tightly across his chest and glanced up and down the road several times as if expecting to see someone he knew.

"Does your First Sergeant know what I was asking Captain Dennison yesterday?"

"He said you wanted to know about Lieutenant Hauck. Said you're trying to figure out why he killed himself. Top said that the CO didn't help you out that much."

"So the First Sergeant sent you out?"

"No, sir. Not exactly. He told me what you were looking for and he told me how to find you. I guess it was my choice whether or not to come out here. I thought about calling, but I wasn't sure if I would back down or not. To tell you the truth, I was thinking about driving away when you came out of the door."

"Why would you not want to talk to me?"

"The word is out to stay away from you, Major. That's why no NCO has approached you, especially on post."

"Who put that word out?"

"I don't know. The Sergeant Major, I guess."

Isen, who had intended to talk to the battalion's senior NCO, mentally moved the Sergeant Major's name to the list for the hostile camp.

"But me and some of the guys in the platoon don't think Lieutenant Hauck's getting a fair deal."

"What do you mean?"

"People are talking . . . no, some of the other lieutenants are talking like Lieutenant Hauck wasn't a good platoon leader. They're saying a bunch of things about how he didn't really fit in, how he didn't belong here."

Isen leaned against the side of the truck; Gabriel followed suit. Across the street, Sue Lynn's next-door neighbor came out to get his morning paper. He waved; Isen waved back.

"Was that the case? Was he a screwup?" Isen asked.

"Nah," Gabriel said. "He was a good lieutenant. A little nervous, maybe."

Isen waited. It was almost mid-morning, and the sun was above the tops of the pine trees that stood in loose groups around the development.

"Lieutenant Hauck went to bat for me when I needed help, see?"

The young NCO was talking with his hands now, allowing them to rise and fall with his speech, to move away from his body.

"Me and my old lady were having trouble, so she went out and bounced a bunch of checks all over post. But it was my ass in a sling, even though I didn't do it."

Isen was familiar with the story. In the tightly ordered universe of the military base, the service member is responsible for anything that goes wrong. Sergeant Gabriel could have been half a world away when his wife passed bad checks: he was the one in uniform, he was the one responsible.

"So the Sergeant Major wants me to get a letter of reprimand," Gabriel said, shaking his head. "Like that's gonna make my old lady change. But Lieutenant Hauck didn't think that was right."

"He talked to the Sergeant Major?" Isen asked.

In his experience, second lieutenants did not bother the senior NCO in a battalion. The Sergeant Major worked for the Colonel. Period. Isen had met more than a few Sergeants Major who would not even speak to second lieutenants, other than to render the proper military courtesy prescribed by regulations: a brisk salute and a curt greeting.

"No. No, sir. The Sergeant Major ain't got time for second lieutenants. So Lieutenant Hauck had to talk to the colonel. He practically had to drag Captain Dennison over there."

Isen watched Gabriel as the younger man spoke. Gabriel would never confide it to another officer, but it was clear that he didn't think much of Captain Dennison. Isen wasn't surprised to hear that the nervous company commander had been unwilling to take on Harlan Veir on behalf of a soldier.

"Anyways," Gabriel continued, "Lieutenant Hauck goes to the colonel's office, and he's got the whole chain of command in tow. He's got this big file folder with all my counseling statements, records and stuff—a whole year's worth that he'd re-copied the night before so that they'd be neat enough for the colonel to read."

"So what happened?"

"Well, I was really nervous. I had just re-enlisted, and a letter of reprimand could have stopped my chances for promotion. Lieutenant Hauck and Captain Dennison and the First Sergeant all went in together. Then the CO and First Sergeant come out, so it's just Lieutenant Hauck in there. And when he comes out, he's not smiling, you know, so I think it's bad news. But he tells me I'm clean. No letter."

"Did something else happen in there?" Isen wanted to know. "Why wasn't he smiling?"

"I don't know. But the lieutenant made me and my wife go to counseling, and that's been the greatest thing for us."

"When did this happen?"

"A month, month and a half before he killed himself."

"As far as you know, Sergeant, was there any sort of

personal problem between Colonel Veir and Lieutenant Hauck? Any kind of personality conflict?"

"You've been in the Army longer than I have, sir, but as far as I know, there's no such thing as a personality conflict between a lieutenant and a lieutenant colonel."

"Good point," Isen said. He shoved his hands into his pockets and looked at the ground, wondering if Michael Hauck would have had the balls to confront Colonel Veir with something he knew, something he had on the battalion commander, in order to get a fair shake for this soldier.

Think horses, not zebras.

"One more thing, sir," Gabriel offered. "There are some rumors floating around about Lieutenant Hauck. Personal stuff. I can't say for sure if they're true or not, but I do know that Lieutenant Hauck was a good man. He cared about the right things."

"What kind of rumors?"

Gabriel paused, watching Isen as if for some sign that he didn't have to say out loud what was on his mind. Then he plunged ahead.

"Some people are saying that he was gay. Just some knuckleheads talking shit when they really don't know anything."

"Who was saying these things?"

"It was just scuttlebutt, you know? Rumors. You can bet that no one says it around me, though. I don't want to hear that shit."

Having said what he wanted to say, Gabriel suddenly became aware of his surroundings again. He looked around the quiet neighborhood. No one was visible, but that didn't seem to make him less uncomfortable.

"I gotta run, sir."

"Thanks, Sergeant Gabriel. It took guts to come out here."

"Yeah, well, I figured I owed the lieutenant one."

Isen and the sergeant shook hands, then Gabriel got behind the wheel and drove away without looking back.

"The implications are huge," Isen said to Sue Lynn. They were unpacking groceries after spending the afternoon shopping. Sue Lynn pulled little jars and boxes of spices from the bags and from the cabinets—ginger, curry, saffron, cilantro, garlic—lining them up like soldiers on the counter. She didn't like boring, she resisted the conventional, the predictable, in the bedroom as well as in the kitchen. Isen, a meat-and-potatoes man, eyed the ingredients warily.

"I mean, if we're really talking about one service or the other being chosen as the rapid deployment force—only one—that means that the Marines and this big slice of the Army are fighting for a decreasing slice of the pie. One of them is going away. Can you imagine the pressures involved?"

"And the Army has decided to pin its hopes on Harlan Veir?"

"It looks like it."

"Based on one magazine article?"

"He has been a successful commander."

Sue Lynn chewed her lip. "You said that some Marine general got relieved trying to get an advantage, right? Who's to say that the Marines were the only ones trying to get a jump on things? I mean, suppose the Army is trying to do something similar with this whole Veir thing, making him a media darling, a celebrity, knowing all along how they were going to use him."

Isen shook his head, but he was not believing. "That's a stretch," he said. "But . . ."

"But it would explain why he feels invulnerable," Sue Lynn said.

She stepped into the dining room and knelt before a large wine rack, examining a half-dozen labels before selecting two bottles.

"What about General Flynn's comments on Savin's leave? You buy all that?"

"I buy it," Isen said. "I mean, I don't think he'd lie to me. But interfering with Savin's leave because he's cynical? That seems like an awful lot of trouble to go through, especially for a guy in the middle of burying his sister's son. He's backing off. Could be pressure from his boss, I guess."

Sue Lynn produced a two-pronged waiter's opener and, in a deft and practiced move, pulled one cork. Isen watched admiringly.

"You know, they have this stuff, wine in a box," he said,

smiling. "You slide it right in the fridge, has a little spigot right there so you don't have to mess around with a cork."

Sue Lynn gave him a lopsided grin. "Go ahead and make fun," she said, "and you'll be drinking tap water and sleeping on the floor."

She pulled two glasses from the cabinet. "So you think there's something with Savin?"

"Yeah. You know, it's funny that a lot of this came back to Savin. Savin doesn't like Veir or Flynn, and they don't like him."

"Could be that Savin blames them for what happened to Hauck," Sue Lynn said.

"Could be that Savin isn't just on the sidelines. I mean, if we believe everything that Sergeant Gabriel had to say, it could be that there was something between Hauck and Veir. Maybe Savin was involved, too."

Isen leaned on the counter, lost in thought. Sue Lynn handed him a glass of wine.

"In vino veritas," she said.

"Cheers," he answered.

They were silent for a while, lost in the possibilities as they moved about the kitchen. By the third glass of wine, the nagging questions had receded a bit. Their focus on preparing supper also faded as they traded kisses and caresses in the kitchen.

"You think you'll get married again, Mark?" Sue Lynn asked as he nuzzled her throat.

Isen leaned back, still holding her in his arms, to look at her face. This wasn't the first mention of his marriage, but it was the first mention of marriage in the future. Isen wondered if his leaving the next day might have something to do with this subject's coming up.

"I'd like to," he said. "The prospect is a little frightening, but I prefer being married to being single. What about you?" he asked.

"Oh, I don't know. There are times when I like having a man around."

She had backed up to the counter, leaning on one elbow so that her hips were thrust forward. Isen stepped up to her, putting his hands on the counter on either side of her.

"Now, would that be any man, as in man-as-interchangeable-part? Or did you have someone specific in mind?"

Sue Lynn licked her lips with a wine-darkened tongue. "Right now I had some*thing* specific in mind."

Some part of Isen told him that wasn't the answer he'd wanted to hear, but other parts of him jangled for attention.

"I swear I get half a dog on just listening to you talk sometimes."

Sue Lynn laughed and took him by the hand to lead him to the couch in the adjacent family room. She unzipped and stepped lightly out of her skirt, then pulled back the tails of her shirt to reveal white panties, cut high on the thigh. Isen groaned deep in his throat and knelt before her as she sat down. They had her panties down on one ankle when the phone rang.

"Don't even *think* about answering that," she said as she placed her hand on the back of his head.

The answering machine clicked on in the hallway. Isen, preoccupied, didn't recognize the voice, but Sue Lynn did.

"This is Jenny Milan. I have something important for you guys if you're there."

"Shit," Sue Lynn said, lifting her legs over Isen and placing her feet on the floor. Isen leaned his upper body across the couch.

"Jenny, this is Sue Lynn," Darlington said in the hallway. Then, after a pause, "Sure, I can put him on the other line."

Isen found the phone on the end table.

"Major Isen, are you there?" That musical voice. Jenny Milan's face floated before Isen's already-frenzied brain.

"Yes."

"I called to let you guys know I'm about to get on an airplane. I'm going to TDY. Tonight."

TDY was the Army's abbreviation for temporary duty, the equivalent of a business trip. And while it wasn't unheard of for soldiers to be called away suddenly, even on a Saturday night, Milan obviously thought there was too much coincidence here.

"Where are you going?" Sue Lynn asked.

"That's why I called you. My boss told me they just got a call from Washington, telling them to send an aviator to

Europe on the next thing out of here. Did you hear anything about that kind of requirement?"

Darlington worked in the Division Aviation Section, and while such requirements did not have to cleared with her, it was unlikely that Darlington or her boss wouldn't have heard something.

"Nothing."

"They asked for me by name," Milan said.

"Who did?"

"It came down from the Chief of Staff. Colonel Kent mentioned me by name."

Isen and Darlington exchanged looks across the room.

"Veir?" Darlington said.

"I think it started with him seeing me in your office," Milan said. "It really doesn't matter, though. I didn't call to complain. I wanted to pass along a few other things before I disappear for a while."

"Go on," Isen said. He was looking about for a paper and pen, but he was focusing on what kind of influence Veir must wield—or his protectors must wield—to make something like this happen.

"This guy Bennett," Milan said. "The one making the lewd comments to me? He hated Michael Hauck."

Isen nodded; Milan was corroborating what Savin had told him.

"How do you know that?" Sue Lynn asked.

"Bennett came up to me after I had talked to Hauck. Remember I told you I thought Hauck was shy? I talked to him for ten minutes or so at Harlan's house. Anyway, Bennett went on for a while about how Hauck was a pussy, a disgrace to the unit, all that kind of stuff. Bennett let on that Colonel Veir wanted him—Bennett—to straighten Hauck out."

"Bennett said that?" Isen asked.

"I don't remember his exact words," Milan said without faltering. "But there was no mistaking what he meant."

"OK," Isen said. "If you think of anything else, anything at all, give us a call. Collect."

Sue Lynn made a face at Isen from the hallway.

"If you think I'm footing the bill for you to talk to your

girlfriend," she said after Milan had hung up, "you're dead wrong."

"What are you talking about?" Isen protested.

Sue Lynn gave him a sarcastic look, then put her arms around his neck but didn't kiss him.

"Sounds like your buddy Harlan Veir can throw his weight around when he wants to."

"If it is Veir," Isen said. "Everything we're hearing is secondhand. There must be other people involved. He can't pull something like this off by himself."

"It's like I told you," Sue Lynn explained, "if Harlan Veir wants to attack, he'll have someone else punch you while he's smiling to your face. But that won't last long if you keep pushing his buttons."

"Well, whoever is helping him out isn't about to let some little aviator captain and some pudknocker Pentagon major get in the way of Veir's chance to save the Airborne from budget extinction."

Sue Lynn, still wearing only a shirt and bra, sat down on the couch once more, then traced the outlines of Isen's thighs with her naked feet.

"Where were we?" Sue Lynn asked as Isen knelt.

He kissed the inside of her knees. "I wonder why she didn't tell us about that thing with Bennett earlier," he said.

Sue Lynn hooked a leg over Isen's shoulder and pulled herself closer to the edge of the couch.

"Mmmm," she said.

He kissed her where she wanted to be kissed, then paused again. "And I'm a little suspicious about. . . ." he said.

"Look," she said, putting her fingers in his hair. "This is something we can talk about later, right?"

"Not the right time, sweetie?"

"Not the right time," she said. "If I want you to talk, I'll let go of the back of your head."

Sue Lynn smiled throughout physical training the following morning, reveling in the feeling of her heart beating, her lungs filling with air, the formation rolling along through the bright morning in boisterous, noisy enthusiasm. She laughed at the corny jokes in the ranks, smiled at the playfulness of the soldiers as they ran, she even smiled all the way through the run. It was a morning of sharp sunlight, everything crisp and new.

It's amazing what a little regular sex can do for your outlook on life, she thought.

There was no doubt about it, she was sweet on Mark Isen. He was, as she remembered him, a good person, honest and forthright. She enjoyed his company, thought he had a fine mind, and she even appreciated the little insecurities he displayed about their lovemaking. He had apologized, that first night, saying that it had been a long time for him. He hadn't actually come out and said "I hope it was good for you," something Sue Lynn couldn't stand, but he was clearly insecure about his performance. She had hugged him tightly and told him she could find nothing ... *absolutely* nothing to complain about.

Darlington left the formation, which didn't run far enough to challenge her. There were hundreds of other soldiers, in small groups and large, crisscrossing the division area. Sue Lynn found a comfortable pace and concentrated on relaxing as she ran.

Darlington knew that Isen was lonely, unhappy in his job and losing something of his identity as a soldier that had been so much a part of him when she knew him before. She told herself that she didn't mind filling that void, that desire for company—but she didn't want Isen to need her, didn't want that clinging possessiveness she found so smothering. She reminded herself that she was complete, self-contained, even when she was alone. She didn't want to be half of a relationship; she wasn't half a circle looking for her matching half, like the sweetheart trinkets teenagers wore.

A small voice somewhere in her consciousness raised an unwelcome question.

So why do you have to keep reassuring yourself?

Sue Lynn was afraid of being needed because she was afraid of needing.

After the PT run, she entered the headquarters building through the back door. A steady stream of headquarter types, most in sweaty PT uniforms, were coming and going. Sue Lynn looked up at one point and found herself behind Private Coates, Kent's clerk and driver.

"Are you Coates?" Sue Lynn asked.

Coates turned around. Isen had been right, she was gorgeous. "That's me," she said lightly.

"Hi," Sue Lynn said, extending her hand. "I'm Sue Lynn Darlington."

Darlington had no reason to believe that Coates would know her, even though they worked in the same building. In PT uniform, without insignia of rank, it was much easier to start up a conversation.

"Patty Coates."

"You work for Colonel Kent, right?"

"That's right," Coates said. The two women stopped in the hallway, where Coates pulled the sleeve of her T-shirt to wipe sweat from her eyes. In the parade of soldiers moving by, it seemed that every second man said hello to Coates.

I remember when that used to happen to me, Sue Lynn thought. *I didn't even realize it had stopped until just now, standing next to this woman.*

"How do you like working up there?"

"It's OK, I guess," Coates said. She ran her fingers through her hair, a nervous gesture. Two more men, walking by, said hello to her; Sue Lynn thought she heard Coates giggle.

"Sometimes I'd like to be someplace a little less ... visible."

"I know what you mean," Sue Lynn said. "Maybe I can help. You got a minute? My office is right down here."

Sue Lynn turned down one of the messy hallways that led to the Operations Section of her cubicle. Darlington opened the door and went in, but did not sit behind the desk. Instead she pulled one of the two visitor's chairs out into the little floor space.

"We could use some help down here," Sue Lynn said when they were in her office. "What would you rather be doing than working upstairs?"

"I'd rather be somewhere where I can work my way into a leadership position," Coates said earnestly. "That's what I want out of this Army experience."

Captain of the cheerleading squad, Sue Lynn thought. Then, in the next instance, *Stop being so catty.*

Coates pushed the door closed, then sat down in a chair in front of Sue Lynn's desk. If the major's insignia attached to Sue Lynn's desk nameplate made her uncomfortable, she wasn't showing it.

"But—" Coates bit off her sentence, shrugged.

"Do they have a good reason for keeping you up there?" Coates smiled.

"Besides, like, decoration, you mean?"

A breakthrough, Sue Lynn thought.

"Aren't they incredible?" Sue Lynn said, raising her voice. She took it as a matter of faith that Coates would know that the "they" in this case meant men.

"What really gets to me is that they think they're so subtle."

"And they think we can't hear all the comments they make," Coates added. She was becoming more animated as she talked. "Like, can you imagine if you were in here and you only kept around male clerks who were, you know, Chippendale material?"

"They'd have a cow." Sue Lynn laughed. "Of course, I don't have as much trouble as I used to, now that I'm getting a little older. And I doubt I ever garnered the kind of attention that you get."

"Officers go through this, too?" Coates asked, genuinely surprised.

"Absolutely," Sue Lynn said. "I have a friend who's an aviator, very pretty. And she's always getting hassled. She's treated differently, you know?"

"I sure do," Coates said sincerely.

"She just got pulled for TDY, all of a sudden, and she has no idea why."

"What's her name?" Coates asked

"Jenny Milan."

"Oh, yeah. Captain Milan. She's the one Colonel Kent sent over to Europe, right?"

"Exactly."

"I thought maybe she shot Kent down. Maybe Kent was trying to date her or something, even though he's *married."*

Coates stressed the last word as if the fact might have escaped Kent.

"What made you think that?"

"Well, it seemed like he went out of his way to make sure that she got sent overseas, you know? I typed the forms for him—something that's normally done down at Personnel—and he stood looking over my shoulder the whole time. I think he hand-carried the paperwork."

Coates pushed a strand of hair behind her ear, then leaned forward and whispered, conspiratorially, "Were they seeing each other?"

"Nah, I don't think so," Sue Lynn said. "Which makes me wonder why he was so personally interested."

"It happens every once in a while."

"Mmm," Sue Lynn said. "Maybe you'd like to come down here and take a look around when we have an opening."

"Oh, I don't know, ma'am. You don't even have any windows down here," she said.

Darlington shrugged, as if she'd been trying to hide that important fact. "Well, you got me there," she said.

Coates stood to leave. "You're friends with that major who came down here from the Pentagon, aren't you?"

"Mark Isen. Yes, I am."

"I thought I saw you two leaving the building together the other day. *He's* not high on Colonel Kent's list."

"What do you mean?"

"Colonel Kent keeps getting calls from that Colonel Veir guy." Coates made a face, as if she smelled something unpleasant. Sue Lynn thought it safe to assume that Veir had come on to Coates.

"And I've heard Major Isen's name mentioned a couple of times."

"In what way?"

"I'm not sure. I mean, I never heard the conversation, just the name. What's he doing down here?"

"Remember that lieutenant who killed himself a couple of weeks back? Well, Major Isen is down here on behalf of the family, trying to find out a little more about it."

"Oh," Coates said. "And that lieutenant was in Colonel Veir's battalion?"

"Right."

"Hmm," Coates said. "Well, I'd better get going. It was nice meeting you, Major. I'm sure we'll talk again."

"I'd like that," Sue Lynn said.

* * *

The contrast between what Isen saw at Bragg—the *real* Army, as he thought of it—and what was waiting for him at the Pentagon on Monday morning was startling. Isen spent the morning moving piles of papers from one side of his desk to another, trying to look busy, shuffling and reshuffling, making "To Do" lists that got longer and longer while he thought about Harlan Veir.

That's it, isn't it? he thought at one point. *You started off this whole thing thinking about Michael Hauck, but he isn't at the center of the story anymore.*

Isen pulled out the little spiral notebook he'd been using to record his notes. Just to satisfy his curiosity, he went through with a red, felt-tipped pen and circled Veir's name every time it appeared.

"The "V" Isen had used as shorthand for "Veir" appeared almost as many times as did the "H" he used for "Hauck."

Isen thought, *Either I'm making this all up because I'm pissed at him, which is what Flynn thinks, or Harlan Veir is really more at the center than I thought.*

He continued to flip through the book until he came to the page where he'd written the name of Veir's ex-wife.

Sara Collins Meade.

That'll go right to Veir, Isen thought. *Even if she tells me nothing, if he finds out about my talking to her, maybe that'll smoke him out.*

Lieutenant Colonel Tynan, Isen's boss, walked by Isen's cubicle. Isen kept his head down over a sheaf of papers centered on his desk. Tynan didn't stop. Isen felt a little foolish, a response that prompted an observation.

Maybe this is all because you're so fucking bored here, Isen, he thought. *Maybe you're so hard up for something to do that isn't Pentagon paperwork that you're inventing things. Even to the point of looking for a confrontation with Harlan Veir.*

There was no margin in trying to deny it: he was drawn to the fight, to the contest. Soldiers called it "marching to the sound of the guns." But like a doctor who will use extreme procedures on even the most forlorn patient, Isen had become interested in the battle for the battle's sake. The importance of Michael Hauck, even the importance of the truth—if ever there was such a thing—was fading. It was being replaced by an obsession.

The question now was: could he go on, obsession or no, and still serve the interests of Hauck's family, still serve the interests of what was right?

The answer to that lay with Harlan Veir.

Traveling from the city center of Philadelphia to the numbing repetition of the suburban sprawl that surrounds the city in all directions, it is easy to miss areas like Bryn Mawr. What was once the country is now sandwiched between the city and the suburbs. And caught there, pinched between the two distinct worlds, are those areas where wealthy city dwellers once fled the dirt, grime, and unpleasant social realities of the cities.

Bryn Mawr sits on a long, low ridge to the west of the city of Philadelphia in an area known as the Main Line. Sprawling stone homes dot heavily wooded countryside, and there are almost as many private schools and academies here, for the education of the privileged classes, as one finds parochial schools in other parts of a city populated by third- and fourth-generation immigrants from the Roman Catholic countries of Europe.

Mark Isen, following the theory that it is easier to ask forgiveness than to obtain permission, more or less played hooky from work on the Tuesday following his week-long stay at Fort Bragg. He had arranged to meet Sara Collins Meade, who had been surprisingly easy to track down through the offices of the local Episcopal charity. What really surprised Isen was the impression he got that Meade didn't think it at all unusual to receive a call from an Army officer who wanted to talk to her about her ex-husband. She had agreed to meet with him—the words she used were "receive him"—on Tuesday afternoon at her home in Bryn Mawr.

Isen followed Interstate 95 north to Philadelphia, skirting the downtown section on the traffic-clogged Schuylkill Expressway. Just past the tallest buildings of the city's center, the river widened through a beautiful park. Isen, traveling in bumper-to-bumper traffic at sixty miles an hour, got a fleeting glimpse of the dun-colored Museum of Art on a bluff on the opposite shore. Below that, Boathouse Row, a collection of ornate buildings housing the rowing clubs that used the wide, flat Schuylkill River for practice.

Three hours and fifteen minutes after leaving Washington's Beltway behind, Isen pulled up in front of an impressive stone building that reminded him of the high school he attended in Georgia. Only bigger. He checked the street address again as he stood beside his car, smoothed out the wrinkles in his khakis and set out up the long drive.

A beautiful woman answered Isen's knock.

"Major Isen," Meade said as she opened the wide door. "Please come in."

Sara Collins Meade reminded Isen of the women one saw in soft-toned portraits from the nineteenth century, something out of Edith Wharton.

Isen stepped inside, heard his heels rap the polished hardwood of a grand entry hall. Meade excused herself to finish a phone conversation on a nearby extension. Isen, nailed in place, looked around.

Bryn Mawr and Fort Bragg were on the same planet, in the same country, on the same coast, but they were light-years apart. He tried to imagine Veir, with his big, booming voice, his exaggerated physicality, entering a room like this in the company of a woman like Meade.

"I see that you were able to find us up here," she said, placing the receiver in the cradle and smiling brilliantly.

"The directions were right on the mark," Isen said.

Meade was about five six, Isen guessed, but her thin frame, her long, patrician neck and thick, straight hair drew pleasing vertical lines that made her seem taller. She had delicate features, a tiny, pointed chin, lively eyes and skin as smooth as a child's.

"Have you eaten lunch?" Meade asked.

Isen had wolfed down a pasty sandwich at a highway rest stop; but he didn't think that this was what Meade had in mind when she mentioned food.

"Yes, thank you," he said.

She led him through a long hallway, lined on either side with the kind of portraits one might expect in a library wing named for a philanthropic family.

"This is my favorite spot," she said, leading him at last

into a sun-washed room that seemed, at first glance, mostly glass. She sat on a wicker love seat, curling one leg under her. She wore a long pearl-colored shirt over tight black leggings; between the leggings and soft shoes, a thin ankle, exquisitely pale and delicate. Her hair, dark blond, was braided in a loose ponytail and tied with a thick velvet ribbon just below her neck.

Isen found an armchair, set at an angle to Meade across a low table decorated with fresh-cut flowers.

"That's a beautiful setting," Isen said.

Meade looked at his eyes for a moment, as if she were expecting some other comment to follow, as if surprised to hear a man, a soldier at that, say something about flowers.

"Thank you," she said. "I have a small garden out back, and I get some of my best blooms in the early fall." She leaned over, touched the flowers with the tips of her fingers, adjusting what didn't need adjusting.

"So you're not stationed at Fort Bragg?" she asked without preamble.

"No," Isen said. "I work at the Pentagon."

"Oh, how interesting," she said, a tiny smile that might have been sarcasm crossing her face. Isen didn't know how long she'd been married to Veir, but obviously she knew enough about the Army to know that the Pentagon was anything but a good assignment.

"What do you do there?"

"Mostly just push papers back and forth across my desk."

"Let me guess, you're one of those men who always want to be out in the field with the troops?"

"I'm afraid so," he said, smiling at her, still unsure if her smile was sincere.

"You mentioned on the phone that you were looking into a suicide. Was that in Harlan's unit?"

"Yes. A lieutenant in Colonel Veir's battalion killed himself a couple of weeks ago. I'm just trying to tie up a few loose ends after my look around down there."

"I see. And what has this to do with Harlan, other than the fact that the man was in his unit?"

Isen shifted in his chair. Meade, for all her soft good looks, cut right to the point.

"The young man's family was quite surprised by this, as

you might imagine. Michael Hauck—that was the dead man's name—seemed to be well adjusted and happy in his new life."

Isen was stumbling badly, and he knew it.

"There seems to be ... ah ... a lot of pressure on the officers in Colonel Veir's battalion, and ... I ..."

"And you want to know what kind of man Harlan Veir is."

"Yes. That's it," Isen said, relieved.

If you're going to screw this interview, might as well do it now and get it over with.

"Why should I help you?" Meade asked.

"I'm going to be frank with you. There are things that point to Harlan Veir's involvement. Colonel Veir runs things his way, and when people disagree with him, well, let's just say he doesn't take that well."

"No, he doesn't," Meade agreed.

"There may have been some tension between Veir and Hauck. I also know that Colonel Veir has quite a colorful reputation—"

"Well deserved," Meade interrupted.

"And I want to find out what kind of man I'm dealing with."

"Do you have evidence of some trouble between Harlan and this Lieutenant Hauck? Or is it just conjecture?"

You're gonna make me work for this, aren't you, lady?

"A little of both," Isen said.

"What is your impression of Harlan?" Meade asked.

"My impression isn't what's important," Isen said, thinking about the PT run. *I hate the bastard.* "I'm interested in hearing from the people who know him."

"Knew him," Meade corrected. "I haven't seen Harlan Veir in a year and a half." She looked directly at Isen as she spoke, but he thought her fingers were pressed hard against the arms of the love seat.

"And I think your opinion of Harlan counts for quite a bit," she continued. "If you didn't think Harlan was somehow involved—more than just the coincidence of being the boy's commander—you probably wouldn't have gone to all the trouble of tracking me down."

Isen didn't respond.

"Why should I help you?"

"I thought about that all the way up here," Isen said. "And I didn't come up with an answer. About all I can say is that I'm trying to find some answers that will ease the pain of this young man's family. And I think some of the answers may lie with Harlan Veir."

Meade looked at him for a long count.

On the drive north, Isen had actually thought that Meade might want a little revenge. But now, in this sumptuous home with this cultured woman, the notion seemed tawdry.

"What do you want to know?"

Everything, Isen thought.

"How long were you married?"

"Six years," she said. Meade shifted her weight, pulled at the bottom hem of her long shirt, looking uncomfortable for the first time.

"This story has enriched a half-dozen therapists," she said, smiling nervously. "And you're getting it for free."

Isen didn't think it a time to crack wise.

"Would you like a drink?" Meade asked, standing.

Isen wondered if a house like this would have beer. Maybe in the servants' quarters. "I could go for a beer if you have one."

"Of course." Meade walked to a bar at one end of the room, no small distance from the sitting area they occupied. Isen studied her as she walked. She was a fine-looking woman, beautiful in a reserved way, and the antithesis of everything he knew about Harlan Veir.

Isen stood and looked out on the back lawn. He thought he could see the edge of a flower bed at the bottom of a gentle slope some fifty meters away. Two wide oaks guarded the hill, dipping heavy branches, all but hiding a generous gazebo that sat above the garden.

"This is a beautiful home," Isen said.

Master of the cliché, he thought.

"Thank you," she said, her voice made small by the distance. "It's been in my family for several generations."

Isen heard the clicking of glass and metal, turned to see Meade handling a silver shaker. She was mixing a martini.

"We used to fill it up with family and friends, back when my parents were living. Wonderful holiday celebrations."

She delivered a small tray set with a frosted mug and a bottle of expensive imported beer, then served him unself-consciously.

"I can remember, as a girl, playing in this room when the snow fell. It was quite beautiful."

"I can imagine," Isen said.

Meade lifted her drink, pursing her lips delicately, barely touching the thin rim of the martini glass.

"I can remember sitting in a bar some years ago, ribbing a friend for ordering a martini," Isen said. "I told him it sounded like a sissy drink."

Meade smiled. "To which he said?"

" 'Sissy drink, huh? Take a little ol' swallow and see what you think then.' So, striving to be a manly man, I shot back a hefty gulp. When I stopped coughing, I said, 'OK, it just *sounds* like a sissy drink.' "

Meade laughed—a delightful chime. She didn't move one exquisite eyelash as she sipped, and Isen guessed at the conditioning that must have gone into that kind of control.

"I think all of this," she said, sweeping her arm in a small arc that couldn't even take in the whole sitting room, "is what attracted Harlan in the first place."

She wasn't talking about the money, Isen knew. She was talking about status.

"Harlan wanted to move beyond his background," she said. "The Army gave him a big jump on that. Bryn Mawr, as he saw it, would put him over the top." She smiled, a pitiful upturning at the corners of her mouth.

"The article in *Newsweek* talked about his background, said he came from 'humble roots.' "

"Fiction," Meade said. "Harlan grew up in suburbia. But he knew, when he was talking to that reporter, what would make better copy. He exaggerated his hardships quite a bit. He's not beyond doing that; he's nothing if not smooth, especially when talking to women."

Isen thought about Veir and the dancer, bent over the fender of his truck in the parking lot outside Jiggles. Nothing smooth or subtle there.

"The only woman he couldn't charm was his mother," Meade said. "He was a completely different person on the few occasions when I saw him around her. She was very strict, in a hardshell Baptist way. Very strict. Harlan wasn't allowed to date when he was a teenager; she thought all the girls he knew were harlots ... that was the word she used. Harlots. To describe little high school girls.

"When Harlan was around her, all his self-confidence and bluster vanished. It was really the most remarkable transformation I'd ever seen. She'd sit at the dinner table and talk about damnation and ask him if he'd sinned ... and it didn't matter who was present. She thought nothing of embarrassing him like that.

"The first time I was in her company was after Harlan and I were engaged. The very first words out of her mouth—after I said, 'Pleased to meet you'—were 'Are you whoring with my son? 'Cause if you are, there's room in hell for both of you.' Can you imagine?"

Meade shifted in her chair, just a slight tensing of her legs and torso.

"When he was away from her, he was a different man. Harlan was so handsome, and so unlike any of the boring ... *vanilla* boys I knew from the schools, from the clubs around here. None of my parents' friends had sons like him.

"The most daring thing I did before I met Harlan was to go pool-hopping with a bunch of teenagers. Pool-hopping. Around here."

She wiped her mouth delicately with a tiny napkin. "Can you imagine how little danger there was in that? Why, I think we knew everyone whose pool we hopped into.

"But Harlan was different. Rough, daring, everything my world here wasn't."

"How did you meet?"

Isen realized, as he said it, that this question had been on his mind since he'd walked in. Women like Sara Collins Meade didn't hang out in Officers' Club bars. At least not in any club Isen had been in.

"My family has a house on Long Beach Island, not too far from here," she said. "I was on the beach one day, reading, watching the surf, when I saw this man swimming nearby." She paused, sipped her drink. She was keeping up with Isen, who was drinking only beer.

"Have you met Harlan?"

"Yes."

"He's very handsome," she said. "And has always been a terrific physical specimen."

Specimen, Isen thought. *There's a word that fits.*

"I guess he noticed me watching him; so he walked out of the water, right up to me, and stood there, dripping salt water onto my feet until I looked up at him."

Isen wasn't surprised that this had been Veir's technique. He was surprised that Meade had allowed him to get close. Isen decided that he already knew more about Veir than he ever would about women.

"We became lovers almost immediately," she said.

Isen swallowed, trying to keep his face impassive.

"Surprised?"

"Yes."

"Not as surprised as I was. But it was the most exciting time of my life. He courted me wildly. Letters, flowers, calls at all hours of the night. I didn't let him meet my family, didn't let him know . . . well . . . let's just say that my family's money had proven a liability in meeting men."

"I can understand."

"I was a little old to be going through the rebellious stage, sneaking around without my parents' knowledge, but there I was. Harlan invited me to visit him in Washington. He was with the Old Guard then. He treated me wonderfully."

Her voice had become soft, sensuous, and Isen imagined the riotous images playing out in her head as she paused, fixing her eyes on the window before her.

"Later, of course, when it was too late, I realized that all the things I saw then, all the things I thought were so exciting, weren't the qualities I should have been looking for in a husband. A lover, yes. A husband, no."

She turned away from Isen and walked back to the bar, where a small pitcher of martinis stood in a puddle of condensation. She poured herself another.

"He had his first affair less than a year after we were married. But I'm sure he'd been fooling even while we were engaged.

"My father was sick then, and looking back, I think my engagement to Harlan hastened his death."

Isen expected her to cry at this point, to at least wipe

away a tear at the admission. Instead, she opened a fresh jar of olives and plopped two into her refilled glass.

Isen, sure that his face gave him away this time, nodded.

"His lieutenants have parties at clubs in Fayetteville," he said evasively, thinking again about Veir holding the dancer bent over the hood of his truck.

"I could never understand that," she said. "Don't get me wrong. Prudish though I may be, I do understand why men go to those places, but I could never understand Harlan. He had half of the wives on any post offering themselves to him—this big, mouthy figure with the great body. And he helped himself plenty, believe me. But he had something for those other women, too."

Isen wondered if any of those vaunted and no doubt expensive therapists had told her what he was thinking. *Your husband was a pig who probably kept you around for some semblance of respectability. The question is, why did you keep him around?*

"Anyway, he never could see how he belittled himself with those women he paid for. He made a fool of himself, pursuing cheap whores and strippers, twenty-year-olds who'd take his money and laugh at him behind his back. He was looking for something they couldn't give him and I couldn't give him and all the slutty wives on post couldn't give him no matter how much they spread their legs."

That comment was a bit sharp, and she must have realized that just as Isen was thinking it, because she resettled herself, pulling back a bit. Her speech would never degenerate into that ribald patois that pervaded so much of the Army, the talk of men who are as aggressive in their language as they believe they must be in everything. Many women picked it up; Meade, Isen thought, was at too much of a remove to slide that far.

Isen hadn't seen her pour the third drink, but it was there in her glass and in her speech and her posture. Almost invisible, well hidden.

"What was that?" Isen asked.

He wasn't sure if Meade heard him; she seemed unfocused.

"Pardon?"

"You said he was looking for something that none of

those women could give him," Isen said quietly. "What was he looking for?"

Meade studied her hands; a small, nervous smile came and went.

"I thought it was about sex, you know? At first I thought maybe there was something wrong with me as a lover. But it turned out that wasn't it at all. It was all about his flouting the rules, about seeing how much he could get away with, what outrageous things he could do. Sex was just the vehicle; he was after the thrill of breaking the rules, getting away with it, always proving to himself that he was better, above average, special."

"How *did* he get away with it all?"

"I used to wonder that myself," Meade said. "Certainly there were times when timid commanders looked the other way, something made easier by the fact that Harlan's job performance has always been outstanding. It was almost as if, once he established a pattern of getting away with things, he was suddenly charmed. You hear stories of men who go through a whole war without a scratch; Harlan was one of those men.

"When we first started dating, I used to call him my Greek god, because of his looks. Later I realized he was more of a character from a Greek tragedy, headed for disaster he cannot see, cannot avoid. But I had my problems, too."

Isen squirmed. If Meade had had retaliatory affairs, he didn't want to hear about them.

"For the longest time I couldn't see that what he was doing was demeaning me, as well. I forgave him for years, telling myself that he had this need for the thrill, that it wasn't about loving or not loving me.

"He filled a need for me, too, you see. I had to fix things, make things better. I convinced myself that I was the one who could make him change. My love was so strong, my perceptions so keen, my caring so unique, that I alone could save him."

Meade smiled. "Quite an ego trip, don't you think?"

She was quiet for a moment, staring at her hands. "I was a fool." She fixed Isen's gaze. "I did have my moment, though."

When he didn't respond, she asked, "You heard about me, didn't you?"

"I'm not sure what you mean."

She pushed her eyebrows together in a dainty scowl that passed quickly.

"The Zippo Lady."

Isen shook his head.

"How quickly our glory fades," she said. "When we were stationed at Bragg he went TDY to Washington, and I heard from one of the other wives—who heard it from her husband—that Harlan had taken up with a cocktail waitress. He was *living* with her."

She pulled herself up straight in her seat.

"The first day Harlan was back the little strumpet called my home—can you believe that?"

Isen shook his head. "Pretty nervy," he said. Actually, he'd run across several similar incidents over the years.

"So I called Harlan at his office. When he answered I shouted into the phone, 'Hurry home, there's a fire.' Then I hung up."

She paused again, for effect.

"He pulled up to the curb a few minutes later, and you could see he was confused. There were no fire trucks, just me standing in the driveway, where I had piled all of his clothes and uniforms. Big pile. Three feet high. I had soaked the whole thing in gasoline. When he got out of the car, I torched the whole pile."

Isen blinked. He wanted to laugh; he wanted to applaud; he was afraid to make a sound.

"It was magnificent."

She moved to a stool; one side of her hair had slipped out of the black ribbon, a few gentle tendrils unraveling beside her face. Isen wondered if she lived alone in this big house.

They sat quietly like that for a few minutes, and Isen became aware of the ticking of a large grandfather clock he'd passed in the hallway, just outside the sitting room. Empty ticking.

"Another time, just a few months later, I caught him red-handed," she said after a pause. "In my house. The house I paid for. My bed."

Her anger had grown larger, filling the room, but without the histrionics Isen might have expected from her ex-husband. This was justifiable, white-hot.

"I walked into the bedroom, and he was on top of this ... this woman. This young woman. Just humping away."

Meade smiled, which Isen found strangely unsettling.

"She was looking at the ceiling with this terrible look of boredom on her face, like she couldn't wait for him to finish."

She'd been looking at the flower arrangement; now she met Isen's eyes.

"I swear, if she'd have been wearing a watch, she would have been looking at it." She snorted. a derisive laugh. "I didn't know whether to laugh or cry."

Meade took another healthy swallow of her drink. Isen sat quietly.

"Anyway, I kicked him out. Right then and there. Him and his little honey. Hired a couple of good lawyers who made sure he got absolutely nothing. *That* really got to him."

"He expected to get money?" Isen asked.

"Yes, but that wasn't what bothered him. What got to him was that I was calling the shots. Well, the lawyers and I. Harlan likes to control things. No matter what it takes."

9

GENERAL FLYNN MET ISEN AT THE DOOR TO THE SCREENED
porch that wrapped around his quarters.

"Hey, Mark," he said, opening the door for the younger
man.

"Evening, sir."

"I thought we'd sit out here, catch a little bit of a breeze."

Fort Myer, home to the Army's Chief of Staff and dozens
of other high-ranking officers, and adjacent to the big tourist
draw of Arlington National Cemetery, received a lot of public scrutiny and so was among the most formal posts in the
Army. Its immaculately groomed lawns and gingerbread
brick buildings—no doubt the vision of the Army that a
schoolboy Michael Hauck would have taken away from visits with his uncle—were a far remove from the seedy bars
and strip joints of rural North Carolina. Here, within walking distance to the Pentagon, even general officers couldn't
hang out on the front porch of their own quarters in a pair
of cut-off pants and a T-shirt. Flynn was dressed down in a
pair of chinos and a short-sleeved madras shirt.

"Beer?"

"That'd be great, sir."

Flynn seemed subdued, his voice a bit heavier than usual. Isen's first thought was that the old man had had a fight with Mrs. Flynn, who packed the same fiery Irish temperament that her husband carried and who was not the least bit intimidated by him. That might also explain why they hadn't gone inside.

"How was your visit to Philadelphia?" Flynn asked.

Isen reported what he had learned from Meade. He ended, as she had done, with the story about the Zippo Lady.

"Sounds like a piece of work," Flynn said.

"She's not the kind of woman who's used to being pushed around."

"So why did she put up with Veir's bullshit? All that running around."

"She thought she was going to save him from himself," Isen said. "In a way, she was stroking her own ego. She knew his problems were huge, but she thought she would be able to get through to him. At least, that's the way she explained it to me."

"Huh," Flynn grunted, mildly surprised at the very simple explanation for such dysfunctional behavior.

"And what about Veir? What drives him?" Flynn wanted to know.

"According to Meade—and I have to say I agree with her so far—Veir is always out to prove himself. He's done that on the conventional playing field: he's a success in the Army. I think he gets bored and so draws new boundaries, new places and ways to prove himself.

"Meade said that even with all the running around, it wasn't about sex. It was about flouting the rules and getting away with it."

Flynn swirled his drink: Irish whiskey, neat. "And what did you think about that?"

"Sounds like the Harlan Veir we know," Isen said. "And that's more or less what his old girlfriend told me," Isen said.

Flynn nodded. "I've seen it happen," he said. "But tell me something, Mark. Why are you spending so much energy on Veir? Was he there when Michael shot himself?"

"He was in the club that night and I know he talked to

Michael. Savin thought that Michael had some problem with Veir. And this Captain Dennison, Mike's company commander, told Michael not to make waves."

Isen had called Flynn that day with details of his talk with Dennison and the visit from Sergeant Gabriel.

"Are you saying that Michael had something against Veir?"

"Or something on him," Isen said. "I mean, maybe Veir did something so outrageous that Michael just couldn't look the other way. Now we have this young sergeant coming out and saying that there are rumors going around about Michael."

"That Michael was a homosexual," Flynn said, pronouncing the word "homa-sex-ule."

"Right."

"So if Michael had something on Veir, maybe Veir or someone else threatened Michael with exposure—even though there was nothing to expose—to keep him quiet."

"Yes, sir. That's what I was thinking."

Flynn sat quietly; he seemed a bit overwhelmed. Isen had to admit it was quite a story; he pressed his point, trying not to sound like an alarmist.

"Even if Veir didn't know about the rumors, he created the atmosphere where that kind of back-stabbing is rampant. Veir fostered cutthroat competition in his battalion, and in that kind of environment, things could get nasty."

"But you told me that Veir said he hadn't heard any of those rumors, right?"

"Yes, sir, that's what he said. But he could be bullshitting; he's certainly capable of lying to cover his ass. I think he lied about meeting Savin at the club; he lied to his wife all the time. But here's the real clincher: I doubt if anything goes on in that battalion that Harlan Veir doesn't know about. Nobody down there moves without thinking about how it will look to the boss.

"I think it bears some more looking, sir. Special Agent McCall wouldn't reveal any names, which makes me think Michael's gay friends were GIs. I mean, if they were civilians, it wouldn't matter if she named them. I think the chances are good that someone in uniform knew something, knew if Michael was vulnerable."

"Great, we're about to uncover a whole cabal," Flynn said. He paused, shook his head. "Look, Mark, I'm not convinced I want to carry all of this to my sister, all the rumors about Michael, that is. And if I'm not going to make anything of it, I'm not sure I want to uncover any more."

Isen was shocked. Flynn was a fighter if nothing else, and here it looked as if he was about to give up before the battle was seriously joined.

"And I'm not so sure there isn't a bit of vendetta between you and Veir, something you want to settle with him because he embarrassed you on that run."

Isen bristled. He realized then that Sue Lynn had been right as to why Flynn had chosen him. Isen knew that people expected him to do what was right, and he was putting his career in jeopardy to do so. Now he was on the horns of a dilemma: either he had been wrong, and was wrong, and he was acting out of petty self-interest in trying to settle this score; or Flynn was backing down because he was getting pressure from above or because he didn't want to find out anything unpleasant about his nephew.

"May I speak frankly, sir?"

Flynn looked at him levelly. "I wouldn't expect anything else."

"I'm not going to try to bullshit you, sir. I don't like Veir. The guy is a prick, no doubt about it. But I'd like to think that that wouldn't be enough to make me want to get him, so to speak. I've met lots of pricks in the Army I didn't investigate.

"Nor have I stopped looking at Bennett and Foote and some of the others. But I really think that there may be more to Veir's involvement than his just getting the ball rolling with a little competition. I also think—and I hope I'm not going too far here—that one of the reasons you might want me to lay off is because you don't want to know whatever else McCall has found out about your nephew's sexuality."

Something dark passed over Flynn's face, and Isen thought that he had gone too far.

Fuck it, he thought. *I said what needed to be said.*

"Now you're making invalid assumptions, Mark."

Flynn shifted in his chair, and Isen had the distinct impression that the general was struggling to hold back his anger.

"My nephew was *not* a homosexual," Flynn said. "But he refused to see that people will tear you down. And all it takes is an accusation, a rumor, to tarnish a career, a . . ."

Flynn trailed off. Isen thought, *tarnish a family?*

"As for backing off of Veir, I'm not convinced that you understand the gravity of this—even this unofficial investigation." Flynn went on. "I know you want to do what is right, but you have to weigh the usefulness of your investigation. Just asking these kinds of questions puts Veir in jeopardy. Is that fair to do? Has he done anything so onerous that we can afford to come in and ride roughshod over the life he's built over the last twenty years?"

This was not a new light. Isen had said all of this to Sue Lynn, but it was a surprise to hear Flynn say it.

"I see your point, sir, and I've considered as much myself. I have tried to be careful with Veir's reputation, and maybe there's room for me to try a little harder."

Isen leaned forward in his chair, elbows on knees.

"But you just mentioned one of the things that really gets me about this—and is probably the whole reason I'm so hot about this stuff. It isn't right to bully people with gossip, to threaten people with character assassination. It's small-minded and wrong. Someone did it to me once and it could be that someone did it to Michael."

Flynn looked at Isen levelly.

"I'm sure that's Veir's point of view; it looks like you're doing that very thing to him."

"I'm sure it does," Isen said. "Look, sir, I'm not saying I can't make mistakes. I'm saying that in this case, I think I'm right."

They sat face-to-face and passed a long half minute like that. Isen felt as if he were sliding backwards down a long slope.

"I want to go back down there and talk to the dancers who were at the party when Michael shot himself, as well as the girls who worked the other parties. They might be able to tell me something new about what was going on, and it's not like they have any influence on Colonel Veir's reputation."

"That seems like a long shot, doesn't it?"

"It might be, yes sir. But I think it's worth a try."

"I'm not sure if I can spring you out of here anymore," Flynn said.

"Have you been told to leave Veir alone?" Isen asked.

"Let's just say that my judgment in sending you down there has been questioned. But the more we push, the more likely we are to attract attention."

"I'd just need a three-day pass, sir. I could leave on Thursday afternoon."

What Isen didn't say was that his boss was going to be out of the office all day Thursday. He planned on leaving at lunchtime. No sense getting the old man all worked up about something like quitting time, especially since Flynn seemed to be getting a little squirrely.

"OK, OK." Flynn sighed. He went inside for a few moments, returning with his billfold and four crisp one-hundred-dollar bills.

"You'll need this."

"Thanks, sir," Isen said.

"I hope we're doing the right thing," Flynn said.

Isen smiled, trying to be reassuring.

I hope so, too, he thought.

On Wednesday afternoon Isen called a buddy who was serving in the Old Guard. Staff Sergeant Tony Cipriotti, who'd served with Isen in Hawaii, returned the call two hours later.

"The Sergeant Major said he was here when this Colonel Veir was a company commander with the Guard. He didn't like the guy, and he made some comment about what he called 'that stupid fucking magazine article.' But he really didn't want to talk much about Veir."

"Do you think I could talk to the Sergeant Major?" Isen asked.

"I don't think he's interested," Cipriotti said. "He said Veir doesn't deserve all these kudos, but he didn't see the margin in badmouthing him."

Isen let his breath out sharply. "Another dead end," he said.

"Not quite," Cipriotti went on. "The Sergeant Major gave

me the name of a retired master sergeant who lives out by Manassass who knew Veir pretty well. He said he thought this guy—his name's Trewick—would be glad to talk to you."

"Thanks, Tony," Isen said.

"Hey, anything to help out the old man," Cipriotti said. "Say, what exactly are you doing with yourself these days, sir?"

"Driving a desk, mostly."

"I mean with all this stuff. Snooping around unpopular officers?"

"That's a good goddamned question, Tony." Isen laughed. "If I figure out what I'm doing I'll be sure to let you know."

Isen drove the short distance to Manassas, Virginia, famous as the site of the first major battle of the Civil War. Washington civilians, driving carriages and carrying picnic baskets, had ridden out to see what they thought would be a glorious show in the clash of armies. They ended the day in the tangle of men and equipment streaming back to the city after the rout of the Federal forces. It often seemed to Isen that the civilians in Washington, particularly in Congress, still had no appreciation of what they were asking when they sent soldiers into battle.

At precisely eighteen hundred hours, Master Sergeant Stanley Trewick, U.S. Army (Retired) occupied a bar stool in the small roadside tavern he'd named when Isen phoned him.

"Master Sergeant Trewick?" Isen said as he approached.

Trewick was about fifty years old, with a broad chest, a salt-and-pepper brushcut and the recruiting poster looks the Old Guard favored. Isen had no trouble picking him out.

"That's right," Trewick said, standing to shake Isen's hand. "Call me Stan."

"Great. I'm Mark Isen. I appreciate your coming out to see me."

Trewick waved his hand in dismissal. "The only reason I agreed was because I recognized the name. I served with your old man at Benning. How's he doing?"

"He passed away almost two years ago," Isen said.

"I'm sorry to hear that. He was a good soldier."

Isen nodded. He had often heard his father, a career NCO, described in exactly those terms. "A good soldier." He wondered what his father would think of Harlan Veir.

Isen pulled himself up onto a bar stool and ordered a club soda.

"I understand you want to talk about Harlan Veir," Trewick said. He was drinking draft beer from a frosted mug. "You're not one of these people trying to make a hero out of him, are you?"

From the tone in his voice, it was clear that Trewick wasn't a fan.

"No," Isen said. He gave a brief explanation of his mission to Fort Bragg, and about some of the comments made by people who knew Veir.

"Yeah, he liked to push the rules all right. I could never understand why that beautiful wife of his put up with his crap."

"They're divorced now," Isen said, feeling as if Meade needed defending. "When I spoke to her she told me about his affairs and so on. I figured someone like that, someone that intent on bending the rules, probably bent a few rules on duty as well."

"Why do you want this information?"

"Because I have a feeling that Michael Hauck, the kid who killed himself, might have seen something he didn't think was right. Maybe he wanted to report it and ... well, who knows?"

Trewick drained his mug and held up a finger to order another.

"You want another club soda?"

"No."

When the draft came, Trewick scraped at the frosted mug with a fingernail.

"Harlan Veir operated by his own set of rules," Trewick said. "I was his first sergeant when he was a captain, a new company commander at the Guard. From the first day, we didn't get along. He was more interested in looking good than in being good. I was pretty sure he falsified training records—fixing up shooting scores and stuff like that—so the company would look better and he'd look better."

"Did you ever challenge him on it?" Isen asked.

"Sure," Trewick said. "About three weeks after he took command the unit started this big marksmanship competition. He had been bragging to the colonel how all of his lieutenants were going to fire these great scores. He made a bet with the other company commanders, really talked it up. Now, I wasn't there to see everyone shoot, but two of the lieutenants in the company who's never done anything better than barely qualify with their weapons were suddenly on the roster as 'experts.' I asked Veir about it and he said he was satisfied with the scores."

"Was it possible that they had a good day at the range?" Isen asked.

"Two of the buck sergeants working the range that day said the scores were cooked. But they weren't sure."

Trewick was silent for a moment, staring into his beer.

"It was usually stuff like that. Hard-to-prove stuff. He was sneaky, no doubt about it."

"Was he concerned that you were on to him?"

Trewick shook his head. "Nah. Somebody like Veir keeps getting away with stuff, he keeps trying more stuff."

That's the pattern, Isen thought.

"I had twenty-one years in when he took command," Trewick said, leaning back on his stool. "I had seen a few things, you know? Kind of thought I'd seen it all. But Veir proved me wrong."

There was a bitterness in Trewick's voice, anger tinged with surprise, perhaps, that this had all happened to him.

"This kind of stuff went on for about a year, a little more. He'd lie and cheat and then cover his tracks. It was like he led a charmed life. I'm not even sure the other officers in the battalion, the ones he was fucking over to get ahead, knew they were being screwed. Veir always came up looking good. That was the thing he did best: he looked good. The unit performed, and there were good NCOs and junior officers who made things work. He wasn't incompetent; he was actually pretty good at his job. It was just that he had no scruples.

"It got to the point where I could barely stand to talk to him, which is hardly the ideal relationship between the two people running an infantry company. I felt like the troops were suffering. So I went to the Sergeant Major, who knew all about my complaints, and told him I didn't think I could do this any more. I guess he went to the Colonel, and I had a feeling that everything was coming to a head. But Veir came in the next day smiling and laughing like nothing happened; and the Sergeant Major said the Colonel was pleased with Veir's performance."

"I figured I had five or six months left as First Sergeant, and all I had to do was ride things out."

Trewick smiled ruefully and raised his eyebrows as if still surprised that all this happened to him.

"But I had crossed Veir, and he wasn't about to let that slide. He doesn't like people to cross him."

Trewick paused, and Isen had occasion to wonder how many Michael Haucks and Stan Trewicks were in Veir's past.

"There was this kid in the company," Trewick said. "Not a great soldier, but with the potential, you know. All he needed was someone to take an interest in him, show him the right way to do things. As far as I knew, Veir had never really noticed him until a rumor started going around that the kid was a homo."

Trewick betrayed nothing with his use of the word *homo*. Apparently, he had covered everything that was important to him when he said the kid had the makings of a good soldier.

"So I made arrangements to have the kid transferred out of the line company and up to headquarters. There was nothing but rumors, you understand, but those were the days when ... well, I'm sure you saw people, good people, hounded out. This kid hadn't done anything wrong, exactly, at least nothing anyone could prove. And at that point he still wanted to stay in the Army. So I told him I'd get him this job up at headquarters and he'd have a chance to clear his name if he worked hard.

"But Veir wasn't going for it. I don't think he cared one way or the other if the kid was queer. I think he saw a way to get to me."

Isen nodded; that assessment fit what he knew about Veir.

"Veir started some rumors among the troops up in headquarters, and they started giving this kid—his name was Quigley—a hard time. Messing up his room and equipment, tripping him, shoving him around, threatening him. So Quigley comes to me and says he wants out of the Army; but the only way to do that is for him to admit he's gay, and he isn't ready for that.

"I went to Veir and asked him if he knew anything about the harassment."

Trewick stopped talking. His mug was empty, and he held the glass between his fingers as he stared at the bar.

"What did he say?"

"He asked me why I was trying to protect this kid," Trewick answered. "Implying that I had more of an interest than I was letting on."

Isen shook his head. Veir the manipulator.

"So the harassment continued, and got worse. One night Quigley ends up in the infirmary after falling down the steps in the barracks. So the next day I hear he's getting a discharge, that Veir had greased the skids. I went to Veir and told him I thought he was behind it all, the beatings, the threats, everything. He told me I should talk to Quigley before I went to the Sergeant Major or the Colonel.

"When I went to see Quigley, he wouldn't talk to me, wouldn't even look at me for the longest time."

Isen shifted his weight on the stool, which squeaked loudly.

"Finally he said that he had to get out, that he was afraid of going back to the barracks. Veir was going to help him."

Trewick turned and looked directly at Isen.

"Veir told him that he wouldn't have to admit that he was gay. But there was a trade."

Isen took shallow breaths.

"Veir had gotten Quigley to make a statement, in front of a witness, that I had propositioned him, made a sexual advance. He got Quigley to say that I had taken care of him, had him transferred, in exchange for the promise of sex."

"But who the hell would believe such a bullshit story?"

Even as he asked, Isen knew the answer; it didn't matter. The mere rumor, just the question, was quite enough. That may have been the lesson Michael Hauck learned.

Trewick shrugged by way of response.

"Why would Quigley say those things?" Isen wanted to know. "Especially after you tried to help him."

"Veir told Quigley that if he cooperated, Veir would get him out of the service. I could get out with my retirement, and nothing bad would happen. If Quigley didn't cooperate, Veir was going to see that Quigley got transferred back to one of the line companies."

Trewick smiled, still surprised at the audacity.

"He told this kid if he went back to a line company, he'd get his ass beat every night and the next time he took a fall down the steps, he'd wind up with a broken neck."

"What did you do?" Isen asked.

Trewick shrugged.

"The kid was scared to death, and I was tired of fighting Veir. Besides that, I figured he just might kill Quigley.

"I retired within thirty days," Trewick said. He raised his hand, signaling the bartender for another beer.

"The worst thing was that I thought getting out would be a relief. But as soon as the door was closed I realized I'd made a mistake. I guess I could have fought him. I thought about putting in for a transfer, but Veir let me know that the story would follow me. And at the time it seemed like this kid was really in some sort of danger."

"What happened to Quigley?" Isen asked.

"Don't know. Just disappeared."

When the bartender brought a fresh mug, Trewick took a long sip.

"The parallels are pretty remarkable, wouldn't you say?"

"Incredible," Isen said.

"I'd say there's a good chance that this kid—what was his name?"

"Michael Hauck."

"I'd say there was a good chance that Hauck saw something wrong, just because Veir does so much that's wrong. Now, I don't know how you get from there to this kid shooting himself in the parking lot of a strip joint, but it seems to me there's a better-than-average chance that Harlan Veir is mixed up in it."

Isen was thinking about other parallels. The pattern was sudden escalation. Veir would keep playing his games and allow himself to be pushed up to a point. Then he'd strike back. Hard, vicious. Isen wondered when, in his own battle with Veir, the gloves would come off.

Trewick lifted his mug in a toast. "And I, for one, hope you're around long enough to pull it all together."

Isen was happy to see, when he went into the office on Thursday morning, that his boss was indeed out for the day. Isen spent a few hours in the morning clearing one or two projects off his desk. He had forgotten, in his time shuffling papers, what a real mission felt like; and now he felt refreshed, enlivened.

He tidied up his station a bit, then decided to head down to the snack bar to pick up a bagel.

"Roger, you want something from downstairs?" Isen asked his neighbor.

Major Roger Smith, the self-described oddball in the office, was hunched over his tiny desk in the adjacent cubicle. Tall and thin, almost emaciated—he often forgot to eat—he favored decidedly unmilitary black cardigan sweaters, which he was always wearing outside of the office against the express guidance of Colonel Tynan.

"Nah," Smith said, pushing away from his desk. He rolled his chair the full seven inches to the divider behind him and raised his arms to shoot a piece of crumpled paper at the trash can. Isen moved to block the shot, but Smith hit his mark.

"Face it, Isen," Smith said. "You're spending entirely too much time away from the office here, neglecting your duties and your trash can basketball. One might begin to think you actually wanted a life outside of the Pentagon."

"How would you know there's life out there? We don't even have a window."

"Ah, yes," Smith said. "But I'm not about to be thwarted. I recently took a look at my *official* Army file, you see, and I noted that some clerk had entered 'married' under marital status."

"Yes?"

"So I began to suspect that these people"—Smith lifted a photograph, a family portrait of him, his wife, and two kids, off the cluttered surface of his desk—"I began to suspect that these people were in some way related to me."

He studied the picture in his hand, squinting at it through narrowed eyes.

"But I honestly can't recall ever having met them."

"Hey, at least you're about done with your tour here," Isen said. "I won't be out of here for years."

"Does that mean you're not making a break for it today?"

Isen looked around. He had told no one of his plans to leave early.

"Not necessarily," he said. "What makes you think I'm leaving?"

"You've been smiling all morning, and I don't think it's just because the beloved leader is gone for the day."

Smith studied him closely, standing and approaching to within inches.

"I think you got laid down there at Bragg. What's more, I think you're headed back."

Isen smirked.

Smith declared, "I knew I was right. Which one did I get right? Both?"

"Both," Isen said. "General Flynn was supposed to try to spring me for a three-day pass, and I was just going to add most of today to that, since the big boss man is out."

"What's going on down there?"

"It's kind of a mess," Isen said, not wanting to go into it.

"Your personal life or whatever it is you're snooping around on?"

Isen just smiled.

"I see," Smith said. "Loose lips, and all that jazz." He turned back to the mass of papers before him on the desk.

"Let's just say that this little personal favor for Flynn has turned out to be messier than I expected."

Smith seemed satisfied with that answer, so Isen left him and worked his way down through various passageways to the underground ring below the great building. A small shopping mall there catered to imprisoned Pentagon employees. Isen bought a bagel and a cup of coffee and made his way into the sunshine of the inner court, still known by its Cold War name: Ground Zero.

Isen found a spot at one of the picnic tables, but had not even had time to take the top off his coffee when Smith walked up to him and handed Isen his hat.

"I don't need this out here," Isen said.

"You need it to get out of the building, though," Smith said.

"I wasn't planning on leaving—"

"There are two plainclothes types up in the office asking questions about you," Smith said. "I was coming back in from the latrine when I heard them ask if you had ever presented yourself to anyone as a CID agent. You know, impersonating an investigator and all."

Isen felt a cold wave of nausea. "What did you say?"

"I didn't say anything. I grabbed your hat off the hook and headed out here. If you're planning on going to Bragg this afternoon, I'd suggest you get going before these guys have a chance to detain you."

Isen left his coffee and bagel on the table as he stood. "Thanks."

"No problem. You want I should throw myself in front of their car if they try to follow you?"

Smith was still smiling, but for Isen, the humor was fading from the situation.

"You OK?" Smith asked.

"Yeah, yeah," Isen said distractedly. "Somebody warned me about this, that's all."

Isen and Smith turned and walked toward the underground exit that led to the Pentagon's Metro stop.

"I'm going to stop by my apartment . . ." Isen began.

"You have your clothes with you?"

"Yeah."

"Why bother stopping home? Just take off. I'll tell Huey and Dewey up there that you'll be back in a few minutes."

Isen blinked at Smith, who still wore a smile, but who was taking things very seriously.

"OK. Thanks," Isen said as Smith turned to climb a staircase.

"Oh, by the way," Isen called.

Smith turned.

"I didn't do anything, you know. . . . I didn't pose as an investigator or anything."

Smith held up his hand. "I never thought that for a minute, my friend. Except for your occasional desire to skip out of work, you're the straightest guy I know."

* * *

Five hours after leaving Washington, Isen let himself into Darlington's house with the key she'd given him. He called Darlington at work.

"I'm back."

"How'd you get out so early?" Darlington wanted to know.

"Hell, I'm probably AWOL," Isen said. "And that's not the end of my problems." He told her about the men showing up at his office asking questions about his investigation.

"Wasn't that what McCall spoke to you about the other day?"

"She warned me about trying to pass myself off as an investigator, which I haven't been doing. I think someone is trying to set me up."

"She's thinking along those same lines," Darlington said. "She came by my office today and asked when you would be back in town. She also asked me if I'd been around when you were talking to any of these lieutenants. I told her about your conversation with Savin, and she asked me if I could see how someone might get the impression that you were an investigating officer. I told her I didn't see it."

"Thanks."

"Anyway, McCall wants you to call her." Darlington gave Isen a beeper number and an office number. McCall answered the page ten minutes later, and Isen agreed to drive on post and meet her at CID Headquarters.

When they were closed in her office, with the ominous red Do Not Disturb sign lit out front, Mccall surprised him by asking, "How's General Flynn?"

Isen looked at her for a moment. She'd delivered the question in the same flippant tone he'd become used to, but she obviously knew that Hauck's suicide was more complicated than her initial report found. What's more, she was pursuing.

"General Flynn is a little worried that we're . . . that I'm on a witch-hunt down here, making trouble for Veir because I don't like him." Isen filled her in on what Meade had said and what he and Flynn had talked about.

"And is that the case? Are you on a witch-hunt?"

"No. I don't exactly know what the connection is between

Veir and Hauck's death, but I believe there is one." Isen shared Trewick's story with her.

"Kind of creepy, isn't it?" she said.

"The similarities are pretty amazing."

McCall nodded, then flipped over a page on the pad before her.

"Major Isen, were you stopped by the Military Police traffic patrol last week?"

"Twice, as a matter of fact."

"You got a ticket for speeding and another for a rolling stop, right?"

"Yes. How did you know? Are you investigating me, too?"

"What do you mean, 'too'?"

Isen told McCall about his visitors at the Pentagon.

"No, I didn't know anything about that. I do know that those two guys, whoever they were, weren't the first people to ask if you'd been impersonating an investigator. As I told you, there have been some inquiries around here, as well."

"Starting where?"

"That's what I don't know," McCall said. "And the thing about the traffic patrols is odd, too."

She studied her notes quietly, as if trying to decide how much to tell Isen.

"I have a friend who is an MP, and he overheard your name mentioned when he was coming off patrol the other day."

"In what context?"

"He wasn't sure, but he thought the desk sergeant gave your license number and name out to the patrols just going on the street, as if they were looking for you. He figured it was an arrest. Then he heard me mention your name, and he told me about it. He checked the log over there the next day and found the citations."

"Maybe they're harassing me?"

"Well, the tickets aren't much by themselves. But it does seem an odd coincidence that your name is being tossed around by the MPs while all these questions are being raised about how you're conducting yourself." She stared at the pad before her.

"Things are starting to look less like coincidence," Isen said, not surprised.

He told McCall about Jenny Milan, about the chance meeting with Veir and her sudden trip to Europe.

"These things aren't necessarily linked," McCall said. "But if they are, we're talking about some fairly powerful connections."

"There may be another reason why golden boy Veir is being protected," Isen said. He told her about the visit by the Secretary of Defense and the fierce budget competition between the Marine Corps and the Army's airborne units.

"That'll get somebody's attention," she said.

"Exactly," Isen said. "So with all this attention focused on him, why does Veir still act like he's invulnerable?"

"He probably feels that way."

"I wonder if he'd use this invulnerability to hide something," Isen mused.

McCall looked up and smiled for the first time Isen could remember.

"What?"

"I was just thinking about how far I'd come in my opinion of you. At first I thought you probably brought all this animosity on yourself because of the way you come across."

"And how's that?" Isen asked.

"No disrespect intended, Major, but that's a pretty big white horse you rode into town."

"So *I* brought this on?"

McCall didn't answer at first; she seemed to relish Isen's self-doubt.

"Maybe. I don't know," she said. "But the fact is that I'm not really convinced that Hauck's death was normal—if you can apply that term to a suicide."

"Meaning?"

"Meaning there were more people involved than just good old Michael Hauck."

"Did you get to talk to Bennett?" Isen asked.

"He's gone. Left Sunday for Fort Benning and some kind of school."

"Another one gone. This looks pretty strange; why would they send away one of their platoon leaders just as the big show is about to go down?"

"Maybe Veir is shipping out all the screwups," McCall said.

Isen nodded. "So are you and I going to cooperate on this," he said, "or are you just using me for information?"

"You and I could cooperate if you were an investigator, but you're not."

"Something that many people would like to remind me of, it seems," Isen said. "On the other hand, I know a few things you might not know, and I am down here to try to help the family sort things out. I should get a little credit for that."

"OK," McCall said. "A little credit."

"Is your report finished?"

"That's what my supervisor tells me."

"What does that mean?' Isen asked.

"The only thing I'm waiting for is the psychologist's report."

"You were waiting for that last week," Isen said. "Is the doctor that slow?"

McCall's expression was unreadable.

"Or did you get him to hold it up because you need ... want more time?"

McCall pursed her lips, an expression that said, all at once, *Who cares, who knows, don't bother me.*

"My boss has been in a conference up in DC for a few days. So I got a reprieve. Besides, you know how busy these doctors are. Let's just say he didn't mind getting a little extension on this."

"So you're still working on this?"

"Not officially," McCall said. "Officially, we have a lot of other cases that need attention, and we don't have the resources to allow me to stretch out an investigation into what is so obviously an open-and-shut case."

" 'Open-and-shut case,' " Isen repeated. "Your words or your boss's?"

"My boss's."

"Don't you think it's odd that such an inexperienced investigator was given such a messy assignment?" Isen asked. "I mean, some officer shoots himself behind a strip club, his uncle the general is rooting around. It's not your nice, neat crime."

McCall bristled, began to speak, stopped, pulled herself up in her chair.

"I got this case because I happened to be on duty at the time," she said. She fidgeted some more, trying to resist admitting what she suspected was true. She was being used.

What was more, Isen had seen that before she did. Yet he hadn't crammed it down her throat; he'd treated her pretty decently, letting her come to the realization on her own.

"Yes, I have wondered why this wasn't given to a more experienced agent. Just the fact that it happened off post should be enough for them to send one of the senior people out on it."

"Do you think this pressure to wrap up early comes from your boss? Or does it start higher?"

McCall took a deep breath. "That's hard to say."

She was conscious of a feeling of disloyalty—talking to Isen about internal CID matters. But she and Isen had something in common that no one else seemed to share: a curiosity about this case and a desire to find out what was behind Hauck's suicide. That made them partners.

She toyed with a pencil in her hand. "I will say that no one would be disappointed if I closed this thing out today. But that can easily be explained: we have a couple of agents off at school, the case load is up. We *are* swamped here and my time could be spent somewhere else. The big show Veir is putting on would be enough of a reason to want you gone. These other things don't have to be connected."

"General Tremmore could just tell me to leave," Isen said.

"He might."

"But he hasn't yet. There may be some heavy hitters at work here, but since they're not prepared to operate in the open, I don't think it goes up to Tremmore."

Isen stared out the smoked-glass window at the elementary school across the street. He didn't like the feeling that he'd gotten a glimpse into something larger than just a few ruffled feathers. Isen wasn't one for conspiracy theories, but there were more than a few unexplained coincidences wrapped around Michael Hauck's suicide.

"When will you get the doctor's report?"

"Today. Next week. Depends." She raised her eyebrows for an instant. Isen was now a co-conspirator.

Isen, who'd been sitting in a chair in front of McCall's desk, stood and took a seat in the chair beside her.

"Since we don't have much time, we'd better have a plan."

Isen went to the post gym at lunchtime, determined to use the running gear he'd been carrying around in his car. Being around all the flat-bellied young combat soldiers at Bragg had underscored for him just how far he'd fallen in terms of taking care of himself.

He pulled on his shorts and an old T-shirt one of his soldiers had once brought back from Fort Benning and a school Isen had sent him to. "U.S. Army Sniper School," the front of the shirt proclaimed. On the back "One Shot, One Kill."

It wasn't the kind of shirt one could wear in polite company or suburban America—say, at the Little League field—but it wouldn't get a second glimpse at Bragg.

Isen made his way outside into the bright sunlight and headed out on one of the sidewalks. Dozens of other runners were visible along the roadway. Many of them, Isen guessed, used the quiet time and isolation to consider their problems.

The whole thing with Veir was disconcerting. Here was a senior officer who solicited prostitutes in the parking lot of a strip joint, caroused with lieutenants and set his subordinates against one another for his own entertainment. Veir had broken faith with the profession. Kent, who had arranged to get Milan shipped out, apparently wasn't much better. Ditto Foote. Flynn had hung Isen out at Bragg and now seemed less than thrilled to support him.

"Mind if I run along with you?"

Isen looked beside him; a young soldier was keeping pace.

"Not at all. Probably do me some good," Isen said.

"How far you going?"

"Just a couple of miles, I think."

They traded banter like that for a while, resting in between comments about their jobs, the weather, the roadway, the hazards of crossing busy intersections at lunchtime. After about a mile, Isen let the younger man, whose name was Hopkinson, take over the talking.

"Been here ten months," Hopkinson said. "I like it. It's hard work, but they tell you that right up front, you know. I mean, it's no surprise that it's hard work."

"You planning on staying in?" Isen asked.

"I don't know," Hopkinson said. "When I joined I was planning on getting out and going to college with Uncle Sugar's help, you know. But it turns out I like the Army all right.

"How about you, sir? You said you're in the Pentagon now, right? What are you going to do after that?"

"Good question," Isen puffed.

The young soldier nodded, probably assuming that Isen simply wasn't sure where the Army would send him next.

I might not have a job after this run-in with Harlan Veir, Isen thought.

"You want to get back to a troop unit?" Hopkinson asked.

Isen looked down at his feet, at the tops of his running shoes as they glided over the background of pavement.

"Yeah," he said. He'd come to Bragg excited about getting closer to the field Army. But he'd touched that Army in one tiny, dirty spot. "Yeah, I can't wait to get back to a troop unit." *Because the Harlan Veirs are rare, thank God.*

Isen looked over at Hopkinson, whose shaved head glistened with sweat.

"Don't let me hold you up," Isen said as he felt himself slowing.

"That's no problem," Hopkinson replied, flashing a smile. "It's easier if you have someone to run with."

They trotted along for another half mile, Hopkinson encouraging Isen all the way. Isen wondered if he looked pathetic or if Hopkinson was a natural trainer.

"What do you do?" Isen huffed.

"I'm an acting squad leader right now," Hopkinson said. He looked over and met Isen's gaze just as Isen realized he'd seen the young NCO before.

"You in Colonel Veir's battalion?"

"Yes, sir," Hopkinson said.

Isen looked at the ground. "You saw me fall out of that run."

"No big deal, sir. Colonel Veir gets lots of guys like that. He always does it when we have a bunch of newbies. He just skunked you, is all."

Hopkinson fell into step alongside the older man, matching Isen's rhythm, pulling him along by example, without cajoling.

"Almost there, sir. Almost there."

Isen thought of a hundred other runs, at Schofield Barracks, at Fort Benning. Lithe young runners, the leaders, shepherded those who were having a tough time. *You can do it, you can do it, you can do it,* like a chant, the mantra of teamwork.

They pulled within sight of the gym; Isen stopped running and started walking.

"Thanks. I don't know if I could have made it without you," he told the NCO.

They walked, hands on hips, for a few yards before Hopkinson picked up the thread of their earlier conversation.

"If I do stay in, I'll probably get some college credits at night. You have to challenge yourself, you know? Or you just get stagnant."

Isen had a sudden vision of this man as a senior NCO, smiling, coaching, teaching the young soldiers who relied on him. And there were hundreds of other Hopkinsons out there, all over Bragg, all over the Army. They far outnumbered the Veirs.

When they got to the door of the gym, Hopkinson stuck out his hand.

"Nice talking to you, sir," he said.

"Good luck," Isen said.

He went inside and stood in line at the water fountain with some twenty-year-olds who were spending their lunch break playing basketball. They looked like high school kids, and many of them weren't far removed from that age. Yet they were also the heirs of the soldiers who had jumped into the night sky above France on D Day; the descendants of men who'd helped blunt the Nazi advance in the Ardennes; the carriers of the banner that had gone first into Saudi Arabia, foot soldiers squaring off against tanks.

Harlan Veir was violating the kind of trust that Hopkinson and these others gave their commanders. It had always been clear to Isen: the subordinates who trusted you in peacetime and promised to trust you in war wanted nothing more than a fair shot and good training and honest treatment by those whom fate and circumstance placed in command.

Isen had struggled to deliver on that deal since his first day in uniform. He wasn't about to quit now.

As they drove out to Jiggles that night, Isen wondered what he and McCall would look like as a couple: a young black woman and a slightly pudgy late-thirties white guy entering a strip joint together.

We'll probably look like cops, he thought. *Which is half true.*

McCall was quiet on the ride out from Bragg, all but ignoring Isen's few attempts at conversation.

For his part, Isen thought about Sue Lynn's comments on the obstacles McCall faced. Her race didn't put her in a minority so much as her gender did. He couldn't help but wonder, noticing her frumpy clothes, complete abstention from jewelry and makeup, and even the way she dropped her voice to something deeper when she questioned someone, if she was trying to hide her femininity.

They parked in the lot where Michael Hauck had shot himself, then went straight into the club after paying the cover. One of the dancers was perched on a stool just inside the door, and as each man came in, she would embrace him, pulling his face into her breasts, and remind him that she was available for table dances.

When Isen stepped through the door, the dancer smiled and extended her arms. When McCall appeared the arms went down.

"My name's April," the dancer said to Isen, the smile apparently glued in place. "I'd be glad to come by and do a table dance for you and your friend."

Isen was a bit embarrassed, though McCall didn't even seem to take notice of the woman, brushing past on her way toward a table in the back.

"Thanks," Isen said lamely.

He caught up with his new partner as she was sitting down. He expected McCall to make a comment, but she remained quiet, taking in the whole room. A cocktail waitress appeared, an apparition in frilly white.

"Can I get you anything?" she said to Isen.

"Coke. You want anything?" he asked McCall.

"Same," she said, and the waitress moved away. McCall seemed intent on blending into the background.

"How many times did you come in here?" McCall asked.

"Just the one time, with Savin. He seemed to know a lot about what was going on. I guess he hangs out here."

"As a front," McCall said, still looking about.

"What?"

McCall looked at Isen for the first time since they entered the room.

"You haven't figured it out, have you?" she said.

"Figured what out?"

"Savin," she said. When Isen didn't respond, she looked back at the floor show. "Savin is the one who's gay."

"Are you serious? You mean Savin and Hauck . . . ah . . ."

"Were lovers? Nah." McCall reached into a basket of popcorn the waitress had dropped off with their drinks.

"So you think someone was threatening to out Savin? Maybe Hauck was protecting him? Or someone was going to make a big deal out of the fact that Hauck was rooming with a homosexual?"

"Those would seem the obvious choices," McCall said. "Funny thing is, I haven't been able to find much to support that."

Isen waited.

McCall, instead of continuing, gestured toward the stage, where a dancer on the far side of thirty-five seemed to be having difficulty picking up the rhythm of the music.

"*That* one had an uphill paper route," McCall said.

"So how do you know Savin is gay?"

"He has a separate life," McCall said. "He even has another apartment up in Chapel Hill."

Chapel Hill, the seat of the University of North Carolina and an island of tolerance in the great conservative sea of the Tarheel State, was about an hour and fifteen minutes north by car.

"As far as I can see, Savin has been absolutely circumspect in keeping that life separate," McCall said.

"Did Hauck know?"

McCall shrugged. "Probably. They were pretty good friends."

Isen sat back in his chair. The dancer onstage had moved to a near corner and was now trying to beckon to him—to his money, more precisely—by gyrating her hips. Isen could see, even from twenty feet, stretch marks that spidered out of the top of her bikini bottom.

"Well, we can't rule out that this is about protecting Savin."

Isen chewed on the little plastic stirrer from his drink.

"Let's go back to the possibility that Hauck had something on Veir," he said.

"What?"

"I don't know. Let's talk hypothetically, OK?"

McCall mumbled something in a disparaging tone; Isen ignored her.

"Let's say that Hauck had something on Veir. If Veir found out that Savin was gay, maybe he could get Hauck to keep quiet by threatening to report Savin."

He chewed furiously.

"Or maybe he got Hauck to shut up by threatening to make it known that Hauck was rooming with a homosexual."

"That would be a pretty serious threat to a kid trying to prove himself to his whole family," McCall said. "And that brings us back to the connection between Veir and Hauck, which is why we're here, right?"

Isen nodded, still turning his theory over.

McCall looked around the room, took a slow sip of her cola.

"All of your friends seem to be a little unsure about coming close, no doubt because they think you and I are together," McCall said. She looked at him with what might be a touch of sarcasm. "Why don't you see if you can coax one of the dancers over?"

Isen talked to three dancers—and spent thirty dollars—before he found one who was willing to sit down with him and McCall. When Isen asked the woman—who introduced herself as Chimera—about working Veir's parties at the club, she chuckled.

"You two cops?"

"Sort of," Isen said.

McCall shook her head in the smallest way, enough for Isen to see.

"You look like cops," the dancers said. "Or at least, you don't look like a couple."

"Thank you," McCall said clearly.

"Those boys are a bit crazy," Chimera said. She folded her arms on the table, resting substantial breasts on her forearms. The sheer pink covering did nothing to hide their medically sculpted symmetry. Isen stared deliberately into her eyes.

"I worked a couple of private parties for them before, here and at somebody's house."

"When was that?"

"Oh, two, three months ago, I guess. The one at a house was somebody's bachelor party, and they brought a couple of the girls down there to liven things up a bit. Not that they needed much encouragement."

"What kinds of things went on at the bachelor party?" Isen asked.

"You've never been to a bachelor's party, honey?" Chimera teased.

McCall actually chuckled. Isen got the distinct impression that her mood improved in direct proportion to his discomfiture.

"I think he means what kind of things, out-of-the-ordinary things that would make you say that those boys were wild," McCall chimed in.

"Well, one of those boys had a gun there, a pistol. And one of the other girls was dancing around the room, you know, just kind of working the crowd. And he tried to rub it against her pussy. He was holding it down near his crotch, like a big metal dick or something."

"Do you remember his name?" McCall asked.

"No, honey, I was a little preoccupied," Chimera said, tilting her head back and winking languidly at Isen. "We throw in a little treat for the groom if he can get a hard-on in front of the whole crowd."

Isen glanced at McCall and thought he saw a tiny crack in her facade of professional detachment. Apparently McCall hadn't been around police business long enough to have heard everything yet.

"The gal you need to talk to is Dee Ann. She was the one the guy tried to bone with the pistol."

"Is she here?" Isen asked.

"No. Tonight's Thursday. On Thursdays she works downtown at the Inferno."

"Thanks for your help," Isen said, standing.

"Would you guys like a round of drinks?" Chimera said, trying to soak them for another twenty bucks.

"I think we'd better run along," McCall said.

Chimera stood and pressed herself up against Isen. Her hair reeked a powerful mixture of cigarette smoke and scented hairspray. A tiny spot of lipstick marked one of her front teeth.

"Then you want to make a donation to the college fund?" she asked, pushing her breasts together with her hands.

Isen pulled a five from the bills in his pocket and pressed it into her cleavage.

"When you come back without your prissy little friend there," Chimera whispered to him, "look me up. I like a man with deep pockets."

Sitting in the Inferno Club and watching the dancer who'd been pointed out to them as Dee Ann, Isen thought that if this woman didn't genuinely enjoy her work, she was an excellent actress. Her smile made her, judging from the wad of bills in her garter and the line of men calling out to her and waving even more money, the most successful dancer in the dim confines of the Inferno Club.

Isen and McCall sat away from the dance floor on a large sofalike seat, cushioned in red velvet, that lined one wall. In keeping with the diabolic theme, the waitresses pranced in skimpy devil costumes, trailing pointed tails.

Dee Ann looked to be about thirty, Isen guessed. She was finishing her set when McCall and Isen sat down, and so was quite naked except for a pair of sparkling spiked heels and—incongruously—a watch. She was extremely fair skinned, almost milky white, with a gentle spray of freckles on her arms and across the tops of her breasts. Thick hair, strawberry blond, pulled back with a bow that dangled near the end of the ponytail. She didn't try to flash bedroom smiles or the come-hither looks that other dancers attempted with varying degrees of success. Her wide smile showed white teeth, and the supporting dialogue might have been, *Aren't you having a good time watching me dance naked?*

The answer, from the thirty or so customers in the place, was a resounding and financially rewarding yes.

Isen sent word with a bouncer, asking Dee Ann to join them at their table when she finished. He tipped the thick-necked man ten dollars.

"It'd be cheaper just to offer a ten-thousand-dollar reward for the truth about what happened to Michael Hauck," Isen said, peering into his wallet as he sat down in front of his soft drink. "I can't afford to buy a beer after—"

"Stuffing all your money into G-strings," McCall finished for him.

"Actually, it's General Flynn's money."

McCall rolled her eyes. It seemed to Isen that she divided her time equally between being pissed off at him and exasperated with him.

"And you're giving it away to strippers."

Isen shrugged. "When duty calls . . ."

Dee Ann finished her set and left the stage, reappearing on the floor in a few moments wrapped in a faux silk dressing gown. Unlike Chimera, she appeared at the table fully covered.

"Howdy," she said as she approached. "Y'all wanted to have a chat, I understand."

Isen held a chair out for her, which drew a sarcastic look from McCall. No doubt she thought his gallantry wasted.

"Can I get you something to drink?" Isen asked.

"Ice water would be nice. Thanks."

Her accent, which Isen had at first thought Deep South, had another edge to it.

"I'm from West Virginia," Dee Ann said.

Isen must have looked startled, as if she'd read his mind.

"No, I'm not psychic, that's just usually the first question people ask." She smiled a genuine smile.

Her speech was rapid-fire, and her rich accent made her

sound like she was overacting for the part of the woman from down in the holler.

"So what can I do for you folks? Who are you guys? Cops? You must be here to talk about that poor boy who killed himself outside of Jiggles."

"A woman named Chimera over at Jiggles told us you'd worked for this group of guys before, the group that included Michael Hauck."

Dee Ann pulled herself up in her chair. Her thin robe fell open a bit, revealing that spray of freckles. Isen wondered if Dee Ann was her real name. It wasn't like the stage names most dancers chose—Desiree, Cheyenne, Amber—which sounded like a collection of cheap perfumes.

"Yeah, I worked for them a couple of times."

"At a private party?" Isen pressed. No response. "And somebody had a pistol?"

"That big mouth told you about that?"

"Was this man, Michael Hauck, at that private party?" McCall asked, producing a photo. She was all business now, and her question came off crisply, maybe even a little off-putting. The tough cop routine. Isen looked over at her; at least she didn't have her notebook out.

"Yes, he was," Dee Ann said. "But he wasn't really into it, you know?"

McCall waited a half beat before asking, "What do you mean?"

"Well, some of the guys obviously want their money's worth. When we dance around the room, those are the guys who'll grab you, rub up against you, all that stuff. There was this one guy who'd flick his tongue out if you got close enough for him to lick. Disgusting."

Dee Ann looked from Isen to McCall and back again, gauging their reactions. If she was waiting for some sort of judgment, she wasn't going to get it here.

"Anyways, this guy Michael kind of hung in the back of the crowd. None of the dancers got near him, far as I could see."

Isen, thinking of Bennett's heckling at the arm-wrestling match, asked, "Did anyone encourage him, or try to bring him up front to see if he would ... participate?"

"Nah, they kind of left him alone. At least, nothing sticks

in my mind." She paused, produced a pack of cigarettes from the pocket of her robe, shook one loose.

"Do you mind?"

Isen and McCall pushed their chairs back from the table a few inches.

"Tell us about the guy with the pistol," McCall said.

Dee Ann took a long, slow drag on her cigarette, then let the smoke drift out of her mouth and nose as she talked. She studied each of them carefully.

"So, you guys cops?"

"I am," McCall answered, pre-empting Isen's vague response. "I'm a military investigator, trying to tie some things up for the Army report."

Dee Ann considered that for a moment.

"Doesn't sound to me like you're trying to tie things up if you're asking about all these other things that went on before the suicide. Sounds like you're trying to find out some new stuff."

She reached over to the next table and found an ashtray.

Smart woman, Isen thought. He sat back in his chair, waiting to see what kind of response McCall would come up with for that one.

McCall said nothing.

"Well, doesn't matter much to me either way," Dee Ann said. "I got nothing to hide. So what do you want to know?"

"Who was the guy with the pistol?" McCall asked immediately.

"Some kid named Bennett," Dee Ann said. "A real sicko, that one."

McCall hesitated a bit, and Isen wondered if she'd assumed that Veir was the one with the pistol.

"Anyone else carry on like that?" McCall asked.

"Not like that guy. We could always count on him."

"Meaning?"

"Well, the deal with the pistol was just one party, but these guys had a lot of parties, and they came around the clubs a lot. So we got to know who was who. And this guy Bennett was always one of the worst."

She leaned forward, resting her elbows on the table, and her robe slipped open a bit more. Isen felt a little foolish, trying to sneak glances down the front of a robe to see the breasts of a woman he'd seen naked just a few minutes before. But then he decided that partially clothed was much sexier.

"A lot of the guys who come in here like to have us talk dirty to them when we're dancing at the tables. Usually it's pretty harmless, and there's not a lot they can come up with that I haven't heard before. But Bennett was something else."

"What did he say that was different?"

"It wasn't that," Dee Ann said. She pressed her lips into a line, concentrating on what made Bennett stand out to her. "It was that you thought this guy was capable of doing what he talked about."

"Sexual acts?" McCall asked.

Dee Ann shook her head. "Violence. Rape. Rip your clothes off, slap you around. That kind of stuff. The dancers tried to steer clear of him, especially after he'd had a couple of drinks. He was just plain mean."

"Did you ever see him with Hauck?" Isen asked. "Talking, arguing?"

"Just that last night. You could tell they didn't like each other. A bunch of the young guys—I think Bennett was one of them—were trying to get Hauck to drink. I remember that because that kid didn't drink very much. He was always pretty sober. Even the few times that they made him carry on—get up onstage, hold some money in his teeth so a dancer could squat over him and pick it up, a sort of initiation for him, I guess—even those times he was almost apologizing, you know."

She chuckled softly to herself. "The shy ones are a lot like the crazy ones in one way."

"How's that?"

"They don't see this as a business. The ones like Bennett think they own you, they think that I'm out here with no clothes on because I like having them stare at me and touch me. The shy ones, like Hauck, act like they feel sorry for you. They forget that I chose to do this instead of waiting tables back in West Virginia."

She shrugged. "Anyway, Hauck was plastered that night, the night he killed himself."

"You saw that?" McCall asked.

"I saw him drinking, and I saw the others encouraging him to drink, and I saw him stagger off to the men's room a couple of times."

Dee Ann answered crisply. She seemed to know that her answers were important, even if McCall wasn't writing them down.

"Do you know who Harlan Veir is?" Isen asked. He thought McCall shot him a look, but he wanted to know what Veir was up to that night.

Dee Ann glanced over Isen's shoulder, a gesture of discomfort. "Sure."

"What was he up to all this time?"

"Just his usual low-key self."

McCall stepped back in. "Did you see Michael Hauck leave the club with anyone?"

"No."

"You're sure?" McCall said testily.

Dee Ann cocked her head, as if she were slightly amused that this woman was trying to lean on her.

"I *do* go on breaks," she said. "Maybe I was in the can."

"Did Hauck argue with Bennett that night?"

"I don't know that they argued, from what I could see, but Bennett kept bothering him. Then again, Bennett bothered everyone."

Isen listened, his finger tracing the little rings of condensation made by their drinks on the table.

"How is it—please don't take this question the wrong way—how is it that you saw so much of what these guys were doing?" he asked. "I mean, there are a lot of customers in here."

"Two reasons, I guess," Dee Ann said. "They spent a lot of money, so I hung around them a lot. They're good tippers."

"And?"

"And I liked to know where Bennett was. He's not the kind of guy you want getting behind you."

In the car on the way back to CID Headquarters, Isen snapped at McCall, "Why didn't you want me asking her about Veir?"

"Because you weren't paying attention," McCall said

quickly. "She was talking about Bennett. He's the one she called a sicko. He was the one with the pistol. He was the one who, according to the other lieutenant, went outside with Hauck. Veir wasn't a part of that."

"Oh, come on. Veir is in charge of these guys," Isen pressed.

"Veir is their battalion commander, and he allows a lot of weird stuff to go on at these parties. But we have no hard evidence of any bad blood between Veir and Hauck other than hearsay about Hauck's opinion of his boss. No one put Veir anywhere near Hauck at the end. Everything is pointing to Bennett as the last person who had anything to do with Hauck before he killed himself. Yet you want to track down this one particular witch."

They were talking fast now, firing comments back and forth.

"I think Veir's control over these guys goes beyond that. I think Veir is the central player here in all this shit that was going on among the lieutenants, and I think he's behind the transfers, the MPs, all that stuff."

"And I think you have it in for him because you fell out of that run," McCall said sharply. "Or maybe because he's a successful battalion commander and you're afraid that you're just a washed-up Pentagon paper shuffler."

"Fuck you," Isen said.

"Thank you. You just proved my point."

They rode quietly for a few miles, and Isen decided that they were either going to move forward or he was headed back to Washington.

"OK," he said. "It is true that I don't like Veir. I'd like to believe that I have professional as well as personal reasons for not liking him."

He waited for a response, but McCall kept her counsel and kept her eyes on the road. They were abreast of World O' HubCaps when Isen started speaking again.

"Let's say I do have it in for him," Isen said. "That doesn't automatically mean he's innocent, does it?"

"No."

"OK, there you go then," Isen said.

McCall looked over at Isen on the seat beside her. "I know you think I'm just some dumb probee," she said.

You read my mind, Isen thought.

"But I do know a couple of things." She smiled, a tiny, almost private grin.

"Tell me something," she said. "When you're in combat, do you hate the enemy?"

"I ... I'm not sure I've ever thought about that before," he said, stalling. "The overwhelming emotion is fear, no doubt about that. Whether it's fear you're going to get killed or maimed, or fear you're going to do something wrong and get other guys killed. Then there's confusion, absolute chaos and maddening ignorance. And mixed in that is some more fear."

He put his elbow up beside the window and tapped his fingertips against the glass.

"There were times when I hated, yes. Times when I saw cruelty, or even ... and this is almost a cliché ... when I'd lost someone close. But hate is not necessary. It probably gets in the way of understanding your enemy, and understanding is the first step toward victory."

"It's the same thing here," McCall said. "When you're pursuing a criminal, you don't keep reminding yourself about the victim. You try to think like the criminal. You *try* to empathize. It's weird, but it's necessary. And you can't do that with Colonel Veir. You're probably not the right person to be working on this."

Isen didn't respond at first. He knew that his judgment was clouded, and he figured that acknowledging the problem was a step toward solving it. The bottom line was: if he left and McCall got pulled off the job, no one would care to find out why Michael Hauck killed himself. Mark Isen didn't think he could live with that.

"I'm not the right person, and you don't have the time," Isen said, watching the neon give way to empty roadsides as they passed the invisible line that divided Fort Bragg proper from Fayetteville. "We're a helluva team."

"Savin has been calling you all night," Sue Lynn said as soon as Isen entered.

Isen walked up to her and kissed her on the lips. "What's up with him?"

"I'm not sure, he seemed—" She was interrupted by the telephone. "You might as well get it."

"Hello," Isen answered.

"Major Isen? Sir, am I glad I caught you."

Isen was having difficulty hearing Savin over the sound of vehicles moving in the background. "What's up, Greg?"

"You'll never guess where I'm calling from. I've over at Pope, and I'm getting ready to get on an airplane."

Pope Air Force base, located next to Fort Bragg, was the point of departure for deploying soldiers.

The first question Isen might have asked one of the infantry lieutenants was "Where you headed?" Savin, as a Finance Officer in one of the support units, didn't usually deploy unless a big slice of the Division—or the whole thing—left Bragg.

"Why?" Isen wanted to know.

"I got a call this afternoon telling me to pick up my bag and be down here by seventeen hundred. I'm headed to friggin' Alaska with an infantry battalion. Thirty days. This unit has been planning this training for months, and just today the battalion commander is told that there'll be a few support types going with him. Including me."

"But there won't be anything for you to do up there. Do you have any idea where the orders originated?"

"The Chief of Staff."

Bingo, Isen thought.

"But I wasn't calling to ask you to get me off the deployment, sir," Savin said. "Actually, I think I'll enjoy getting away from Bragg for a while. I had some other information to give you."

Isen wondered if Savin was about to tell him about the other life, about the apartment up in Chapel Hill. He wasn't sure he was ready to hear all that. "What's that?"

There was a pause at the other end as what sounded like a forklift roared by.

"About six weeks before he died, Michael became involved with this woman. He met her at a laundromat, if you can believe that. Anyway, I think they were seeing each other up until he died, although their relationship was a bit weird."

"What do you mean 'weird'?"

"Well, he hardly talked about her at all, like he wanted

her to be a secret. Frankly, that's why I didn't think of it sooner. And they didn't have regular dates or anything. Every once in a while he would go out real early in the morning, like one or two, to see her."

"What's her name?"

"I only met her once, and all I got was a first name. Cindy."

"Was Hauck serious about her?"

"Hard to say. Like I said, he didn't bring it up. If I had to guess, I would say he was pretty taken with her. I mean, he used to drag himself out to see her, then go to PT at six in the morning."

"I wish you would have told me about this sooner," Isen said. "Any idea how to contact her? You know where she works or anything?"

"No, sir . . . but I think she was a stripper."

Isen mimed surprise; Sue Lynn sat on the arm of the couch next to him.

"Michael was dating one of the dancers?"

"Now, I don't know for sure that she's a dancer. He never said anything and I never saw her in a club. But the hours and all that. And she looked like she might be a dancer, you know?"

There was another loud noise, a grinding of metal that forced the two men to pause.

When he could hear again, Isen asked, "Why didn't you tell me about this before?"

"Look, sir, I screwed up. I know that. But I'm not sure this is great news, anyway. You came down here to look into the suicide of a proud family's favorite son; I'm not sure the folks at home will like finding out that Michael was smitten with a stripper."

Isen shook his head. "Is there anything else you want to tell me?"

Savin was quiet.

"Greg, is it possible that Michael was taking a lot of heat because he was protecting you?"

Somewhere behind Savin, Isen could hear men laughing.

"It's possible," Savin said at last. "You ought to ask General Flynn."

*   *   *

Isen called McCall at home to tell her about Cindy and that someone else involved with the Hauck case was being sent away.

"It's starting to look like a conspiracy," McCall said. "But I can't get past how many people would have to be involved with something like that."

"That's not even the part that bothers me," Isen said. "It's the trail. Milan. Bennett. Savin.

"It's as if someone is trying to protect Veir or keep a secret. But the means of doing it is so obvious, so sloppy."

"So you're thinking what?" McCall asked.

"It's almost as if whoever is doing all this wants to leave a trail, wants to get caught."

"Veir?"

"I'm not sure Veir has that kind of clout. He has influence, but not the power."

"So that leaves us with Tremmore and Kent," McCall said.

"Kent," Isen said. "I don't think Tremmore's been around the division long enough, and from what I hear, that kind of underhanded maneuvering isn't his style."

"So you think we should talk to Kent?" McCall asked.

"No. If he's leaving a trail on purpose, we've already discovered what he's offering: he's pointing to Veir. If he isn't doing it on purpose, if we're wrong, then approaching him will just alert Kent and Veir."

"OK," McCall said after a pause. "What's next?"

"I've got to find this Cindy."

"*We've* got to find her," McCall corrected.

10

NEWS OF THE IMPENDING VISIT BY THE SECRETARY OF DE-
fense was made public Thursday evening. On Friday morning Isen drove over to Veir's battalion headquarters. There
might have been people on Fort Bragg who had not heard
the announcement the evening before, but everyone around
Harlan Veir's headquarters knew what was happening and
how important this show was going to be.

The small waiting room just inside the door had been
turned into something of a war room. There were large maps
posted on boards and covered in clear plastic overlay sheets.
Two of the larger boards, each some six feet by four feet,
showed the training and demonstration areas on Fort
Bragg's massive westward sprawl. Another board showed a
training grid—a detailed schedule of training times and sites
for each company in the battalion.

Green field tables, littered with printed orders and the
thick black binders the army used to hold operational plans,
stood in untidy ranks. Someone had tacked up a poster on
one wall: "D minus 14." Fourteen days until the big show.

Soldiers came and went hurriedly, all of them in helmets
and field gear. If Mark Isen hadn't watched the news that

morning, thus confirming that the nation was not at war, he might have been a bit apprehensive. Veir and his men would be under intense scrutiny from the rest of the Army—this was to be the service's one chance at showing the folks from Washington what they could do—so it was no surprise to Isen that the headquarters had the feeling of combat preparation.

"Well, well, well. Major Isen. I thought we'd seen the last of you."

Leonard Foote stepped into the small room, filling it with his voice and what could only be described as a malevolent smile. He was probably still gloating about the PT run.

"Doing any running up there in Washington?"

"Good to see you again, Major Foote," Isen said. He wondered what the young kid sitting at the runner's desk would do if he heard these two field grade officers cursing each other across a room crowded with junior enlisted men.

"Is Colonel Veir in the area?" Isen asked.

"Colonel Veir, as it so happens," Foote said, "is not in the area. As a matter of fact, Colonel Veir—and the rest of us in the real Army around here—have become quite busy lately. I doubt if Colonel Veir would have time to see you even if he were in his office."

"How go the plans for the big show?" Isen said, strolling over to the map board that showed the demonstration area. A timetable overlay marked the major events: a parachute drop of the entire battalion, followed by firepower demonstrations. Once the soldiers were in place and the fireworks were over, Colonel Veir would meet the Secretary and introduce him to a selected group of soldiers.

Face time for Hollywood, Isen thought.

"We'll shine, as usual," Foote said smugly.

"You've got a practice jump on Saturday?" Isen said, reading the training schedule.

"That's right," Foote said.

"Mind if I come out to the drop zone and watch?"

"It's a free country," Foote said. "Just be careful you don't get something heavy dropped on your head."

Isen could hear, from an office behind him, the Battalion Sergeant Major chewing out someone over the telephone. "I don't care how many people you have to bring in or how long you have to stick around or how many times you have to do it. Get it right; get it done. We're at war here, got it?"

"Looks like things are pretty torqued up around here."

"Nothing we can't handle," Foote said. "Look, I'd love to stay and chat, but we're pretty busy."

He had already turned to walk away when Isen said to his broad back, "Too bad Bennett is going to miss the show."

Foote stopped but did not turn around.

"Yeah, too bad," Foote said. He seemed less argumentative, somehow. "But he is. So why don't you just go away."

Isen was about to say something further when Veir came into the room trailed by a handful of officers and NCOs like royal retainers. The private at the reception desk sprang to attention, fumbling his "Airborne, sir."

Veir didn't miss a beat as he returned the youngster's salute. Directions came out in an unbroken stream while his entourage took notes.

"And I want those goddamned vehicles cleaned up, but not spit-shined. There's nothing worse than having the whole thing look like what it is, a friggin' dog-and-pony show. If they wanted a cheap show, they'd have asked one of these other limp-dick battalions to do it."

The staff chuckled appreciatively.

Gosh, aren't we lucky to work for someone who keeps a sense of humor when the chips are down, Isen thought.

Veir saw Isen standing by the map boards.

"Major Isen," he said tonelessly. "You're back."

And aren't you glad, you bastard.

"Yes, sir, I was wondering—"

Veir cut him off with an upraised hand. "Sergeant Major," he called into the office nearby. The battalion's senior enlisted man appeared at the door to his office a second later.

"What about those uniform and equipment inspections?"

"All laid on, sir, and I have the folks at the issuing point standing by to replace whatever we need. If a trooper has a piece of fucked-up equipment, we'll trade it in right on the spot."

"Good. Did we get rid of those lob-cocks down in Alpha?"

Isen could only assume that Veir was weeding out any soldier who didn't fit the recruiting poster image he wanted to present to the Defense Department's highest ranking policy maker.

"Out of here by tomorrow, sir."

"Excellent," Veir said. Then, turning, "Major Foote."

Foote was standing by in the doorway to his own office. "Yes, sir?"

"We having any trouble getting what we need in terms of training areas?"

"No, sir. We're getting everything we ask for. Seems like *just about everyone* knows how important this job is for the Army."

Isen turned to Foote to see if that last comment had been directed at him. Foote was looking at Veir.

"That's the way it should be all the time," Veir said. "By the way, you make sure you get out of here for that appointment."

"I was planning on missing it this week, sir," Foote said, a bit uncomfortable.

"Bullshit," Veir said. "Besides, I can just work you all night long if I need to."

Veir leaned over the desk where the private had nervously taken his seat again. "Isn't that right, son?"

The private jumped up again, slapping his hands to his sides in an exaggerated position of attention. "Yes, *sir.*"

"Hooah," Veir shouted, spraying spittle onto the boy's uniform.

"Hooah," the soldier yelled back, the cords on his neck straining as he tried to give as much volume as he was receiving.

Veir laughed, then turned sharply into his office. The men who'd been following him, not dismissed but clearly not invited inside, shuffled about in confusion for a moment before leaving. Foote disappeared into his office, and Isen was left alone with the private, who still stood nervously by his desk, which offered him scant protection.

Isen walked over to Veir's office door. The colonel was on the phone and the office, which had been as sterile as an operating room the last time Isen had seen it, was almost as much of a shambles as the outside room.

Isen knocked on the doorframe. Veir looked up and saw him but made no move to invite him in. Isen watched him issuing crisp orders and demands in a my-way-or-else tone of voice. Isen noticed that Jenny Milan's picture was gone. When Veir finished, Isen knocked again.

"What is it?"

"Sir, I'd like to ask you a few questions."

"Come back in two weeks," Veir said. "When this mission is finished."

"I only need a few minutes, Colonel."

Veir had been reading, or pretending to read, something on his desk. Now he looked up at Isen.

"I think I've given you plenty of cooperation since you dropped in here, Major. But right now I'm smack in the middle of the biggest mission, short of war, the division has undertaken in years. You're dismissed."

Veir lowered his head, and Isen started to go. Fifteen years of military courtesy told him it was time to leave the room. To do or say anything else was a challenge to Veir's authority, right here in the man's own office. Isen looked at the top of Veir's head, where his thick hair had been all but shaved away in his paratrooper haircut. Two seconds clicked by, and during that time Isen wondered why he was risking so much for this unofficial mission.

"Something isn't right here, sir," Isen said, surprising himself.

Veir looked up as if startled that Isen was still standing before him.

"Yeah, I'll tell you what's not right, you're still standing in my fucking office, that's what's not right, Major."

"Something's not right with the explanation of why Hauck killed himself, and I think—"

Veir stood suddenly, punching the chair with his legs, sending it careening back into the credenza, shaking the trophies there. "I think you need your goddamned hearing checked. Either that, or you need to figure out that you're in *my* office, in *my* battalion area."

Isen resorted to an old trick. *When the other person starts shouting, lower your voice. Drives them crazy.*

"I think Bennett knows more about Hauck's death and. . . ." Here he put his hands in his pockets. Casual, matter-of-fact. "And frankly, Colonel, I think you know more about it, too."

Isen pulled his hands from his pockets, drew himself to attention and saluted. Veir did not return the salute. Nor did he scream and yell, as Isen thought he might. Instead, he straightened up calmly, his eyes becoming hooded, threatening. Just before he turned to go, Isen thought he saw Veir smile.

"You did what?"

Now it was McCall's turn to be angry.

"I wanted to see if I could get a rise out of him," Isen said. "You know, smoke him out."

"You watch too much TV, Major Isen," McCall said. "If we're going to get anywhere on this, that means you and I had better cooperate. And cooperation does not mean that you go off like a loose cannon and just confront anyone you want, any time you want."

She was lecturing him now. Isen knew that he'd taken a chance with Veir. But in the aftereffects of the colonel's little explosion, he felt as if he'd accomplished exactly what he wanted. If they were running, he wanted to see their backs.

"Right," he said to McCall.

"I think you ought to stay away from Veir and Foote and that whole crew," she said.

"Right," he agreed. He found he was smiling.

"At least until we've had a chance to talk to this Cindy person. Can you do that this afternoon?"

"Give me a call at Major Darlington's," Isen said. "I'll be standing by around eight."

"Make it six," McCall said. "It's a Friday night. We want to make the rounds before the crowds start coming out."

"Airborne," Isen said.

Sue Lynn had an afternoon appointment at the hospital, and Isen, who had a couple of free hours now that his partner had put Veir's men off-limits, rode with her.

"So what made you decide to pull that little stunt in his office?" Sue Lynn wanted to know.

"I'm not sure," he said. "Something told me it was time to stop bullshitting around. I told Veir exactly what I think: there's more to this than we've yet heard; I think Bennett knows more; and I wouldn't be surprised if the good colonel knows more, too."

"What about all this flack that's coming down that looks like someone's trying to protect him, or them, or at least discourage you from snooping so much?"

"I thought about telling him that I was on to that, too," Isen said, filling her in on the sloppy paper trail Colonel Kent was leaving. "I just can't see that all of this, all these people getting shipped out—Bennett, Milan and Savin—is a coincidence, along with the stuff from the MPs and the visitors at the Pentagon."

They parked and locked her car, then walked toward the main entrance, exchanging salutes with dozens of soldiers headed in the other direction.

"Don't look now. . . ." Sue Lynn said.

Isen looked anyway. On the sidewalk up ahead he saw the unmistakable figure of Major Leonard Foote.

"It's my buddy, Lenny," he said to Sue Lynn.

As they got closer, Isen could see that Foote was not alone. A tall, very attractive woman walked beside him, her hand on his arm, her gait easy, relaxed. Foote walked slowly too, pushing a wheelchair that held a small boy. The child, who looked to be about six or seven, had his head turned to the side and was talking to his mother. His legs were tiny black wires peeking out from khaki shorts and finding their way down to blindingly white sneakers.

They were on the same sidewalk; there was no way Isen could avoid Foote.

"Hello, Major Isen," Foote called to him in a surprising voice. Isen realized it was the first time he'd heard Foote speak without hostility, sarcasm or outright threats.

"Hello," Isen said, slowing. If Foote was going to go through with this charade, he thought, he might as well play along too.

"Honey," Foote said to the woman beside him, "this is Mark Isen, down here from the Pentagon. This is my wife, Elizabeth."

Elizabeth Foote showed a gentle smile and held out her hand. "How do you do?"

Her voice, her regal carriage, even the way she held out her hand had a soothing character, like soft music. Isen wondered how she ever got mixed up with a man like Foote, who had all the delicacy of an exploding hand grenade.

"This is my friend Sue Lynn Darlington."

Sue Lynn took Elizabeth's hand, then her husband's.

"And this is Peter," Foote said, putting his hands on the boy's shoulders.

Peter looked up at them, his head cocked slightly to one side. He raised his left hand, which Isen took in his own left.

"I'm glad to meet you, Peter," Isen said.

"Do you work with my daddy?" Peter asked.

"Well, sort of," Isen ventured.

"I didn't think you did because you don't have a beret." He pronounced the word "bray."

"That's true, I don't," Isen said. "That's why I stick close to Sue Lynn here, 'cause she does have one."

Peter looked up at Sue Lynn, who wore the headgear Peter was used to seeing on soldiers.

"You must be a leg, then," Peter said, turning back to Isen.

Isen laughed. "Yes, I guess I am."

Elizabeth smiled and put her hand on Peter's shoulder. "That's what we get for steeping him in this whole Airborne culture," she said. "No offense."

"None taken."

Foote smiled, though he wasn't relaxed. Isen thought that the big man might be embarrassed, afraid that Isen might say something to reveal his alter ego, the asshole. His wife might find out what he was really like when she wasn't around to pacify him.

"Did you serve in Hawaii?" Elizabeth asked Sue Lynn.

"Yes, I did."

"I thought so. I believe we met once, briefly, at some parade or something."

"Mark served in Hawaii at the same time," Sue Lynn said, including him in the circle.

"Oh, do you know the Benningtons, by any chance?"

Isen found that he was staring at Foote, who had bent over and was rubbing Peter's shoulders, one of which was lower than the other. He'd been trying to catch Foote's eye, give him an I'm-on-to-you look.

"Pardon? Oh, yes," Isen said, coming back. "I did know them. Are they friends of yours?"

"Very dear friends," Elizabeth said.

They exchanged pleasantries for a few minutes, comparing lists of who knew whom and when, a standard meeting ritual in Army circles. Isen felt himself watching Foote again. The big man was gently stroking his son's hair; Peter was falling asleep. Foote's hand was bigger than the top of the child's head.

"Fort Bragg is tough on family life, of course," Elizabeth was saying. "Lots of separations. But thank the Lord for the medical care." She looked over at Peter, whose head had come to rest on his tiny chest. "They do take good care of him, and he needs a lot of care. I don't know what we'd do. . . ."

She let her voice trail off, but not before the final notes turned to concern, worries about this sick child, Isen thought, or some glimpse of the burden she must carry.

"We have a lot to be grateful for, that's for certain," Foote said evenly. His voice didn't match the image Isen had of him. It matched the picture of the big man caressing the head of a sleeping child.

"Well, we've kept you long enough," Elizabeth said. "I think we'll take Peter home so he can sleep in his own bed instead of out here on the sidewalk."

"It was nice meeting you," Sue Lynn said to both of them.

Isen shook hands with Elizabeth Foote. Her husband nodded at him but didn't take his hands off the wheelchair.

When they were headed into the building, Sue Lynn said, "That explains why he wants you out of here."

"Pardon?"

"That explains why he acts the way he does to you, why he wants you out of here."

"Oh, c'mon. That little act he put on for his wife was a joke. The guy's a flaming asshole, that's the only explanation I need."

"Don't be such a thickheaded Neanderthal," Sue Lynn said in her school principal voice. "Did it ever occur to you that we just saw his real personality? That maybe he's trying to scare you off because he's afraid that if his boss goes down, he goes down, too? You know, if it turns out that

Veir had some sort of role in Hauck's death, or if somebody decides that Veir has just been amoral in all these goings-on with the dancers and such, it's not going to go well for Major Foote, either. His record will reflect what happens to Veir. And with things as competitive as they are, that could mean that Foote will be looking for a new profession. One without medical coverage."

She stopped and put her hand on his arm.

"It doesn't look to me like he's willing to take that chance, not with a child who needs that much medical care. He has to stay in the Army, and for now, at least, that means he's stuck with Veir."

"But if he's such a gentle soul, how can he stand to put up with Veir's bullshit?"

"How far would you go to take care of your child?"

11

Isen and McCall started their Friday night at Jiggles. The club was still full of the after-work crowd: men in dirty overalls and workboots; others in suits, ties loosened and shirtsleeves pushed up; grinning loosely with beer and good spirits. They waved fists full of money, vibrant pennants summoning half-dressed women who hurried from one table to another, pressing the flesh and raking in the cash.

"So much for having the place to ourselves," Isen said as he and McCall found their way to the back. They stood at the bar; McCall ordered a soda, Isen ordered a beer. The bartender told them that Dee Ann had worked the day shift and was off for the night.

"You lookin' for work?"

This from an obese man in a garish floral print shirt who was draped over a stool several places down from where McCall stood.

"Pardon?" Isen said.

"I was talking to your girlfriend here," the man said.

McCall turned out of curiosity. "Sorry, I didn't hear you," she said politely.

"I asked if you were looking for work. I'm the manager,

and I noticed you in here the other night." He let his watery eyes run the length of her. "You look pretty good. 'Course, I'd have to see you with your clothes off—we could do that in the back, in private—but we could use another black dancer."

McCall was standing closer to the man than Isen was, her sensible black purse clutched tightly under her arm, her little blue oxford cloth shirt buttoned almost to the neck, black shoes, navy blue pants. *What the hell,* Isen wondered, *is this guy thinking?*

Isen bit his lip, but it didn't work; he snorted, then laughed out loud. Isen wondered if McCall would pull her pistol on the fat man.

"No, thanks," she said. "I already have a job."

She turned back to Isen, who pulled his lips into a pucker, trying to make his smile disappear.

"Very funny," she said. "You put him up to that?"

"No," he said, shaking his head. "But only because I didn't think of it first."

McCall moved closer to the manager, sliding her soft drink down the bar.

"You have a dancer named Cindy?" she asked.

"Did," he said. He had a tiny mouth that almost disappeared in the big doughnut of flesh that clung to his chin like an inflatable bib. "She hasn't been around in a while."

"Do you know where she went?"

"Nope. Lots of these women just cut out, you know? I mean, she wasn't a professional or anything. I think she was just in it for a few quick bucks."

He put his beer to his lips, then spoke around the mouth of the bottle. "She made good money, but she was kind of a pain in the ass."

"Why's that?" McCall asked.

"Kept jumping around from club to club. And she wouldn't always tell me. A couple of times, she'd booked herself for two places at once."

He shook his head and pulled on his beer, the weight of business responsibility heavy on his shoulders.

"Did she have any relationships with customers?" McCall asked.

He swiveled dark eyes toward her. "Who wants to know?"

"We're from Fort Bragg, and we're looking into the suicide of that young guy who shot himself out here a couple of weeks back."

"I thought you guys have already been through all this."

"Takes time to do a good job," McCall said. "So did she have any relationships with customers?"

"You mean relations?" he corrected. "As in turning tricks?" He wiped his mouth with the back of his hand, then used a single pudgy digit to press his lips together as he belched. McCall edged back a fraction; Isen was out of stench range.

"Look, I run a respectable business here. No drugs, no hookin', none of that shit."

"Nobody is suggesting anything different," McCall said.

"But some of these women ... I mean, I can't count on them all the time, you know? Some of them got drug problems, some of them like to pick up a few bucks on the side, banging guys out in the parking lot."

"Was Cindy one of those?"

The fat man stayed quiet for a moment. McCall added, "You're not under suspicion; we're not investigating you or your business."

"I know that," he said. "But I'm looking for an upside to cooperating."

McCall, standing between Isen and the manager, shifted her weight from one foot to the other. Isen stepped around her and put a twenty next to the manager's elbow.

"Yeah," he said, sliding the bill to the far side of his beer. "Cindy didn't mind being friendly to somebody with an extra hundred or so. Although I can't figure out why."

He turned on his stool, facing them fully for the first time. Even in the dim light from the neon beer signs above the bar, Isen could see the purple tracks of broken blood vessels on his nose.

"She was beautiful. Absolutely gorgeous. She had this sweet look about her—used to drive the guys crazy. Some of these other girls ..." He gestured to the stage, where a dancer was squatting before a customer, scissoring her knees open and closed, open and closed. "Some of these other girls look a little rough, you know? But Cindy looked like she should be on her way to class at some swanky college up north."

"She date any customers that you know of?"

"Nah. But she didn't exactly confide in me, either."

"Was she friends with any of the other dancers?"

"Her and Dee Ann seemed pretty tight."

"We'll have to talk to her again," McCall said over her shoulder to Isen. She pulled a small notebook from her purse and said to the fat man, "Now, what were the names of these other clubs where Cindy danced?"

They left Isen's car in the parking lot of the club and climbed into McCall's sensible little sedan. It was not a government car, Isen saw, but it might as well have been for all of the individuality it expressed. If a car could wear blue oxford cloth shirts, this one would.

When they were on the road, Isen said, "His comment about dancers turning tricks out in the parking lot put me in mind of my buddy Colonel Veir. He was a patron of that little side trade. And he certainly has a taste for the best-looking ones."

"So you think he might know something about this Cindy girl?"

"I'd be surprised if he didn't at least know who she was."

Isen was looking straight ahead, out the passenger side window, but he could feel McCall studying him.

"You're not planning on busting into his office and shouting at him about this, too, are you?"

"No," he answered, looking at her. "I thought I'd let you handle it this time. If you think you're up to it."

Beyond the fact that she'd left town two or three weeks earlier, visits to three other clubs turned up nothing, not even a last name, on the dancer named Cindy.

"Right about the time that Hauck killed himself," Isen said as they sat in McCall's car outside a club called, for some reason, *Thee* Doll House.

"Could be a coincidence," McCall said. "Everyone we've talked to said she was a bit flaky, prone to taking off whenever the urge hit her."

"It's a coincidence that she disappears at the same time her boyfriend kills himself?"

"You're making an assumption that she disappeared, for one thing. She may have just moved. And no one except Savin has suggested that Hauck was her boyfriend. Maybe he was just another john to her."

Isen folded his arms.

"You know what your problem is, Special Agent McCall? You don't watch *enough* cop shows on TV."

They rode back to Jiggles, where they tried to get the manager to give them Dee Ann's phone number.

"Do you know how many weirdos try to get these girls' numbers?"

That was all the response they got until Isen put three crumpled ten-dollar bills on the bar.

The big man pocketed the money, then pulled his round shoulders up in a small shrug. "Best I can do is call her and see if she wants to talk to you."

He rocked from side to side on his stool, slowly shifting the mass of his weight—or at least the part in contact with the stool—toward the edge. He reached for the floor with one foot, then waddled toward an office.

"Wait here," he told them.

He was back in less than three minutes, and his features, noticeably devoid of expression to this point, were screwed up as if he was in pain.

"Something's going on out there," he told them.

"Out where?" McCall wanted to know.

"Out at her trailer. She was crying, said somebody beat her up."

"Is she alone now?" McCall asked, getting to her feet.

"Yeah, yeah, yeah. She thinks the guy left, but she sounded scared."

"She have a boyfriend who would do this?"

"I don't know."

"Take us out there," Isen said.

"I'm not getting involved in this," the manager answered quickly.

"But there may still be someone there, hiding outside. Or the guy may come back later. You know where she lives?"

"I know where she lives, but I can't go out there. I . . . I have to stay here and run this place."

Isen saw that the man was scared. It wouldn't be unusual, in this line of work, to run into the occasional abusive boyfriend.

"We'll go out there. Just tell us where it is."

The man turned his head from side to side, working his mouth and staring at each of them in turn, as if he couldn't remember how he got there.

"Are you guys cops?"

"I am," McCall said. She produced her badge and ID.

The manager seemed relieved. "OK," he said. "OK. You can take care of this, then. I've got to stay here. Business like this doesn't run itself, you know."

Isen rode to the trailer park, which was on the east side of Fayetteville, with his feet pressed against the floorboard of McCall's car, his right hand gripping the dash, as if that would make her drive faster.

"Can we speed it up?" he asked.

"Ain't gonna do us much good to crash on the way out there," McCall said calmly, her hands at ten and two on the wheel. "Besides, in case you haven't noticed, I don't have lights and a siren on this thing."

When she came to a full stop at an intersection that was clearly empty, Isen snorted.

"Relax," McCall told him.

The Greenwater Trailer Park crouched in some low ground off the side of a state road east of town. Tall pine trees shaded rows of aluminum trailers, once white, now marked in gray and green where the trees dripped sap. Number twenty-seven, Dee Ann's trailer, was off the third driveway.

Isen was out of the car before McCall even had it in Park. He took the crooked redwood steps two at a time.

"Don't startle her," McCall said from somewhere behind him. "Lots of gun owners in these parts, and she may be a little jumpy if somebody's been slapping her around."

Isen looked back over his shoulder at McCall, and as he did so he noticed that the driver's side door on the rust-marked car in the driveway—he assumed it was Dee

Ann's—was open. What looked like the contents of a purse were strewn across the seat and onto the ground, little pieces of debris barely visible in the courtesy light.

"Dee Ann," he called, facing the door again. "It's Mark Isen and Terry McCall. Are you OK?"

The door was shut, but after McCall's comment about the gun, Isen didn't think he wanted to try it just yet.

"Dee Ann, it's me, Mark Isen. Are you OK?"

A light went out in one of the windows down at the end of the trailer. "Go away."

"Are you OK?"

"I was fine until I started talking to you people."

The light went off in the front room, but Isen thought he saw someone moving inside. Dee Ann might have been checking him out. Or drawing a bead on him.

"We'd like to see you to make sure you're OK. Are you alone? Why don't you open the door?"

Isen heard McCall mount the steps behind him. He realized, when she started speaking softly, that he had been screaming in the excitement. He looked around to see what neighbors might be watching.

"Dee Ann, this is Special Agent McCall. Your manager told us that you were upset, that you said something about someone beating you up. Now, you know you don't have anything to fear from us. But unless you open the door, I can't be sure that someone isn't holding you hostage in there, and I'll have to call the sheriff."

Isen didn't like the sensation he had, that he was being watched. Especially if there was someone inside besides Dee Ann. He had never liked being a target.

They heard the bolt slide back in the door.

"I'm alone," Dee Ann said. "Don't call the cops."

"Can we come in and look around?" McCall asked politely. "It's for your own good, really."

Dee Ann saw the logic in this, apparently, as she pulled back the door, turned on the light and turned away from them to go inside. Isen and McCall followed. When Dee Ann turned to face them, Isen came up short.

Her lips were already swollen, and there were abrasions on both cheeks that would soon swell into purple bruises.

She was holding a purple washcloth to her arm, but couldn't cover the whole of the vicious scrape there.

"Who did this to you?" McCall asked. She holstered her weapon, which Isen hadn't seen her draw.

"I don't know," Dee Ann said, the tears coming back in a generous flow. "Somebody who didn't like me talking to you guys, though. I know that much."

Isen approached Dee Ann to check her wounds, but the woman recoiled.

McCall stepped forward, waved Isen back. "What did he say that makes you think that?"

"He kept calling me a bigmouthed bitch. Told me I ought to know better than to talk to nosy fuckheads who can't mind their own business. Then he said I wouldn't be able to talk so much if he knocked my teeth down my throat."

Dee Ann let McCall pull the washcloth back. There was a deep cut on her upper arm, and parallel scrapes that traced the arch of her tricep from shoulder to elbow.

"He dragged me up those stairs," she cried. "I thought he was going to kill me in here."

McCall's soothing gestures made Isen feel useless. "I'll get some water to wash that," he said, ducking into the kitchen.

"Did he say anything else?" McCall asked. "Did he mention us? Or the investigation? Anything specific that you remember?"

"I don't know," Dee Ann said. She was regaining some of her composure now. "I was too scared. I know for sure he didn't want me talking, and you guys are the only new people I've talked to recently."

"Did you get a look at him?"

She shook her head. "He came up from behind me when I opened the car door to get out. He put his hand over my mouth ... and ..."

Dee Ann faltered again, and McCall led her to the couch, where she sat next to her and rubbed her back for a full minute until the dancer could speak again.

"He put his hand over my mouth and dragged me in here. It was dark."

"Any idea how tall he was?" McCall asked. "Compared to you, I mean."

"I wasn't standing. I was on the floor, and he'd pick me

up and smack me. He ... he was pretty strong. He picked me up with one hand."

She had her eyes shut tightly, and as Isen stood there with a basin of water and a dishcloth he'd found in the kitchen, he tried to imagine what it would be like to feel so powerless. Isen had been frightened before, and there were times in combat when he'd been sure he was going to die. But he'd always been able to fight back. His experience was nothing like Dee Ann's.

"We should call the sheriff," McCall said softly.

Dee Ann was suddenly animated. She stood abruptly, pushing McCall's hand off her. *"Fuck* that noise," she said, her chest heaving again. "I'm getting out of here."

"Where are you going?" McCall asked. "You don't have to leave."

"Are you kidding me? Do you see this?" She was screaming now, pointing at her bloody arm. "And this?" Her face.

"Someone almost *killed* me because I *talked* to you people. Do you think I want to stick around to see what happens? I'd rather be back in fucking West Virginia."

Isen looked at McCall, who'd done all the talking so far. *Do something,* he mouthed to her.

But McCall apparently saw that they weren't going to keep Dee Ann around with some lame promises about protecting her. Instead, she focused on their original mission.

"Dee Ann, do you know anything about your friend Cindy and a guy she may have been seeing named Mike?"

Dee Ann was stuffing clean laundry, which had been sitting neatly folded on the only chair in the tiny room, into a nylon bag. She was still crying, and her tears splashed the bag's bright blue fabric like raindrops.

"No."

"What was Cindy's real name?"

"I told you I'm not talking to you people. I'm leaving."

"I won't try to stop you," McCall said. "I'm sure you'll be safer somewhere else.,"

"That's right," Dee Ann insisted.

"But there may be other girls in danger back here. Once you leave you'll have nothing to worry about. But you can't let this guy get away with beating you."

Dee Ann didn't respond. McCall repeated the question as if she expected an answer.

"What was Cindy's real name?"

Dee Ann wrestled with her conscience and her fear. Finally, she spoke.

"That was her real name. Cindy Racze. Almost all the dancers use stage names, but Cindy didn't care. She said she wasn't afraid of those guys, that they were just little boys with tiny peckers."

"Was she involved with anyone?"

"Cindy used a lot of those guys," Dee Ann said, her voice cracking. "I mean, I like her and everything, but she used as many of them as she could, taking presents, turning tricks. She even let two guys fight over her once, right there in the parking lot." She shook her head. "She used to do all that kind of shit, and I'm the one who gets beat up."

"Did she have any special friends, regulars or anything like that?"

"No," Dee Ann said. She zipped the bag, but something caught in the zipper. "Shit!"

She flung the bag to the door, then looked around the dreary room.

McCall persisted. "Did she have any regulars, any favorites?"

"No, but *she* was somebody's favorite."

"Whose?"

"The big guy named Veir."

Isen felt something snap into place.

"He was the one in charge of the guys who ran all those parties," Dee Ann continued.

"Did she ever date him?"

"I think she might have at first ... this was a while back. Could you hand me that stuff?"

She gestured to the tiny counter in the kitchen. Isen handed her a half-dozen bottles of pills, mostly vitamins.

"But then he got kind of weird on her, so she dumped him." She retrieved the bag from the floor, stuffed the bottles inside. "Not that she wouldn't still take his money."

"What do you mean about it getting weird?"

"This guy used to follow her around like a puppy dog. Wherever she was dancing in town, this guy would show up."

She used to dance up in DC every once in a while, and he even followed her up there. She told me that he got this fancy suite in some ritzy hotel right near the White House, and he offered it to her. When she went, she realized that he was going to spend the night there, too."

"Did she stay?"

"I'm not sure; she didn't tell me. She liked to leave a little mystery to her stories, you know? I know she did him a couple of times, but then he started asking for other stuff. B and D, anal sex. He wanted to take a video of her with a couple of other guys he was going to hire. She tried to let him down easy, you know? I mean, the guy was spreading some bucks around. But he forgot that it was about money. He thought he owned her."

She stopped talking, looked around the tiny living room once more, pulled her bag on her shoulder.

"She told me she had that problem figured out, though."

"How's that?"

"Some other poor sucker she had on the line was gonna get this Veir guy off her ass. At least, that's what she was hoping."

"Who was the guy?"

"Don't know. If I had to guess, I'd say some GI. Young, probably. She said she let the guy think they were dating or something. The guy was all set to defend her honor. Can you fucking believe that? She even laughed when she told me about it."

McCall and Isen exchanged looks.

"Where's Cindy now?" McCall asked.

Dee Ann looked at McCall, then at Isen, who thought he smelled fear.

"Don't know. She was staying here, kind of off and on for a while before she split. Last time I saw her was the night that boy shot himself."

Isen and McCall sat in McCall's car in the trailer park after Dee Ann had pulled away. McCall had tried to get the dancer to give her an address or a phone number, but the woman was badly frightened. She finally gave her brother's name and number, saying that she'd tell her brother what had happened and that he'd kill anybody who tried to get near her.

"You think she knows more than she's saying?" Isen asked.

"Undoubtedly. But she's scared to death; I can understand why she doesn't want to cooperate with us."

"You think that Cindy's knight in shining armor was Hauck?"

"Seems to fit," McCall said.

"Now what do we do?"

"Well, we have no Cindy, no Dee Ann, Bennett is gone, Veir threw you out, Foote isn't giving anything up ... did I miss anything?"

"No, I think that's the whole list," Isen said. "We do know that someone doesn't want people talking to us. As of yesterday, there might have been a benign explanation for that. But after this"—he gestured toward Dee Ann's trailer—"I'd say some lunatic wants to get rid of us."

"If there is something behind the coincidence of Milan, Bennett and Savin getting shipped out, that doesn't mean the same people had Dee Ann beaten up."

"OK, I'll grant you that," Isen said. "But it could be that Veir has enough influence to get all three of them sent away, and at the same time turns around and uses methods that are a little more crude to get rid of Dee Ann."

"Mmm-hmm."

"We went around to these clubs to see if anyone knew where Cindy is," Isen said. "Maybe we didn't ask the right questions."

It was just a little after eleven when they pulled into the parking lot at Jiggles. McCall was going to drop Isen off at his car and then spend some more time talking to bouncers and club managers.

When he spotted his car, Isen's first thought was that there was frost on the windshield. Before he could even discard that as illogical—it wasn't cold—he knew what had happened.

"Oh, man," McCall said.

The windshield still filled the space above the hood, but it had been smashed into a silvery foil of broken safety glass.

The side windows were completely knocked out, the headlights caved in like wounded eye sockets.

Isen got out of McCall's car and walked around his own.

Judging from the impression on the hood, it looked like the work had been done with a baseball bat. There were large oval dents on every door, on each quarter panel. The tires had been slashed; one of them still held a large screwdriver, which stuck out like a knife handle in a B-movie stab wound.

"Looks like Dee Ann isn't the only one who's being told to shut up," McCall said.

Isen woke at seven on Saturday morning; Sue Lynn was on her back beside him. He wormed his arm under her neck and hugged her close; she responded by turning on her side, her cheek on his shoulder, one of her legs thrown across his body. She did not wake. Isen looked up at the ceiling and wondered if Dee Ann had driven all the way to West Virginia last night.

He had been shocked by what had happened to her, not because he didn't know it happened all too often but because he could not imagine how a man could strike a woman. He was disgusted by that kind of weakness.

He had also been shocked because the attack on Dee Ann had changed everything. Before they reached the trailer park, it was a stretch to think that the sudden departures of Milan and Savin were connected—Dee Ann's attacker had made his point clear—the opposition had dropped from the civilized to the barbaric. His wrecked car was merely redundant.

Sue Lynn stirred beside him, nestling deeper into the seam between the bed and Isen's body. He put his hand on her back to feel her breathing.

Dee Ann had gone home to family, that much was clear when she told them her brother would kill anyone who tried to bother her. But it wasn't until the middle of the night, some time after three according to the orange numbers on the bedside clock, that Isen had thought about that in any detail.

If he had already succeeded in pissing off the powers that be, if he had torpedoed his career by chasing down Veir in what McCall referred to as a witch-hunt, Isen had no place to go. Both of his parents were dead; he had no siblings; his wife had left him because, as she'd put it, he'd "married the Army first." He didn't own a home or enough furniture to fill a good-sized apartment; he didn't even have what he could call a hobby. He had the Army, and his memories, and nothing more. And if the Army were pulled away from him, well. . . .

Sue Lynn ran her fingernails lightly across his chest, the first sign that she was awake.

"Rough night, huh?"

"Yeah."

"What are you thinking about, studly?"

"I was thinking about how much I'm risking down here, jousting with Veir and all that."

"Your career, you mean?"

"Everything. I'm risking my career, and that's all I have in my life."

Sue Lynn pushed her hair away from her eyes and leaned back so that she could see his face.

"Sounds like you did a little two o'clock in the morning soul-searching."

"It was after three, actually." He still had his arm around her, and he liked the closeness there. She kissed him in the crook of his elbow, then put her hand to his face.

"And what do you want?" she asked.

"I guess that's the question I've been shying away from," he said.

"Don't feel left out," Sue Lynn said, rolling over onto her back. "Lots of folks spend their whole lives avoiding that question. What's important to you?"

"My identity as an Army officer, I guess. I mean . . . well, that's a little vague. But I'm tied up in this profession. I like being around soldiers; that's what I like best. I don't get to do that nowadays, which is why I hate my job at the Pentagon."

"So it's not the Army, because an assignment at the Pentagon is part of the Army, and you have to go through that to get back to troops. It's the soldiers, right?"

"Yes," he said.

"What else? What makes you happy?"

Isen rolled over on his side so that he could face her. He propped his head on his hand.

He wanted to tell her what a calming influence she was for him, how she had shown him that there were things not adrift. But the words eluded him.

"This closeness. Being with you."

"Being with someone you care for, someone you can talk to."

"Being with you," he said.

Sue Lynn looked at him; there was a fluttering in her stomach, like a muffled alarm.

"You're just lonely," she said, making light of it. "When you got here you were horny, but we've taken care of that."

"No," he said, still serious. "It's more than that. I'm not much different from Harlan Veir, in a way."

"What the heck are you talking about?" She sat up and slid over to the far side of the bed to put her feet on the floor. Isen pulled himself closer on his elbows.

"Let's assume he's behind all this stuff. I was thinking what might drive someone to that extreme. The Army is all he has; take away his career and he has nothing."

He looked into Sue Lynn's eyes. "Just like me."

"You're talking crazy," she said. "You have a career, he has a career. You have integrity. Harlan Veir, if he is behind *any* of this crap, can't check that box."

"Maybe not, but we have more in common than I'd like to think." He put his hand on her leg. Sue Lynn stood and retrieved her jeans from the floor. She kept her back to him as she pulled a long-sleeved shirt over her head.

"So are you going to ditch the Army?" She still had her back to him, brushing her hair in front of her dresser mirror.

Isen leaned back. Over the years he had come to believe that people acted to seek pleasure or avoid pain. Sue Lynn, this beautiful woman who had flown through storms and enemy fire, was afraid of being touched. There were doors she wouldn't—couldn't—open.

"Nah. I'm too old to learn a trade. Maybe I could get work as a private eye."

"I doubt it," Sue Lynn said, leaving the bedroom.

* * *

McCall called Isen at ten o'clock.

"I talked to a dozen bouncers and dancers last night, asked them about Cindy and Hauck. Zilch. Then I asked about Veir maybe following this Cindy woman. Turns out she was taking his money for a while, then she got tired of him. Problem was he wouldn't let up. One of the bouncers at Jiggles said Cindy once asked him to drive her home because she thought she was being followed."

"Veir?"

"Turns out the bouncer didn't see anyone that night. But Cindy got kind of scared there in the weeks before she left. Seems like Veir was there, no matter where she was dancing."

"Did he harass her?" Isen asked.

"Not really. More like the puppy dog that Dee Ann described."

"Doesn't sound much like our man Harlan," Isen said. "The submissiveness, I mean."

"Well, he's full of surprises. There was one guy, one bouncer, who remembered Cindy complaining that Veir kept other guys away from her."

"You mean in the clubs?"

"Yeah," McCall said. "They make a lot of their money doing those table dances. But when Veir was around, well, he just didn't like her doing those for other guys. She complained to the bouncer once, who talked to Veir."

"What did Veir do?"

"The guy said Veir was very cooperative. Told the bouncer that he couldn't imagine why anyone would think he wanted to interfere with Cindy making a living. He left quietly when the bouncer asked him to."

"No problems?"

"Not with that guy. Of course, the guy is about seven feet tall, big enough to have his own zip code."

"So we don't have much, right?" Isen said.

"Well, we don't have as much as I'd like to have. But it looks like we've connected Veir to Cindy and Cindy to Hauck."

"We could use some hard evidence," Isen said.

"Yeah, OK. It's still pretty shaky, but it's something to go with."

"I wonder if Veir behaved differently when he was out of town," Isen said. "Remember that Dee Ann said he followed Cindy to DC and had a hotel suite there for her? Maybe the rules about behavior didn't apply in other places."

"So where does that get us?"

"Maybe it'd be worth taking a look around DC, trying to find out where she worked up there. Dee Ann said the room was in a hotel near the White House. Wouldn't hurt to see what's around there."

"You going back tomorrow?" McCall asked.

"Yeah. And I've got to meet with General Flynn. Keep me posted on the search for Cindy," Isen said. "And call me if Bennett shows up."

Isen sat at the kitchen table, spread the morning paper before him and fixed a cup of coffee. When Sue Lynn came in the room, Isen felt an awkwardness that hadn't been there before.

"Look, Sue Lynn, I didn't mean to run you off this morning," he said. "I just think we've got something good going here."

"So do I, Mark," she said. She stood on the other side of the table, tapping her fingernails on the wood, measuring, Isen thought, what she was about to say.

"And I don't want to ruin it with a lot of sentimental BS. You're not in love with me; you're just so thrilled that some woman will treat you right, with a little consideration and no mind games, that you think we're headed into a relationship."

"It is possible, isn't it? There are lots of ways to make a long-distance relationship work. People in the Army do it all the time."

Sue Lynn was about to say something but was interrupted by a knock at the door. She got up and returned a moment later with an express package.

"It's for you," she said.

"Isen checked the return label. Bryn Mawr, Pennsylvania. Inside, a manila envelope and a single piece of fine stationery, without letterhead, that listed two sets of dates.

"Whose handwriting?" Sue Lynn wanted to know.

"I'm not sure," Isen said. "Meade, Veir's ex-wife, lives in

Bryn Mawr, and she looks like the kind of woman who would have stationery like this."

Isen used a kitchen knife to slice the envelope. He reached inside and pulled out a sheaf of enlarged photographs, many of them in black and white and all of them, apparently, taken without the knowledge of the subjects. Most of the pictures showed two people: one was always Harlan Veir, the other an attractive young woman.

"Surveillance photos," Sue Lynn said. "They're photos of Veir and ... I'm going to take a wild guess here, his girlfriends."

The settings of the photos varied from bars and expensive-looking restaurants to strip joints. Isen recognized the stage of Jiggles in one shot. Some of the enlargements were fuzzy, and the young women were not all clearly visible in the photos. It was obvious the photographer was interested in Veir.

Isen started to make a couple of small piles.

"Sorting them out by women," he said.

When he was finished, he'd counted thirty-one photographs and seven different women.

"Busy little devil, wasn't he?" Sue Lynn said.

"I guess she used this stuff in the divorce," Isen said. "There's certainly plenty to choose from."

"What about those dates?" Sue Lynn asked, turning the paper over to see if there was anything on the back side.

"Well, let's see," Isen said. There were two pairs of dates, in chronological sequence. The start and end dates of each pair looked to be three or four years apart.

"Look," Sue Lynn said. She'd turned over the photographs, which had been dated with a stamp.

"All of these pictures fall within the second time period listed there."

"Think these could be the dates of Veir's assignments to Bragg?"

"That's what I'm thinking."

"But what did she want to give us this stuff for?" Isen wanted to know. "To prove that he was as big a jerk and philanderer as she said he was? And why didn't she sign the note, or indicate what the dates were for?"

"You said that you thought Dee Ann knew more than

she was letting on, and that she was keeping quiet out of fear," Sue Lynn reasoned. "Maybe it's the same with the former Mrs. Veir."

"You mean she'd like to screw him over but doesn't have the guts to say so?" Isen said.

"That might be a little harsh on her, considering what happened to Dee Ann. Maybe Meade has been slapped around a bit, too."

Isen shuffled through the stacks.

"Maybe one of these women is Cindy."

He looked at the photos again, then tucked everything back into the envelope.

"I'm going out to Sicily DZ to watch Veir's battalion jump this afternoon," he said. "You want to come along?"

"No thanks," Sue Lynn said. "I get my fill of airborne ops with my own jumps. Falling out of an airplane once every few months is enough for me. I can't imagine wanting to watch other people doing the same thing."

"Not even Hollywood Veir? I'll bet he sprouts wings or something."

Sue Lynn didn't answer.

"We'll continue that other conversation later, OK? The one about you and me."

Sue Lynn picked up the newspaper and unfolded it in front of her. "Mmm-hmm," she said.

"Say, Mom," Isen said. "Can I borrow the car?"

"Goddamn pussies should have let us jump from five hundred feet," Harlan Veir shouted over the roar of aircraft engines.

Veir was seated at the end of one of the webbed jump seats that ran along the center of the C-141 Starlifter. Like the rest of the paratroopers in his battalion—three hundred and seventy-one of whom were making this jump—Veir was a prisoner of his parachute harness and the combat gear he had to take out the door with him. It pinched his shoulders, pulled at his crotch and constricted his chest. His rucksack, sixty-five pounds of field gear hanging a few inches off the floor, tugged at and tightened the straps across his groin. Sweat ran down his face—painted with thick green camouflage stick—in greasy tentacles. Two men across the tiny aisle from him had already puked their breakfasts onto the aluminum deck and the boots of a half-dozen or so men around them—including Veir.

And this was the glamorous part of being a paratrooper. Veir loved it.

When the aircraft dipped one wing to turn back on its racetrack pattern toward the drop zone, or DZ, Veir let out a whoop.

"Is this fucking great, or what?"

"Airborne, sir!" a few men shouted.

The doors were already open, the jumpmaster—responsible for everything that went on in the back of the aircraft—was already into his incredible high-wire act. The NCO leaned out of the aircraft door for a visual check of the drop zone, hanging on by his hands like a man leaning over a balcony. Satisfied with what he saw below, he turned to the troopers in the aircraft and shouted to be heard above the thundering engines.

"Get ready!"

All eyes were on the jumpmaster.

"Inboard personnel, stand up!"

Almost as one, the paratroopers along the center benches struggled to their feet, fighting gravity, nausea and the rocking of the airplane.

"Outboard personnel, stand up!"

Now there were four files of heavily laden men trying to merge in two tiny aisles. Veir, facing aft at the rear of the aircraft (he would be the first out the door) could no longer see his men, but he heard someone else vomit.

"Hook up!"

Veir grabbed the end of his static line and hooked its metal clip to the cable that ran overhead. The webbed strap would pull his parachute open as he left the aircraft.

"Check static line!"

The commands were a litany now. More than just simple checks of procedure and equipment, their predictability was also a talisman, comforting the superstitious and the faithful alike.

"Check equipment! Sound off for equipment check!"

Veir tugged at the chinstrap on his helmet, eyed the metal quick-release disk on the front of his harness. There was no one in front of him for Veir to check; but he felt the hand of the man behind him patting his packed chute, touching the static line coiled there, looking for errors, deadly oversights.

Starting at the rear of the line, or stick, the signal came up to the jumpmaster as each man slapped the man in front of him.

"OK!"

When Veir felt the thump on his shoulder, he pointed at the jumpmaster and bellowed, "All OK."

Through the open door just a few feet away from him, Veir could see the pointed tops of pine trees speeding away underneath the belly of the aircraft.

The jumpmaster held up an index finger.

One minute.

The engines boomed like a giant waterfall; hot air shot around Veir's legs and face, thick with the smells of jet fuel, sweat and vomit.

The jumpmaster held up his hand, thumb and forefinger held together in a pinch.

Thirty seconds.

Veir stepped up to the jumpmaster, handed over the trailing end of his static line and waited for a few interminable seconds.

Then the red light by the door went out and the green light came on. He was out the door as the jumpmaster's command, shouted into his ear, registered.

"GO!"

The air rushing by at over a hundred knots sucked him from the aircraft, spinning his legs upwards so that he could see the dark green rectangle of the plane's horizontal stabilizer pass over his head.

Veir counted *one thousand, two thousand, three thousand, four thousand* and then the chute opened, tugging at his shoulders, painfully tightening the harness's grip around his torso. He looked up; above him, the thin canopy fluttered and filled, a green disk against the blue Carolina sky.

Mark Isen sat in the bleachers at the edge of Sicily Drop Zone and watched the paratroopers stream from the doors on either side of the aircraft. There were soldiers working around the bleachers, cutting and trimming the grass around what would be the ringside seat for the Secretary of Defense. One of the young men, manning a swing blade and hacking away at some thick weeds, paused to watch.

"Air-fucking-borne!" he said enthusiastically. "That's why I signed on the dotted line."

Another soldier, also within Isen's hearing, paused and leaned on the handle of his blade. He watched the drop with mild interest, then looked at his enthusiastic comrade.

"You mean it wasn't to cut weeds and paint bleachers?"

"C'mon, man," the true believer said. "You gotta admit that jumpin' is the coolest thing."

"Shit," the second soldier said, turning back to the resistant weeds. "They drop boxes of ammo out of planes, too. So that means we gotta be at least as smart as a box of bullets to do the same thing, right?"

Sue Lynn wasn't home when Isen returned to her house. There was no note. He was stuffing some of his clothes into a bag when he heard her come in.

"I'm up here," he called.

She came into the room and walked by without kissing him.

"Hi," she said as she sat on the bed. "How was the drop?"

"Standard, I guess," Isen said, offering her a smile she didn't return.

"Something wrong?" he asked.

"No."

Isen balled up a couple of dirty shirts and pushed them down inside his overnight bag. Sue Lynn, her leg hanging off the bed, swung her foot nervously.

"I heard some kid say something funny about airborne ops," Isen said. "I thought you'd get a kick out of it since you were so fired up about the Airborne this morning."

"Oh?"

"One soldier said that jumping out of airplanes was 'the coolest.' The other one said, 'Hell, they drop boxes of ammo out of planes. So that means we have to be at least as smart as a box of bullets to do the same thing, right?' "

Isen smiled; the joke fell flat.

Sue Lynn leaned up against the headboard.

"Did you ever think that maybe your attitude is making your job down here harder than it has to be?" she said.

"What?"

"Your attitude. You can't come in here making fun of the whole idea of airborne forces—something these people around here have dedicated a great deal to—and expect them to welcome you."

"Sue Lynn, you were the one this morning talking about how you didn't see anything special about jumping."

"I didn't say that," she replied, folding her arms across her chest. "I said I'd seen enough jumping for the time being."

Isen felt as if he'd missed part of the movie.

"Well, excuse me for having an opinion," he said. "In case you've forgotten, I have a few jumps under my belt, too. I think I'm entitled to an opinion."

"I'm just saying you're not very tactful about the way you express those opinions," Darlington said. "You can't come here, attack us and expect us to cooperate."

"Now it's 'us'?" he said.

When she didn't answer, Isen zipped up his bag.

"Look, I don't know what's gotten into you. I'm sorry if I said anything to offend you. I'll try to be more circumspect in the future."

But Isen didn't sound sorry. Nor did Sue Lynn budge.

"Look, I'll call you from DC, OK?"

"OK," she said, offering her cheek as he leaned to kiss her.

"G'bye."

"Good-bye."

When she heard his rental car pull away, Sue Lynn turned and punched her pillow.

"Damn, damn, *damn,*" she said thumping away at the lacy shams.

She plopped back on her bed and stared at the ceiling.

"Now why the hell did I do that?"

Outside, a neighbor fired up a lawn mower. She rolled over onto her stomach and listened to her breathing until she calmed down.

You've staked a claim here, she told herself. *You've put a great deal into the Army, and any attack on that denigrates your choice.*

She turned that argument over in her mind and saw facets of it she found unsettling.

Maybe that's been your mistake, she thought. *You've spent all this energy struggling to succeed in a man's world, and where has it gotten you?*

She thought about something a friend of hers, another woman aviator, had said when she told Sue Lynn she'd decided to leave the Army.

"You know many Aviation Brigade Commanders who have breasts?"

But that was only part of the problem. Sue Lynn had been telling herself for years that she was independent, that she could operate completely on her own. And whenever she felt any doubt about that, she lost herself in frenzied activities—skiing in New Zealand, rafting the Grand Canyon, scuba diving Truk Lagoon—as if to prove that she *did* have a life.

Mark Isen had rattled that. But admitting that she wanted something more than an affair was a shift of continental proportions. Mark was ready to say it out loud. Sue Lynn first had to accept that a change wasn't a repudiation of who she was. Who she'd been.

Sue Lynn propped herself up on one elbow and looked at her bedside clock.

It would take Mark four or five hours to drive to Washington.

Four or five hours, she thought. *No, make it five or six. Then maybe I'll call.*

Isen called General Flynn from a rest stop in Virginia; the two men arranged to meet at the general's quarters as soon as Isen could reach Fort Myer. Some of the strain of their last encounter lingered as they sat on the porch, drinking cold beer against the heat as the light failed. Isen recounted what he'd found in his talks with the dancers and what he thought of the express package he'd received. As he spoke he wondered if Flynn would interrupt his report.

A lot's happened. Maybe that'll move him.

"Did you contact Veir's ex to ask why she'd sent that stuff?" Flynn asked.

"I tried, sir. No answer. Maybe she's out of town."

Flynn shook his head. "In order to connect the sudden departures of Savin, Bennett and Milan with the attempt to keep this dancer . . . what's her name?"

"Dee Ann."

"With the attempts to keep Dee Ann from talking to you, that would mean that Veir almost certainly has to be involved. You told me your theory about the Division Chief of Staff, but there's no reason to believe that other high-ranking officers are this involved with these dancers, is there? I mean, no one else knows them well enough."

"Not as far as I know," Isen said.

Flynn picked at the label on his beer bottle, rolling the paper up into tiny balls and putting them in a potted plant on the table beside his chair. He was distracted, and Isen didn't think he was running through theories about what had happened at Bragg.

"Have you talked to your sister lately, sir?" Isen ventured.

Flynn looked up a second later. "Pardon?"

"Have you talked to your sister lately? Are you keeping her apprised as to what's going on?"

"I talk to her, but I haven't been filling her in, no. I guess I want to make sure it'll do some good before I subject her to all of this. Right now all we have is a bunch of speculation. I can't see the sense in letting her ride a roller coaster as we develop these theories."

"I see," Isen. Then, slowly, testing the waters. "Lieutenant Savin implied that you gave Michael some heat about their rooming together."

"Did he?"

"Yes, sir. I inferred that you were against it because Savin is gay and you didn't want Michael mixed up in any trouble over that."

"Savin is right. I was against it. I told Michael that. He just decided not to listen."

Isen nodded, not completely satisfied.

"There's something else," Flynn said, setting his beer on the end table and pushing himself back in the big wicker chair.

"The White House just put Veir's demonstration on the President's schedule."

"Damn," Isen said, more impressed than surprised. "Now he'll really be unreachable."

"Yes. Exactly. The Chief thinks that the President is only a month or two away from making a decision on force structure that's going to completely change the way the Department of Defense works. He's tired of all the squabbling, the interservice rivalry. He wants to come out, as he put it, 'representing the American taxpayer,' and see what we're getting for our defense dollars."

"Is he thinking about doing away with the current structure?" Isen asked. 'Are we going to just have a Defense Force, like the Canadians?'"

The idea of eliminating the separate services had been tossed about for years. Countries who'd followed that line found themselves with more efficient organizations—it was the military equivalent of downsizing, as well as the giant bogeyman that stalked the nightmares of countless generals, admirals and defense contractors.

"There are some people who think he might go that far. The stated objective of his visit is to choose one service that will be the nation's primary response force."

Flynn drummed his fingers on his thighs.

"So the pressure is on Veir," Isen said.

"Unimaginable pressure," Flynn said. "And not just on Veir."

Here it comes, Isen thought.

"I got a message from General Santangelo yesterday."

Isen nodded, listening. General Santangelo was the commander of the Eighteenth Airborne Corps, headquartered at Bragg. The Eighty-second Airborne Division, of which Veir's unit was a part, was a subordinate unit of that Corps. Santangelo was Veir's boss. Three echelons up.

"General Santangelo, who had called me when Mike died, expressed his sympathies again. Then he asked me if I understood the importance of the mission they were undertaking down there at Bragg. I told him I did."

Patrick Flynn was up for his third star. Even the least politically minded soldier in the Army would know that tangling with senior officers over something as sensitive as the upcoming demonstration wasn't a great idea. Isen waited to be told to drop the whole investigation.

"He asked me if I knew you, too," Flynn said.

"He mentioned me by name?"

"Absolutely," Flynn said.

He paused, as if to let Isen consider that he was known to—and probably not appreciated by—powerful senior officers.

Fuck them, Isen thought.

"He told me that he trusted my judgment—and that he wanted me to consider whether whatever I had you looking into down there could wait two weeks."

"In other words, until after the President's visit."

"Roger that."

"Isn't that interfering with an investigation?" Isen wanted to know.

"Hardly, Mark. You're not an investigator." Flynn's tone had changed to something that made Isen think that they weren't on the same side of the issue any longer.

"What about McCall? She's an investigator."

"Yes, General Santangelo mentioned her. It seems that Special Agent McCall has been deliberately stalling in not completing her report. On Monday her boss is going to call her in and tell her to file or be written up for poor performance."

"They got to her, too?" Isen asked. "I thought the CID is supposed to be separate."

Flynn leaned forward carefully. He looked as if he might feel sorry for Isen's lack of understanding.

"The CID is part of the Army too, Mark."

"So what you're saying is that anyone can be reached? Is that it?"

When it was out of his mouth, Isen realized what Flynn might infer from that question.

"If you're accusing me of knuckling under," Flynn said, his eyes flashing angrily, "I'd like to remind you that's my nephew lying under that hill over at Arlington."

How the hell did I get myself in this position? Isen wondered. *This whole thing was his idea, and now I'm about to get reamed because I've taken a serious interest in it.*

"I'm sorry, sir. I didn't mean to discount your feelings.

It's just that ... well, it doesn't feel to me like I'm after Veir. To me it feels like I'm on to something."

He looked up to see how Flynn was following. The old man still looked pissed off.

"Well, it's going to have to wait," Flynn said. "This thing is bigger than both of us."

"Sir, that's just not right," Isen persisted. "I'm not interfering with the preparations. I won't go back to Veir's battalion headquarters, even."

"I guess somebody thinks that messing with Veir's mind, following him around and asking a bunch of questions about him, is enough to rattle him. And no one wants that to happen when the big show is less than two weeks away."

"But if he is successful," Isen said, "then it's going to be even harder to get close to him. He won't just be the division's fair-haired boy, he'll be the Army's hero. There'll be no chance of finding out what really happened. In fact, maybe that's what he's counting on. If the thing with the President goes well, he might as well get a pardon."

"You know, Mark, I asked you to do this job because I think that you can see the right thing, and you have the guts to go after it."

Flynn paused. Isen remained quiet; somehow he didn't think congratulations were forthcoming.

"But that doesn't give you a monopoly on what's right and what's wrong. You still have to take into account the fact that you may be wrong."

"So what's the final word, sir?" Isen asked.

Flynn ran his fingers over the gray stubble of his hair. He had the look of a man tormented.

"Let me sleep on it, Mark."

An hour after Mark Isen left his quarters, Major General Patrick Flynn knelt in a dimly lit Roman Catholic church in Alexandria. He had been driving around, trying to decide what to do about the events he'd set in motion, when he spotted the church. He called at the rectory and asked the priest who answered his knock if he would hear Flynn's confession.

"I'll be with you in a few minutes," the priest said. "Why don't you go sit in the chapel for a few moments."

Patrick Flynn clung to the faith he'd been raised in. He tried to adhere to the teachings of the Church and to attend the sacraments. He'd often thought that the guilt his Roman Catholic upbringing had saddled him with made it necessary that the Church offer solace to the penitent.

There had never been a time when he'd walked into a confessional and been unable to recite a list of sins, mortal and venial, he'd committed since his last visit. He preferred the clear-cut rights and wrongs. Looking with lust at another man's wife. That was pretty straightforward. He hadn't stolen anything since he was twelve or thirteen, and he attended the Sabbath, but he could always count on a few impure thoughts to round out what was mostly a litany of garden variety transgressions.

He wondered, as he sat, if he honored his father and mother. He took that one seriously. And though both his parents were dead, he honored their memory by looking out for the family, and the family name. That embrace reached out to his sister, to his nieces and nephews, including the dead Michael Hauck.

There was no question in Flynn's mind that homosexuality was a sin. Countenancing such behavior, Flynn believed, must also be sinful. He had tried to warn Michael of that. What Michael had called open-mindedness was fraught with dangers, spiritual and temporal.

The priest joined him, sitting in the pew directly behind Flynn. When he turned, Flynn was surprised at how young the man was. He wore a green pullover and a pair of khakis. No belt.

"Is this OK here?" the priest asked.

Flynn would have preferred the darkness and anonymity of the confessional, but it seemed kind of silly since the man was sitting right behind him.

"Sure, I guess so."

The young priest pulled a long rectangle of purple cloth—a stole, Flynn knew from his altar boy days—from his pocket and put it around his neck.

"What can I help you with?"

The suicide had shocked Flynn. The church taught that it was wrong to take your own life, a terrible sin. He wondered if Michael's soul was lost. And he wondered about his part in it.

Flynn crossed himself.

"Bless me, Father, for I have sinned."

That part came easily. The rest was difficult.

Back in his apartment, Isen called McCall at home to warn her about what was going to happen on Monday morning.

"Looks like the end of our little crusade," Isen said, fishing. He had decided, before he called, that he wasn't going to try to badger her into helping if her career was at risk.

McCall sighed on the other end. "Yeah, I guess it is," she said. "Do you think you'll come back after the President's visit?"

"I'm not sure what I'm going to do," Isen said.

"You're not thinking of continuing if Flynn tells you to lay off, are you?" She wasn't lecturing him; she sounded concerned, maybe even unsure herself.

"Hey, you're the one who said I was just a washed-up old Pentagon paper shuffler," he said. "What difference does it make?"

"Well, I worked hard to get here," McCall said, "and I don't want to risk it."

"Uh-huh."

"What does that mean?" she demanded.

"What does what mean?" Isen teased.

"That 'uh-huh' business."

"I don't know. It's a listening technique, I guess. It means I hear and understand what you're saying.

"Something's been bothering me," he went on. "We figure that Bennett, the only lieutenant we haven't questioned after your initial interview, is the one who called Veir, right? Did that bear out with Veir's phone records? I mean, did Veir's call to Foote fit the time sequence?"

McCall hesitated. Isen knew then that she hadn't checked.

"They'd be local calls," she said. "No record."

"Veir lives in Fayetteville; Foote lives on Bragg. Are you sure?"

There was a pause, a few silent seconds as they both thought the same thing.

"Don't think you're going to get me to come on this little adventure with you, trashing my career with a bad performance review the first time out, just because you have it in for Veir."

"You know what I hate?" Isen said. "I hate the fact that my little personality conflict with Veir gives everyone a convenient excuse to back off when we encounter a little resistance in taking on the division water-walker."

"I said it before, Major. You're not the person to handle this case," McCall said.

"Yeah, but if you chicken out, I'm the only one left. Right?"

He was about to repeat the question when McCall hung up on him.

There were no messages from Sue Lynn when he got home. He thought about calling her, but wasn't sure if she wanted to hear from him or if she missed him as he missed her.

We've only been together for a little more than a week, he reminded himself. *Maybe you ought to lighten up on her.*

He lay on his bed fully clothed, light on, because to do anything else would be to admit she wasn't going to call. He woke at one o'clock in the morning, the light still on. He was thinking about Veir.

It's a shame we started off pissed at each other, he thought. *If we were buddies and I suspected him, no one would be able to say I was just out to get him.*

Isen reached over and turned off the bedside lamp, plunging the room into darkness until his eyes had a chance to become accustomed to the gloom and the glow from the streetlights outside.

He went over, again, all the facts that he and McCall had gathered. Veir wasn't tied to Hauck's suicide, but there was an awful lot of interesting stuff going on that Isen felt needed more attention.

He tried to clear his mind of his personal feelings for Veir, to see if the facts looked any different in that light. Sue Lynn, who wasn't one to shy away from popular psychology and what Isen referred to as "touchy-feely shit," had talked to him at some length about how to *let anger go,* how to *move beyond anger.* After her suggestion, he closed his eyes and visualized his animosity toward Veir as a rock, held tightly in one hand. He stretched the hand out over a stream, as if from a bridge, and let the rock go. He watched it hit the water and disappear, then he took several deep breaths, as she had instructed him.

He opened his eyes; light from the window drew skewed rectangles on the ceiling. Before he could say "New Age," Veir's face was back. The bastard.

Must you hate your enemy? McCall had asked him

"Well, I don't know if I must hate him," Isen said out loud. "But I'm afraid I do."

12

S<small>UE</small> L<small>YNN</small> D<small>ARLINGTON</small> <small>CALLED</small> I<small>SEN AT WORK ON</small> M<small>ONDAY</small>
morning. "Is this the one-nine-hundred number for lonely
Army officers?" she asked when he answered.

Isen looked around quickly to see who might be within
earshot. "I might be able to help you, young lady," he
purred into the phone.

"It was awful lonesome in my bed last night."

Isen picked up his coffee mug, sipping around a small
grin. "So you miss the great sex?"

"Oh, no," Sue Lynn said. "I had great sex. It's just so
much better when there's someone there to share it with."

Isen tried to laugh and swallow at the same time, which
sent hot coffee shooting through his nose onto his shirt and
the papers spread on his desk.

"*Nice*, Sue Lynn," He said when he could speak again.

"The old coffee-through-the-nose trick?" she wanted to
know.

"Through the nose, onto the desk, onto the uniform."
Isen found some napkins in a desk drawer and began to
blot his shirt.

"Well, now that I've gotten a rise out of you, so to speak," Sue Lynn said, "I'm sorry I bit your head off the other day."

"That's OK. I probably crowded you. Last night I was thinking that's it's been less than three weeks since I called you out of the blue. I just hope I didn't scare you off."

"Not yet," Sue Lynn said. "Truce?"

"Truce."

"So I can get on with the news?"

"What happened now?"

"First Coates called me to tell me that Kent was involved in sending Bennett off to that school at Fort Benning, and she thought he was involved in having Savin sent off, too. She said he did the paperwork himself and apparently he left something on her computer."

"So it is bigger than just Veir."

"Looks like it, buddy boy," Sue Lynn said. "And did you hear that the President is coming for this demonstration?"

"Yes, I certainly did," Isen said. He recounted a bit of his interview with General Flynn.

"So he said to knock off the investigation?"

"Not really," Isen said. "He was a little shaky at the end, but he called me this morning to say that we could proceed cautiously."

"Well, if you're still on a witch-hunt," Sue Lynn continued, "You'll be able to do it a lot closer to home. Veir is scheduled for some meetings in DC on Wednesday. He has to see the Chief of Staff on Wednesday morning, and he's having lunch with a couple of White House flunkies that day to brief them on what's going to happen at Bragg."

"How do you know this?"

"He's taking a VIP flight out of here, and so the request had to come across my desk."

"Why, you sleuth, you."

"But that's not the most interesting thing. The pilots were bitching because Veir wanted the flight plan changed so that he could stay the night in DC, even though he said his meetings end in the afternoon."

"He's already acting like a general," Isen said.

Sue Lynn was quiet on the other end. "Are you thinking what I'm thinking?" she asked after a moment.

"Cindy may be up here."

"Right. He's got everyone down here working practically around-the-clock on this show for the President, yet he's going to take the night off in DC? That doesn't make sense unless there's some strong reason."

"Like he wants to find Cindy and shut her up, too."

"If he had something to do with beating up that other girl," Sue Lynn said, "then there's good reason to be concerned about Cindy."

"So I've got until Wednesday to find Cindy Racze," Isen said.

"You've got to get to her first, Mark. If there's even the slightest chance that Veir is behind all this stuff that looks like cover-up."

"OK. Listen, I want you to find me a picture of Veir and a picture of Cindy and send them up overnight."

"The picture of Veir will be easy. But where am I going to get a picture of Cindy?"

"You could take those glossies around, ask if Cindy is in one of those pictures. I also seem to remember some pictures hanging in some of the club entrances. You know, promo shots. Maybe there's a shot of Cindy."

"You're not going to try to follow Veir, are you?"

"I'm not sure I'm cut out for that stuff. Besides, I want to get to her first, before he spooks her."

There was a moment of quiet between them, just the soft hiss of static.

"This has sure come a long way fast," Sue Lynn said. "Too fast."

"Yeah."

"When you came to my house the first time, you were doing someone a favor. Now people are getting beaten up and you're sneaking around like some amateur detective. I'm worried about you, Mark."

"I'll be all right. I might not have a career left, but I'll be all right."

More quiet. The background noise seemed more emphatic.

"What about us?" Sue Lynn said.

Isen was surprised to hear her refer to them as an "us." She had brushed him off the other day; now she was back. Isen remembered a bumper sticker he'd once seen: *There*

*are only two ways to understand women. And nobody knows
either of them.*

"I've been thinking about taking some leave when this is
all over," he said. In fact, the thought had just occurred
to him, but he felt he was doing well making it up as he
went along.

"Maybe the two of us could take a trip somewhere. Sort
things out without this pressure cooker."

"Somewhere warm," she said. "Where we'd only have to
pack bathing suits and T-shirts and suntan lotion."

She was talking in that warm liquid tone she used when
she was randy, and Isen paused for just a second to wonder
if she was in her office.

"Slow-turning ceiling fans, cotton sheets . . ."

"Breezes through the open windows, the scent of flowers
coming in at night . . ."

Isen heard someone nearby. He looked up to see Colonel
Tynan standing outside his cubicle, watching him and, judging from the look on his face, listening.

Isen put his hand over the mouthpiece of the telephone.
"Can I help you, sir?"

"I realize it's tough to get back in the habit of working,"
Tynan said, rocking back and forth on his feet as he did
when he was agitated. "But give it a shot."

When Tynan left, Isen went back to Sue Lynn.

"Sorry, honey, but the galley is pulling out and I've got
to man my oar."

"I'll man your oar for you."

"That kind of talk will get you . . . whatever you want,"
Isen said. Colonel Tynan walked by again, and Isen thought
he heard a *tsk.*

"Listen, Mark, be careful, OK?"

"I can't catch a disease in a DC club that I can't catch
in Fayetteville."

"That's not what I mean, and you know it," she said.
"Just be careful of the kind of chances you take. If Veir is
somehow behind this stuff . . . well, just be careful."

"I'll do my best," Isen said.

In the dimly lit halls that make up the inner rings of the
Pentagon, it is not unusual to find visitors roaming aimlessly,

sometimes covering the same stretch of corridor for an hour until some experienced local recognizes the distress signals.

The two men in suits outside the suite Isen shared with five other officers had that lost look. Isen, on his way downstairs to grab a sandwich, got some other read from them as well.

It's Huey and Dewey.

"Can I help you gentlemen?"

"Yes, we're looking for . . . you, actually," one of the men said, reading Isen's name tag.

Isen stuck out his hand.

"Mark Isen," he said. "You must be Huey."

"Beg your pardon?"

"Nothing," Isen murmured. "Do I know you?"

"I'm Special Agent Clark," the first man said. Isen shook Clark's hand, then turned to the other man.

"This is Special Agent Brush."

"As in Fuller Brush?" Isen asked.

"The same."

Clark launched into the preliminaries; Isen kept quiet and studied the two men.

Clark was older, maybe thirty-five or forty, with a thick ring of dark hair that circled the very bald and very shiny top of his head.

He wore a brown suit.

Even Isen, whose civilian clothes tended to imitate a uniform—pressed khakis and jeans, solid-colored knit shirts tucked in snugly and secured with neat leather belts—even Isen knew that a brown suit was bad news.

Brush was younger and better dressed; he even smiled when Isen looked at him.

Obviously not from the same CID as McCall, Isen thought.

"We're here to talk about the conduct of your investigation at Fort Bragg," Clark said.

"You want to walk with me while I get something to eat?" Isen asked. "I only have a little bit of time."

Clark nodded and the three men set out on the circuitous route to the underground mall and its fast-food havens. Brush, still smiling, read Isen his rights—the same ones a civilian has against self-incrimination—from a card as they walked. The experience was somewhat less intimidating in the hallway on the way to get lunch than it might have been in an interrogation room.

"We understand that you've been conducting an unofficial investigation into the suicide of a lieutenant down at Bragg," Brush said. "We're interested in how you're going about that."

"OK," Isen said cheerfully.

"How have you identified yourself to the people you want to question?"

"I tell them I'm conducting an unofficial investigation on behalf of the dead man's family."

"Have you ever identified yourself as a CID investigator?" Clark asked.

"Never."

"Have you ever threatened any junior officers, telling them your mentor"—here Clark flipped open his notebook—"General Flynn, will either go hard on them or take care of them depending on how they cooperate?"

"Never even close."

The questions went on for the whole walk down five floors, around to the sandwich shop, through the slow-moving line and all the way back to Isen's office. Clark and Brush exchanged looks more and more often as the questioning continued.

There was no trace of the hostility that McCall had brought to their first meetings. Isen had a sneaking, hopeful feeling that the agents believed him.

"Look, why don't you go into your office, and Special Agent Brush and I will join you in a minute," Clark said when they'd come full circle.

Isen obliged, leaving the two CID men in the hallway. Four or five minutes later, the two men came in.

"Look, Major," Clark said. "We have no sworn statements about your behavior down at Bragg—"

"Were you sent here to harass me, scare me away?" Isen interrupted.

Clark looked down at his notes. Brush smiled again, although he tried to hide it this time.

"We do need to warn you, however, that impersonating a CID investigator is a serious offense, OK?"

"Got it," Isen said.

Clark, looking no happier, closed his notebook.

"One more thing," he said.

"What's that?"

"Can you help us get the hell out of this building?"

Lieutenant Colonel Tynan found plenty of work for Isen to do on Monday afternoon. Isen amused himself with daydreams of Sue Lynn as he plowed through the mostly makework tasks. By the time he was able to leave the office at a quarter to eleven that night, he thought it a bit too late to go cruising around Washington looking for strip joints. Even the area around the White House wasn't always safe enough to invite evening strollers once the tourists were gone.

Tuesday and Wednesday were replays of Monday. Throughout Wednesday afternoon Tynan came by Isen's desk at what seemed like ten-minute intervals, each time dropping off some bit of minutia that needed attention. Isen thought about calling Flynn to see if the general could help him out from under the piles of work. In the end he decided that Flynn, shaky as he was, might use Isen's workload as an excuse to drop the whole thing.

"See to this before you go home this evening," Tynan said when he brought a fresh stack of requirements by Isen's desk at seven.

"I'd like to get out of here before twenty-one hundred, sir," Isen said. "If that's OK."

Tynan spoke in that singsong voice that encouraged thoughts of homicide among his subordinates. "I'm glad that you showed the presence of mind to *ask,* Major Isen, instead of just *leaving* whenever you thought it appropriate."

He must know about me playing hooky, Isen thought. Then, in the next instant, *Well, fuck him.*

"My job is difficult *enough,*" Tynan droned on, "what with all these pressures placed on me by the Army Staff, *without* my having to keep tabs over which of my officers is leaving work *early.*"

Spare me the lecture, Isen thought. *Do I get the night or what?*

"I understand, sir," Isen said.

"I'll be here with you this evening," Tynan said. "We can leave at about the same time."

*I wonder if you're hiding from your family or they made
it clear that they like when you stay away.*

"And what time would that be, sir?"

Tynan got edgy.

"Just a ballpark figure," Isen said. Then, in an inspired
moment, "I have someone coming in from out of town, and
I was hoping to meet him later."

Not the whitest lie you've ever told, Isen thought. But
not untrue.

"We'll see how it goes," Tynan said. He motioned Isen
back to his desk with an imperious finger. "Duty first."

Isen wandered into Tynan's little cubicle at eight and was
sent out again with another letter to draft.

By eight-thirty Isen was convinced that someone was leaning on Colonel Tynan to keep Isen at the office. The promise
of a few points with a superior, Isen thought, would certainly
be enough to turn Tynan into a jailer. Tynan had probably
moved quickly and happily through most of his career. But
all the rules had changed in the shrinking Army and, like a
lab rat conditioned to respond in one way, the stress of
change had all but rendered him ineffective. The poor bastard wasn't sure which lever to push to get his pellets. Unfortunately, in Tynan's case, the uncertainty had turned him
into an asshole.

Now you're starting to see everything as a conspiracy, Isen
thought. *This guy was a jerk long before you ever heard of
Harlan Veir.*

At nine-fifteen Isen stood in the tiny opening that served
as a doorway to Tynan's small world. The colonel was bent
over a desk swept clean of all papers except the one he held
in his pudgy fingers. The desk itself was larger than the
standard: Isen supposed it gave Tynan some sort of status
to have a bigger desk than his subordinates. The plan failed,
in Isen's view, because the desk completely filled the little
cubicle.

Maybe he keeps it clean so that it looks bigger, Isen
considered.

Whatever else he thought of Colonel Tynan, Isen knew
that this kind of future—senior paper pusher—was nothing
to aspire to.

"Sir?" Isen said. "I'd like to leave now."

Tynan took his time looking up. He stared at Isen for four or five seconds before answering.

"Where is it you have to go in such a *hurry?*" Tynan wanted to know.

Isen felt a loosening at the seams of his control, like the trembling lid of a pot left too long on the burner.

"Sir," Isen said as evenly as he could, "it is now"—he looked at his watch—"twenty-one fifteen. I arrived at work fourteen and a half hours ago. In the past three days I have worked thirty-eight hours. As we are not in the midst of a combat action, I think I should be allowed to leave the office for a few hours."

Tynan blinked and did not respond immediately. When he did, he stuttered at first.

"I ... uh ... this work, this work *has* to be done, Major. We cannot wait on *your* social obligations to see this friend or that friend ... and, besides ..."

"Who got to you?" Isen said.

"What? What are you talking about?"

"Who got to you? Who told you to make sure that I don't leave the office all week?"

Tynan looked down at the desk for an instant, convincing Isen that his theory was right.

"I'll see you tomorrow morning at zero seven, *sir.*" Isen brought his heels sharply together, snapped his fingers to his brow and away again. "Good evening, *sir.*"

He cursed all the way to the parking lot, relishing his anger, turning it over in his mind, touching its hot places. But as much as he knew it would embolden him for what he was about to do, he also knew from experience that anger clouded his judgment.

When he got to the car, he faced it squarely and placed both hands on its roof until he felt the heat subside.

Well, McCall, he thought. *You'd be proud of me, exercising self-control and all that.*

Isen had a change of clothes in the back seat of his car, left over from the weekend at Bragg. The pants were wrinkled and the shirt, upon the kind of close inspection he'd seen only men do—sniffing the armpits—was a little ripe. But he didn't have time to run home. He changed in the front seat, stuffing his uniform on the floorboard of the passenger side.

Isen drove across Key Bridge into northern Virginia, then out to a little club by the Beltway; one of the dancers Sue Lynn had spoken to thought Cindy had worked there. He had a hard time finding the place, which was as low-key—one small neon sign in the window—as Jiggles was tacky. He showed the glossy promo shots Sue Lynn had sent him to the bouncers and manager.

"Yeah, she used to work here," one of the bouncers told Isen when he produced Cindy's picture. He wore a name tag, helpfully identifying him as Mason. "Her name ain't Cindy, though. Least, her stage name. She went by Angel. She ain't been around in a while."

"How long?"

"Four or five weeks, I guess."

"You ever see this guy in here?" Isen asked, showing Veir's photograph. "Maybe talking to her? Maybe she complained that he was bothering her?"

Veir's picture was from the Fort Bragg newspaper, the *Paraglide*. Isen held his finger over the beret.

"Yeah, I seen that guy in here. But I don't remember her complaining. In fact, I think she was taking him for a few bucks, you know?"

Isen folded the photographs up and slipped them back into his shirt pocket.

"You're not a cop, are you?" Mason asked.

"No, I'm not," Isen said. "How did you know?"

"Because you left out a big question, and I figure a cop would have asked that question." He was smiling as he looked away to check the IDs of a gaggle of four boys trying to pass themselves off as men. He held up one of the tendered cards. "This one's fake," he said to the group. He slipped that card into his own pocket. "So you all lose." Mason pointed to the door. "Good-bye, and have a nice day."

Two of the youngsters made sounds, as if they wanted to protest or wanted the card back. Mason simply raised an eyebrow.

"Good-bye," the last one said as he closed the door behind them.

"Now, what were we saying?" Mason said, turning back to Isen.

"You were yanking my chain about some question that I would have asked if I were a real cop," Isen said.

"Oh, yeah." Another smile.

"Look, I'd love to stay around and entertain you with my ineptitude," Isen said, pulling out a twenty. "But I really don't have the time now."

"A real cop would have asked when was the last time I saw the guy," Mason said. "The one with the funny hat."

Another smile. Another few seconds.

"OK, when was the last time you saw the guy with the funny hat?"

"About an hour ago," Mason said. "He was in here looking for Angel."

"Jesus Christ," Isen said. "Why didn't you tell me?"

"I'm telling you now," Mason said. "And don't swear at me."

"Sorry," Isen said. "Did he say why he was looking for her or anything?"

"Nope. He came in and sat at the bar for a little while. I did notice that he kept watching the door, though. I mean, the front door. I thought it was odd because if Angel was going to come in, she probably wouldn't use the front door. But maybe he didn't know that."

"Did she have any other hangouts around here?"

"Some of the girls go up to Georgetown sometimes, let the college boys buy them drinks."

"You know the names of the places they hang?"

"Just head to M Street, right below the university. There's a good half-dozen places there. You'll see all the college kids on the sidewalks—looks like a feeding frenzy."

Isen made his way back toward the city. He had to park four blocks off M Street, the busy main thoroughfare now packed with tourists and students returned for the fall semester. The sidewalks were crowded enough so that he had to step down off the curb if he wanted to walk more quickly than the casual stroller.

Gotta have a plan, he told himself after he'd been jostled along both sidewalks in the five-block range the bouncer had given him. He ducked into a crowded club and, after wading through customers three-deep at the bar, ordered a beer. The music was loud and—to Isen at least—unrecognizable. The clientele was mostly college age, and the uniform seemed to be baseball caps, turned sideways or backwards, the bills rolled carefully to give them a weathered look that didn't seem to go with the expensive shirts and jewelry and leather backpacks. These were kids who would never see the inside of an Army barracks.

Isen pushed his way to a stool, feeling like someone's grandfather.

Cindy was proving difficult to find. There didn't seem to be a fresh trail.

Maybe Veir is having better luck, Isen thought.

It was now after ten o'clock, and Isen felt he had to get closer to Cindy, or at least to Veir, in a hurry. He had a small tourist map of downtown Washington that he'd carried from the car; he pulled it out to study. Sue Lynn had given him the names of two clubs, the one in Virginia, and one— she thought the name was Kryptonite—that he hadn't been able to find in the phone book.

Dee Ann had told them that Veir had offered Cindy a suite at a hotel "around the corner" from the White House. It hadn't occurred to Isen that the club in which Cindy danced might also be near the White House. Then he remembered how surprised he'd been to find so many homeless people sleeping on benches in the park at Lafayette Square—within sight of the Executive Mansion's windows. Maybe there were some other surprises close to the center of official Washington.

His tourist map showed a half-dozen luxury hotels within a few blocks' walk from the White House. Isen got a few dollars in change from the bartender and took his beer with him into one of the old-fashioned telephone booths by the rest rooms. He began making calls, telling the hotel operators he wanted to leave a message for a guest named Harlan Veir. On the fourth call, to the Hotel Washington, the operator connected him to a room.

Isen let the phone ring six times while he thought of Dee Ann and what had happened to her in Fayetteville—right next to Bragg. If Veir was behind that, then there was no telling what he'd do this far from the flagpole. Isen hung up and located the Hotel Washington on his map. It was on Pennsylvania at Fifteenth, separated from the White House by the hulk of the Treasury Building. Close enough to walk.

Isen scooped the change off the small shelf and walked back to his seat at the bar, glancing through the big window that looked out on the crowds. Short blond hair. Walking quickly. Just a glimpse.

Harlan Veir was on the sidewalk across the street.

In the seconds it took Isen to pull his change off the bar and take two quick steps toward the door, Veir was gone.

Isen hurried out onto the sidewalk and turned left to parallel Veir on the south side of the street.

No sign of him.

Isen walked faster, glancing back in case Veir stopped on the other side to window-shop.

Maybe he went inside somewhere.

No sign of him. Something told Isen he'd be too close if he crossed the street, but it wouldn't make much difference if he lost Veir.

He stepped off the curb and into traffic. Four kids in a BMW swerved away from him. The driver leaned on the horn and a pretty young girl in the passenger seat, sitting with the window rolled down, yelled, "Watch where the fuck you're going."

Isen dodged traffic in the westbound lanes and made it to the curb. Still no sign of Veir.

Isen turned west again, running the broken field around people walking arm in arm and in groups of three.

No sign of Veir in front of him. Isen turned around, wondering if he'd outdistanced his quarry. Or maybe Veir had been walking faster than the crowd.

"Shit," he said aloud, turning around on the sidewalk in an agony of indecision.

Isen turned back, walking east now, looking into the windows of the bars and restaurants he'd already passed, thinking that perhaps Veir had gone into one of them. He moved along the sidewalk in an odd, jerky gait, looking both ways, darting up to the windows, annoying or even alarming some of the passersby who noticed him. He checked his watch. Eleven o'clock.

Isen began a slow run back to his car, which was parked

off M Street near Thirty-fourth. As he ran, he looked at the traffic passing him, hoping for a glimpse of Veir.

He was sweating by the time he reached his car. He thought about calling the hotel again to see if Veir had returned. He could let the phone ring and simply hang up if Veir answered. As he put his key into the ignition, Isen had a sudden, sinking thought.

What if Veir saw me looking for him?

The bouncer, Mason, had said that Veir had kept his eyes on the door of the bar the whole time, as if waiting for someone. But Angel/Cindy would not have used the front door.

If Veir knew that, Isen thought, *who the hell was he looking for?*

He swiped at his brow with the back of his hand and turned the key. *Goddamn, this is getting weird.*

Isen endured the stop-and-go traffic of M Street for several miles until he crossed Rock Creek Park and joined the faster traffic on Pennsylvania Avenue. Isen looked into the windows of the half-dozen taxis he could see. No Veir.

The bastard just disappeared.

Suddenly the White House was on his right, reassuringly familiar, lit starkly and framed by the thick foliage, now blue-black in the darkness and artificial light. Isen could see the white-shirted guards of the uniformed Secret Service detail manning the little booths at the corners of the grounds.

He found the Washington Hotel and parked in the garage, which was shared by the Willard Hotel, the Washington's more famous neighbor. He went into the lobby, feeling a little ridiculous as he slipped along the wall, hoping that Veir wouldn't appear from an elevator. What would he say?

Isen found a house phone and had the operator ring Veir's room.

No answer.

It was eleven-thirty.

Isen went outside and showed the now dog-eared pictures to the doorman, who was understandably suspicious about answering questions put to him by a man in wrinkled, soiled clothes who looked as if he'd just run all the way from Virginia.

"I can't help you," the man said.

Isen folded a twenty-dollar bill alongside the little photo of Veir and extended his hand again.

"Try it in this light," he said.

"Oh," the doorman said as if he just now understood what Isen wanted. "That guy. Yeah, he looks a little like Andrew Jackson, right?"

Twenty dollars poorer and unamused, Isen asked, "Seen him?"

"He left here about ten minutes before you got here. Maybe not even that long. A taxi dropped him off. He went in and came out again, real quick."

"Did he get another cab?"

"No, he left on foot."

"He ask for directions or anything?"

"No, he seemed to know where he was going."

"Which direction was that?"

The doorman, who was rapidly losing interest, pointed north, toward Pennsylvania Avenue.

"Any topless bars within walking distance?"

"Sure. There's one right on K Street, just up from Lafayette and around the corner. It's got some funny name."

"Kryptonite?"

"No," the doorman said, shaking his head. He looked down, studied the sidewalk. "Sybarite," he said, smiling, pleased with himself.

"Damn," Isen said, setting off immediately.

He walked quickly, wondering why Veir would go back to the hotel for a few moments. He wondered, too, what he would say if he ran into Veir. The bar was a public place, but it would be pretty obvious that Isen was following him.

Doesn't matter, Isen reminded himself. *If he does find Cindy, I need to be right behind him.*

At midnight Isen was walking along K Street, two blocks north of the White House, when he spied a small, elegant sign that said "Sybarite: A Gentleman's Club."

Well, that's a far cry from Fayetteville's "Jugs-O-Rama," Isen thought.

He checked the street, nearly deserted at this hour, and went in.

Yes, we are a long way from Fayetteville, he thought as he followed carpeted steps to a clean tile landing. There, a framed sign announced "guest fees" and a young man in a white shirt and bow tie said, "Good evening, sir."

By the time he set foot into the room, Isen realized that the place was too small to avoid Veir if the other man was here. He waited a minute by the door to see who came out of the rest room—but there was no sign of his man.

The room was long and narrow, with a polished wooden bar along one wall and floor-to-ceiling mirrors opposite. A narrow aisle separated the bar stools from two rows of little tables. A small platform, only eighteen inches high, held a single dancer. At her feet, a brass rail framed the stage. Unlike the formidable constructions that protected dancers at Jiggles, this rail was delicate, almost an imaginary line signaling to patrons that they should—really, now, gentlemen, please—leave the ladies some room.

Isen doubted he'd run into any soldiers here, although the clientele certainly wore uniforms. Dark suits, white shirts, the occasional blue, and the slightly bemused expressions of men trying to look as if they chose to be here only because, gosh darn it, tickets to the opera were sold out.

The dancer on stage was different, too. While it was certainly possible to run across beautiful young women dancing in the altogether in Fayetteville, one was just as likely to see women who were on their way down, sporting scars, loose flesh, mother lodes of subcutaneous fat rippling like cottage cheese. In contrast, the woman on stage here looked like a fitness instructor, like someone, Isen thought, who could keep up with Harlan Veir on a PT run.

The bartender, whose plastic name tag read "Mario," greeted Isen cheerfully.

"You have a woman who dances here by the name of Cindy Racze?" Isen asked, producing the photo. "Or maybe she goes by Angel."

"Who wants to know?"

"She used to date a friend of mine," Isen said. He was about to say *who recently died,* but thought better of it. "I'm supposed to pass her a message. Maybe you could get it to her."

Mario was polishing glasses, pointedly uninterested in Isen's story. "She hasn't been around in a while."

I'll take that to mean she did dance here. "Uh-huh," Isen

said. "When she was dancing here, did you ever notice a guy hanging around who might have been bothering her? Big guy? Short hair?"

"You a cop or something?"

"Or something," Isen said. He put Veir's picture on top of Cindy's. "This guy here, maybe. Ever seen him around? You see him tonight, maybe?"

Mario seemed intrigued that Isen was carrying photos; he became more interested. "No, not tonight. But I think I've seen him before."

Isen was about to pull out another twenty—they were going fast, and soon he'd be drinking water—when Mario got a little more helpful.

"He used to come around some. Not every time. She said he was in the Army, but that he wasn't stationed around here. I wouldn't say he bothered her, though."

"Why's that?"

"They were pretty friendly. I'd guess he was probably a sugar daddy, you know? He did her favors, maybe helped her out with some money or something. And she did him favors."

Mario cupped his hand, making a circle of his thumb and forefinger. He held it to his open mouth and pushed his cheek out from the inside with his tongue.

"How long did this go on?"

"Not too long. Started this past summer, I guess. But I think they had a falling out. Cindy liked to have a couple of friends, you know, keep the field wide open. I don't think this particular guy liked that very much."

Mario answered a waitress's call at the other end of the bar, leaving Isen to wonder where he was going to get more information on Cindy. He thought about hanging out to see if Veir showed up—he was almost certainly in the area—but then reminded himself that he was after Cindy, not Veir.

He got up, threw a buck on the bar and headed outside. When he pushed the door open, Harlan Veir was standing outside.

"Hello, Isen."

Isen pulled up short. Although he'd been thinking about the man, he hadn't been expecting to run into him. He tried to salvage some composure, but he was sure Veir had intended to startle him.

"Good evening, Colonel," Isen said after a pause. "What brings you to Washington?"

"Oh, I had a little business to attend here." The cold fish smile appeared. "I'm headed back in the morning. What about you? I thought you lived in Alexandria."

"I . . . uh . . . I was in the area," Isen said. "Thought I'd stop for a beer."

That was about as lame as it gets, Isen thought.

"Would you care to join me?" Veir asked. "I've got some time to kill."

Isen was surprised again, and something in him told him to stay, to see what Veir could tell him.

Find Cindy, he reminded himself. But what was the best way to find her?

"No, actually, I'm meeting someone. I'd better be going."

Veir smiled his empty grin. "She's not here, is she?"

There was a perceptible pause, a weighty few seconds when both of them, Isen was sure, were thinking about Cindy.

"Who's that, sir?"

"Whomever it is that you're meeting," Veir said. "I guess I assumed it was a woman. But then again, you're seeing that major down at Bragg, aren't you?"

"Major Darlington, yes, sir," Isen said, remembering how Veir had forgotten Sue Lynn's name several times.

"Well," Veir said. He reached for the door handle and was past Isen when he dropped his voice to a whisper, almost as if he were talking to himself. "I hear she's a great cocksucker."

Veir was inside before what he'd said registered with Isen. Isen almost reached for the handle before realizing that that was probably what Veir wanted.

Go ahead and bait me, asshole, Isen thought. He grabbed the handle, pulled the door open a few inches and slammed it shut. *I've got your fucking number.*

He turned and walked east on K Street, jamming his hands in his pockets.

All these people who are so concerned about a vendetta should meet you, Isen thought. *Maybe they wouldn't be so squeamish about your reputation if they saw what a douchebag you really are.*

Isen turned south on Fifteenth Street, crossing I Street to the front of the Veteran's Administration Building. He could feel his anger growing sharply, and he fought against it, knowing that it would keep him from thinking clearly. He tried instead to concentrate on everything that had happened.

Could it have been a coincidence that Veir was outside the door? he quizzed himself. *It sure looked as if he were waiting for me.*

Isen crossed H Street, trying to get some objective distance from the whole thing. But Veir's smug face kept coming back to him, smiling that eerie smile. *Great little cocksucker.* Isen was sure that was what Veir had said.

Maybe Sue Lynn had had a fling with him. She certainly seemed to hate him as if she had.

She told you she didn't, Isen. Now you're going to start doubting her because of something that jerk-off said.

At the corner of Lafayette Park he looked up at the statue of Kosciuszko, the Polish military engineer who'd come to the aid of the Colonies during the American Revolution. Isen had visited the garden, hidden on a slope at West Point, where Kosciuszko sat to gather his thoughts as he built the Hudson River fortress upon which so much of that struggle depended.

I need someplace like that, Isen thought. *Got to clear my head.*

Isen glanced around Lafayette Square. He could clearly see the White House, alight across Pennsylvania Avenue. He could just as clearly see the homeless camped on the benches that lined the semicircular walkways. During the warm months, this park was a center of daytime activity, with workers from the many buildings that fronted it coming out to enjoy the fresh air.

At night it belonged to another segment of society.

Isen decided he could walk around the park as long as he walked fast and looked like he knew where he was going.

He set off along the northern edge of the square, just across from St. John's Church, where so many presidents had worshiped. A man in a long raincoat and dirty yellow pants, his hair half-captured under a swollen watch cap, passed him going in the opposite direction. He gave Isen a wide berth.

There was nothing to indicate that Veir had expected to see Isen, except the feeling Isen had that Veir had been waiting outside.

Isen imagined himself on General Flynn's porch, with the general asking the questions.

What made you think that?

The way he looked at me, sir. Like he was satisfied that I'd come out right there, like he expected to see me.

What else?

That's it, sir. That and the fact that some bouncer thought Veir had watched the door an awful lot tonight, like he was expecting someone, someone other than Cindy.

You're positive that Veir knew that Cindy or Angel or whatever her real name is could only come through the stage door, or from the dressing room?

No, sir. I can't be positive of that.

Isen heard footsteps behind him. He turned, and the man in the watch cap and yellow pants, who'd been following him, halted some twenty feet behind him.

"You want something, partner?" Isen asked. Not cheerfully. More in the tone of a warning.

Yellow Pants turned away and walked back toward Kosciuszko.

At the northwest corner of the park, Isen turned toward the White House and walked south, the park on his left. There was some movement under a huge pile of blankets on one bench. Isen told himself that the fact that the homeless slept out here at night meant it was relatively safe. In dangerous neighborhoods, the homeless slept during the day and stayed awake at night, when the demons were on the prowl.

One of the streetlights was out, and Isen looked around behind him again when he was in the middle of the darker passage, but there was no sign of Yellow Pants or anyone else.

None of the bouncers or managers he'd talked to in Fayetteville or D.C. had said anything about Veir being abusive or threatening to Cindy. He was a sugar daddy, they said.

Deep pockets, a little shot of leg now and then. A bit miffed, perhaps, that he wasn't the only one, but he didn't lose his mind over it, either.

Yet someone had beaten Dee Ann, probably to keep Isen from learning more about Cindy.

Isen turned along one of the diagonal walks toward the center of the park. He walked with his head down, watching his feet and thinking how much Veir might know about the inquiries he'd been making. Maybe Veir would give up his search, knowing that Isen was following him; or maybe he'd just be more careful about the trail he left.

Or maybe, Isen thought, *he'll become even more emboldened by this thing.*

There was a shuffle behind him, as of someone beginning to run. Isen turned to see Yellow Pants jogging toward him on the same brick walk, talking to himself.

"Talk about spending *my* money, eating *my* food. *Sh-e-e-et.*"

"Something I can help you with, pal?" Isen said when the man got closer.

Yellow Pants looked up and stopped suddenly. He placed his feet shoulder-width apart, then leaned forward at the hips so far he looked as if he might fall.

"Look out for yourself," the man said solemnly. "I look out for me. You look out for yourself."

"I'll try," Isen said.

Yellow Pants seemed satisfied with this; he turned around and shuffled off in the direction he'd come from.

When Isen turned back to the front, he was looking at the ground and so saw only a pair of legs before something crashed into his face.

Isen's eyes suddenly filled with painful shards; his head snapped back and his body followed. He put his arms to the side to break his fall, and so his face was uncovered when the next blow—a vicious kick—came again at his face.

Isen shut his eyes and brought his hands up, but his attacker was quick enough to land more blows to his uncovered face. Isen heard a crunch, followed by an explosion of pain from the center of his face; his nose was broken. He pulled his legs up into the fetal position as his assailant smashed him again and again in the head, in the stomach, in the kidneys. He was vaguely aware of the feet dancing in front of him, looking for an opening. He could see nothing else, not even the color of the shoes; nor did he see the foot that went straight up and down again quickly on the side of his face, closing him off in merciful darkness.

At six-fifteen the following morning, Mark Isen was sitting in his car on the street outside General Flynn's quarters when a Military Police Officer approached the car from behind.

"Step out of the car, please."

Isen couldn't turn his head—there was too much pain in his neck—so he rotated his body halfway around in his seat. He couldn't see the soldier's face, just part of a uniform and the heavy black leather belt laden with cuffs, pistol, radio.

"Step out of the car, please," the police officer repeated.

Isen opened the door.

If you thought I looked suspicious sitting down, he thought, *wait 'til you get a glimpse of the whole picture.*

He still wore the clothes he'd had on the night before: a bloody shirt, torn at the neck; trousers streaked with grime from where he'd rolled on the ground, trying in vain to protect himself. He'd spent the night in the emergency room, after having been found by District Police, nursing a broken nose, one cracked rib and a host of bruises and abrasions.

"Don't even bother asking for ID," Isen said while the soldier was still staring at him. "My wallet got stolen when I got jumped last night. My name is Major Mark Isen, and I'm waiting for General Flynn, who is not expecting me."

The MP, a tall, skinny private first class with an enormous Adam's apple and bad posture, stepped back and looked over the roof of Isen's car at the quarters' nameplate to determine if they were, in fact, in front of General Flynn's. Confirmation seemed to do nothing to lessen his suspicion.

He looked back at Isen, narrowing his eyes a bit and examining Isen's bloody clothing as if he were an interesting photograph in a police training manual.

"What did you say your name was, sir?" he asked.

"Isen, I-S-E-N. Major Mark Isen. I work over at the Pentagon. Last night I got attacked down by Lafayette Park. I stopped by here this morning to see General Flynn—"

"Turn around and put your hands on the roof of the car, please, sir," the MP said.

"Oh, this is great," Isen said in exasperation. "Just fucking great."

He turned toward his car and slapped his hands down on the roof. A woman, walking her dog on the sidewalk a few feet away, stared at the little tableau of crime and punishment, then hurried by.

The MP stepped up behind Isen and patted his arms, then slid his hands down Isen's side. Isen cringed, anticipating the sudden pain if the soldier patted his ribs.

"Don't ..." he began, bending over quickly.

The cop didn't like the sudden move. He'd placed one foot inside Isen's. Now he kicked outward, and Isen pitched forward into the side of the car, smacking his forehead on the edge of the roof.

"God*damn*," he said. "What'd you do that for?"

The MP had backed up. Isen was almost afraid to turn around, certain that the young crimefighter had drawn his weapon.

"My ribs are all bruised from being kicked around last night," Isen said. "Just don't bang on them anymore, OK?"

Isen looked up. No pistol, but the soldier had pulled out the cuffs.

"Stand up, face the car and place your hands behind your back."

"You're not going to *cuff* me, are you?"

"Stand up, face the car and place your hands behind your back."

"I heard you the first time," Isen said sharply, fully aware that he was digging a deeper hole every time he shot his mouth off. "You don't need any cuffs; I can barely lift my freakin' arms."

But it was too late. A few minutes earlier, he'd been an officer, sitting in dirty civilian clothes on a U.S. Army base. Now he was a suspect, and the police officer's attitude had changed drastically.

"If you're such good buddies with General Flynn," the

MP said, grasping one of Isen's wrists, "why didn't you just call?"

Isen was experiencing something he'd only heard and read about before, something that generally didn't happen to thirty-some-year-old, middle-class white males: he was being singled out by the police because he didn't look like he belonged in this spot.

"Mark, is that you?"

Isen felt a palpable relief at the sound of General Flynn's voice; but the MP held his arms, and he couldn't turn around.

"Jesus, Mark, what the hell happened to you?"

Flynn walked around the car and into the street to get a closer look at what was going on.

"I found this man sitting in front of your quarters, General," the cop said. He was talking to Flynn as if the two of them were sharing a confidence about someone they both knew and disliked.

"He claimed that he didn't have any ID . . . says he was robbed."

"Well, it seems pretty obvious that something happened to him, don't you think?"

The MP wilted a tiny bit and, in his defensiveness, reverted to copspeak.

"The suspect exhibited aggressive moves when I was in the process of searching him for weapons, sir."

"Weapons? Jesus Christ, son, this man is a soldier, a trained killer. He doesn't have to carry weapons. Why, if he'd wanted to resist, you'd already be dead."

Isen turned to watch; the MP was blinking nervously, too frightened to laugh at what might not be a joke—who the hell knew what generals were going to say?

"Now take those goddamned handcuffs off him before he gets pissed off and kills both of us."

The soldier tried an insincere smile; Flynn scowled in return.

Isen turned away from the young MP and offered his wrists. The soldier removed the cuffs gently.

"Thank you," Flynn said. "You can leave now."

The MP fumbled at his belt, trying to put the cuffs back in their holder. When Flynn repeated himself, the youngster tried saluting while his left hand was still struggling against the resistant cuffs. Isen and Flynn walked to the house.

"That kid looked like he almost believed the stuff about the bare-handed killer," Isen said.

"Judging by the look I saw on your face when I came out of the house, he should believe. Now, what the hell happened to you?"

"I ran into a little trouble last night down in Lafayette Park."

"What were you doing down there?"

"Following our friend Harlan Veir."

Something dark passed over Flynn's face; Isen wasn't sure if it was anger at him, anger at what had happened to him, or just a general distaste for hearing Veir's name yet again.

Flynn took him by the arm and led him up onto the porch of the big brick quarters.

"You want some coffee?"

Isen nodded and Flynn went inside, returning a few moments later with two mugs. Isen sipped at his and burned his swollen lip.

"Damn," he muttered. "Maybe I'll skip the coffee."

"How did you know Veir was in Washington?" Flynn asked.

Isen was about to tell Flynn about the VIP flight and Sue Lynn's call when he paused at something in Flynn's tone.

"Did you know he was coming up here, sir?"

Flynn nodded. "Yes. I got a call from his boss down there, Larry Tremmore."

"He tell you to lay off, too?" he asked.

Flynn narrowed his eyes; he would only tolerate so much smart-ass, Isen knew.

Fuck it, he thought. *I'm the one who got his ass kicked last night.*

"We're done with this thing, Mark," Flynn said. "We've got to lay off Veir. You and I are getting a reputation around here; people think we're after Veir. People think that you're just a loose cannon with no respect for the law, no respect for procedure, no respect for a brother officer's reputation."

Flynn leaned back in his chair, slump-shouldered.

"I may have to just accept not knowing all the details of Michael's death."

Isen wanted to scream. "It's not just about Michael anymore, sir," he said. "If you had seen what happened to Dee Ann—"

"Do you know it was Veir ... know for sure that he was involved with the beating of this girl or what happened to you?"

"Veir was waiting for me when I left that last club," Isen said.

"He was waiting for you? Or was he outside?"

Isen sat back in his chair. It pissed him off that Flynn was cross-examining him, that Flynn was unwilling to take the risk of fighting the system when he, Isen, was wearing several dark purple badges of his own commitment. And he believed, in his heart of hearts, that Veir had ambushed him. *But the truth is ... I can't be absolutely certain.*

"He was just ... outside, sir."

"And this was right before you got jumped in the park?"

"Yes, sir. Minutes before."

Leaning forward now, Flynn put his coffee mug down on the table in front of him.

"Do you think he could have followed you around the corner to Lafayette Park and jumped you?"

"Yes, he most certainly could have, sir. I believe he's capable of it. He knows that I'm causing—or trying to cause—him all sorts of problems. For that matter, everybody in the Army thinks so."

Flynn folded his hands carefully, examining his fingernails.

"Did you see who did this to you?" Flynn asked.

The million-dollar question, Isen thought. *Say yes, and chances are that Flynn will let me do whatever I have to do to go after Veir. And I'm sure it was Veir.*

"No sir. I didn't see who attacked me," Isen said.

Flynn sat back, relaxing for the first time. There was even the hint of a smile on his face.

"Did I say something funny, sir?" Isen asked.

"No. Not at all, Mark," Flynn said. "But you did just prove something to me."

"What's that?"

"That you're not out to get Veir at all costs, no matter

what the people at Bragg say. If you were, you just had the opportunity to finger him."

"Well, sir," Isen said, lightly touching his swollen nose with the tip of a finger, "I wish I could sit here and tell you that it never occurred to me to lie."

He smiled, a wry grin on the side of his mouth that wasn't swollen.

"But I will tell you that I'd be willing to bet whatever I have left of a career that it was Veir who attacked me."

The smile dropped from Flynn's face. A telephone rang inside the house, making Isen think of Colonel Tynan, who would soon be looking for him. Isen resisted the temptation to look at his watch.

"There's a lot riding on this presentation that Veir is doing at Bragg, Mark," Flynn said without enthusiasm. Isen had the feeling they were in a shoving match; he'd push a little, Flynn pushed a little.

"Yes, sir. But that doesn't mean that we can let slide our responsibility to look hard at things that are . . . out of line."

Flynn was wavering. That third star, that nice job at some major headquarters away from Washington, it was all on the line. On the other hand, Flynn already had enough years to retire. Isen, if he got canned, would be out looking for a new profession at the age of thirty-five.

"We have to remember our duty to the whole organization, Mark. We're talking here about the future of the Army."

"Sir, you said yourself that the folks at the Pentagon are blowing this thing out of proportion; that they're treating this like it's . . . I don't know, like the whole future of the Army is riding on this. Like we're about to cut the cards, and that will be it. Don't you think that's a little simplistic?"

Flynn ran his hands over the gray stubble of his hair. It looked to Isen as if the old man were looking for another place to dig his heels in.

Isen pressed, driving in on Flynn's uncertainty. This wasn't an unfamiliar investigation; this wasn't paper shuffling anymore. This was a fight. And Mark Isen knew how to fight.

So why is it so difficult? Isen thought.

"We have a duty to do what is right, too, sir. We have

a duty to Michael, to Dee Ann, to everyone Harlan Veir has mistreated."

Isen hesitated. Everything he was saying was true, but part of him wondered if he was addressing the real problem.

"If Veir is somehow involved in these things, well—"

"And you still have no proof of that," Flynn came back.

"Not yet," Isen said. "Let me go back down to Bragg, see what I can find out about Veir's trip up here. Maybe I can smoke him out, get him to admit something about this attack."

"Oh, come on, Mark," Flynn said. "You think he's going to tell you he smacked you around? He's not stupid."

"OK," Isen said, still fishing. "Maybe my partner down there, Special Agent McCall, has come up with something. Maybe there's something to ... I don't know ... maybe there's something to this packet I got from Veir's ex-wife. Give me some time to look into that."

Flynn shook his head, but it was more confusion than forbidding.

Isen sat back in his chair. Just about everything he'd touched in the course of this so-called investigation had turned to shit.

So who's wrong here? he wondered. *Am I nuts, or is it everyone else?*

It had occurred to him more than once that working in the Pentagon, in a job he hated, had skewed his view of how he was supposed to conduct himself. Here he was, sitting with a two-star general who'd been a friend and a mentor, and he could think of only two options. Walk out or get into it with Flynn.

Isen looked out onto the quiet street, where the woman who'd been walking her dog and had seen him with the Military Policeman was returning. The dog, a little white ball of hair with four tiny legs, was straining against the leash.

Isen turned back to Flynn. "Why are you fighting me on this, sir?"

"What the hell does that mean?" Flynn shot back.

"You know exactly what I mean. There's more to this than you're letting me know," Isen said, his voice rising to match Flynn's.

"If you're afraid of losing that third star, afraid of pissing off the wrong people, then . . . well, I just wish you'd thought of this before. Don't send me out to get my ass kicked, to ruin my name and reputation."

"Just who the hell do you think you're talking to?" Flynn spit. "I think somebody knocked your friggin' brain housing group loose last night."

"And I think you sent me out to beat the bush and now you're not willing to back me up."

Flynn stood up and took a step toward Isen's chair, obliging the other man to lean back. He was shouting now, and Isen wondered for a second if the woman with the dog was still within earshot. Quite a day's gossip, all before breakfast.

"I couldn't give a flying *fuck* about that third star," Flynn said, shouting now. "And I couldn't care less what those bastards down at Bragg say either."

Isen dropped his voice; it was barely a whisper.

"So what are you afraid of?"

Flynn crumpled into his seat, pressed his knuckles to his temples.

"Oh, Jesus," he said, his eyes tightly shut, his breathing suddenly rapid and shallow. "Oh, Jesus, forgive me."

They sat like that for half a minute: Isen sore, dirty and exhausted; Flynn wrestling with some private demon.

"I knew about Savin," Flynn said at last, his head still bowed. "And I was afraid that if word got around that Mike was living with a homosexual that it would ruin his career.

"I told him that he had to move out. He said he didn't care about Savin's private life. We got into this big thing about the policy, see, and I . . . well, I guess I was too old-school for Michael."

"So the pressure Michael felt to conform came from you?"

"A lot of pressure, I'm afraid. Too much. I told him that he could disgrace the family if he got kicked out under that cloud. I told him he had no right to do that to a reputation built up over generations."

Isen let the silence hang for a moment before he spoke.

"You don't know for sure that's why Michael killed himself," Isen said.

"And you're saying we should look for other reasons?" Flynn asked.

"It's just that . . . if he stood up to you, face-to-face, why would he fall apart later? There's got to be more."

Flynn hid his face in his hands. "I've been over this again and again. I don't know."

"Was anyone else at Bragg aware of your concern?" Isen asked.

"No," Flynn said.

"You didn't talk to anyone else about this objection to Michael's choice of roommates?"

"No."

"Did you talk to anyone else about Savin?"

"No," Flynn said. "Wait. I did have someone from my office call down there to ask where he worked. That was after my first visit, a couple of months ago. And I told you I interfered with his leave request."

Isen stood.

"You may have left your nephew feeling like he didn't have any support, sir," Isen said. "But I still think that's only part of the problem. He didn't have the support he needed from family, but he could have gotten along if everything else was going well. I think maybe something else happened that made him need that support. That's what we're looking for."

"And where do you think you'll find that?"

"I want to find out if Veir knew about Savin."

"He already told you he didn't know anything about Savin," Flynn said. "How are you going to get him to admit something different now?"

"I don't have an answer for that," Isen said. "But, for a change, at least I know some of the questions."

13

"**A**ND WHERE EXACTLY DID YOU COME UP WITH THIS THEORY?" McCall asked.

"Sitting on the front porch of Flynn's house," Isen said. He was sitting in Sue Lynn's kitchen, twirling the phone cord and imagining McCall's disapproving look.

"And this was after you'd been assaulted, right? After you'd been kicked in the head a couple of times."

"You said you found no one at Bragg—at least not in Veir's battalion—who would admit to knowing about Savin. He kept his life separate, right?"

"Right," McCall said.

"Flynn knew. Hauck knew. If we want to test this theory that someone else here at Bragg leaned on Hauck about Savin, then we have to find out who else knew. Right?"

"With that hypothesis," McCall said, "right so far."

"Flynn called Bragg, probably Savin's boss, after Flynn visited Bragg a couple of months ago. Even if Flynn didn't say 'I don't want him around my nephew because he's a bad influence, a homosexual,' Savin's commander might have guessed."

"Assuming he knew about Savin's other life," McCall said.

"Check. Maybe it's possible that Savin's boss told Veir all this."

"It's possible, though I'm not sure why Savin's boss would tell Veir any of this. It's shaky, but let's say we establish all that. Are you saying Hauck killed himself because someone was threatening to accuse him of homosexuality?"

"My guess is that's only part of it," Isen said. "Right now we have to find out if Savin's boss talked to Veir about Savin's other life."

"He'd just about have to admit that he let Savin get sent off on that bogus trip, too," she said. "What reason does he have to admit all that?"

"None that I can think of," Isen said.

Isen was sitting in the food court of Bragg's massive Post Exchange when McCall sat down across from him.

"You're early," Isen said around a mouthful of food. "I'm not supposed to meet you for another fifteen minutes."

"You look terrible," McCall said, studying his bruises.

"Yeah, well, next time there's an ass-whipping to be had, I'll let you take a turn," Isen said, looking at his watch.

"Relax and finish eating," McCall said. She leaned over the table and looked at the bed of nearly colorless iceberg lettuce that covered Isen's paper plate.

"That's your meal?"

"I decided I needed to trim down a little bit," Isen said. "And luckily they serve these salads—I think it's surplus chow from Vietnam—so I'm never really tempted to finish one."

McCall's expression remained fixed.

"Listen," Isen said. "If you ever consider smiling or anything drastic like that, let me know. I'd like to see it."

"I guess I just don't find you funny, Major," McCall said. "And everyone else at Bragg has been so amused with my visit."

"Any sign of Cindy?"

"None," Isen said. "She's been out of sight—at least in the places we checked—for several weeks. Since about the time of Hauck's suicide."

"You think she found out and decided to hide?"

"Possibly."

McCall got up and walked over to get a soft drink; Isen watched from his seat. She wore a pair of loose-fitting khaki pants, sensible black shoes and yet another oxford cloth shirt, white this time. Plain, plain.

"Where do you carry your piece?" Isen asked when she returned.

"Pardon?"

"Your weapon. Where do you carry it? You're not carrying a purse today, so I was just wondering."

She gave him a look that a young woman might reserve for a particularly annoying preteen brother. "Humph," she said.

Isen, who'd tangled with a major general not twenty-four hours earlier, was feeling a little reckless.

"You ever wear any dresses?" he asked her.

"Not anyplace you'd ever see me," McCall answered coolly.

Isen chewed quietly.

"I have a plan for questioning this guy," she said. In forty-five minutes they were to meet with a Lieutenant Colonel Win Murchison, who was Lieutenant Greg Savin's commander.

"I'm sure you do. By the way, how do you keep your boss from finding out that you're still bugging people about the Hauck case?"

"I'm not sure I can," McCall said.

"And you're willing to take that risk?" Isen asked. "That he might slam dunk you?"

"I'm here, ain't I?"

Isen nodded.

Whatever else I might think about you, he thought, *you got balls.*

Isen kept the observation to himself.

"So what's your plan? What are you going to ask this guy?" Isen said.

"Just let me handle the talking, OK?" McCall said.

Isen stabbed another fork full of translucent lettuce, lifted it to his mouth and said, "The food really sucks here."

* * *

"Follow them."

"Follow them?"

"Just for a while. See where they go from there."

Command Sergeant Major Hendrix, Veir's top NCO, was talking to his boss on one of the pay phones banked just off the food court where Isen and McCall sat talking. Hendrix, who'd been running errands all over the post, had stopped in to grab a sandwich. He figured—correctly—that Colonel Veir would be interested in a meeting between Isen, who'd become a pain in the ass around the unit, and the woman Hendrix recognized as the CID agent who'd investigated Hauck's suicide.

He didn't expect to be told to trail them.

"I'm supposed to meet with the First Sergeants in an hour, sir," Hendrix said into the phone. "OK if I give it up in time to make that meeting?"

"Fine," Veir said. "Keep me posted."

Isen and McCall were ushered into Lieutenant Colonel Murchison's office after twenty minutes of waiting in a gray hallway lined with government issue chairs and the same government issue prints from the U.S. Army history series that decorated Veir's conference room.

"This place has all the warmth of an unemployment office," Isen said.

"We both might just get the chance to find out what those places look like," McCall answered.

Isen leaned back in his chair just as a gnomish figure appeared in the doorway at the end of the hall.

"You two can come in now."

McCall and Isen answered the summons, with Isen leading into a large, sunny office dominated by an outsized American flag that hung from the wall behind the desk. If Murchison was trying to look like George C. Scott's portrayal of General Patton, the effect fell short after the flag.

Murchison presented the two visitors, who were left standing, with the shiny and rather pointy top of his head. The rest of him, visible from this angle mostly as a pile of camouflage cloth, fell away in sharp slopes; the man in the chair was shaped like a bullet.

Murchison didn't look up; Isen scuffed his feet impatiently. McCall, perhaps more used to being left waiting, put her hands behind her back—relaxed, but not far from what the Drill and Ceremony Manual called "parade rest."

Murchison signed a few forms, hunched over, his face close to the paper like a first grader struggling to master those tricky letters. When he looked up, he checked out Isen's bruises and matching black eyes, then scanned his civilian clothes.

"Are you with the CID?" he asked Isen.

Isen played along, although Murchison undoubtedly knew the answer.

"No, sir, I'm not. But this is Special Agent McCall of the CID, who is heading the investigation into Lieutenant Hauck's death."

"I thought that the investigation of Lieutenant Hauck's *suicide,*" Murchison said, emphasizing the last word, "was complete."

McCall gave Isen a look that said, *I told you to let me do the talking.*

"I'm about finished, yessir," McCall said, taking a half step forward to move Isen into the background. "I'm just trying to wrap up a few loose ends, get some answers for questions I still have."

Murchison pushed his glasses up his nose with a quick stab of his index finger. "I'm listening," he said.

"Lieutenant Hauck's roommate was Lieutenant Greg Savin, who is one of your men. Did you receive any calls about Savin in the weeks before Hauck's suicide, before the sixteenth of September?"

"What do you mean?"

"Did anyone ask you any questions about Savin? Did his name come up in any way that wasn't immediately connected with his duties?"

McCall was speaking very quickly now, though her tone had not changed. Murchison pulled his chair in tighter to his desk.

"Did anyone ask about his personal life, his relationship to Hauck, what kind of officer he was?"

"Yes. I got a call from General Patrick Flynn," Murchison said. "That was a while ago." Then, to Isen, "I understand you know him."

"I already know about General Flynn's involvement," McCall said.

She was determined to keep the floor, Isen thought, even if it meant stretching the truth just a bit.

"I want to know who else was interested in Savin," she finished.

"What has all this to do with that suicide?" Murchison said. It wasn't a question; it was a weak stall.

"I won't know until you answer me, sir," McCall said.

"His name may have come up," Murchison waffled.

"With whom?"

Murchison opened and closed his mouth a few times, but the phone rang before he could coax any sound out. He grabbed at the receiver as if it were a life preserver.

"Murchison here."

The reaction was almost comical, Isen would think later. Murchison's eyes grew wide. He looked up at the pair in front of his desk—he had not asked them to sit—then down again quickly.

"Yes, yes, they are," he said. He lowered his voice, then decided to try to act as if there was nothing wrong.

"No. Of course not." He seemed to compose himself a bit, as if someone had just given him a satisfactory answer to a nagging question.

"Yes, I'll call you," he said before hanging up. He had the trace of a sneer on his face and was about to speak, but Isen beat him to it.

"That was Veir, wasn't it?" Isen said.

There was no hiding the surprise. Murchison's mouth actually dropped open, a small, dark circle.

"Did he tell you to threaten us? Did he tell you that nothing was going to happen to you? That you didn't have to tell us shit?"

McCall wheeled around to face Isen. "Major," she said sharply, trying to startle him back to his senses.

"No," Isen said, putting his arm out to her and stepping up to the desk, pushing it a little with his thighs so that Murchison could feel the shove.

"Veir called and asked you a bunch of questions about Savin, didn't he? Before Hauck killed himself."

"I didn't say that," Murchison managed.

McCall had her arm on Isen's now, gently trying to pull him away from the desk. Some part of Isen's brain registered that she wasn't pulling very hard.

"Did Veir ask you if Savin was gay? Did he ask you how much you knew about that? What did he say?" Isen demanded, his voice tight with anger. He put both hands on the desk, shoved the blotter back so that it stabbed Murchison in the chest.

"What did he say?" Isen continued. "Did he pound on his chest and tell you he was going to weed all the queers out of his Army? Did he tell you it was your duty to help him?"

McCall put the palm of her hand on Isen's shoulder and shoved him away from the desk.

"Colonel," McCall said when Isen quieted for a moment. "Although my report is all but finished, you must know that if I find any evidence of impropriety—on the part of *any* service member—I'm obliged to report it. I would appreciate your answering questions about any conversations you had with Colonel Veir."

McCall paused to let it all sink in. Murchison's eyes clicked back and forth, from Isen to McCall and back again. He licked his lips.

Veir was the most visible officer on post. But McCall had a badge.

"I told Colonel Veir that Savin was a good officer. That he worked hard and that he cared about soldiers," Murchison said. "But he wouldn't let up. Veir kept saying that he knew what was going on over here, that he knew I wasn't policing my ranks."

Murchison shook his head, clearly troubled by what he'd done in caving in to Veir.

"Was Veir behind this bullshit mission you sent Savin on?"

"That tasking came from the Chief of Staff," Murchison said. "But Veir was probably behind it. He has the ear of every general officer on post. They all listen to him."

"What did you tell him, sir?" McCall said calmly.

"I told him that I had heard that Savin kept an apartment in Chapel Hill, that he had another life up there. I told him that I didn't pursue it, that I didn't want to pursue it. I told

Veir that I didn't see where it was any of his business. That's when he told me that Savin roomed with one of his lieutenants."

He slowed, then stopped talking. McCall coached him.

"What did Colonel Veir say then, sir?"

"He said he'd take care of everything," Murchison said.

"What the hell was that little display about?" McCall fumed when she and Isen were outside the headquarters.

"Hey, it worked, didn't it?" Isen said. "Murchison wasn't going to cooperate until I leaned on him. Hell, Veir even called him while we were in there. He's playing hardball, so I'm going to play hardball."

McCall grabbed him by the arm and spun him around. The movement was so unexpected that Isen nearly lost his balance. She leaned in close to him, her voice cracking with the effort to keep from screaming at him.

"Just who do you think you are? You can't make up the rules as you go along. If you want to play cowboy, I'll do this alone."

"Yeah, you've done a great job up to this point," Isen said, his own anger up like a storm flag. They were squared off now, their faces inches apart. "You would already have written this off and gotten your little pat on the back, a little 'atta-girl' for your file."

McCall turned away quickly, headed to her car. Isen threw his head back, took a deep breath, then took off after her.

"McCall," he said, jogging to catch up to her. "Look, I'm sorry I said that. That was a low blow."

She fumbled with her keys at the locked car door, dropped them, picked them up, dropped them again.

"*Fuck,*" she said.

Isen went around to the passenger side as she opened the driver's door.

"Hey, I went too far," he said again.

"You sure did," she said. She slammed the door without getting in and looked at him over the top of the car.

"Look, any mistakes I made ..." She put her hands on the hot roof, suddenly looked tired. "Any mistakes I made were honest ones. I got pushed around in this investigation.

I see that now, but people with a lot more rank than me have gotten pushed around, too."

Isen nodded agreement.

"I want to find out the whole story, just like you do. And I'm taking chances, too—just like you—in continuing to ask questions. I can accept that risk. But I don't think we need to deliberately antagonize everyone just so we can prove we can send our careers down in flames. OK?"

Isen, acting if not feeling penitent, nodded.

McCall got in the car, leaned over and unlocked his door; Isen climbed in. They drove in silence for a few minutes before Isen spoke.

"You've got to admit I was pretty good in there."

"Oh, right," McCall said, rolling her eyes. "Real cool customer. A regular Joe Friday."

"So where to now?"

"We've still got to find Cindy, track down Meade, maybe confront Kent about all these bogus transfers," McCall said. "But right now, I think we should go see Colonel Veir."

"The lion in his den, huh?"

"I have a feeling that this thing is going to break open soon," McCall said.

"Right over Harlan Veir's head," Isen said.

The division area, on the south and west sides of main post, was in an uproar. Squads of soldiers armed with brooms, shovels and rakes moved about in little clusters of activity, trimming and cutting and sweeping away the random blade of grass or clump of dirt that might scream out, to a presidential motorcade whizzing by at forty miles an hour, that Fort Bragg—and hence the Army—was anything less than perfectly maintained.

"They're really going overboard, aren't they?" McCall commented.

"Well, not if you believe that this really is the last big showdown," Isen said.

McCall had to park two blocks away from Veir's headquarters, which was surrounded by military vehicles, many of them piloted by young soldiers intent on indicating, by their speed, that they, too, understood just how tense things really were.

Isen and McCall walked into Battalion Headquarters unnoticed, so intent were the people scurrying back and forth. A master sergeant, walking quickly as he flipped through a thick stack of photocopies, walked right into McCall.

"Sorry," the man said without looking up.

Isen could hear Veir's voice as soon as they entered the building. A few steps inside and he could see the boss through the open door of his office. Veir had his feet on the desk and was holding a big coffee cup out with one hand so that a young soldier could fill it from a nearly full pot.

"No," Veir shouted into the phone, slopping some coffee onto his desk. "No pictures at the rehearsal. Yeah, well, that's too fucking bad."

He pointed with his index finger to the coffee spotting the desk's glass top. The soldier, still holding the steaming pot in one hand, looked around, but apparently found nothing to blot up the mess. Instead, he leaned over the desk and used the bottom edge of his uniform blouse.

"Call the old man if you want," Veir shouted into the handset. "I doubt if he'll go against my recommendation."

With that, he tossed the receiver onto its cradle, stood up behind his desk and bellowed. "Major Foote!"

Isen and McCall stepped up to the door; Isen tapped the frame.

"Good morning, Colonel."

Veir looked up. "It was until you showed up," he said.

When Isen came into the room, Veir smiled. "Say, what happened to your eyes? Run into a light pole?"

Isen didn't respond. A soldier appeared in the doorway behind him.

"Sir, Major Foote stepped out."

"Find him," Veir said.

When the soldier hurried away, Isen shut the door.

"I'm a little busy right now, in case you haven't noticed." Veir swept his hand over the desk, which was covered in papers, black binders, maps of the training areas and several large folders with the printed legend "The White House."

Much as Veir wanted the attention, Isen figured, the pressure had to be tremendous, as close as one could come to combat without hearing real bullets zip by. It might or might not turn out to be true that the President was going to decide, as a result of this mission, whether to make the Marines' or the Army's light forces go away. But the fact that so many people in the Army believed that decision was coming brought Veir the same kind of pressure.

To judge from appearances, the man was thriving on it.

"We have a few questions to ask you, sir, about Michael Hauck," McCall said.

"I've already spoken to you once," Veir said, annoyed. "And I've been available ever since. Yet you wait until I'm in the middle of the biggest mission of the year to come here and take up more of my time. I should call your boss."

Maybe he knows that McCall isn't supposed to be doing this, Isen thought.

"That option is always available to you, sir," McCall said coolly.

"Talk fast," Veir said, falling back into his chair and smiling. "I got an Army to save here."

"Jesus," Isen said out loud.

"Why did you call Colonel Murchison, in the weeks before Lieutenant Hauck's suicide, with questions about Greg Savin, Hauck's roommate?"

"I don't recall," Veir said.

"You don't recall having the conversation?" McCall said. She pulled out a small notebook and flipped it open importantly. She hadn't taken a single note in Murchison's office; Isen knew that, Veir didn't.

"I don't recall the substance of the conversation," Veir allowed.

"Why were you interested in Savin?"

"I was interested in the welfare of one of my junior officers," Veir said. "I thought Hauck was under a lot of pressure."

"You told me you found his behavior wasn't all that remarkable in the days before his death," Isen interrupted.

"Are you asking the questions, or is she?" Veir said.

The smile was still there, the eyes still cold.

"Why were you interested in Savin, sir?"

"Is this part of your official investigation?"

"Just answer the question, please, Colonel."

"Because if it isn't, you ought to think twice about wasting my time with this bullshit," Veir said. "The whole post, hell, the whole fucking Army is going to be watching this battalion in the next week."

Then, to Isen, "You remember the Army, don't you."

The gloves were clearly off now. McCall was still talking, but the two men were ignoring her.

"What's your problem with me?" Isen said.

"I got a problem with you going around and impersonating an investigator," Veir said. "Which, by the way, is illegal. I've taken the time to find that out."

"I'm down here in a unofficial capacity and have never represented myself in any other way," Isen said, cringing at how much he sounded like a lawyer.

"Yeah?" Veir said, his voice rising. "How about up in Bryn Mawr, talking to that cunt Meade? What were you doing up there?"

Isen thought Veir winked at him, just a quick movement of his right eye. But then he realized it was a tick, a nervous tick. Isen was delighted.

"Hearing all kinds of stories about you," Isen said, managing a smile.

"Gentlemen, please," McCall tried.

"I might have to file a complaint with the Inspector General that you're going around trying to fuck with my good name," Veir said.

"That's a laugh."

"You think I won't," Veir said, standing now, teeth clenched.

"I meant the part about a good name," Isen said.

"Colonel," McCall went on bravely, "did you suspect that Michael Hauck was a homosexual?"

"What?"

"Did you suspect—"

Isen felt his chest burning. He cut McCall off. "Were you out to get Michael Hauck? Did you threaten him? Tell him you were going to let it be known that he was gay—even though you knew it wasn't true?"

"You're out of your fucking mind, Isen," Veir said. He was struggling to keep his voice in check; thick cords stood out clearly alongside his throat.

"And you called Murchison while we were in his office," Isen said, his voice rising. "Did you threaten him, too?"

There was a strange repetition; it was his own voice echoing off the walls.

"What did you tell him you were going to do? Huh?"

"I don't have to threaten little fuckheads like that, they do what I fucking tell 'em. I would have thought you'd have figured that out by now," Veir said before he caught himself.

The room was suddenly very quiet, and for a few delicious seconds Isen felt as if he'd—finally—taken the right turn.

McCall closed her notebook, then she and Isen turned around to see Major Foote standing in the open doorway. He met their eyes in turn, then stepped aside as they walked by. When they were outside the office, Isen heard Foote behind him. "You called me, Colonel?"

Isen was practically giddy by the time they reached McCall's car.

"He folded," Isen crowed. "Did you see that? Big Hollywood Veir cracked under the pressure...."

"Calm down, will you?" McCall said. "All you found out is that he tried to make some connection between Savin and Hauck beyond just the fact that they were roommates."

"But suppose he tried to lean on Hauck about that? Make an issue out of it? Suppose he wanted Hauck to stay away from the elusive Cindy and he thought threatening to out him would be just the ticket. It's all tied in to the same sicko-sexual theme."

"Suppose he did," McCall said. "How are you going to prove it? Hauck's dead, remember. Our man Veir was too smart to threaten a junior officer in front of witnesses."

Isen stubbornly refused to let the facts get in the way of his enjoyment of the moment.

"Our man Veir is just as likely to make mistakes as anyone else. He proved that in there; we just have to keep looking."

They paused at a crosswalk as a platoon of soldiers in full combat gear double-timed through the intersection.

"Tighten it up, *tighten it up,*" one of the NCOs yelled.

"All he proved in there was that he's under a tremendous strain," McCall said. "As you would be if the President and the Secretary of Defense and every general between here and the Potomac were about to descend on your little world."

"There's more stuff out there, McCall. I can feel it."

"Feeling is great, Major Isen. But we have to actually find it."

She was still walking as she spoke, but Isen had stopped. He was staring at a red pickup in the parking lot across Ardennes Road.

"What is it?" McCall asked.

"That's Veir's truck," Isen said. "The big red one."

"Doesn't surprise me," McCall said. "Something wrong?"

"See that little antenna on the back?"

"*Damn*," McCall said. "Veir has a car phone."

"So you didn't check those records? See what kind of calls he made on his car phone?"

"No. I didn't know he had a car phone, and until recently, we didn't suspect him of anything."

"That was then," Isen said.

"And this," McCall finished, "is now."

McCall dropped Isen off at Sue Lynn's house. Isen squatted next to the car and talked to McCall through the open passenger side window.

"I'm curious about that packet that Veir's ex-wife sent me," Isen said.

"I don't know. Doesn't sound to me like she's on our side. I mean, she sent you the packet and then disappeared—or is at least ignoring your calls."

"Veir found out that I visited her," Isen said. "Maybe she decided to disappear for a while."

McCall put the car in Park. "Could be. If so, that's another dead end."

"I'll keep calling anyway."

"OK. I've got some paperwork to do at the office." She put the car in gear and shooed Isen off with her hand. "You can reach me there if you need me."

"Don't forget to check on calls from Veir's car phone," Isen said as the car pulled away.

McCall waved over her shoulder. "Yeah, yeah, yeah."

Alone in the house, Isen spread the contents of the package from Meade on the floor of the family room. First he arranged the photos by subject, grouping them together according to the women. He stood up and walked around the room, looking at his handiwork, but no pattern came to mind. Next he tried arranging them according to location, grouping together the ones taken in bars, the ones taken outdoors.

He stood up, stretched his legs and went into the kitchen for a beer. When he came out again, wiping his mouth with the back of his hand ... he still saw nothing of note. He called Sue Lynn at work.

"I have all these pictures spread out on the floor, trying to figure out why Meade sent them to me."

"Did you try calling her again?"

"Yeah. No answer."

Isen told Sue Lynn that Veir knew about his visit to Bryn Mawr.

"Scary dude," she said.

"But capable of making mistakes."

Isen moved the photos around the carpet with his foot. "So what do I do with these things?"

"Well, we know that none of those pictures are of this Cindy woman; I checked that."

"Right," Isen said. "And we know that these women aren't around anymore."

"How do we know that?"

"I thought you asked the managers and bouncers if they recognized anyone," Isen said.

"No. I concentrated on Cindy," Darlington said. "I'm sorry."

"That's OK," Isen said. "We've got to find out if any of these other women are around. Maybe Veir beat up on some of them."

In one thirty-minute period Harlan Veir fielded no fewer than six calls asking for changes in the itinerary for the demonstration that was less than a week away.

Major General Tremmore, the Division Commander, had someone call to ask if Veir was interested in having the Division Staff prepare a briefing book on the current administration. That way there'd be less of a chance that some junior officer or NCO would mistake the third assistant deputy undersecretary for the fourth assistant. Veir said that would be just fine, just fine, thank you very much.

An excited staffer from Corps Headquarters called with the hot news—this from White House protocol—that the President preferred to be photographed from the right side and that Veir should stay on his left whenever possible.

"Airborne" was the only answer Veir could think of for that one.

Veir held the phone pinched between his ear and his shoulder while his Brigade Commander droned on, somehow connecting marksmanship records with sharpened bayonets.

On the desk before him lay a large printout that showed the exact time sequence of the President's visit to Bragg. Someone in Veir's Operations Section had highlighted in yellow the times that the President would be with Veir's battalion. The soldiers had taken to using the White House's own shorthand—POTUS, for President of the United States—to identify the Commander in Chief. Veir stared at the numbers and the abbreviated instructions—"1407-1420: CDR AND POTUS TALK TO SELECTED SOLDIERS AND JUNIOR NCO'S"—trying to imagine how he could keep the President going where he, Veir, wanted him to go, seeing only what was in the plan.

He hoped the soldiers wouldn't clam up. He hoped none of them would say anything stupid, he hoped the President wouldn't ask any of them how much time and energy and how many tight budget dollars they'd put into this little show, he hoped it wouldn't rain, he hoped he could stay on the President's left, he hoped that the network news people would ask to interview him instead of talking to Major General Tremmore.

Veir felt his eye move again, involuntarily. That twitch. He rubbed his face with both hands and turned to the window; his driver waited outside by a humvee.

"Shit."

He was supposed to be on his way to the training and demonstration site to watch his companies go through another rehearsal. He was supposed to be concentrating on the plan, looking for the things that his subordinates, capable though they were, might have missed. He was supposed to be getting ready for what would undoubtedly be the most important day of his whole career.

And all he could think about was how much he'd wanted to reach across his desk and smash his fist into Mark Isen's face.

"I've got to get this guy off my back," he said to the time charts and the calendar and the relentless clock.

"What's that, sir?"

Veir turned around to see Foote standing before his desk, a sheaf of papers tucked under his arm. The accordion-fold computer printouts looked like a stack of index cards beneath Foote's massive forearm.

"Thinking out loud," Veir said.

Foote looked down at the papers in his hand but did not speak. Had Veir been less distracted by all that was tormenting him, he would have noticed his subordinate's discomfort. Veir was an astute enough observer that he would have seen that Foote was backing off from this confrontation with Isen and the investigator McCall. It was there in his body language, it was there in the fact that he didn't immediately offer to help with whatever it was that was troubling his boss. Foote knew that things were getting a little twisted, and he didn't want any part of it.

But Veir wasn't thinking clearly, and although he never would have admitted it, he was dangerously close to being overloaded with the concerns heaped on him by this visit. He had gladly taken on every challenge, banking that a good performance would make his career for the next ten years. But he hadn't gambled on Isen's persistence.

"This Isen is turning out to be a real pain in the ass," Veir said.

Foote merely looked up.

"I think he's got a chip on his shoulder because he's stuck in that dead-end job in the Pentagon."

"I did some asking around about him, sir," Foote offered.

"Good. What did you find out?"

"He's a straight arrow—"

"That much I knew," Veir interrupted. "What did you find out that could help get him off my . . . our . . . case?"

"Nothing. Everyone who's ever worked with him says he's a stand-up guy. He tries to do the right thing—"

Veir slammed his hand on the desk, palm down. "I don't want to hear this *shit!*"

Foote turned and calmly closed the door, catching a glimpse, as he did so, of the soldiers in the anteroom studiously avoiding looking to the commander's office. When he turned around, Veir was standing, looking out the window again, hands on his hips. When he turned back to face the executive officer, he was smiling.

"I can't afford . . ." Veir began. "No, the Army can't afford to blow next week's demo."

He sat down at his desk, straightened some papers there. The transformation amazed Foote. The man was a consummate actor; everyone around this headquarters knew that. But under the stress of what looked as if it would be the ultimate test of his career so far, everything was exaggerated. Veir's fuse, already short, had become shorter still; his pyrotechnic tantrums more dramatic, his ersatz politician's smile even shinier.

"Now, I'm not one of these people who think that next week is going to be the end of either the Army or the Marine Corps. But there certainly are enough people, many of them wearing stars, who think that's the case. And we can't disappoint them. We have to do a good job for those soldiers out there," Veir said.

Foote's face remained unchanged. *Here it comes,* he thought.

"If we screw this up, a lot of people are going to suffer unnecessarily. Lots of wailing and gnashing of teeth."

Foote didn't answer. Veir, his mind clouded by anger, his concentration fragmented like so many pieces of broken glass, didn't notice his XO drifting away. Veir was in his own world now, a world he'd created and would maintain at all costs.

"This Isen is going around impersonating an investigator, getting people all stirred up with the idea that there's some sort of criminal investigation going on into Hauck's suicide. He's got to be stopped before he screws up the whole week. It doesn't look good for us, and this week, above all others, we must be aware of how we look."

Foote knew he was expected to ask, at this point, what

he could do. He shifted the printouts from one arm to the other.

"I just want that word around the battalion, around the division. Isen is trying to derail next week's show. I don't want anyone getting all worked up about stuff he asks. I want people to stay focused on the mission."

Lest we look at what, sir? Foote thought.

The executive officer stepped closer to Veir's desk and put the pile of paper on its crowded surface. "I understand, sir," he said.

Isen made the rounds of the clubs in the early part of the afternoon, taking with him those photos that showed full-face, or nearly full-face shots of Veir's collection of girl-friends. The only thing he learned was that he was becoming a regular; half a dozen managers and dancers recognized Isen from his previous visits. None of the people manning the fort in this part of the day saw anything in the pictures Isen showed them.

He sat in the dim light of one of the clubs, flipping through the photos and absentmindedly ordering a beer. The waitress delivered a warm bottle—the coolers had apparently just been stocked for Saturday night—and replaced the ten on the table with four ones. Isen, whose entire time at Bragg had been one big hemorrhaging of cash, decided that he'd better find another place to sit while figuring out an alternative course of action. He was on his way out the door when someone called him.

"You the guy with the pictures?"

Isen turned to see a huge bearded man in a black T-shirt that read "Free Mustache Rides."

"Yes, I am. I was asking around to see if anyone recognized these women," Isen said, pulling the folder from under his arm.

"That's what I heard in the back." He extended one arm, and Isen placed the folder in a hand the size of a baked ham.

"You must have pissed somebody off real good to get a couple of shiners like those."

"I walked into a door," Isen said. He gestured to the pictures. "So, did someone recognize one of these women?"

"Let's just say that you made some people nervous," the

man said as he flipped through the shots. "Part of my job is to keep things calm around here. These are surveillance photos, right?"

Isen had been studying the man's attire, which ended at the floor in a pair of workboots pulled on without laces.

"What's that?" Isen asked "Yeah, surveillance shots. You recognize any of those women?"

"You a cop?"

"No."

"Somebody's pissed-off big brother?"

"Actually I'm interested in that guy in the pictures," Isen said.

The big man grunted and pulled one photo out with pudgy fingers. Isen noticed a ring made up of entwined snakes.

"This one," he said.

"What about her?" Isen asked, taking the print.

"She's dead. Got herself murdered a few years back."

"They catch the guy who did it?"

"They didn't catch nobody. The police dicked around a little bit, couldn't find nothing. Then they let it leak that she was hookin', too. Not a lot of big public outcry over the death of a whore, you know? The case kind of went away."

The narrator brought a hand up to his mouth, searching his back teeth for some piece of food that was apparently annoying him. He retracted his finger and studied something on the end of it before sucking the digit clean.

"What I think happened is that they couldn't make anything with the shitty leads they had, so they let it die."

Isen flipped the photo over and showed the man the dates. "This about when she was killed?"

"Hard to say. Around that time, I guess. Yeah."

"You ever see this woman hanging out with the guy in the picture?"

"No," he said stabbing one sausagelike finger on the print that showed Veir kissing the woman, his hand cupping her breast. "But I'd say she knew him."

"Yeah," Isen said. "Thanks."

Isen was walking out the door when he thought of something else.

"You said they developed some leads," Isen said to the man's back.

"Shitty ones, I said."

"Any idea what those were?"

"Word on the street said they suspected a soldier, but hell, that narrows it down to about thirty thousand of the horny bastards, right?"

"I guess," Isen said.

Isen telephoned McCall and asked her to meet him. Then he drove to the Fayetteville library and pulled out the bound copies of the local newspapers covering the dates around the woman's murder.

The body of Barbara Ann Yonders, twenty-three years old, had been found by hunters out near Kinston, which lay some eighty miles east of Fayetteville. The first article, light on details about her life in Fayetteville, apparently catered to the public's fascination with gruesome crime.

She'd been beaten, the coroner said, then strangled. The police weren't talking about a weapon, which led the reporter to speculate that they had not found one. Isen, on the other hand, wondered if the beating was delivered with fists, as Dee Ann's had been. He reached up and gingerly touched his blackened eyes with the tips of his index fingers.

Death was by strangulation. Isen knew he could probably find out, or have McCall find out, if the woman had been strangled with a cord or at someone's hands. But he didn't think it important at this point.

Isen flipped through two sections of furniture store ads and stories about high school football to the next day's newspaper.

Barbara Ann Yonders' picture was on page one.

Isen opened the folder of surveillance photos, spreading them across the yellowing pages of newsprint.

The woman in the picture did not much look like the murder victim.

Another picture, a different one this time, on the third day after the body was found, looked even less like the glossy Isen had packed in his folder. The story had also been relegated to the second section, where the headline, "MURDERED GEORGIA WOMAN WAS PROSTITUTE, POLICE SAY" pushed Barbara Ann Yonders a little farther away from the public's conscience.

Didn't take them long to lose interest in this, Isen thought. "What did you find?"

It was McCall, standing behind him and looking over his shoulder.

"A guy at one of the clubs said that this woman"—he pointed at the newspaper photo—"was this woman. It doesn't seem so clear to me."

"Let me see," McCall said, leaning closer. "Well, cut the hair and change the hair color. I don't know, I think it could be the same woman. This one"—she pointed to the surveillance photo—"isn't all that clear. Not even a full-face shot."

She was behind Isen, and she put her hand on his shoulder as she bent over the table for a closer look. Isen felt her small, hard breast brush his arm; at the same moment he heard movement in the stacks nearby. Isen looked out past McCall and saw a man standing just a few feet away. He wore a suit that looked at least two sizes too small, a white shirt opened to three buttons, no tie. He was aiming a camera at them.

"What the hell?"

Isen stood as the flash went off, once, twice.

In two steps he'd closed with the man, who put the camera behind his back, as if Isen might try to grab it.

"Who the hell are you?" Isen asked.

"Fuck you, pal," the man said, turning away.

Isen had no idea what to do or say. Some stranger had taken his picture in the public library, then refused to tell him why.

OK, so what's the big deal? he asked himself.

When he turned around, he saw McCall standing at the table. He got a glimpse of what the picture was about.

"What was that?" McCall asked.

Instead of answering, Isen asked, "You married?"

"No. Why?"

"I was just wondering what might be of interest in pictures of us," he said. "Have you ever heard the dictum 'Sow discord in the camp of your enemy'?"

"Can't say I have."

"Well it looks to me as if we have someone backed into a corner."

14

At seven-thirty on Saturday evening Veir chased most of his staff from the Battalion Headquarters and sent the staff duty NCO to the line companies to urge the commanders and First Sergeants to let the men go home.

"We'll be in here most of the day tomorrow anyway," Veir said, smiling at his weary subordinates.

An orderly answered a ringing phone, placed his hand over the mouthpiece and told Veir, "Sir, it's for you."

Veir took the call in his office.

"Colonel Veir."

"I got some pictures," the voice on the other end said.

Veir turned his back to the door, which was open to the anteroom and the dozen or so people milling around outside his office. "Any good?" he asked.

"These two are no lovebirds, I can tell you that. I got a couple of shots that show them close, but that's about it."

"I want you to follow them tonight," Veir said. "See if you can get something I can use."

"That'll be another buck and a half," the voice said.

Veir fumed. "You said the rate was one-fifty a day."

"My workday ends in the evening, just like most people's.

You want me to throw in a night, it's gonna be another day's fee."

You fucking sleazeball, Veir thought.

"Fine. Whatever. You'd just better come back with some good pictures."

"I can tell you right now that there aren't going to be any cum shots with these two. They barely talk to one another."

"Spare me, OK. Just do your job."

The line went dead.

And just maybe I won't pound the living shit out of you when I see you, Veir thought.

He pressed his finger on the disconnect button, pulled out the post telephone directory and looked up the number for the Inspector General.

Let me launch a couple of bullets your way, Isen, he thought, skimming through the pages. *See how you react.*

The Inspector General, like the Criminal Investigation Division, was part of a command structure separate from any on post, and for the same reason: to avoid command influence. While the CID handled criminal investigations, the Inspector General, or IG, handled everything from soldiers' complaints about services or unfair treatment to allegations of misconduct.

Harlan Veir made good on his threat to accuse Isen, in official channels, of impersonating an investigator. He also went beyond that.

"I also think he's banging the CID agent he's supposedly 'working' with," Veir told the major who'd taken his call.

"Let me get this straight," the officer on the other end said. "This guy came down here to look around in an unofficial capacity, yet has been throwing his fictitious weight around, and the whole time he's doing this special agent? What rank is she?"

"Buck sergeant, I think," Veir said.

"Well, sir," the IG representative said, "I know you don't need this right now."

The major, like Veir an infantry officer, would be looking for a job as a battalion exec or operations officer when his time with the IG was up. At first he'd been piqued that he'd been called at home on a Saturday evening. Now he saw it for the great opportunity it was: here was a chance to score some major points with the most well-known and well-connected commander on post.

And this week, the major thought, *the most well-known lieutenant colonel in the Army.*

"You've got a lot on your mind," the IG continued, "and I'll make sure that none of this interferes with your job this week."

"Thank you, Major," Veir said. "You've been most helpful."

Veir left the headquarters and drove off-post in his big red pickup. As always, he drove carefully on Yadkin, which was really just a gauntlet of overpowered cars driven by eighteen-year-olds who fell out of airplanes for a living. A dark blur came up behind him, too quickly, swerved into the passing lane and sped by, the driver leaning on the horn. Veir pounded one fist on the steering wheel and thrust the other hand, middle finger extended, up to the windshield.

"Fuck you, motherfucker!"

He took his foot off the accelerator and took a deep breath.

This fucking Isen is getting to me, he admitted.

Throughout most of his life, most of his Army career certainly, Veir had been able to throw off unwanted scrutiny. His shining job performance, his trustworthy looks and, for a while, at least, his trophy wife, all served him with an air of respectability. Then came Isen, hounding him and worrying all the inconsistent details of Veir's public persona.

The funny thing was that until he'd crossed swords with Isen it had always been the women who could get to him, the women who were toughest to control. That pattern had started with his mother, who alternated between ignoring him and criticizing his every move. When the old bitch died it was all he could do to keep from dancing at her funeral.

Beginning in high school, when he'd reached his physical maturity, there'd always been a parade of women: the cheerleaders and homecoming queens; the thirty-something housewives who hired him to cut their lawns, then watched him hungrily as he sweated, shirtless and powerful, through the hot summer days. At an early age Harlan Veir tapped into a mother lode of willing women, young ones, older ones, all of them clamoring for his clumsy attention. No matter how badly he treated them.

The trouble with his taste, he considered in rare moments of what passed for self-examination, was that he liked them with spirit.

Meade, who'd been wildly thrilled with him at first, finally turned out to have too much spirit. He'd hit her only once—a sharp backhand that left no mark and did nothing to keep her in line. But she had exacted a painful revenge, humiliating him when she'd torched his clothes and uniforms. That was exactly the kind of public rebuke his mother so loved.

He had tried to hang on to Meade, tried to bring her in line. But there had been a few other missteps, and finally she'd broken it off, a bevy of lawyers covering her retreat.

He'd found solace close by, with the dancers whose wantonness had always touched him in some dark place. There, too, he liked the lively ones, the ones who didn't always give in to him at first, the ones who fought back.

There'd been one, years ago now, who'd turned her mouthiness into a kind of foreplay—exciting him tremendously. But the resistance was only good when he knew the outcome: dominance, wet release. Every time she refused him, every time she jerked him around, he wanted her more; and as long as the buildup was let go in orgasm, everything was fine. As with anything so intoxicating, he built up a tolerance. Over a period of a few months she had to resist him more strongly; his dominance, his final triumph had to be more dramatic, more physical.

"Sometimes it feels like you're raping me," she'd said to him once in mousy complaint.

"I am," he'd told her.

And the more the women played his game, the more they refused him—as he wanted, as he needed—the more inevitable the final outcome.

Cindy Racze was the master of the teasing resistance.

She'd never been the least bit intimidated by him, which stoked his fire. The more attention and money he lavished on her, the more she scorned him. Almost unknowingly, Veir had given her the upper hand. He begged for sex—that was part of the game—and his pleading had two results: she disdained him even more, and he wanted her more still.

The more she made him beg, the more he paid her. He begged for coitus, he begged for fellatio, begged and paid for things she wouldn't do. And even her refusals were exciting.

Cindy once took a hundred dollars from him, promising to show up at his house to let Veir videotape her banging two guys—an amateur porn film. He flew into a dangerous rage when she didn't show, and drove at breakneck speed to catch up with her outside of Jiggles. He screamed and swore and punched dents in the quarter panel of his truck, working himself into a perfect frenzy of frustration. She had only smiled at him, which pushed him even further. And just when he recognized the dangerous red veil that preceded violence, just when he thought he should leave rather than hit her, she took his hand, pulling him into the manager's office and locking the door behind her. When he took her—when she allowed herself to be taken—he entered her from behind, his big hands pressing hard on the small of her back, his whole weight pushing her forward and face down onto the desk top where she'd doubled over, ramming her as hard as he could as he tried to exorcise whatever demons she'd released in his heart.

"You bitch," he said over and over.

Her scripted response: "Fuck me hard, harder."

Cindy thought the game would go on indefinitely—her teasing him, coaxing him higher and higher to frightening states of excitement where control vanished and the primal came rushing to the fore.

Then, abruptly, she had tried to move away. After she'd conditioned him so that he wanfed only her, the bitch tried to dump him. There came a day when she told him no, and incredibly, she meant just that.

She tried to give him back some of the money she'd taken, some of the gifts. But Veir wasn't about to let her go. She appeared at his home once, five hundred dollars in cash in a plastic bag. She begged him, crying, to leave her alone.

He'd pushed her to her knees, watched her plead and weep, watched her supplicant role long enough to see that it was real, that she wanted the games to end.

He laughed when he opened the bag and saw what was inside.

"I've got something for you, too, honey," he'd told her,

grabbing her hair and freeing himself from his pants just in front of her face.

That was a good one, he remembered. The cash strewn on the floor, her cheeks wet with tears, her crying muffled as he'd thrust deeper into her throat where, surprisingly, the tremulous quivering of her sobbing titillated him directly.

You were so good, Cindy, so smart, he thought. *The best player. But not smart enough to see that you couldn't go back, that you couldn't hide from me. Not behind your tears, not in another city. Certainly not behind Michael Hauck.*

Stopped at a red light, he glanced to the parking lot of a convenience store and the pay phone sitting there and was struck with an idea that could well wrap everything up for him, Isen and all the other loose ends. It was a risk, but his whole life was a risk.

Harlan Veir was nothing if not decisive. He considered the possibilities for less than a minute, honked at the car stopped in front of him and drove his big truck over the curb to the phone booth. It wouldn't do to make this call from his car phone.

At a quarter to eleven on Saturday night, Mark Isen and Sue Lynn Darlington were sitting in the recreation room of her home, four empty beer bottles on the table between them.

"I'm telling you, they're all going nuts in there," Sue Lynn said.

She'd gotten home only a half hour before, having spent the evening rehearsing a presentation the Division Aviation Section had to give to the Secret Service on Monday. She'd pulled off her blouse and kicked off her boots and sat, in BDU trousers and olive drab T-shirt and socks, while Isen rubbed her feet in between sips of beer.

"They had us running around all afternoon, calling the Marines who fly him around, rushing over to Pope. I mean, it's *only* a few aircraft."

"Even if one of them is Air Force One," Isen said.

"Thank God the Air Force guys at Pope have to worry about that."

She'd pulled her T-shirt free of the top of her trousers and ran her hands absentmindedly across her stomach.

"All we have to do is handle the helicopters that'll take him out to the demonstration area."

"It looks like the pressure is on all over the place," Isen agreed. "Even our man Veir is starting to show a few cracks."

The knock at the door startled both of them.

"You expecting someone?" Isen asked, standing.

"Hardly."

Sue Lynn followed him to the hallway. Isen turned the porch light on and peered out the long glass windows on either side of the opening.

Major Leonard Foote waved at him through the glass.

May I come in? he mouthed.

Isen put his hand on the knob, then had a second's hesitation as he remembered Foote's hostility. But surely he and Darlington were safe in her home.

He pulled open the door, and Foote—dressed in jeans and a University of Alabama T-shirt—stood there for a few awkward seconds.

"I'm sorry to disturb you so late," he said. "But I didn't think this could wait."

"Come in," Isen offered.

Foote entered, ducking his head under the hanging light in the foyer, and followed Sue Lynn to the recreation room. She grabbed her uniform blouse, which had been balled up on the floor, and her boots, then broke the awkward silence.

"Why don't you sit down. Can I get you something to drink? A beer, maybe?"

"Ice water would be just fine, thank you."

Foote looked around the room. Sue Lynn, out of his line of sight, raised her eyebrows at Isen. Isen shrugged; he had no idea what was going on.

"Sorry to barge in like this," Foote said again.

Isen got the odd feeling that he was looking at yet another Leonard Foote: not the gentle father he saw outside the hospital, certainly not the raving lunatic of their first confrontations.

Maybe there is a conscientious soldier under there, Isen thought.

Isen held his questions in check until Sue Lynn returned. She had tucked her T-shirt back into the top of her trousers.

"I'm a little surprised to see you here," Isen said.

Foote smiled at the understatement. "I'll bet," he said. "I'm a little surprised to find myself here, to tell you the truth."

"Has something changed?"

"I'm not sure," Foote said. "Maybe I'm just seeing things differently."

He took a long sip of water from the tumbler Sue Lynn had given him. Isen sat in a chair opposite Foote; Sue Lynn sat on the arm of the chair.

"When you came down here the first time," Foote began, "I really believed that you were stirring things up unnecessarily. I was satisfied that the CID had done a complete investigation and that Hauck had shot himself for reasons we might never discover. I saw you as a threat."

"That much was clear to me," Isen said.

"I may have even been a little ... overzealous," Foote said, clearly uncomfortable. "It doesn't take much to ruin someone's reputation, and one bad report card these days and you might as well start looking through the Help Wanted pages. The short version is this: if you trashed Colonel Veir and this battalion, some of that was going to rub off on me, and I can't afford that, for a lot of reasons."

Foote met Isen's eyes, then Sue Lynn's. He was completely calm, in contrast to the man Isen had come to know. Although this confession was clearly not easy for him, the self-appraisal that preceded it was nothing new to this man. In spite of all Foote's bluster, Isen realized, thinking again about the scene outside the hospital, Leonard Foote was an introspective man.

"I have to think about my family. In particular, I have to think about my boy's medical care."

"I understand," Isen said.

"We even talked about that after we saw you outside of the hospital," Sue Lynn added.

"And that was OK as long as I thought we—Colonel Veir and I—were doing the right thing."

Foote paused again, took another long drink. He held the glass between his knees in two enormous hands.

Isen started to speak, wanting to prompt Foote, but Sue Lynn touched his arm.

"I just wanted to get you out of here," Foote said, looking at Isen. "It was nothing personal."

"I thought maybe you just didn't like white guys."

Foote smiled, lowered his head. When he looked up again there was some trace of relief on his face, something in his eyes that marked a passage; he had turned a corner.

"In the last couple of days, it seems, Colonel Veir has gone too far. He's beyond trying to protect the unit. I think he's hiding something."

"What makes you think so?"

"I talked to Bennett tonight," Foote said. "I'm bringing him back to Bragg tomorrow. We need all of our lieutenants for this week's festivities."

Isen leaned forward in his seat.

"He's the only one of those lieutenants you didn't talk to, right?"

"That's right," Isen said.

"That wasn't by accident," Foote said. "Colonel Veir wanted him out of here fast."

Isen didn't mention that, thanks to Darlington's friend Coates, they knew about the special attention Bennett's trip had gotten.

"Did you tell Colonel Veir that you were bringing him back?"

Foote shook his head.

"But you're doing it anyway?"

"Yeah. It's a loose interpretation of his guidance to have everyone on board. Actually, I only decided to bring Bennett back here after I spoke to him."

Foote leaned back, brought one leg up, resting the ankle on the opposite knee and tucking a finger into the back of his running shoe.

"Bennett asked if you and Special Agent McCall were still around asking questions. I implied that you weren't, that the heat was off, thinking he'd say something. Sure enough, he started shooting his mouth off. He bragged about how he'd managed to avoid you, about how Colonel Veir had run circles around you and that you weren't about to find out anything."

"What is Veir hiding?" Isen asked.

"I'm not sure what Colonel Veir knows. But Bennett . . ."

Foote put both feet on the floor again, leaned forward as if plunging in. "Bennett was out there with Hauck. Bennett was the last one to talk to him, the last one to see him alive."

"Did he say something about that?" Isen asked. "Something about what happened out there?"

"Yeah," Foote whispered, nodding. "He said, 'I'm glad that pussy Hauck took our advice.'"

Foote dropped his head, rubbing his brow with thumb and forefinger.

"I called Colonel Veir, told him what Bennett had said. Told him I thought maybe Bennett had been taunting Hauck, that maybe Bennett knew more about what happened out in the parking lot than anyone suspected and that I thought Bennett should talk to the investigator."

"What did Veir say to that?"

"He exploded, started talking about how you"—he gestured to Isen—"weren't an investigator, that you were just a troublemaker and that he should have gotten rid of you when he had the chance. I told him that when I said 'investigator' I was talking about McCall."

"What did he say to that?"

"He told me that loyalty worked both ways, up and down the chain of command."

He threatened you, Isen thought.

The three of them were quiet for a long moment, then Sue Lynn asked, "You want that beer now?"

"Yeah,'" Foote said. "I think I might."

"It took a lot of guts for you to come over here," Isen said.

"Well, I might have gone to see McCall first, but I wasn't sure where she lived. Besides, she might not have let me in."

Sue Lynn returned with three beers, already opened.

"I think Colonel Veir and Lieutenant Bennett are hiding something about Hauck's death ... Hauck's suicide," Foote said.

He took a long pull on his beer. "Hauck was pretty drunk, and that was unusual for him. Bennett is a pain in the ass, always taunting people, and he had something against Hauck. Other than that, I'm not sure what happened. But I figured you and McCall might have a theory, and I couldn't live with myself if I just sat on this. So here I am."

"You really think he'll ding you on your evaluation?" Sue Lynn said.

"Absolutely," Foote answered. "Just the fact that I talked to you guys should be enough to make him explode. And although Veir didn't specifically say to leave Bennett at Fort Benning, I think he'll have another fit when Bennett shows up."

"Maybe just McCall and I should meet with Bennett," Isen said. "Keep you out of this."

"Bennett won't talk to you guys," Foote answered. "Hell, he may not even talk to me. But we have a better chance if I'm there and we get to him before Colonel Veir sees him."

"What about taking care of your son?" Sue Lynn asked. "Don't you think it's worth trying it without you there, without your being implicated?"

"I think we'll get only one shot at Bennett, and he's the key."

Sue Lynn chewed her lip, trying to think of another way. Isen shook his head; he didn't like it either.

"Look," Foote said. "I appreciate your concern and all. But I not only have a responsibility to take care of my son, to make sure he has the medical care he needs. I have to be able to look him in the eye, also. And right now, I'm not sure I can do that. OK?"

"OK," Isen said.

Sue Lynn nodded.

"Well," Foote said, standing. "I'll let you folks get some rest."

"You, too," Isen said.

"Yeah," Foote said. "I'll probably sleep a little better tonight."

Harlan Veir woke at six on Sunday morning, showered, shaved and put on a pair of jeans and a long-sleeved pullover. He checked himself out in the mirror. Tucked the shirt tighter around his trim waist and headed out the door. He bought a Raleigh paper on the way to his favorite greasy spoon restaurant on Yadkin Road, then flirted with the waitress as he thumbed through the front section looking for articles about the President's visit. There were two, and neither one mentioned his name.

The waitress brought his plate—fried eggs, creamed chipped beef on toast and home fries—just as his visitor joined him.

"Coffee."

The waitress, a pretty young high school cheerleader type, hesitated.

I guess we make quite a pair, Veir said, studying his companion.

"You look like ten miles of bad road," Veir said after his smile sent the waitress away happy.

"You payin' me to look good or take pitchers?" the man asked, scratching what had to be at least a three-day growth of beard. He pulled a bent cigarette from his shirt pocket and stuck it in his mouth; the end, turned down like a spigot, pointed at the floor.

Veir started to speak, but the man held up his hand.

"I know, I know. No fuckin' smokin' *anywheres.*"

He rolled the cigarette around on his lips while he pulled an envelope from his pocket.

"You printed them up already?" Veir asked, pulling the envelope toward him.

"Not all of them. Weren't no point. There ain't nothing goin' on between those two."

Veir opened the envelope and looked inside. The top photo showed Isen and McCall walking into one of Fayetteville's clubs.

"What'd they do last night?"

"They went around asking the same questions about this woman Cindy," the PI said. "And some other women in some old photos. From what I heard, you was in the pitchers, too."

Stupid fuckers, Veir thought, smiling.

"You said last night you got a couple of shots that might be of use," Veir said.

"They was touching each other, but there wasn't anything sexy about it. Check the bottom of the stack."

Veir pulled out the photos and thumbed through to the last ones in the pile.

The light was brighter, and he could see that McCall was

touching Isen, but just barely. Maybe her breast was touching his shoulder, but they were both intent on something else.

"Where'd you take these?"

"In the fucking *library,* if you can believe that. I'm telling you, these people ain't doing the wild thing."

Veir looked at the picture again. *What the hell were they . . .*

"They was looking at some old newspapers. Local stuff. I went back after they left and wrote down the dates," the PI said proudly.

Veir felt something cold flush down inside him. He looked up; the PI was holding out his notebook so that Veir could see the dates.

"Mean anything to you?"

Veir swallowed; not trusting his voice, he shook his head.

"How much?" he asked after a moment.

"Three-fifty," the PI said.

Veir reached into his pocket, producing a packet of folded bills held with a paper clip. "Here's two seventy-five."

"Maybe you didn't hear me . . ." the PI began.

Later the PI would tell himself that he should have known something was up by the way the guy reacted to the news that the two people in the photos were looking at old newspapers. Even so, he wouldn't have been ready for the change.

The PI had his arm out, his fingers touching the money. Veir's arm shot forward and grabbed the man's fingers in his own. He bent them backwards viciously, just short of snapping bone; one little tug and the PI knew he wasn't going anywhere. He thought about whacking the guy with the blackjack he kept on his belt, but he decided, in a panicked instant, that the soldier would break his hand.

"Get the fuck out of here," Veir said. He kept the pressure up while the PI took his money with the other hand, then released his grip. The man left without looking back.

Veir shoved the photos back into the envelope. He hadn't counted on Isen and McCall getting that close to him. There were a few things that probably could have waited.

Fuck them, he told himself. *On Friday I brief the President. By Saturday . . . hell, on Friday night I'll be in the club, drinking the general's booze and celebrating. Let them try to touch me.*

He handed the young waitress too much money, putting his hand on the small of her back as he left and running his fingers over the straps of her bra.

"Keep the change, sweetheart," he said, smiling his invincible smile.

McCall met Isen at Pope Air Force Base on Sunday morning, forty-five minutes before the scheduled arrival of the transport on which Bennett was to arrive and a half hour before they were to meet Foote. Isen used the half hour to brief his partner on what had happened at Sue Lynn's the night before.

"Did you consider that this may be part of a ruse? That maybe Foote and Veir are in on this together and just want us to spin our wheels some more?"

"Frankly, no," Isen said. "I don't think Foote operates that way. The guy was really troubled. You'll see the difference in him when he gets here."

"So you think he's ready to give us something else on Bennett, maybe even on Veir?"

"I don't think there is anything else on Bennett or Veir. I don't think Foote knows anything more than we do at this point. The difference today is that he's willing to help us try to get Bennett to talk, help us figure this all out."

"Well, I'm not optimistic," McCall said. "They've managed to avoid giving up anything of substance up to this point, and I can't see that anything has changed."

Isen looked at her. She was dressed in khaki pants and another oxford cloth shirt, pink this time. Her leather belt had a silver tip, the sole ornamentation on her entire outfit.

"You part Amish?"

"What?"

"Forget it," Isen said. "So why are you here?" he asked, feeling his exasperation with her come back.

"The elusive Bennett," she said. "I guess my curiosity got to me."

Foote was late, arriving just as the aircraft taxied over to the edge of the tarmac. The three of them walked over to the bottom of the aluminum stairs that an airman wheeled up to the dark green fuselage. Bennett was the first one off the plane.

"Airborne, sir," he said when he saw Foote. He saluted as he reached the bottom of the stairs.

"Welcome back, Lieutenant Bennett," Foote said. "You remember Special Agent McCall?"

"Yes, sir," Bennett said without looking at her.

"And this is Major Isen."

Bennett didn't acknowledge the introduction. Isen was about to say something when he thought better of it. He'd let Foote handle the talking as much as possible.

"What brings you out this early on a Sunday, sir?" Bennett asked.

"We want to ask you a few questions about the night that Lieutenant Hauck killed himself," Foote said.

"Roger that," Bennett said cheerfully. "You want to do it right here?"

"No, we'll go inside," Foote said, gesturing to the door of the waiting area.

If the welcome committee makes Bennett nervous, Isen thought, *he's doing a good job of hiding it.*

Bennett, carrying his duffel bag, followed the other three into a large waiting area of blue plastic chairs and cheap carpet. A television droned in the corner and a bored airman flipped through a magazine behind a counter marked "Information."

Bennett dropped his duffel on the floor and waited to be told to sit down. He took a seat on one side of a small aisle; McCall, Isen and Foote sat across from him.

"We'd like you to reconstruct what happened on the night that Lieutenant Michael Hauck killed himself," McCall said. "Paying particular attention to what he said when you last spoke to him, and what you said to him."

Bennett reached into his shirt pocket and pulled out a pack of gum. He peeled one stick, shoved it into his mouth and began chewing loudly.

"You're the cop, right?" he asked McCall.

"I'm a Special Agent with the Criminal Investigation Division," McCall said evenly. "I'm—"

"I thought all this shit was over with, you know? Am I

being investigated?" Bennett interrupted. "Am I being accused of something?"

"No," McCall said. "Not at this time. We'd just like you to answer a few questions, that's all."

Bennett turned to Foote. "Do I have to answer her questions, sir?"

"Technically, no," Foote said. "But it would help if you cooperated."

"Hell, sir, I don't mind cooperating with you. You know that. We're *compadres.*"

He lowered his voice, but not enough so that he couldn't be heard. "But I'm not real excited about talking to this bitch."

Isen looked at McCall. She was breathing deeply, either to maintain control, Isen thought, or as a prelude to pulling out her piece and pistol-whipping the lieutenant.

Foote was at a loss.

"Maybe ..." Isen offered, "maybe Special Agent McCall wouldn't mind if Major Foote asked the first questions."

"Not at all," McCall said icily.

"In private," Bennett added.

McCall stood and walked to a chair some fifty feet away.

"That's better," Bennett said. "I don't like having that hose-bag around. She dresses like a dyke."

He propped his boots on the duffel bag, leaned back in his chair and put his hands behind his head.

"How's everything down at the battalion?"

"Busy," Foote said.

"I'll bet. You know, it's great to be back. I wouldn't want to miss this for the world; this is a real chance to shine," Bennett said. "A real chance to shine."

He smiled at Foote. "I'm glad Colonel Veir wanted me back in time."

Isen wanted to look at the executive officer's expression, but he held his curiosity in check.

"What can I do you for, sir?" Bennett said. He did not even look at Isen, which made Isen wonder why he didn't ask to speak to Foote alone.

"I know you've been through this before," Foote said. "We all have. But I'm looking for a little more clarification. You were the last one to see Hauck alive, right?"

"Roger that, sir," Bennett said.

His tone was still lighthearted, as if they were talking about catching the game on TV. And just that quickly Isen saw why Bennett, who had avoided Isen until now, didn't care if Isen heard what he had to say. Foote was there, and Bennett could not imagine that Foote would do anything outside of Colonel Veir's wishes. Which meant that the little incident with McCall had nothing to do with her status as an investigator; it was because she was a woman.

"Was Hauck upset that night when he came to the club?" Foote asked.

"Yeah. His girlfriend had dumped him, and he was bent outta shape about that. But hell, she was a stripper. I told him there was plenty of other pussy where that came from."

"Did he say why she'd broken up with him?" Foote asked.

"He didn't have to. Everybody knew the bitch was using him. He was all kinds of in love with the little twat, and she was using him. Then she dumped him. At least, that's what I heard."

"From whom?" Isen wanted to know.

Bennett looked him in the eye, taking his time answering. "It was just, you know, general knowledge."

"One of the others at the club that night said that you were giving Hauck a hard time," Isen said.

"What's a hard time?" Bennett asked.

Isen wanted to stand this kid at attention, maybe leave him there for an hour or so, then come back and talk about how to address a superior. But he doubted the effectiveness of that questioning technique.

Foote stepped in. "Following him around, keeping after him."

"Aw, hell, sir, I was just teasing him. I think the little fruitcake was too sensitive, that's all."

Isen watched as Bennett walked right into the minefield.

"Little fruitcake?" Foote said, leading him without a struggle.

"Yeah." He leaned forward, a conspirator. "Hauck's roommate is a dick-smoker, a faggot. I told Hauck that maybe his girlfriend got a little suspicious, him living with a queer and all."

Bennett smiled, pleased with himself, and leaned back in his chair.

"I told Hauck I'd be glad to straighten her out."

Thinking, perhaps, that the other men might miss the double entendre, Bennett extended one overmuscled forearm, slapping the opposite palm in the crook of his elbow.

Foote spoke again, more calmly than Isen could have managed. "That's all you said?"

"I told him that he needed to be careful. That people would talk and the next thing he knew, they'd be calling him queer and tossing his ass out of the Army."

"Is that true?" Isen asked.

"What?"

"Were people talking? Did you think there was a chance that Hauck would be accused of being gay?"

"Not only did I think it could happen," Bennett said, "I thought it was a great fucking idea. Now, don't get me wrong, I didn't want the guy to kill himself, and it's sad for his family and all that happy horseshit. But this battalion isn't any worse off—maybe we're even better off without him."

"Is that the way Colonel Veir felt, too?" Isen asked.

Bennett started to speak, then caught himself, apparently unsure of what Veir would want him to say. He smiled his inane smile, but there were two or three glistening spots of perspiration just below his hairline.

"I'm not sure," Bennett said.

"But that's your call, huh?" Isen said. "No great loss."

Bennett shrugged.

"What can I say, sir? It's a fucking jungle out there."

Foote and Isen left Bennett waiting while they pulled McCall aside and filled her in.

"He's going to run to Veir as soon as we let him go," McCall said.

"And that's the end of the line for me," Foote said.

Isen stood with McCall and Foote but watched Bennett across the terminal. "Veir already knows he's back."

"What makes you say that?" McCall asked, glancing in Bennett's direction. Bennett waved.

"I think he called Veir as soon as you told him to come

back," Isen said to Foote. "Veir told him what to say here, what to give us. Why else would he be suddenly willing to talk? Why else would the little smart-ass be so smug?"

"Because he thinks the investigation is closed?" McCall said. The tone was a question; she was testing theories.

"Because shooting his mouth off is as natural to him as breathing," Foote added. The executive officer was growing more uncomfortable by the minute, anticipating his commander's reaction.

"Nope. Veir coached him," Isen said. "This door is temporarily closed. We gotta work another angle, then come back to Bennett and what happened in that parking lot."

"Bennett, asshole that he is, may have pushed too hard on Hauck," McCall reminded them, *"but he didn't shoot him."*

"What about the tie-in with Veir?" Isen persisted. "He was obsessed with this Cindy. I'll bet he knew Hauck was seeing her."

McCall shook her head, showing exasperation with Isen's refusal to let go more than anything else. "Veir had the hots for half the women in town who took their clothes off for money."

"He followed Cindy around, for chrissakes," Isen said. "He went up to DC to see her there—"

McCall's beeper went off, interrupting Isen. As she walked off to use a pay phone, Foote gestured to Bennett. "What about him?"

"Just hold him for a few more," McCall said.

Isen felt as if things were slipping away from him. The big break he'd expected to get with Bennett had failed to materialize. He was sure that Veir had closed that road.

Isen looked over at Bennett, who was using a folding knife, taken from a sheath at his belt, to clean his fingernails.

Veir-Hauck-Cindy, Isen thought.

Dee Ann said that Cindy had found someone to help her with her Veir problem.

Michael Hauck, Isen thought. *That's what Veir had against him.*

Foote was sitting in one of the plastic chairs, his chin in his hand. Isen sat down next to him.

"You see all this stuff go on that night?"

"Some of it," Foote answered.

"Where was Veir?"

"Veir didn't pay much attention to Hauck. I think he might have talked to him for a minute or two, but no more than he did to any of the others. Besides, he left early."

McCall came back from the pay phone.

"That was the state police, the guy I called to ask if they had any word on Cindy Racze," she said as she finished writing something in her notebook.

"Well?" Isen asked.

McCall looked up. "They found her body about thirty miles from here," McCall said. "Looks like she's been dead for a while."

Isen and McCall spent the rest of the day and most of the evening hanging around the county coroner's office in Fayetteville. Normal procedure, because it was Sunday, called for Cindy Racze's body to be stored until Monday morning. McCall wanted more than that. She talked to the coroner twice and to his assistant once.

"Somebody's coming in," she said after the third conversation. "But only because it's starting to rain."

"What's that got to do with it?" Isen asked.

"Cancelled tee time," she said.

The deputy coroner showed up a half hour later, still dressed in loud golf pants and a sun hat that wouldn't be of much use today.

"You Special Agent McCall?" he asked after pushing through the swinging steel doors.

"Yes, Doctor," she said respectfully.

"I can't believe you want to drag me in here on a Sunday—" The doctor stopped, his hand on the morgue door. "You have any jurisdiction here?"

"Well, we've been looking for this woman to ask her some questions about a military case. The fact that she turned up dead makes me even more curious about what she knew."

The doctor grunted and disappeared into the autopsy room.

"Smooth," Isen said.

A few seconds later the doctor stuck his head out the door. "You want to watch?" It had the ring of a challenge.

Isen shook his head, but McCall stood bravely, dropped her small purse on Isen's lap and followed the doctor inside.

She reappeared ten minutes later, her face covered in a fine sheen of perspiration. She was breathing through her mouth.

"You OK?" Isen asked.

McCall shook her head. "No."

Isen waited, then asked, "What'd you learn?"

"That I could never be a coroner."

"Not that ..."

"He said she's been dead four or five weeks."

"She died around the same time Hauck did," Isen said.

McCall nodded, then continued. "Some damage to the bones in her neck indicates that she might have been strangled. There don't appear to be any bullet holes, but then a lot of the flesh was gone ... animals, uh, animals ..."

She swallowed hard.

Isen walked to a water cooler at one end of the drab waiting room, filled a paper cup and brought it to McCall.

"Sit down," he said. "Drink this."

McCall collapsed into a chair and took the cup. Once composed, she continued.

"He said a closer examination of the skeleton might reveal knife marks or wounds made by bullets."

"He's going to classify it as a homicide?" Isen asked.

"He won't make that call until he's finished, but it looks that way."

"Sure looks an awful lot like what happened to Barbara Ann Yonders," Isen said.

"Sure does," McCall allowed.

It was after midnight by the time McCall drove Isen back to Sue Lynn's house. Fourteen minutes into Monday; the President was due on Friday.

"You up for coffee?" Isen asked.

"Sure," McCall said. "I might as well stay up and enjoy all twenty-four hours of what may be my last day in the Army."

Isen's banging around the kitchen brought Sue Lynn downstairs. She wore a long nightshirt, blue with a big white star and lettering that said "Don't Mess With Texas."

"Evening, ma'am," McCall said.

Sue Lynn blinked at the light and ran her fingers through her hair, which was already pointing out of her head at odd angles.

"Nobody who looks like this needs to be called ma'am," Darlington said. "Sue Lynn is fine. What have you sleuths been up to this evening?"

Isen told Sue Lynn about Cindy Racze, then backed up to the meeting with Bennett and filled in the rest of the day.

"So what have you got for theories?" Sue Lynn asked after taking it all in. The three of them were drinking coffee now. It promised to be a long week.

"Major Isen's pet theory—Veir is responsible for everything from the national debt to dental plaque—is looking more plausible," McCall said. "The problem is going to be proving it."

"He's connected pretty strongly," Isen said. "Two women he was messing around with turned up dead."

"What about Hauck?" Darlington wanted to know. "You said that neither Foote nor Bennett put Veir close to Hauck that night. Maybe Hauck was thin-skinned. Maybe he had other things on his mind, failings real or imagined that made him even more vulnerable."

"It just seems odd that Bennett hit the very nerve that was exposed," Isen said. "General Flynn told me he made too much of an issue about Hauck's rooming with a reputed homosexual. Flynn was worried that he made Hauck more nervous, more susceptible."

"But how would Bennett know what Flynn said? Maybe Savin's proclivities were common knowledge, or nearly so. And Bennett just hit on it hard at precisely the right ... or wrong ... time."

"Or maybe Veir knew that Hauck was vulnerable there," Isen said. "Maybe he pushed Bennett into baiting Hauck."

"Doesn't sound to me like Bennett needed much pushing," Sue Lynn observed.

"He's a piece of work, all right," McCall agreed. Then, to Isen, "Why would Veir have it in so bad for Hauck?"

"Cindy Racze."

"A lover's triangle?"

"Why not?"

"Threatening to out him was only the how. The why might have been Cindy Racze," Isen said.

"Forgive me for sounding like Bennett," McCall said, "but you really think he killed himself over a stripper?"

"There may be more,'" Isen said. "Or that might be enough. Remember the first time we met over at CID Headquarters? And you told me you had a kid commit suicide because his girlfriend dumped him."

"That was a teenager," McCall said.

"What about the woman who committed suicide because her boss was mean to her?"

"Mental case."

"And the young NCO who killed himself because he finished second in his class at BNCOC?"

McCall didn't respond to that one.

"Or the fact that our own good Dr. Severin wants to say that Hauck committed suicide because he didn't get his goddamned EIB?"

"OK, OK," McCall said. "You've proved your point. Sometimes people do things that would be unbelievable in the movies, even."

"Like the Zippo Lady story," Sue Lynn added.

"That" would make a great movie," McCall said.

She studied her hands for a moment while they listened to the ticking of the big clock in the hallway, all three of them considering the same possibility. McCall spoke it first.

"So you're saying that Harlan Veir killed Cindy Racze?"

"Cindy Racze, Barbara Ann Yonders, Michael Hauck," Isen said. "There's a lot of blood out there; I think Harlan Veir has some on his hands."

Special Agent Terry McCall dragged herself out of bed on Monday morning after getting only two hours of sleep. Still, she found herself surprisingly alert, a condition she didn't expect to last all day.

The prospect of moving forward with her investigation of Veir's role in Hauck's suicide elicited conflicting responses. The professional, if inexperienced, investigator in her was excited at the challenge of working through this maze of unclear connections to find something that approximated the truth. The soldier in her was angry that men like Veir and

Bennett wore the same uniform she did. The human side of her—if she thought about it, she might even have admitted it was a maternal side—was saddened by what had happened to Michael Hauck. In spite of his chosen profession and the martial history of his family, in spite of the fact that he'd decided to stand by his roommate and friend at great cost to himself, Hauck had turned out to be quite vulnerable.

All of her brainstorming on the way into work pointed toward action, to the point where she forgot—momentarily—that she was violating the spirit, if not the letter, of her orders.

"Special Agent McCall."

Colonel Berry, her commander, signaled to her from the door of his office down the hall from her own. He was back; her grace period was over.

"Come here, please."

The phone inside McCall's office rang, and she considered asking Berry if she could go in and answer it first, but thought better of it. Voice mail would pick it up.

McCall knocked on the frame of the open door.

"Come in," Berry said. "This is Major Gerhardt, from the IG."

Major Gerhardt, tall and thin with thick red hair, sported the grotesque military issue eyeglasses that the troops called BCGs, for Birth Control Glasses. ("Put these babies on and you couldn't get laid in a whorehouse with a C-note taped to your dick," McCall had heard one uniformed comic explain.)

"Sir," McCall said, extending her hand to Gerhardt.

"Major Gerhardt is here to talk about your conduct," Berry said with melodramatic emphasis, "in the investigation of Lieutenant Hauck's suicide."

McCall, not offered a seat, continued to stand while the two men sat.

"I understand that you've been working with a Major Mark Isen," Gerhardt said.

When McCall didn't answer—this was no bombshell—Gerhardt continued.

"You know that he is not an official investigator, don't you?"

"Yes, sir," was all McCall offered.

"We've had some reports that he's been presenting himself as an investigator in order to coerce information from people. Is that correct?"

"No, sir. Major Isen has not, in my presence at least, presented himself as an investigator. Furthermore, I know that he understands the seriousness of such a move."

"And how do you know that?" Gerhardt asked.

"We spoke about it, sir," McCall said evenly.

"Which means you had a conversation about the very thing Major Gerhardt just spoke about," Berry added.

Shit, McCall thought.

"Tell me, what occasioned that conversation?"

"My concern that Major Isen might be accused of impersonating an investigator."

"Did this come up out of the blue?" Berry pressed.

Gerhardt, a little slower on the uptake, caught on and nodded approval to Berry.

"No, sir," McCall said. "I had heard the concern raised before."

"So you warned him off?" Gerhardt said.

"Yes, sir. And I told him that if I found he was doing anything illegal," McCall said, turning to face her boss, "such as impersonating an investigator, I'd be happy to haul him in myself."

"Are you having sexual relations with Major Isen?" Gerhardt asked.

McCall's head snapped around.

"What?"

"I said, are you having a sexual relationship with Major Isen?"

"That is a ridiculous question and I resent your asking it."

"Is that a yes or a no?" Gerhardt persisted.

"That's a no, Major," McCall said, fighting to control her temper.

"So these rumors about the two of you are untrue?"

"What rumors?" McCall wanted to know.

McCall didn't know too many women in uniform who hadn't been the subject of rumors, often vicious, that were spread by people who would never consider themselves gossips.

Gerhardt reached over to Berry's desk and pulled several photos from some papers there; he handed them to McCall.

The black-and-white shots showed McCall and Isen looking over the bound newspapers in the library stacks. In one photo, McCall's hand was on Isen's shoulder.

"So what's this supposed to mean?" McCall asked. She wasn't giving them anything.

"You tell me," Gerhardt said.

McCall laughed in his face.

"You've got a lieutenant colonel down the street who's banging strippers in the parking lot, you've got soldiers soliciting blow jobs at private parties, somebody's going around beating up women because they talked to me, and you want me to take *this* seriously?"

She shook the photos in front of him. "I have my hand on his *shoulder.*"

She dropped the photos on Gerhardt's lap.

"But I bet I can tell you who initiated this complaint. For that matter, I bet I can tell you who paid the sleazy guy in the bad suit to take these pictures."

Gerhardt blinked rapidly behind his glasses. She knew, and he knew she knew.

"Let me guess . . . you're sucking up to him because you think he's going to be the next division commander or something, right?"

McCall took a step forward, closing the space between them to less than a foot. "A little warning, Major. You'd better be careful about which wagon you hook up to. Know what I mean?"

She turned to Berry, who seemed somehow amused by all of this.

"You know that even the appearance of this kind of impropriety can ruin a good investigator," Berry said to her. "It doesn't even have to be true, mind you. That's the sad part. I've seen rumors such as this one effectively end careers."

"Your warning sounds like a threat, sir," McCall said.

"Stay away from Isen," Berry continued. "Stay away from anyone who had anything to do with Michael Hauck or Michael Hauck's unit. That's an order. Got that?"

McCall was having difficulty holding her tongue. "There have been quite a few new developments—"

"Write me a report," Berry said. "And while you're at it, write me a report detailing what you and this Isen have been up to. Take your time; you'll have plenty because you're off the Hauck case. As a matter of fact, I want you to spend a couple of days at home."

McCall waited for him to confine her to her quarters, but he didn't get quite that specific.

Maybe he's anticipating having to explain himself to some-one later on, she thought.

Berry looked at the calendar on his desk. "Things are going to be pretty crazy around here until the President's visit is over on Friday. Come back after that."

Mark Isen's morning didn't start off much better than had McCall's. He called General Flynn to report on the conversation with Bennett. Isen didn't relish the prospect of telling Flynn that his harping on Hauck's rooming with a homosexual might have made him more vulnerable to the taunts of his peers. But Isen didn't get a chance to deliver his bad news before Flynn dropped something of his own.

"I got a call last night from a friend of mine at the IG, Mark," Flynn said.

"Let me guess," Isen said. "They want to ask me some questions about my so-called impersonating an investigator."

"It's a little more formal than that," Flynn said. "Word is that they already have some statements and a formal com-plaint. You're under investigation."

"It's a smoke screen, sir," Isen said.

"And an effective one, too. There's also word up here that you've been sleeping with the Special Agent in charge of the investigation."

"Not true, General. Veir dreamed that one up, too, I'm sure."

"Doesn't much matter at this point," Flynn said. "I also got a call from the Vice Chief's office."

The bad news is piling up fast, Isen thought.

The Vice Chief of Staff, a three-star rank, reported to the Chief of Staff of the Army.

"Actually, it was one of his flunkies who called, sort of unofficially, to warn me . . . us, I guess . . . to lay off."

"If people are so concerned about our interfering with his big show, why doesn't someone just order us to stop?" Isen asked.

"I was thinking about that myself," Flynn said. "Maybe Veir's patrons don't want to look like Veir's patrons. Doesn't much matter, the message is pretty clear."

"Is General Tremmore involved in this?" Isen asked.

"I haven't heard anything from him directly since that first call," Flynn said. "What are you thinking?"

"You said he was a pretty straight guy," Isen said. "Let me go to him, present what I have and let him make the call. If he says get out, I'll leave."

"Just like that?" Flynn asked.

"It's time to come out with what we have. If I just continue digging, somebody's going to throw me off Fort Bragg anyway. At least this way I get to present my side."

Flynn hesitated. If Isen kept pushing, the speculation about Hauck's sexuality was bound to come out; Savin would probably be dismissed. And the rumors damaging Hauck's reputation would be just as painful to his family now—maybe more so since Hauck shot himself when he could have turned to his family for help.

"I'm not sure that'll work, Mark," Flynn said. "This presidential visit is sure to steamroll everything. I doubt if Tremmore will even have time to see you."

"I can ask, sir. And I can take Special Agent McCall with me if she agrees. She *is* the official investigator."

Another pause. Isen switched the phone from one hand to the other.

"OK," Flynn said at last. "But keep in mind that General Tremmore plays only one game."

"What's that?"

"Hardball."

Isen hung up after promising to let Flynn know if the meeting would take place. Then he dialed McCall's office number and heard a voice mail message saying she'd be out of the office until the following Monday. Isen dialed her home number.

"What's this stuff about your being out of the office?" he asked when she picked up the phone.

"Berry told me to take the week off. You're not going to believe the story they hit me with this morning."

"Who?"

"Some jerk from the IG." She filled him in on the details, including the ridiculous story about their sexual liaison.

"I was hoping to have you come with me if I got in to see Tremmore," Isen said.

"Doesn't look like that's going to happen," McCall answered. "But I think you should go through with it. Ask Tremmore to appoint an investigating officer, someone you can turn all this stuff over to. Tell him what Bennett said and about Veir calling around to find out about Savin. Tell him about the sudden moves of Milan, Savin and Bennett."

"Should I tell him about Cindy and that other girl? The stuff Meade sent me?"

"You can tell him about this alleged triangle. You can tell him what we know about Cindy. It's not time to talk about that other dead girl. Make sure you take notes, 'cause he's probably going to challenge everything you say. You might get rattled if you don't have it written down. And remember to try to make it as simple as possible. His natural reaction will be to side with his own man. And you're the outsider."

"You can say that again," Isen said. "At least with you there I'd have a bit more legitimacy. What are you going to do now?"

"I got a message from my buddy at the state police. I asked him to check Veir's car phone records. I'm going to give him a call."

"Aren't you taking a chance, disobeying Berry like that?"

"Hell, I started taking chances the minute I said I'd help you out with this stupid, no-merit case you're trying to make," McCall said. "Hasn't killed me so far."

15

Mark Isen went to Sue Lynn's office in Division Headquarters and called the commanding general's aide, a captain, requesting twenty minutes with the general.

"I can squeeze you in week after next," the aide said cheerfully.

"Today."

"Pardon?"

Like many aides, this captain had the kind of perpetually happy demeanor that made Isen think *Salesman of the Quarter.*

"I want to see the CG today," Isen said evenly. "No, make that this morning."

"Well, sir, the general is pretty busy this week. The President is coming to Fort Bragg this week and—"

"I know all about the general's schedule and the President's visit," Isen said. "I'll tell you what, Captain. Tell General Tremmore that Major Mark Isen asked to see him as soon as is convenient for him. You got that?"

"Yes, sir," the captain said, his voice going cool. "I got it that time. May I call you back?"

"Right away." Isen gave him the number.

He hadn't even time to refill his coffee cup before the phone on Sue Lynn's desk rang.

"How fast can you be here, sir?" the aide asked without preamble.

"I'm already in the building."

Isen had two blue index cards on which he'd sketched an outline of what he wanted to say to General Tremmore. It looked pretty lame when he had it on paper.

The general's aide looked just like someone with his telephone voice ought to look like. Earnest, unlined face, close-cropped hair, with all the right hero badges on his uniform and the kind of poise one could only get from breeding.

The aide, sitting behind a nameplate that read "Captain Grace," stood and smiled when Isen walked in.

"Major Isen?"

Isen fought the urge to tap the name tape on his uniform that identified him as "Isen." No sense in trying to piss the kid off right away.

"Thanks for getting back to me so quickly," Isen said. "The general said he'd see me?"

"He's on his way back from a meeting downstairs," the captain said, glancing at the plain government issue clock above his desk. "He told me to have you stand by."

Isen nodded and looked around. The aide's office wasn't an office at all; it was more of an extension of the hallway with two desks jammed in tightly. The captain's beret and a maroon briefing folder—probably the general's schedule—lay on one desk. The other desk belonged to a civilian secretary who was not in at the moment.

Grace flipped through a three-ring binder that held various typed sheets and calendar pages, all tabbed, neatly arranged. Everything one could ever want to know about the Eighty-second Airborne Division was there: from how many soldiers were in the hospital to how many vehicles were in service bays to re-enlistment rates to AWOL cases. The aide had to be ready to answer the general's wide-ranging questions at any time, and this book was his armor. He probably ironed the pages.

"Is this your first visit to Fort Bragg?" Grace asked.

Isen wondered if he had a page tabbed "Questions for Visitors."

"No. I've been here for a few weeks now."

The aide was too professionally polite to say "Stirring up a shitstorm," but Isen figured that's what he was thinking behind his smile.

Isen was about to sit down when General Tremmore walked into the room.

"What's going on?" Tremmore said to the aide as he strode toward his office door. Spotting Isen, he cut back across the small room.

"Major Isen, right?" Tremmore said, extending his hand.

He was a bit shorter than Isen, about five seven, brown hair beating a retreat from a thinning widow's peak, his features square-cut, friendly. He moved quickly, confidently, but he did not smile.

"What happened to you?" Tremmore asked, noticing Isen's bruised face.

"Ran into a little trouble up in DC," Isen said, shaking the man's hand. "Thanks for agreeing to see me, sir."

"In here," Tremmore said, motioning for Isen to follow him through a door marked "Commanding General." Tremmore dropped into a chair beside a small coffee table, motioning Isen into an adjoining chair.

At least we're not facing off on either side of his desk, Isen thought.

"What can I do for you, Major?" Tremmore asked.

"I'm not sure how much you know about the purpose of my visit here," Isen began.

"Fill me in," Tremmore said. His voice was neither hostile nor friendly. He hadn't said he knew why Isen was here, nor had he feigned ignorance. He was going to let Isen set the stage for whatever happened.

Isen glanced down at the notecards he'd pulled together at McCall's suggestion, swallowed once, and began.

Tremmore interrupted him only twice, asking for clarification on the initial CID report and General Flynn's specific instructions. Satisfied, he let Isen go on.

Isen talked about the parties, the rowdy behavior, the dancers. He talked about how Hauck had been bothered and disappointed by everything he saw. He weaved together the stories of the sudden transfers of Milan, Savin and Bennett, revealing his source in the Chief of Staff's office. He told the general about the late-night call from Carroll and Veir's meddling in the investigation. Isen drew the connection between Hauck, Cindy and Veir; about how Veir used to follow Cindy around from club to club. He brought up McCall and the pressure to have her conclude an investigation that she didn't think was finished. He told the general what Bennett had said about Hauck, about how the unit really hadn't lost anything. He lined up his evidence, simplifying, trying to remain objective; and he was conscious, the entire time, that he was exposing himself as well. His and Veir's careers and Isen's professional reputation were laid out now in front of the general, who sat inscrutable as Solomon.

"So your theory is that Lieutenant Colonel Veir . . . what? . . . encouraged Bennett to *tease* Hauck into shooting himself?"

Isen thought "tease" a poor choice of words—as in *Doesn't look good for my side*—but he nodded.

"I believe Bennett, and maybe some others, threatened to spread a rumor to the effect that Hauck was gay. I think Colonel Veir wanted Michael Hauck out of the picture somehow, either because Hauck was going to complain publicly about the antics of his fellow officers or because he perceived Hauck as a threat to his relationship with Cindy."

"It seems to me that it would be helpful to talk to this Cindy," Tremmore said. "Have you done that?"

"No, sir. She turned up dead the other day. Died around the same time Hauck did, although the report's not done yet."

Tremmore considered that point for a moment, and Isen wondered if he'd gone too far. He had nothing on which he might claim that Veir was a murderer.

"I think all of this bears further investigation," Isen said. "The CID should re-open the case or you should appoint an investigating officer."

Tremmore sat quietly for a moment, watching Isen as if expecting more. Isen studied his cards again, as if he could make something more appear there.

Tremmore pulled himself out of the chair, walked around behind his desk, sat down and folded his hands.

Not a good sign, Isen thought.

"I must admit that I'm surprised by a great deal of what you tell me, Major Isen," Tremmore said slowly. He paused, and Isen, now standing before the commander's desk, felt as if he were being lifted by strong wings. He hadn't been wrong to insist on this interview.

"I'm also surprised that you would come down here, conduct an amateur investigation, draw startling conclusions from circumstantial evidence, and use those conclusions to sully the name of a brother officer."

Oh, shit, Isen thought.

"I think that you have a point about an investigation," the general continued. "And I am not going to have this hanging over our heads during this very important week. I'm not going to do anything that could lead someone to accuse us of covering this thing up just because the President is coming."

Isen's mind was in overdrive, trying to anticipate the general's options.

Tremmore flipped open his desk calendar, scanning the page with the tip of a pen.

"Today is Monday," Tremmore said. "On Thursday morning I'll have you and Colonel Veir in here. Just the two of you—we'll leave the CID out of this just yet—so we can get this thing sorted out. I'll let him answer your accusations, confront his accuser, as it were. And at that time I'll decide if I want to appoint an investigating officer or if I want to ask the CID to re-open the case."

"Sir," Isen said. "That's the day before the President's visit."

Tremmore gave Isen a look that was somewhere short of tolerant.

"I'm well aware of when the President is coming, Major. I don't want this hanging over the division. If your argument has some merit, we'll proceed."

Tremmore closed the book, pulled it to the center of his blotter, where he tapped it with his pen.

"If it turns out that you're full of shit, Major, if it turns out that you've been causing all this trouble out of some personal motivation, rest assured that I'll roll over you like a freight train. You understand?"

"Yes, sir," Isen said.

"Thursday, eleven hundred hours. You're dismissed."

Isen saluted, executed a wobbly left-face, and left the office. The aide, who'd probably listened to the last exchange through the open door, said, "Good day, sir."

Isen wandered in a daze to the first floor and Sue Lynn's office.

"What did he say?" Sue Lynn wanted to know as he took a chair in front of her desk.

"The big showdown is Thursday. He's going to hear my side and Veir's right there in his office. If Veir can talk his way through Thursday morning, he'll survive and Tremmore will see to it that I get to make a career change."

"Isn't that what you wanted?" Sue Lynn asked. "A showdown, I mean."

"No," Isen said, wondering why it wasn't obvious to everyone else. "I thought he'd appoint an investigator *after* the President's visit, after things had calmed down around here. Or they'd let McCall re-open the case. Then the investigator, an *official* investigator with a mandate from the local commander, would have time to fill in all the gaps in this story."

Isen thought about his phone call to the aide, how he'd insisted that he needed to see the general right away.

"Now that I've forced the issue I'm left with only the same circumstantial evidence—Tremmore's words—and all Veir has to do is rebut. I'd say the chances of Tremmore relieving his star on the day before the show are slim to none. But if he can get me out of here on Thursday, so much the better."

Isen pulled the phone around to the front of Sue Lynn's desk and dialed Flynn's number. When the general came on the line, Isen told him about the interview.

"Yes, sir, I got to see General Tremmore. But I think I just built my own gallows."

When Sue Lynn went off to brief the Secret Service about air operations during the President's visit, Isen sat at her desk with the door closed. He considered calling Foote, but his own situation seemed so far gone that he'd just drag Foote down with him. There was no doubt that Bennett would tell Veir about the little interview at the airfield, but it might still be possible for Foote to salvage something of his career.

I wish I could say the same for me, Isen thought.

Sue Lynn's phone rang. Isen was going to let it go—he couldn't help anyone with questions about aviation—but he picked it up on the third ring for want of something better to do.

"Major Darlington's office. Major Isen speaking."

"Just the person I wanted to talk to." It was McCall.

"I thought you weren't supposed to have any contact with me," Isen said.

"I'm not, but I didn't think you'd turn me in," she said. "I just got a call from the guy who was looking at Veir's phone bill, the bill for the car phone."

"And?"

"He called Dee's trailer on the night that Hauck shot himself. He called her right before he called Foote; he must have known Hauck was dead when he phoned."

"Why would he call Dee?" Isen asked.

"Cindy was staying there at the time, remember?"

Isen sat up. "So he called Cindy that night. . . ."

"Dee might be able to tell us if Veir spoke to Cindy," McCall said.

Isen pulled a yellow legal pad from Sue Lynn's drawer. "What time was the call?"

"Twenty-two forty-four," McCall said. "He called Foote at twenty-two fifty."

Isen wrote the time on the sheet. "And Hauck shot himself?"

"Between twenty-two thirty and twenty-three hundred," McCall said.

"So if we can determine that Cindy talked to Veir at a quarter to eleven . . . what?"

Isen was frustrated. He knew he should be able to fit this into the puzzle somehow, but the pieces seemed to change shape even as he watched.

"If we can determine that Hauck was at the club when Veir called Cindy," McCall said, "and that he didn't leave the club and she didn't go there, then we know that Hauck died first."

"OK," Isen said. "What about Veir?"

"What about Veir?" McCall said. "You're looking at this from the wrong end. Start with what you know rather than with the assumption that Veir is involved in everything. Veir's call might help us determine that Hauck killed himself before Cindy was murdered, and that's about it so far."

"So we'd know that . . . what? Hauck didn't kill Cindy?"

"Right," McCall said. "But that's not the same as saying that Veir did."

"OK, OK," Isen said. "I'm jumping around a bit because I'm trying not to panic here."

"Has something changed?"

Isen told McCall about the showdown in the commanding general's office.

"So it could all be over by Thursday at lunchtime," she said.

"Probably will be. Tremmore said he didn't want this hanging over the division."

"The general didn't give you much time to put things together," McCall said. "Maybe he knows what he's going to decide on Thursday, but he's going through the motions so that it looks like he's doing something, like he's trying to be objective."

"I've thought of that," Isen said.

"So the only way to avoid getting crushed on Thursday is to come up with something more," McCall said. "I think you should start with Dee. See if she can connect Veir and Cindy on that phone call to her trailer."

"And then what?" Isen wanted to know.

"Well, somebody threatened to kill her once. It seems pretty obvious that she knows something dangerous. Dangerous to her and to whoever else is involved."

"Dangerous to me, too," Isen said.

The orderly stood by quietly until Veir, who was already on the phone, looked up at him.

"Colonel Kent is on line two for you, sir," the soldier said.

Veir punched the hold button, watched the light blink five

times, six, thinking, *Don't get squirrelly on me, Kent,* before he picked up.

"Veir," he said into the receiver.

"Colonel Veir," Kent said.

"Colonel Veir?" Veir said, trying to lighten the moment. *"That's* not a good sign." He considered making a joke about the fact that he wasn't banging Kent's daughter, but he let it go for the moment.

"I just had a conversation with General Tremmore," Kent said. The Chief of Staff was trying to sound official, but it was coming off as nervous.

"I've been talking to him quite a bit myself, lately," Veir said.

"He wanted to know about these little transfers and TDY requests," Kent said.

"Do you mean Lieutenant Bennett?"

"I mean Bennett, Milan, Savin. All of them."

Veir considered pointing out that Milan and Savin were not in his unit and so were not his responsibility, but he bided his time.

"Yes?"

"He wanted to know if requests you made got special treatment," Kent said.

"And what did you tell him?"

"I told him that the division staff was doing whatever it could to support you in your mission. I told him that I had instructions from his predecessor to do what I could to make sure the Army got as much ... publicity mileage as possible out of your sudden notoriety."

"Sounds like a fair answer, Colonel Kent," Veir said. He was calm now, in control. Kent seemed to be slipping.

"General Tremmore wanted to know if that extended to transferring officers who were not in your command."

Isen, Veir thought. *That fucker is putting all this together.*

All around him the headquarters operated in chaos. Soldiers hurried back and forth, computer printers hammered out stacks of paper, phones jangled, radios squawked—the casual observer might wonder if it were all going to come together in time for the big day. Everything cried out for the commander's calming influence.

One of Veir's staff officers appeared next to him, holding

out a paper that needed the commander's attention. Veir covered the mouthpiece with his hand.

"Can you see that I'm on the goddamned fucking phone here?"

The captain disappeared.

Veir regained his composure. There was nothing he could do about Isen at the moment, and there was always a way to handle Kent.

"And you said?" Veir asked.

"I said it didn't."

Veir smiled.

"So if your guidance said nothing about sending these other motherfuckers on TDY, Colonel, and you did it anyway . . . sounds to me like you're in this up to your asshole."

At his office in Division Headquarters, Kent put the phone gently into its cradle and sat down at his desk.

"Exactly the conclusion I reached," he told himself. "The question is: can I come clean?"

Dee Ann had left Isen and McCall with the name of a brother in her West Virginia hometown. Although Isen wouldn't have been surprised to find out that the brother's given name was Moon, it turned out that there was no telephone listing for a Moon James. It was just as easy to call all the Jameses listed for the area around Smoke Hole, West Virginia; there were three. It was six o'clock by the time he connected.

"Is this Moon James?" Isen asked.

"Uh-huh."

"My name is Mark Isen, Mr. James. Your sister Dee Ann gave me your name in case I needed to contact her."

"That's a crock of bullshit," Moon said, dragging out the first syllable—"*bool*-sheet."

"She gave you my name because she knew I'd kick the shit out of anybody who tried to bother her again. You the fella that beat her up?"

"No, no," Isen said. "I'm the one who tried to help her. I'm a major in the Army."

"From what my sister tells me, that don't mean much when it comes to figurin' out who's nice and who needs to get whomped."

Thanks to people like Harlan Veir, Isen thought.

"Look, Mr.—"

"Call me Moon."

"Look, Moon. I'm trying to get the man who beat your sister. I think the same man might be responsible for other things, other attacks on women. But I need Dee Ann's help to stop him."

"Last time she helped she damn near got killed."

"She's safe down there with family. . . ."

"You're damn right, she is."

"I just need to talk to her. Ask her a question."

"Gimme your number," Moon said. "I'll get back to you."

Isen read the number off Sue Lynn's phone, then gave him the home number as well. Moon hung up without saying anything else.

While he waited for the return call, Isen pulled a road atlas off of Sue Lynn's tiny bookshelf. Smoke Hole was as far north as Washington, D.C., and almost directly west of the capital in the mountains that divide West Virginia from its larger namesake cousin. Isen figured he could fly to Charleston, then take a puddle jumper north.

Moon called back a few minutes later.

"She says she don't want to talk to you," he told Isen.

"Can I ask her a question through you?"

"Nah. I ain't gonna keep calling you back, playing games like two kids passing notes in school. Get yourself somebody else to help you."

The line went dead.

Dee Ann might be the only person who could connect Veir and Cindy on the night of Hauck's death. He couldn't let her go.

Isen pulled a stack of metal routing trays from the corner of Sue Lynn's desk. One was marked "In," another "Out." The third one was marked "Hover." He found a yellow legal pad in the third tray and drew a rectangle on the page; inside he wrote "Cindy."

If Cindy died after Hauck—something he might be able to determine with Dee's help—the best he could do was absolve Hauck; he wouldn't be any closer to Veir. Isen thought about Barbara Ann Yonders, the stripper friend of

Veir's who'd turned up dead a few years back. The coincidences and similarities were chilling.

There was plenty to do: Sue Lynn was still trying to contact Meade; she would also canvass the clubs and Dee Ann's trailer park once again to see if anyone saw anything of note. McCall was out of the net. Foote might or might not want to help; at any rate he was in the middle of preparing for the President's visit.

Isen had to connect the still-living Cindy to Veir, had to put them together after Hauck's death. That was one part of the puzzle. Veir might just provide him the other part.

Isen looked at the map again. He could fly up there in a couple of hours, five or six if the connections didn't work out. He could drive it in seven.

Harlan Veir stood on the short, forward-slanted hood of his command vehicle and glared at the infantry squad taking up positions in the undergrowth that stretched away from the road. His jaw was set, his fists propped on his shiny new pistol belt, his feet spread shoulder-width apart in a perfect, magazine cover pose. Someone nearby was speaking. He looked down.

"What did you say?"

One of the battalion's medics stood below him, eyes squinted almost shut as he looked up toward the sun. His arm was extended.

"I brought you the painkillers you asked for, sir."

"Thanks," Veir said, squatting. He popped the two capsules into his mouth, unstrapped the canteen on his belt and took a long swallow of lukewarm water.

"You got something for this?" Veir said, holding out his hand. His knuckles were scraped and bleeding. "I beat the shit out of some motherfucker who deserved it," Veir said, but the medic was already moving away.

"Fuck it," Veir said, standing. He looked around at the little knots of officers and NCOs who stood nearby. All of them seemed as intent on keeping some distance between themselves and the old man as they were on watching the demonstration unfolding before them.

Veir began to practice his speech, the one he would deliver to the President of the United States. The Commander in Chief.

"You've seen what our knockout punch looks like, sir," Veir said. "Those five hundred men you saw descending on the drop zone are ready for violent action as soon as they hit the ground. Now I'd like to show you the other side of our capability, the infantryman's art, if you will."

He turned half-left and gestured with outstretched arm, a move he'd practiced before one of the three full-length mirrors he kept in his bedroom.

"In the field before you is a squad of infantry, eleven men expertly camouflaged and moving toward us even as we stand here. Keeping in mind that this is daylight, and the American infantryman's best friend is the night, see if you can spot any of our soldiers out there, sir."

Veir had wanted to say "I challenge you . . . ," but his chicken-shit brigade commander had thought that wording a little strong.

Veir looked out at the field and saw movement to his front.

"I see somebody fucking moving out there," he yelled.

He looked around for the NCOs, but they seemed to have moved farther away. Then there was the unmistakable sound of helicopter blades cutting the air close by.

Veir turned around and looked at the sky above the tree line behind him.

"It's the President's chopper, sir," the Sergeant Major, suddenly close again, said.

"He can't be here yet," Veir said, trying to hold the desperation out of his voice.

"Too late."

That voice. Veir looked back over his shoulder to see Mark Isen standing up amid the squad of soldiers, all of them suddenly visible. He was camouflaged as they were, but he had no weapon.

"WHAT THE FUCK ARE YOU DOING HERE?" Veir screamed. "SOMEBODY GET HIM OUT OF HERE!"

"Can't, sir," Leonard Foote, now standing by the vehicle, said. "He just won't go away."

"I'll make him go away," Veir said, tugging at his pistol. "He's not going to fuck me over."

Veir pulled his weapon. Isen now had a rifle; he was trying to raise it, point it at Veir, but he was too slow. Veir squatted, held the pistol in two hands, felt the small recoil of the nine millimeter, but heard no sounds.

"Get him out of here," he shouted, but the people around him were looking for the helicopter, which sounded close.

Veir jumped down from the vehicle hood and ran to where he'd dropped Isen. He kicked through the choking weeds and brambles, felt something beneath his foot. Bending over, he plunged one arm through the branches of a small bush which tore at his face as he pushed them aside.

Cindy Racze lay on her back, a single entry wound just above her left eyebrow, her pretty throat ringed in vicious purple bruises.

"Sir."

It was Foote's voice, just behind him. He was afraid to turn around.

"Sir, it's the President. We'd better tell him what happened. . . ."

Veir sat up quickly, banging his head on the top of the vehicle's doorframe.

"What?"

Foote stood beside the vehicle, his hand on Veir's shoulder.

"Looks like you dozed off a minute, sir," Foote said. "No big deal. Everybody's pretty ragged out. I wouldn't even have bothered you, but the CG's aide just called and you're supposed to call the old man right away."

"Uh . . . thanks," Veir said. He worked his jaw, which felt as if it had been clamped shut.

"Was I talking in my sleep?" Veir asked.

"Talking and grinding your teeth," Foote said.

Veir gave his XO a questioning look.

"You didn't say anything I could make out," Foote added.

Veir's driver carried a cellular telephone which had been given to Veir so that he'd be available during the weeks leading up to the President's visit. Veir, who'd initially been flattered—only the highest ranking six or seven officers in the division had such phones—considered his new constant accessibility a perfect example of the curse of technology.

He dialed the number for the CG's office, checked in with the aide and waited for the general.

"Harlan?"

"Yes, sir," Veir said, trying to sound upbeat. Foote was about ten yards away. Veir smiled at him, gave him a thumbs-up.

"I had a talk today with this Mark Isen," Tremmore said. "I assume you know all about him."

That could mean a lot, Veir thought. For a moment he wondered if the old man was trying to smoke him out.

Not this close to the big show, he assured himself.

"I know he's been following me around, sir. Trying to make something more out of Lieutenant Hauck's suicide. He's been a pain in the ass."

"Has he interfered with your preparations?" Tremmore asked, characteristically cutting to the root of the problem.

Veir wanted to say *Only when I dream about shooting the motherfucker.*

"I've got everything under control for the President's visit, sir," he said into the tiny phone. "It'll take a lot more than some douchebag from the Pentagon to knock me off track."

"Good," Tremmore said without enthusiasm.

Veir made a mental note to play his bluster hand a little more lightly with this general.

"Is it safe to say that you'd rather not have him around?" Tremmore asked.

"Yes, sir," Veir said happily, anticipating the gift that was coming. *Throw his ass right off post.*

"Good," Tremmore said. "We're going to get this thing straightened out this week. Before the President's visit."

"Sir?" Veir said. His jaw tightened again, his teeth pressing together painfully.

"Thursday morning, my office. Isen will be here to present his side. You'll be here to present your side, if you think it's necessary."

Veir felt something like a cold breeze pass over the back of his neck, where the tiny hairs bristled.

"I don't want any of this hanging over us for the President's visit," Tremmore said. "I want to get it over with. I also don't want anyone saying we covered this up. So it'll be clear by . . . let me see, when's the dress rehearsal?"

Veir could hear Tremmore sliding a calendar across his desk.

"The rehearsal is at thirteen hundred, sir."

"Good. Excellent," Tremmore said. "Be here at eleven hundred. I'm eager to put this behind us."

"Yes, sir," Veir said. "I am, too."

Tremmore hung up; Veir snapped the phone shut, then stood with his hands at his sides. Behind him, NCOs were shouting instructions to the soldiers who crawled and sweated, trying hard to make themselves invisible, all at the behest of a commander who wanted to be the most visible officer in an Army uniform.

It took Mark Isen the better part of Tuesday to cover the three hundred and fifty miles between Fort Bragg, North Carolina, and Smoke Hole, West Virginia. At the end of four airline connections and two and a half hours on the road he was driving his rental car through a steady rain over slick and winding blacktop that wouldn't have made a safe driveway, much less a two-lane road.

He hadn't told Flynn about the trip; the old man hadn't been much help. McCall—who reminded Isen "I'm not even supposed to talk to you"—wasn't all that impressed with his plan. She thought he would find Cindy's story in Fayetteville. Sue Lynn had urged him to confront Kent; Isen thought the time for that was later. More than once during his long day of traveling he'd told himself that Sue Lynn had been right in warning him against going to West Virginia.

"You're wasting time," she'd said. "And you're down to your last few days."

"If I don't have a better case to make with Tremmore when I see him on Thursday," Isen had replied, "I'll be down to my last few days in the Army."

He found a tiny motel and woke the desk clerk to get a room. Five minutes later he collapsed on the bed in his rain-soaked clothes and dialed Moon James's number. Someone answered on the sixth ring.

"Yeah?"

"Mr. James, this is Mark Isen. We spoke yesterday, remember?"

"Yeah, I remember," James said. "You remember how to tell time? It's past friggin' midnight."

"I'm in Smoke Hole, Mr. James. Down at the Blue Rock Motel. You know where that is?"

"Yeah, I know where you are," James said.

"I need to see your sister, Mr. James. It's vitally important."

"Must be, to get you to come all the way out here."

"Can I talk to her, then?"

"Nope. I told you that yesterday."

"Can you at least ask her if she'll see me?" Isen asked.

James yawned loudly into the phone.

"I might," he said.

"Call me back in the morning?"

"Nope. Best I can do is talk to you tomorrow afternoon," James said.

Shit, Isen thought. The meeting in Tremmore's office was less than thirty-six hours away.

"I'm afraid I don't have a lot of time, Mr. James. I have to be back at Fort Bragg by Thursday morning."

"Have a nice trip, then," Moon James said just before he hung up.

"*Fuck*," Isen said, slamming the phone onto the cradle. The sudden movement shot pain through his still-sore ribs. He counted to ten to calm himself.

"You're the one asking for favors here, Isen," he said out loud. "Best keep that in mind."

He dialed the number again, breathing deeply to relax his tone.

"Tell me where to meet you," he said when James answered the phone.

Lieutenant Brian Bennett paced back and forth, back and forth in the darkness along the line of cars parked behind Jiggles. He wasn't sure what had brought him back to this spot; he just knew that, at home, sleep wasn't coming.

"You lose something, pal?"

Bennett looked up. There was a middle-aged white man not two feet from him; he smelled of booze and the end of his necktie was jammed into the breast pocket of his shirt.

"What?"

"I asked if you lost something," the man repeated. His words slurred on a thick tongue.

"Get the fuck out of here," Bennett said.

"Hey, I didn't mean nothing. . . ."

"I said GET THE FUCK OUTTA HERE!" Bennett screeched. "Get out before I fuckin' kill you, too."

The man turned clumsily away, but before Bennett lost sight of him he thought about what he'd just said. *Before I kill you, too.*

He jumped into his own truck, started the engine and punched the accelerator. The pickup swerved onto the road in a loud screech of rubber, and Bennett looked in the rearview to see if he was being followed. He thought he saw Michael Hauck come out of the club's front door.

Bennett thrust his cowboy boot onto the brake pedal; the truck fishtailed into the center of the road, heeling over dangerously. He looked back—there was no one by the club door.

"Fuck," he said as he put the truck back in gear and eased into the center of his lane. "I'm fucking losing my mind."

Brian Bennett didn't like ambiguity. In fact, he wasn't all that keen on making choices; he preferred to have his options worked out for him by someone else. He wasn't perceptive enough to see that this made him the perfect subordinate for Harlan Veir; it was also the trait that led to war crimes.

Harlan Veir had shipped him out, had tried to get rid of him. That much was clear now.

Bennett had called Veir from Benning after Foote told him to come back to Bragg. Veir had exploded, calling Foote a "disloyal prick" before calming down and lapsing into an eerie, distant silence. Veir had coached Bennett on what to tell the investigators, had encouraged the lieutenant, telling him that everything was fine.

Then Veir had shut the door on him, leaving Brian Bennett with nothing but his imagination and his imperfect understanding of everything that had happened to Michael Hauck.

"I ain't done nothing 'cept what I been told to do," he said to reassure himself.

He snorted, then forced a laugh because he felt something like tears coming on.

"And look what the fuck doing what I been told got me," he said. "Fucking ghosts in my rearview fucking mirror."

Major Leonard Foote spent Tuesday night on a cot in his office. Sue Lynn Darlington, driving by at five-thirty on her way to PT, spotted Foote's car and pulled in to the lot. She startled the duty NCO, who'd been sitting with his feet up, reading *Penthouse*.

"I see Major Foote's car out there," Sue Lynn said as she walked in.

The duty NCO put his magazine down, quickly shoving it into an open drawer when he saw the woman—who heard her come in?—standing right in front of his desk.

"Is he in?"

"Yes, ma'am. That is, he slept in his office last night. I don't know if he's up yet."

Sue Lynn walked by the NCO and the runner, a private, toward a door marked with a big stenciled "XO." The soldiers were admiring the way she looked from behind in her gym shorts before they realized where she was going.

"He's probably sleeping in there, ma'am," the NCO stammered. "I don't know that it's a good idea—"

"Relax, Sergeant," Sue Lynn said. "I just want to have a chat with him. I promise not to attack him in his sleep."

Darlington turned the knob and pushed the office door open, throwing an oblong of light into the room. She could feel the men behind her watching, waiting to see what she would do.

They probably think I'll act like a girl, she thought.

"Major Foote," she said loudly, entering the room and switching on the light.

Save for his big feet, which stuck out over the edge of the cot, Leonard Foote was completely covered with a camouflage poncho liner.

"Rise and shine," Darlington said cheerfully.

One hand snaked out from under the lightweight blanket and tugged at a corner, exposing Foote's eyes. He studied Darlington as if she were an apparition.

"What the hell are you doing here?"

"We need to have a chat," she said. Darlington turned to close the door; the duty NCO and his runner were staring, openmouthed. She could almost hear their imaginations running at full steam.

When she turned back around, Foote was sitting on the edge of the cot, the poncho liner wrapped around his waist. She noticed his trousers and blouse folded neatly on the chair.

Foote stretched, and Darlington thought of a magnificent Greek statue, executed in ebony instead of marble. She tried not to stare.

"Forgive me if I don't stand up," he said, pulling the liner around him more securely. Darlington saw that Foote was embarrassed.

"Mark called me last night," she said. "He went up to West Virginia to find this dancer named Dee Ann. She might be able to connect Veir and Cindy Racze."

Foote looked around the room, as if trying to get his bearings. He nodded.

"He and I thought it would be a good idea for you to go to General Tremmore's office tomorrow at eleven."

"Are you nuts?" Foote asked evenly.

"Mark talked to the commanding general. Tremmore wasn't even close to being convinced that Mark's story has merit. Under other circumstances, Tremmore might allow the case to play itself out. But with the presidential visit, with the spotlight on Veir, he wants it taken care of now. Tremmore has made it so that he can put an end to this tomorrow. Eleven hundred. Isen and Veir in the CG's office. Kind of like a duel.

"You and McCall are the only other people who heard Bennett, and McCall is practically under house arrest. If Veir got to Bennett, Bennett won't say anything more. Mark is the bogeyman; you have credibility."

"Is Isen going to be there?"

"He's planning on it," Sue Lynn said.

"What the hell does that mean?"

"OK, he's going to be there," she said, telling herself it was the truth.

"So what does he need me for?"

Sue Lynn heard some soldiers laughing in the outer office.

She had come here thinking that Foote was on their side. He had come forward to help Isen, but something was shifting.

"Look, you know that Veir had something more to do with Hauck killing himself than anyone has suspected so far," Sue Lynn said. "If you don't help us bring that out into the light, you're part of a cover-up."

"Cover-up of what?" Foote demanded. "You've got nothing but a bunch of rumors and innuendo. You're trying to piece it all together to make a picture that isn't there."

There was a photograph of Foote and his family on the wall. Foote held his son; there was no wheelchair in sight. Sue Lynn did not want to push this man.

"Not exactly," Sue Lynn said. "We want to let General Tremmore decide if there's something there. But we need your help."

"Are you going to be there?"

"If Mark needs me, or if I find out something new."

"What if Isen doesn't show? Doesn't make it back in time?"

"He'll be there," Sue Lynn said, surprised at the confidence in her voice.

Foote was quiet for a moment.

"He'll destroy me," he said softly.

Seconds passed. Outside the window, Foote and Darlington could hear soldiers gathering for the day, joking, shouting at each other, swearing at the early hour—the sounds of an Army that had been their home for a decade and a half.

"Sorry to barge in on you like this," Sue Lynn said as she made ready to go.

"Tell me something, Sue Lynn," Foote said to her back. "Do you really think right always wins?"

Sue Lynn turned around at the door.

"Nah. But it's always *right*."

Harlan Veir saw Command Sergeant Major Hendrix in the company street talking to two of the company first sergeants. The NCOs came to attention and saluted as Veir approached.

"Good morning, good morning," Veir said. He wore the

dazzling smile that some of the NCOs in the battalion called his *Newsweek* smile.

Veir spent a few minutes looking interested while the senior NCOs talked about how their preparations were going. He thanked them, saluted and made ready to walk away before turning back as if remembering something.

"I almost forgot," he lied. "Amid everything else that's going on, I need you guys to do something else for the battalion. I heard a rumor yesterday afternoon that is potentially damaging to unit morale, and I want to make sure we do everything we can to quash it."

The NCOs nodded, acknowledging their commander's concern and his respect for their roles as leaders in the unit.

"There's a rumor going around," Veir said, dropping his voice, "that Lieutenant Hauck killed his girlfriend before he ate his pistol."

"Holy shit," Hendrix said.

"Now, I don't have to tell you men that we don't need that kind of irresponsible gossip flying around here. Not only does it do a terrible disservice to that young man's reputation and family, but it's not going to help us this week, either.

"If you hear somebody talking that shit, I want you to tell them to shut the hell up. Got it?"

"Got it, sir," Hendrix answered as the others nodded. "You can count on us."

Veir smiled. He couldn't have spread the rumor faster with a megaphone.

"Thanks. I appreciate your help," he said as he saluted again and turned away. "Carry on."

Isen saw an orange neon glow come up suddenly on his left; he slowed and pulled into the gravel parking lot and deep puddles of Possum Holler Pizza. There were two patrons inside, a fortyish man and woman who looked up as his headlights swung across them through the big front window. Isen parked, ran the few steps to the door and pushed his way in. He'd been bored out of his mind all this rainy day, with nothing more to do than badger Sue Lynn and McCall by phone. He showed up an hour early to meet Moon James.

The couple at the table nodded as he walked in. A pimpled teenager behind the counter said, "Howdy."

"Hey there," Isen responded. He sat down and ordered a slice of pepperoni pizza.

The teenager, who wore an incongruous combination of a Bass Angler's hat and a gold cross earring, dropped a cold slice onto a paper plate and slid it into the oven.

"Drinkin'?" he asked.

"Diet," Isen said.

Isen watched the kid pour his soft drink.

"I'm looking for a fellow by the name of Moon James," he said. "You happen to know where he lives around here?"

The counterboy looked at Isen from under his eyebrows without raising his head. He put the cup on the counter, turned and pulled Isen's pizza from the oven. The paper plate spun when he slid it across the counter. Isen was about to repeat the question when someone behind him spoke.

"You a friend of his?"

Isen turned to look at the man in the single booth. He wore his hair in a shiny ponytail, and there was a Rorschach blot of dried salt that dropped in remarkable symmetry from the collar of his black T-shirt. He had a single blue letter tattooed below each knuckle of his right hand. Isen couldn't make out the word from across the room.

Isen considered answering yes but figured there was a chance, at least, that in this small town everyone knew the story already.

"We talked on the phone for the first time the other night," Isen said. "And I told him it was important that I see him."

The man hadn't looked up again. He chewed and studied his pizza as if every change he made by biting it rendered it more interesting.

"Would you know where I can find him?" Isen asked politely.

"I'll bet he didn't know you were coming," the man said. His companion, a woman for whom the bright fluorescent lights of the room were no friend, looked sideways at Isen.

"Frankly, no, he didn't know," Isen said. "Sounds like the two of you are pretty close."

"You could say that," the man said.

He turned in the booth, swinging his legs up onto the seat beside him and producing a toothpick from the pocket of his shirt. He picked at his teeth delicately for a moment before continuing.

"I know he's pretty upset about what happened to his sister down there in North Carolina." His accent was more remarkable than Dee Ann's. Isen thought of the expression "You could fry hush puppies in his mouth."

"So am I," Isen said truthfully. "I'm trying to get the guy who did that to her."

"But you ain't a cop," the man said. There was nothing of a question in his voice.

"No, I'm not," Isen said. "But I am conducting an investigation."

"You a private investigator?"

Isen thought about that a moment. "I'm about as close to a private investigator as you can find in the Army," he answered. "And I'd like to talk to Dee Ann."

"I heard that's what got her in trouble last time, talking to somebody who was nosing around."

"Dee Ann was beaten up because someone thought she knew something damaging. She was beaten up to keep her quiet. But if she keeps quiet, the man I believe is responsible will get away with this and some other things as well."

All speculation, of course, Isen thought.

"You got proof?" the man wanted to know. "You got proof you should go to the police, don't you think?"

"That's what I plan on doing," Isen said. "But there are a couple of pieces missing."

The man pulled the toothpick from his mouth, studied the end of it before putting it back in his shirt pocket. He took his time standing, sliding across the seat toward Isen, lowering his boots to the floor, then pulling himself upright. Flat-bellied, with the wide shoulders of a working man, he stood three or four inches taller than Isen and probably had him by forty pounds. When he reached to push a loose strand of hair from his eyes, light and shadow played across the muscles in his arm.

He walked over to Isen, who stood and held out his hand.

"I'm Mark Isen. And I'll bet you're Moon James," Isen said.

"That's right," James said. "Pretty good for somebody who's not even a real detective."

He shook Isen's hand. Isen noticed that the blue letters on his fingers spelled "Moon"; a long blue-and-yellow dragon curled on the inside of his forearm.

"I'm sure my sister told you that I get real upset when somebody hurts her," James said. "And I was going to say something like that to you. But it looks like somebody already kicked the shit out of you."

"I think it was the same person who beat up your sister," Isen said.

"You seem pretty sure. Dee Ann said she thought you guys were taking shots in the dark."

"I've learned a lot since then," Isen said. "I need to know what Dee Ann knew that would make someone want to shut her up."

"I decided you can't see her," James said.

"What? Last night you said ... when did you decide this?"

"Just now."

Isen had the strange sensation that he could close his eyes and he'd be talking to Leonard Foote.

"You kept me waiting all day," Isen said. "You don't have any reason to jerk me around like this; I just want to ask her a few questions. That's all."

"Maybe you don't hear so good," James said. "I said you can't see her."

"Maybe I can talk to her on the phone, then," Isen tried.

"She don't want to talk to you, neither."

"Look, she's safe down here with you. . . ."

"And I intend to keep it that way," James said. "If your little investigation is so damned important, why aren't the real police handling it?"

"I've stuck my neck way out for this," Isen said, feeling the old frustration that had been his since his first day on Fort Bragg. "But I can't do everything myself."

A woman's voice said, "What makes you so sure I can help you?"

Isen looked up at the door; Dee Ann James stood just inside.

Her face was healing, but was a long way from the unsophisticated prettiness that had appealed to so many young soldiers in Fayetteville. She held a brown paper sack in her arms.

"How did you know he was here?" Moon James asked his sister.

Dee Ann pointed to the counter, where the pimple-faced teenager was watching them. Undoubtedly this was the most entertainment Smoke Hole had seen in a long time.

"Ricky called me," Dee Ann said. "So I thought I'd come down and see if you was going to beat the hell out of this guy."

"You want me to?" her brother asked.

Isen, sucker punched in Washington, edged to his right, calculating the angle he'd need to bring his foot up to Moon's crotch.

"Nah. Looks like somebody already did."

Dee Ann moved to an empty table, where she placed the bag and removed two six-packs of beer.

"I guess we might as well sit and talk to the man," she said. "He did come all the way up here to see me."

Isen joined Moon and his sister at the table, where they each opened a beer. Moon's wife—she wore a wedding ring, he didn't—walked over, kissed Moon on the cheek, took the keys to his truck and left without saying a word.

When the woman left, Moon looked at the kid behind the counter. "Why don't you find something to do in the back," he said.

Ricky disappeared.

"So what the fuck do you want?" Moon said to Isen.

Isen, almost used to being addressed that way, was about to answer when Dee Ann interrupted.

"You got no call to talk to the man like that, Moon," she said. "He ain't the one who beat me up."

"He's a soldier, ain't he?" Moon said.

Dee Ann reached out and touched her brother on the arm.

"Don't mind him," she said to Isen. "Moon's just angry at anybody who's seen me with my clothes off."

"Oh, now don't start that, Dee Ann," Moon said, embarrassed.

Dee Ann kept her hand on her brother's arm as she spoke; she had a calming effect on him.

"So, Mr. Major Isen, what was so important that you had to come all the way to this godforsaken place to ask me?"

Isen looked at the young woman across from him. Her eyes were ringed with purple half-circles. Her lip had healed most of the way, but there was still a long dark blotch along her jaw; it was shaped like Cuba.

He realized, as he watched her, that he'd put all of his hopes in this woman. He had a couple of flimsy backup plans, but he wasn't convinced they'd save his ass. If she told him nothing new, he'd race back to Bragg to stand in front of Tremmore and Veir with his laughable little notecards of circumstantial evidence. His career—the only life he'd known since boyhood—could very well be at an end by this time tomorrow.

Maybe I just won't go back, he thought for a moment to amuse himself. *I'll just disappear. Better yet, I'll stay here at fucking Possum Holler Pizza.*

"Thanks for coming," Isen said.

Dee Ann nodded.

He took a breath, knowing he was about to shock her.

"Dee Ann, I'm sorry I have to tell you this. Cindy Racze is dead."

Dee Ann flinched, a quick spasm that shuddered through her neck and shoulders and pulled her scarred lip up in one corner, as if Isen had reached out to strike her.

"I'm sorry," he said again.

"Did she get killed because she talked to you?" Moon asked.

It had not occurred to Isen that James—more importantly, his sister—might think that.

"No," Isen said quickly. "Not at all. In fact, she was probably dead before I even came to Fort Bragg."

"That just means it was one of those other fuckhead GIs," Moon said. His lips were pulled back over his teeth; the dragon tattoo on his arm seemed to writhe as he opened and closed his fist.

Dee Ann had her eyes closed. Isen, figuring that Moon might throw him out at any moment, pressed on.

"She was killed about the same time that Michael Hauck killed himself," Isen said.

Moon had taken his sister's hand.

"I think we've heard enough," Moon said to Isen.

"We know that Veir—that was the guy who used to follow Cindy around, remember?—we know that Veir called your trailer that same night. Dee Ann? Can you help me here?"

Moon kicked Isen under the table, catching him just under the kneecap with the pointed toe of his boot. It wasn't meant to be a reminder; it was meant to hurt. The only thing keeping the brother from lunging at Isen was his sister's hand, which he held tightly.

"I said that's *enough*," Moon said.

Dee Ann was crying now, shiny tears lining through the dark bruises under her eyes, making them darker still.

"Dee Ann," Isen said, "tomorrow may be my last chance to bring anything to light. I want to find out what happened to Cindy—"

Moon held his sister's hand with his right; with his left he swung at Isen across the table. Isen pushed back in his chair, but one of the legs must have caught on the tile, because he tumbled over backward, smacking the back of his head on the floor.

He saw Moon coming around the table, whatever concern he had for comforting his sister apparently dissipated in the looming clash. Isen knew that all of Moon's anger over what had happened to his sister was about to be released in a major ass-whipping.

Isen rolled to his left and sprang to his feet. Moon walked right into the short jab, a closed fist that Isen pulled after just tapping the man's Adam's apple.

Moon fell as if he'd been dropped from a great height.

"Will you *stop* it," Dee Ann screamed. *"Just stop it!"*

Isen leaned over the big man, who was gasping for breath. He'd turned an interesting shade of blue, but Isen heard air rattling through, so he figured he hadn't killed the guy.

"Sorry," he said, reaching down and patting Moon on the arm.

"I'm sick of all this macho bullshit," Dee Ann said. She was still crying, but her voice had no trace of waver, nothing of uncertainty. She knelt at her brother's side.

"That's at the bottom of all this anyway, you boys and your silly games."

Isen and Dee Ann helped Moon into his chair, where he continued to gag.

"I'm sorry," Isen said again.

"Oh, stop saying that," Dee Ann insisted. "You'd be a lot more sorry if he'd hit you first."

"Dee Ann," Isen said, sitting again, "tomorrow morning I have to go see General Tremmore, the commander of the Eighty-second Airborne Division. He's going to give me a chance to tell everything I know about Harlan Veir. Can you connect Veir with Cindy that night? Did he talk to her on the phone while she was at your trailer?"

Dee Ann pushed her short hair straight back from her forehead. Slumping into a chair, her chin nearly resting on the table top, she looked up at Isen warily.

"I don't know if they talked that night or not," she said. "I wasn't home."

"Well, he talked to somebody at your number," Isen said. "And if you weren't there, it was probably Cindy, right?"

"Cindy weren't the only one who stayed there."

Isen closed his eyes. Tremmore would eat him alive.

"But they're connected, all right."

Isen opened his eyes.

"What?"

"They're connected," she said again. "Or they was connected. That night, I mean."

Dee Ann patted her brother's shoulder as she told Isen the story.

"Here it is," Coates said.

Sue Lynn Darlington stood behind Coates's chair, watching as the soldier searched her computer files. Although it was nearly twenty-one hundred, the two women were not alone in the Division Headquarters two nights before the President's visit. Through the open door of the office suite, they could hear the comings and goings of those whose day hadn't yet ended and those whose Thursday had already begun.

Coates scrolled the data up the screen. Only the desk light

was on; Sue Lynn could see their faces reflected dully on the glass.

"Bennett, Milan ... and here's Savin's name," Coates said, reading. "But here's the best part."

She tapped a fingernail on the corner of the screen that showed the file name under which her boss had stored this information.

It said "veir-1."

"See, I told you I could find this stuff," Coates said, proud of her detective work. Darlington touched her on the shoulder.

"Good job. Thanks."

Sue Lynn didn't say that the detective work had been so easy as to be suspicious.

"When did you notice this?" Darlington asked.

"There was something on here last week when I called you. But I saw this file for the first time this afternoon," Coates said.

"Is it possible that the file was added today?"

"I guess so," Coates said. "But why would that be? If anything, I would think he'd take stuff off the computer today."

"Unless he *wanted* us to see it."

The overhead fluorescent lights came on. "What's going on?"

The two women turned around to see Colonel Richard Kent standing quietly in the doorway. He had his helmet tucked under one arm; he leaned against the doorjamb. Sue Lynn had the feeling that he'd been there listening for a while.

Coates jumped to attention.

"Sir, I'm Major Darlington."

"I know who you are," Kent said. There was nothing threatening in his tone; it was a flat statement of fact. He wore the same smug look that Sue Lynn hated on Harlan Veir. Isen had kept putting off this confrontation with Kent; Sue Lynn was tired of being circumspect.

"Private Coates is showing me the Veir file," Sue Lynn said. She felt Coates wilt beside her, as if Darlington had just volunteered the two of them for a suicide mission.

Kent smiled.

He did want us to find this, Darlington thought.

"That's pretty bold, Major," Kent said. Turning to Coates, he said, "You're dismissed."

Coates grabbed her beret, mumbled a perfunctory "Airborne" and walked quickly out of the room.

"I understand Major Isen is to meet with General Tremmore again tomorrow," Kent said. "Do or die, from what I gather."

"Yes, sir. You could say that."

Kent had been locked out; Tremmore had barely discussed with him what was going on with Veir. Kent didn't think he was being paranoid in assuming that, come morning, his name would come up in the big office down the hall. Darlington wasn't a cop, but she didn't need to be. Kent's career might not survive a revelation that he'd sent people around the world at Veir's behest.

Kent walked past Darlington and into his own office, dropping his helmet and pistol belt on his desk. There was a fearful rush of blood in his ears.

"What about these files?" he asked, forcing his smile. He didn't want to believe his career could come down to this. And even as he tried to spin-doctor what he'd done, he didn't have much hope.

"Well, sir, it looks like Colonel Veir got some help from you in getting rid of the people he found troublesome."

"Not exactly, Major," Kent said gently. "It's important that you get this right. Harlan Veir *did* get some help from me with some transfers. He didn't tell me why he wanted these people to go away for a while. Naturally, since Colonel Veir is carrying such a heavy burden for the division—with Friday's briefing, that is—I wanted to help him."

Kent lifted himself onto the top of the desk, then clasped his hands on one bent knee, trying hard to look casual.

"Naturally it occurred to me that this was very odd, so I made sure that these clues were available to Major Isen." Kent smiled. "And to you, too, of course," he added condescendingly.

"Are you saying you left an obvious trail to steer us here?"

Kent smiled again as if at a bright pupil.

"Naturally," he said. "You see, my job was to protect the

division; Major Isen's job was to find out what was going on with Colonel Veir. This was the only way we could both do those things."

"Well, sir," Sue Lynn said, trying to achieve the same smug look, "it sounds to me like you were afraid to ask Harlan Veir what the hell was going on. Now, I don't know if that's because he's such a big shot or because he has something on you."

Sue Lynn thought she saw one corner of Kent's smile twitch and falter. He nailed it back in place quickly.

"It sounds to me like you were covering all your bets," she continued. "If Veir came out OK, then you hadn't done anything to piss him off. If Isen turned out to be right, you claim you were helping us. Why didn't you just turn Veir in?"

"For what?" Kent asked. The plastic smile was still there, but there was a ragged edge to his voice now. He took a long breath, as if to gain control over his voice. He had let go of his knee; his shoulders dropped.

He's got to hear how stupid he sounds, Sue Lynn thought.

"See, I understood that there might have been certain improprieties before and after this . . . er . . . suicide," Kent said rapidly.

Not like this, he thought. *It can't end like this.*

Kent's sense of the absurd noted the irony: the great warrior was being done in by two women.

"Yes, sir, I'd say there were improprieties," Darlington said. "But instead of asking . . . no, instead of demanding to know what the hell was going on, what Veir was up to, you took the chickenshit way out. You looked the other way and left this little file here to try to cover your ass."

She pulled her beret from the cargo pocket of her trousers, unfolded it and shaped it with her fingers.

"It might work, Colonel," she said. "Personally, I hope it doesn't."

"Get the hell out of here," Kent said. It came out flat, defeated; he couldn't muster the anger. In ceding something to Harlan Veir he'd given up his right to be indignant, and a lot more.

16

W HEN THE DINING HALL OPENED AT SIX, LEONARD FOOTE made his way past the two dozen or so soldiers already lined up at the headcount table.

In the field, officers and NCOs ate last, which sometimes translated, when there was not enough food for everyone, to not at all. In garrison, it was their privilege to go to the head of the chow line when they had pressing business. Foote had a busy day ahead of him.

"Good morning, sir," several of the men said.

"Morning," Foote repeated to each, like a chant.

The soldiers who saw him guessed that he was preoccupied with the day's activities. They would be right in a sense; however, he was not, at the moment, thinking about the dress rehearsal scheduled for that afternoon.

Foote pushed his tray along the steel rails while the cooks shoveled a big pile of scrambled eggs onto his plate. Four pieces of bacon, three sausage links, and two biscuits with a generous river of red-eye gravy poured over the whole thing. Foote picked up two glasses of whole milk, one of orange juice, an apple and an orange, a fresh-baked Danish, then stood by while the ancient toast machine dragged three pieces of white bread over the heating element for him. It was going to be a long day, and he was determined to be fortified.

Foote put the tray down at an empty table, then walked back to the serving counter for a cup of coffee. When he returned to his seat, Brian Bennett was standing next to the table, holding his own heavy-laden tray and shifting his weight from one foot to the other as if keeping time to music only he could hear.

"Mind if I join you, sir?" Bennett asked.

Foote didn't answer; Bennett sat down anyway.

"Big day today, right, sir?" Bennett said. He held his fork like a screwdriver and worked it like a shovel, pulling big mounds of mixed eggs and gravy toward his face. Foote looked at him, wondering if he chewed his food.

"You could say that," Foote said.

Bennett was nodding, watching Foote, waiting for the older man to say more. He kept lifting his chin up and down, up and down, and Foote thought of the little dog statues that bobbed up and down in the back windows of cars.

"What?" Foote asked to put an end to the nodding.

Foote put his fork down, placed his hands flat on either side of his tray. Bennett dragged a napkin roughly across his face, laughed nervously as his eyes shifted from Foote's to the plate and back again.

"Uh ... I talked to Colonel Veir about all those questions Major Isen asked me the other day," Bennett said. He didn't mention Veir's explosive response.

"Yes?"

"Colonel Veir told me that this would all be over before the President's visit."

The lieutenant paused again, shifting in his chair as if in pain.

"That's tomorrow," Bennett said. "I mean ... I was just wondering what was going to happen, you know, if something was going to happen today, maybe."

You're wondering if Veir's going to let you get screwed, Foote thought.

"What do you want to tell me?" Foote asked.

Bennett blinked rapidly, then laughed, a little snort through his nose.

"Do you think I was being disloyal when I talked to you the other day, when I answered questions for you and Major Isen?"

"Disloyal to whom?" Foote asked.

"To ... uh ... to Colonel Veir, I guess." He ran his fingers over his cropped hair. "Yeah, to Colonel Veir."

"Why do you ask?"

Bennett tilted his juice glass toward himself and looked inside, as if there might be an answer there.

"Colonel Veir didn't like Hauck," Bennett said. "I'm not sure why. I mean, I don't think Hauck was a faggot, even if his roommate was, you know?"

Foote looked around. The room was crowded now, the soldiers boisterous. They were all tired, but excited at the prospect of the notoriety that tomorrow would bring their unit, by the spotlight about to shine on all their hard work. In spite of the noise, Foote thought he could hear his own heart beating slowly, imagined he could hear the sandpaper movement of his tongue in a dry mouth.

"Colonel Veir didn't like Hauck," Foote repeated. They had crossed the line now. He was subverting his commander.

"Right," Bennett said, eager for understanding. "And I gave him a lot of shit, you know. Gave Hauck a lot of shit. But I didn't think ... I mean ... oh, god*damn* it."

"If you want to come clean, Brian, now's the time to do it," Foote said. "Colonel Veir isn't going to help you. You know that. He sent you away, right?"

Bennett nodded.

"And he coached you on what to say to the investigators, right?"

Another nod.

"He's only going to protect himself, Brian. And if that means you get bowled over in the process ..."

Foote turned his hands out, palms up, in a gesture that meant "the answer is obvious."

Bennett had a white-knuckle hold on the edge of the table.

"Did you see the pistol, Brian?" Foote asked.

Bennett looked up quickly, drew a breath through his open mouth.

"What have we here? A meeting of the minds?"

Harlan Veir put his tray on the table and fell into an empty chair beside Bennett.

"How are you men this morning?"

"Great, sir," Bennett said a little too enthusiastically. He chanced one more look at Foote and tried to smile as if nothing had happened.

Bennett was not the actor his mentor, sitting beside him, was.

"You have your plan for the day, Lieutenant Bennett?' Veir asked.

"Yes, sir. We're all set."

"Good, good," Veir said. "Since you're almost finished, would you mind excusing us?"

Bennett pushed his chair back and stood quickly, grabbing his tray as if just freed from a particularly onerous task. He didn't look at Foote when he said, "Airborne, sir."

Foote sipped from his coffee cup and watched his commander. Veir was wearing what looked like a brand-new uniform, and his scalp shone where some barber had buzzed over it with electric shears in the last twenty-four hours. But there were lines around Veir's eyes that Foote didn't remember seeing before, and a half-inch-wide swath of beard just below his jaw that he'd missed with the razor.

"Sleep well, sir?" Foote asked.

"Like a baby," Veir said, his mouth full of eggs. "How about you?"

"Off and on," Foote answered honestly. Apparently Veir was going to pretend that nothing had changed between the two of them. For his part, Foote didn't plan on telling Veir that he'd been awakened at twelve-thirty in the morning by a call from Isen.

"I didn't go by headquarters yet this morning," Veir said. "Did they get all that shit cleaned out of there? All those briefing charts and maps and things?"

"I'll check right after I leave here, sir," Foote said.

"You see the paper this morning?" Veir asked. He downed an entire glass of orange juice. "Big write-up about the President's visit, fucking three pages' worth, and they didn't even mention us."

By which you mean you didn't see your name, Foote thought.

"We'll get plenty of attention come tomorrow, sir," Foote said. "More than we need."

"That's where you're wrong, Leonard. You can't get too much attention these days," Veir said. "You know, when you came in the Army, about five to ten percent of infantry officers got to be battalion commanders, got to sit where I'm sitting. Now it's somewhere around two to three percent, and the number drops every year. It's not enough to do a good job anymore. You have to do a good job for the right people."

Foote nodded slightly. This was the leverage he'd given Veir all along.

Here comes the report card threat, he thought.

"You want to be a battalion commander, don't you?" Veir asked.

"Yes, sir," Foote answered. "But I have to admit I'm not as sure about it as I was a few years ago."

Veir looked up as if Foote had just announced a mutiny.

"That's no way to talk, Lenny," Veir said. He raised his fork, runny with eggs, and waved it at Foote.

"You've got to keep the edge. You've got to *want* it," Veir said, eyes narrowed, tone sharpened. "What the fuck is there besides command? Huh?"

Foote didn't answer. Veir stabbed at a piece of sausage with his fork, sending several shiny links flying on to the front of his blouse.

"Fuck," Veir barked, pushing his chair back. There was a small rectangle of grease right in the center of his chest. That was all it took, Foote noted, to push him over the edge.

"Will you fucking look at that?" he raged. He grabbed at the napkin dispenser, upsetting salt and pepper shakers and pulling a wad of paper out. He stuck a handful into his water glass and dabbed at the spot.

"I can't fucking believe this," he said. "This is just what I need."

Looking up, Veir spotted a soldier from headquarters.

"McCarthy!" he shouted.

Men around the room were watching him now; they glanced away when he looked in their direction.

"McCarthy, find my driver and tell him I need him to go to my apartment and get me another uniform."

McCarthy, who'd been just about to enter the chow line, turned and handed his tray to the man behind him.

"Airborne, sir," he said, turning on his heel.

"Make it fast," Veir boomed at McCarthy's rapidly disappearing back. "And tell him to come here and get the keys."

Veir looked around, realizing that the noise had died down and that many of his men were watching him.

"Let's get moving, men," he shouted to the whole room. "We're burning daylight, here."

Subdued, the soldiers hurried again.

Veir turned back to Foote.

"Where the fuck was I?" he said.

Disintegrating, Foote thought.

"I've got this meeting with General Tremmore this morning," Veir said. He chewed vigorously, talked with his mouth full, nodded to soldiers passing by the table—working hard to look nonchalant.

"It's time to put an end to all this bullshit."

"I read in the paper where they found that girl's body," Foote said. "The one Isen and McCall were looking for. She's been dead for a while, too, I hear."

"That's what I understand," Veir said. He slouched down in his chair and held a glass of orange juice to his lips. He smiled mirthlessly. "Sounds like she died about the same time that Hauck killed himself," he continued. "You knew that they were seeing each other. This chick and Hauck, that is."

Foote knew it because Isen had told him about it. Isen had also told him all about Veir's obsession with the woman. And at almost one in the morning Isen had advanced an even more outlandish theory, based on what he'd learned in West Virginia.

Foote held Veir's gaze.

"Kind of odd timing, don't you think?" Foote said.

"I heard a rumor," Veir said, leaning forward, lowering his voice, "that Hauck was pissed when she dumped him."

He leaned back again.

"You gotta wonder, now that she turned up dead and he checked himself out . . . just how pissed was he?"

Foote studied Veir, but the colonel had thrown up his inscrutable smile like a parapet.

This is what Isen had predicted: Veir would call it a murder-suicide.

Foote was stunned, not so much because Isen was right, but because in spite of all that had led to this point, he didn't want it to be true.

"I appreciate your loyalty through all of this, Lenny," Veir said. He'd discovered the patch of unshaven whiskers alongside his jaw and was scratching them with his fingertips.

"And just between you and me and the wall, I think I'll be in a position to reward that kind of loyalty."

Veir seemed satisfied that Foote had no answer.

"Remember, it's not enough to get noticed. You have to get noticed by the right people," Veir said. "And you and I are about to be noticed by the Commander in Chief and everyone between him and us. This is going to be the greatest week of your career, Lenny."

"Yes, sir," Foote said, toying with his coffee cup.

Loyalty had been bred into Foote from the first time he'd pulled on a pair of combat boots, and it was hard to abandon. He looked around the room at the soldiers who offered their trust every single day to the leaders who deserved it. He could stick around the Army and make a difference for those guys. Or he could play dangerous games he was bound to lose.

"I think I'll shove off now, Colonel. I've got a ton of stuff to check before the rehearsal this afternoon."

"Excellent," Veir said, smiling. "Great. I'll let you know if anything interesting happens up in the CG's office."

Foote picked up his tray and walked from the table.

Whatever happens is bound to be interesting, he thought.

Mark Isen woke when he felt the pickup decelerate. He opened his eyes to see the windshield wipers on the passenger side making little headway in keeping the rain off the glass. He could barely see outside and couldn't read a large lighted sign that was no more than a few hundred meters away.

"Where are we?" he asked.

"Just south of Richmond," Dee Ann said.

"The storm looks worse." Isen rubbed his neck and checked his watch. He'd been asleep for several hours after his shift on Interstate 81, which paralleled the slant of the Virginia–West Virginia state line.

"It is worse. And best I can tell from the radio, it's going to be like this all the way down."

It had been Dee Ann's idea to drive Moon's truck to Fort Bragg when a low pressure system parked over the Atlantic seaboard and plunged the eastern third of the country into a monsoon, canceling many flights. Her brother had been against it, although in general his objections had been less strident after Isen had punched his Adam's apple to the back of his throat.

"There's a girl dead down there, Moon," Dee Ann had told her sibling. "This ain't no little thing anymore. Somebody's got to stop that guy 'fore he kills someone else."

Dee Ann headed into the truck stop for another cup of coffee; Isen pulled the road atlas out to calculate—again— how long it would take them to make Fort Bragg. He counted on arriving an hour or two before his meeting with Tremmore.

As he thought about what was ahead, Isen felt a familiar sort of unease in his stomach, and as he watched a big tractor-trailer rig pull up to the nearby fuel pumps, he recognized it as the same feeling he'd had going into combat for the first time. He'd dreaded what was about to happen, but knew he had to go through the fire to come out on the other side. One way or another, this time at his own personal Purgatory of Fort Bragg would soon be at an end.

Dee Ann raced through the sheets of rain and got back into the cab. She wore a short white shirt that did not reach the top of her jeans. Thanks to the rain, Isen—and no doubt all the truckers inside who weren't too bleary-eyed to notice—knew that Dee Ann wasn't wearing a bra.

"He gave me the coffee for free," she said when she caught Isen looking at her breasts. "Imagine that."

Isen smiled and shook his head.

"Looks like we'll make it in plenty of time, unless this storm knocks out part of the highway or something," he said.

"Quit worrying," Dee Ann told him. "You want to worry about something, worry about what you're going to say to that general."

"I've thought about that," Isen said as she eased the truck back onto the access road. "Have you thought about it?"

"Hell," she said. "Little ol' general don't scare me."

"Wish I could say the same," Isen admitted.

"You afraid of the general or afraid of what the general might do to you?"

"What he might do to me," Isen said. "There's a chance that my career could be over by lunchtime."

"So why are you doing this?" she asked. "I mean, the kid who killed himself wasn't even your kin, right?"

"Right," Isen said.

He watched the horizon out the passenger side window, where a feeble dawn was struggling to break through the thick clouds and sheets of water.

"Except that he was a soldier," Isen said. "Corny as it sounds, I do feel a connection. And I'm not sure he got a fair shake in the investigation."

"So you want to straighten it out," Dee Ann said.

"Yeah, I guess that's it. I don't like people messing around with my Army."

"You feel like you're doing the right thing?" she asked.

"Yeah," Isen said.

Outside, the water snaked and danced across the road's surface in curling waves that came and went quickly as the truck sped by.

"Yeah. I think I'm doing the right thing. I think I'm doing the only thing I can do."

"Well, then," Dee Ann said, "whatever happens, it'll be OK. 'Cause you did what you had to do, right?"

"Airborne," Isen said.

They both laughed.

The storm that was hammering Virginia dragged its southern edge across the Carolinas, so that by nine o'clock on Thursday morning the rain was steady, hard and increasing in intensity.

Leonard Foote sat in his office with three of his staff and two of the rifle company commanders, a shortened version of the President's itinerary in front of him. There was an inclement weather plan, of course, but nothing that anticipated the drenching that was going on now. Foote was trying to keep his staff from panicking as he game-planned another version of the demonstration they'd worked so hard to perfect, some idea that wouldn't include having the President standing outside wearing a life preserver.

"There won't be any jump, of course," his operations officer was saying. "Which leads me to believe they'll cancel the whole visit."

"You mean he just won't come?" one of the company commanders asked, real pain in his voice.

"Why should he? The only thing we do around here that's really special is fall out of airplanes. If we can't do that, what's the point in having the show?"

"Our guys are going to be pretty pissed off," another junior captain interrupted. "They've worked really hard at this."

"So have my guys," the other commander said.

"I wasn't implying that your guys didn't...."

"They won't be as pissed as the rest of the Army will be if the Marines get the nod because of a fucking rainstorm."

"We won't melt in the rain. I don't see why we just can't do the whole thing as planned. We'd do it in combat."

Foote was staring out the window, trying to ignore the bickering. Visibility was falling, but he could still make out the parking lot across the street. He thought he saw someone run from a dark pickup. Bennett.

Foote stood abruptly and walked toward the door.

"Don't worry about the President canceling," he said. "We have to be ready no matter what, so just assume we're going."

He pointed at his operations officer. "Modify the inclement weather plan we already have. Keep in mind the Commander in Chief hasn't spent a lot of time standing around in the rain with soldiers. Keep him dry."

The officers were making notes.

"And stop your whining."

Foote hurried to the front of the headquarters building and opened the door. Rain was spilling off the roof as if poured from a huge bucket, the sidewalk and grass were awash in an inch of water; the world outside was colorless, washed-out shades of gray. Out on Ardennes Road, traffic had slowed to a crawl, and plenty of vehicles had simply pulled to the side of the road to wait out the deluge.

"Major Foote."

Foote turned to see the orderly holding up a telephone receiver.

"It's Colonel Veir, sir. He's out at the demo site and he wants to talk to you."

Foote looked at the kid, then back out into the storm where a lone figure moved toward the company area.

He glanced back at the private, shrugged.

"He just missed me," Foote said before he turned and dashed out into the storm.

He was soaked before he'd gone five meters. He hadn't put on his beret or his rain jacket, and the water, surprisingly cold, ran down the neck of his blouse. His trousers stuck to his thighs as he jogged after the figure moving away from him.

"Lieutenant Bennett," he called.

The figure hesitated, then headed away again. Foote ran faster.

"Lieutenant Bennett," he called again. He closed a few more steps, then the dark rain gear started to jog off.

"You there, HALT," he yelled in his best parade ground voice.

The figure halted.

Foote approached from behind. The hard rain pressed the hood down into a cone; the man looked like a monk. Foote walked around front, blinked against the rain that was driving directly into his face, stinging his eyes shut. It was Bennett.

Foote shouted to be heard above the storm. "Why were you running from me?"

Bennett had the drawstring of his hood pulled tight around his face, pinching his cheeks in. His eyes were all but closed.

"Do you hear me?" Foote demanded. He could feel the water streaming off his chin now, running in ten rivers off the ends of his fingers.

"Why were you running from me?"

When Bennett didn't respond, Foote reached out and grabbed him by the shoulder, turning him to the back wall of the headquarters building, where there were no windows. Foote could hear better in the lee of the building, but he had to contend with the water pouring off the roof like sheet metal unrolling.

"Bennett!" he yelled.

"What?" Bennett finally responded. "Why don't you leave me alone? Why won't you all just leave me alone?"

His eyes were closed tightly, his mouth a dark circle as he screamed against the rain and rising wind.

"I didn't do anything I wasn't supposed to do."

He leaned over, bending at the waist and putting his hands on his knees like a tired runner. Without standing, he said, "Colonel Veir said he'd get me kicked out of the Army if I turned on him."

"It doesn't matter what he threatened, Brian," Foote said. "It's time to come clean."

Bennett didn't respond, didn't move. Foote ran his hands over his face; his uniform felt ten pounds heavier with water.

"What happened out in the parking lot with Hauck?" he shouted at Bennett.

The lieutenant stood upright. He might have been crying; it was hard to tell in the rain.

"I didn't think he'd go that far," Bennett said.

Even amid the sounds of the storm, Foote knew that the bravado was gone from this voice.

"Honest," he pleaded. "I didn't."

"OK," Foote said, touching the lieutenant. "What happened?"

"We fucking tortured that guy," Bennett said, talking rapidly now. "We ragged on him for weeks about his dick-smoker roommate and about how he was probably a faggot, too and how it would make all the papers and shit. This big military family and his fucking big shot uncle the general, how it was all going to come apart. We were going to fuck him over: him, his roommate and his uncle."

"Who's 'we' Brian?" Foote asked. "Other lieutenants?"

"No," Bennett said. "No other lieutenants. Just me and Colonel Veir."

Foote tried to imagine this little vendetta, this limited war directed against Michael Hauck.

"That's why he killed himself?" Foote asked.

Bennett wiped his nose with the heel of his hand; his face was awash in rain. He shook his head.

"There was something else between Hauck and Colonel Veir," Bennett said.

"What?"

"That Cindy chick," Bennett said. "Out in the parking lot, Hauck said he had all kinds of dirt on Veir. About how he beat up women and shit like that. I thought he was just drunk, you know? Making it up. But he was talking about Cindy."

Bennett shook his head, throwing raindrops off the end of his nose. He grimaced in pain.

"I saw it," he yelled into the tempest. "I saw the pistol. Hauck took it out of the glove compartment."

"What did you do?"

"I went inside and told Colonel Veir that Hauck had a handgun. I asked if I should take it away from him. Veir said not to worry about it. He said Hauck was a pussy and he wouldn't do anything."

Bennett's face was upturned; the rain seemed to be melting it into a long mask of grief.

"What did you do then?" Foote yelled.

"We laughed," he screamed. "We fucking laughed."

They'd lost an hour and a half stuck in traffic just east of Lake Gaston, right over the state line from Virginia. Isen had even driven on the shoulder, passing a half mile of cars, most of them with their engines off, before coming up behind a North Carolina State Trooper. Isen thought about calling Sue Lynn, asking her to go to Tremmore's office to explain that Isen was on the way, but there were no phones, no rest stops nearby.

When Isen pulled the old truck off of I-95, it was eleven o'clock—he was supposed to be in Tremmore's office—and they were still some dozen miles from the post. He pushed the truck over the little county roads, approaching Fayetteville from the south. They hit four red lights in succession, and at each one Isen looked at his watch and swore.

"Let me see that a minute," Dee Ann said, taking her hand off the dash for the first time in a good while.

She took Isen's hand, pulled his arm toward her and unbuckled his watch. Then she rolled down the window and threw the watch out into the storm.

"Look at the road," she said. "That's the only way we're gonna get there in one piece. Got to be somebody left alive to tell the general the story."

At eleven hundred hours Lieutenant Colonel Harlan Veir knocked on the door of the Commanding General's office.

"Come in," Tremmore said.

Veir treated the aide to one of his supreme confidence smiles before he walked in.

Tremmore looked up over the top of half-glasses he used for reading. Veir had seen the old man wear the glasses before, and he had always thought, on those occasions, that if his eyes started to fail, he'd get contacts. The little glasses looked more professor than warrior.

Veir centered himself before the general's desk and rendered a sharp salute. "Airborne, sir."

"All the way," Tremmore answered, returning the salute and removing the glasses. "Where's Isen?"

"I don't know, sir," Veir said, trying not to smile too broadly and leaving off the obvious *I guess he's late.*

Tremmore looked puzzled, as if he couldn't fathom that someone might miss his summons.

"OK," Tremmore said. "You look a little tired, there, Colonel Veir."

Veir reached up and touched his face, as if he might wipe the exhaustion off.

"We've all been working very hard, sir. Nothing I can't handle."

"Sit down and tell me what problems concern you about the visit tomorrow."

Veir took his seat, telling himself to be confident.

Didn't he just ask you about tomorrow? He isn't going to do anything to jeopardize the President's visit. You've got nothing to worry about.

But in spite of this testimony, Veir felt his stomach lurch a bit. He tasted the sausage again.

"We've got everything under control, sir," Veir said. "We've planned and practiced and all that. Today I plan on talking to the men about 'expecting the unexpected.' You know, all the things that crop up—Murphy's law—that can kill you. I plan on giving them the Commander's Intent, just like this was a field operation. That way, no matter what goes wrong, every last swinging dick knows what we want the end result to be."

"And what is that, in your words?" Tremmore asked.

Veir leaned forward in his seat, elbows on knees.

"We're going to impress the hell out of the Commander in Chief. He's going to leave here thinking that we need two or three more divisions like this one."

Tremmore, who did not put a lot of stock in bravado but wanted the facts, nodded tiredly.

"We're going to show these people some things, sir," Veir continued. "I swear, if this stuff doesn't make your dick hard, you're queer."

Tremmore looked unimpressed; Veir scratched his jaw. He'd shaved again after breakfast, but by then he'd already rubbed the spot raw.

"Captain Grace," Tremmore said testily. The aide appeared in an instant.

"Yes, sir?"

"See if you can find Major Isen. Tell him I'm not in the habit of waiting around for majors."

"Airborne, sir," Captain Grace said before scuttling off.

"I was going to let Isen do the talking in here," Tremmore went on. "Give you a chance to hear what he has to say so you could answer him. Looks like he found something more important to do."

"I'm not surprised," Veir said. "Major Isen hasn't been very responsible. He's harassed members of my command, spreading gossip and rumors. He's even bothered my ex-wife."

"Why would he do all these things?"

Veir smiled as if they were talking about a child they both understood but couldn't help.

"I think he's jealous," Veir said. "He tells everyone how he hates his job at the Pentagon; maybe he wants to get noticed here."

Tremmore nodded.

If you're gonna lie, Veir thought, *lie big.*

"Why don't you tell me about Michael Hauck," the commanding general said.

Veir swallowed, scratched at his jaw again.

"Michael Hauck was basically a good officer," Veir said. "Although obviously plagued by personal problems."

Comforted by the familiar sound of his own voice, Veir continued more smoothly.

"I believe he felt a great deal of pressure to perform up to his family's expectations. He was somewhat sensitive— maybe overly sensitive—and I think that these things, in concert with some personal problems most people his age would have been able to handle ... well, I think it was all too much for him."

Tremmore put his half-glasses back on and opened a folder on his desk.

"This Special Agent McCall seemed to think ... you know who she is, right?"

Veir nodded, his breathing shallow. Tremmore apparently had McCall's report right in front of him; Veir had no idea what it said.

"Anyway, Special Agent McCall seemed to think that someone might have accused Hauck of being a homosexual, or that someone threatened to accuse him."

Tremmore turned a few pages before he looked up at Veir.

"Do you know anything about that?"

Veir brought his hand up to his jaw and scratched himself viciously.

There were little half-moons of light reflected in the general's glasses.

What do you know? Veir thought.

"Hauck had a girlfriend, sir," Veir offered, hoping Tremmore would go for the red herring.

"Is that right?"

"Yes, sir. He was dating a woman ... well, I wouldn't want this to get back to the family, and I don't like to speak ill of the dead, but he was dating a stripper. That girl who turned up dead just the other day."

"Yes," Tremmore said. "I saw in the paper that she'd been dead for some time."

Veir leaned forward, lowering his voice. "She died around the same time Hauck did, sir."

"What are you saying?"

Veir straightened up in his chair; he was leading confidently now. People always believed him.

"A few days before the suicide, I had a talk with Hauck. I warned him about getting mixed up with the wrong kind of woman. See, there was talk around that this woman was also a prostitute."

Tremmore nodded.

"He just didn't see that this was a business for these women. That happens to a lot of these young guys with their first piece of tail." He smiled at the general, two old hands sharing inside knowledge. Tremmore did not respond.

"Anyway, maybe they had a fight that night," Veir said, wanting Tremmore to make the connection. "Maybe he knew he couldn't keep her, but also couldn't stand the thought of losing her."

Tremmore propped his elbows on the desk and put his fingers to his temples. There were voices in the outer office. Veir looked up; one of the voices undoubtedly belonged to Foote. Veir's first thought was that something was wrong down at the battalion, something wrong with the demonstration. He was about to speak when the aide appeared in the doorway to close the door.

"Are you suggesting that Michael Hauck killed this woman and then took his own life?" Tremmore asked.

"I'd have to say it's a very real possibility, sir, what with the timing and all."

Tremmore closed the folder and pushed it toward the corner of his desk.

"Well, I have to admit that's the most straightforward explanation I've been offered," he said.

Veir held his breath. *Could that be the end of it?*

"Sir, I thought I heard my executive officer in the outer office. I can't help but wonder if something's gone wrong. Since we're so close to rehearsal time, I wonder if I might be dismissed?"

"Of course, Harlan. Thanks for coming by to help straighten this thing out. I'll have someone contact the local authorities about this possibility you've suggested."

"Yes, sir."

Veir bit his lip and put on a concerned look.

"I understand the necessity of that, of course, General. I just hope we don't have to expose Hauck's family to any more pain."

Tremmore came out from behind the desk. "That's considerate of you," Tremmore said. The two men shook hands. "I'll see you at the dress rehearsal."

Veir smiled. As Tremmore walked back to his seat, Veir sized up the office.

Eight, ten years tops, he thought. *I'll have it painted when I move in.*

Mark Isen pulled Moon's pickup onto the sidewalk in front of Division Headquarters at eleven-twenty. The rain had abated somewhat, though it was still hammering down in impressive amounts.

"Let's go, let's go," he said to Dee Ann as she ran from the passenger side.

The first thing he saw when he pulled open the door was a Military Policeman.

"Can I help you, sir?" the MP asked.

"Yeah, I'm twenty minutes late for an appointment with General Tremmore," Isen said. "So you can help me by getting out of my way."

Another voice came from behind the security glass. "And you are?"

"Major Mark Isen. I'm here to see General Tremmore."

Isen hurriedly pulled his military ID from his wallet and tossed it onto the steel counter.

"I'll have to call upstairs, sir," the voice said.

"Look, can't you do that after you let us in? I told you I'm late. I just finished driving from—"

"You both want to go in?" the voice asked.

"Yes, this is Miss Dee Ann James, and she's coming in with me," Isen said.

"And she has an appointment with the Division Commander?" the voice asked. "Dressed like that?"

Isen looked at Dee Ann. The rain had completely soaked her thin cotton shirt. Her nipples stared out at Isen, the MP and whoever was watching her from behind the glass.

"Besides, if she doesn't have an ID card . . ."

"Look, I'm telling you she's with me, OK? I'll vouch for her."

Isen had both fists on the counter now. The MP, backed up by a steel-and-glass door, watched impassively.

"Look, Major Isen," the voice continued. "Security is a little tighter around here this week. I'm sure I can get someone from the CG's office to come down and talk with you in a few minutes—"

"And I'm telling you I don't have a few minutes. I'm late for a meeting with General Tremmore."

Isen peered into the hole in the glass; he could see a mouth.

"I'll call right now, sir," the mouth said. "Although General Tremmore may have left the building."

Looking for his watch, Isen turned up an empty wrist.

"Sorry about the clothes, Mark," Dee Ann said.

Isen turned to look at the MP. Behind the soldier and through the glass door, he could see a bunch of uniforms moving about. One separated from the group.

"Mark!"

It was Sue Lynn.

"What are you doing out there?" she asked. "You're supposed to be upstairs."

"I know, I know."

Sue Lynn pushed the door handle from the other side, bumping into the MP.

"I'm sorry, ma'am, you can't come out this way," the MP said.

"Well, I don't want to come *out* this way, silly," she said. She reached past the MP and grabbed Isen by the upper arm. "I want him to come *in* this way."

Before the MP could react, Isen was in the headquarters and taking the stairs two at a time.

"I need Dee Ann up here, Sue Lynn. Right away."

"Airborne," Sue Lynn said, winking.

Veir left the general's office, pulled the door shut behind him, then looked up to see Leonard Foote dripping into a large puddle in front of the aide's desk.

"Something wrong down at the battalion?" Veir asked his executive officer.

"Yes, sir," Foote answered. "You could say that."

He motioned toward the chair behind the secretary's empty desk. Veir turned to see another wet uniform huddled there; it was Bennett.

"What's going on here?"

"I found out some interesting things about what happened in the parking lot that night," Foote said, trying to sound more confident than he felt.

Veir didn't hesitate. Parry and *thrust*.

"You found out *shit*, Major Foote," he said. "Innuendo and hearsay. And what do you think you're going to do? March into the CG's office and tell him ... what? That you're on Isen's side? *That's* not going to be real impressive, Major. Isen fucked up big-time when he didn't show up here. He's done. If you want to jump on board a sinking ship, be my fucking guest."

"Lieutenant Bennett," Veir snapped.

Bennett jumped up to a rigid attention. "Yes, *sir*."

"I'm not sure what you think went on at that strip club on the night Lieutenant Hauck killed himself. But whatever it is you were thinking about doing ... I'd think *real hard* about it."

Isen came tearing up the steps behind Foote, catching himself just before he ran into the big man.

"Well, look who decided to grace us with his presence," Veir said.

Isen tried to catch his breath. He was unshaven, soaked to the skin and bedraggled after spending the night in a cold pickup truck.

"Uh, Major Isen," the aide asked.

"Yeah," Isen said. "You want to tell the general I'm here."

"A bit late," Veir added smugly as Captain Grace struggled to squeeze by. The little anteroom was crowded now, with Veir in front of the CG's door, squared off against Foote and Isen. Bennett stood at attention in the only floor space left.

"Get in here, Isen," Tremmore called a few seconds later.

Veir smiled as he stepped aside to let Isen pass.

Isen marched inside to a spot two steps in front of the general's desk, executed a sharp left-face and snapped his hand to his brow.

"Sir, Major Isen reports, with apologies for my lateness."

"I don't want your apologies, Isen," Tremmore said. "I want to know who the hell you think you are—"

"Sir, I can explain—"

"You missed your chance to explain," Tremmore said as he glanced at his watch. "By half an hour. But I guess I shouldn't be surprised. This little show you've put on this morning is indicative of the cavalier attitude you've shown in all your actions down here at Bragg."

Isen was still at attention, staring at a spot above the general's head. His only chance was to wait for Tremmore to give him a chance to explain himself.

"You came down here without an official mandate as an investigator; you operated in a haphazard manner, questioning all sorts of people according to your whim while ignoring the advice of experienced investigators and the word of fellow officers. You dug and dug and fabricated stories to satisfy your own fantasies, apparently. All of this with no thought to what you were doing to the reputation of an officer who has an outstanding service record and who, incidentally, is in the middle of what may prove to be an extremely important week for the entire Army. Your actions have been completely irresponsible."

Tremmore paused and Isen wondered if he'd been wrong to trust the general's impartiality.

"Sir," he began.

"Silence," Tremmore said. "I've wasted enough time listening to you. It's time I talked to General Flynn."

Tremmore picked up the phone and punched the intercom.

"Get me General Patrick Flynn at the Pentagon," he said into the speaker. He put the phone down, studied Isen for a moment, checked his watch impatiently.

"OK," he said to Isen. "While we wait, you can talk, but only as long as it takes General Flynn to reach the phone."

Captain Grace, the aide-de-camp, pulled a reference sheet from his top desk drawer. The sheet listed the dates of rank of all general officers in the Army. When two officers wore the same number of stars—as did Flynn and Tremmore—rank was determined by who'd worn those stars longest. And the lower ranking man, general or not, would come on the line first and wait for the senior man.

"Who's he want to talk to?" Veir asked.

"General Patrick Flynn," Grace answered.

Veir leaned against Grace's desk, folded his arms and cocked his head at Foote.

"Sounds like my good buddy Major Isen arrived just in time to rearrange the deck chairs on the *Titanic*. You sure you don't want to join him?"

"Bennett told me he saw the pistol and told you about it," Foote said. He was a little unnerved by the confidence Veir displayed—suppose he'd picked the wrong side?—but he was committed. "You told him not to worry about it."

"That's not the way I remember it," Veir said. "Lieutenant Bennett was drunk, as I recall, so his memory might be a tad hazy. But even if it did happen that way—which I doubt—the most I could be accused of is an error in judgment. Should I have foreseen that Hauck was going to shoot himself?"

Captain Grace was on hold with the Pentagon. He did not want to hear what was going on, nor was he free to abandon his post. He tried to squeeze by Veir, thinking he'd use the phone in an adjoining office, but the colonel and his executive officer were blocking the small passage.

"I ... uh ... gentlemen, would you excuse me, please? Please excuse me."

Veir did not move; he did not appear to hear.

Grace sat on his desk, swung his feet over the top and ducked into the hallway.

Veir moved closer to Foote, dropping his voice to a near whisper.

"It's a real shame that fucking pussy killed himself, but not everybody is cut out for this stuff," Veir said. "Take you, for instance, Lenny. I'm not so sure anymore that you're meant to be a combat commander."

"Getting a little crowded in here, isn't it, men?"

Veir and Foote turned to the door, where Sue Lynn Darlington stood, hands on her hips. Dee Ann stood at her shoulder.

"So nice to see you again, Colonel Veir," Darlington said, smiling. "Of course, you've always had trouble remembering me, but maybe you'll remember Dee Ann here."

Veir's eyes widened. "What the hell is she doing here?" he demanded.

Darlington was happy to see Veir agitated; it meant that they'd struck a nerve. But Dee Ann felt something icy touch her. She wished she'd brought Moon along.

"I believe she and Major Isen have something to tell General Tremmore," Sue Lynn said.

Darlington stepped aside and looked at Dee Ann, who crossed her arms nervously across her chest. Captain Grace appeared behind her, bobbing from one side to the other like a nervous bird.

"I don't think that she can go in there, Major," he said to Darlington. "I mean, she's not really, well, dressed appropriately."

Dee Ann dropped her eyes, ran one hand over her wet hair, then hugged herself tightly.

"Shut up, Captain," Darlington said.

"She's practically naked," Veir insisted.

"You never minded before, Colonel," Darlington said. "Are you suddenly rethinking your habits?"

Dee Ann spoke, so low she almost wasn't heard. "He's the one," she said.

"What?" Darlington asked.

"I recognize his voice," Dee Ann said. She looked up, her eyes lined with silver tears. "From my trailer. He's the one that beat me up."

"Captain Grace," Veir shouted. *"Get this fucking whore out of here."*

The aide gently put a hand on Dee Ann's arm. Foote reached out and touched Grace's hand, just as gently, with a single finger. When he had the captain's attention, he shook his head.

"What the fuck do you think you're doing, Major Foote?" Veir screeched. He was not even pretending to control his voice now.

"You're fucking finished, do you hear me? Finished!"

A voice squawked over the intercom, too indistinct for Darlington to hear above the commotion.

An MP appeared beside Grace. Now there were seven of them crowded in and around the little room.

"Sir," Grace pleaded with Veir. *"Sir!"*

Veir's eyes were wide, his voice high and strained. This was too much; there were too many of them lining up against him.

Veir shouted at the MP. "Get these fucking *bitches* out of here."

When the young police officer hesitated, Veir grabbed the telephone off Grace's desk and slammed it to the floor.

General Tremmore threw open his office door. "I said, 'What the hell is going on out here?' "

Harlan Veir chose that moment to try to push Dee Ann and Darlington out of the office. He stepped in front of Foote, approaching the two women. Dee Ann shrank back, but Sue Lynn stood her ground. As she anticipated, Veir pushed her, hard, his wide hand splayed across the top of her chest.

"Get the fuck out of here," he said through clenched teeth.

He was a big man, and Sue Lynn almost fell, but in a split second she found her balance, rocked forward off her right foot and drove her fist directly into Veir's nose.

She heard the crunch of bone and saw the run of scarlet. She followed her first punch with a left cross, aiming for the jaw, catching his throat. Harlan Veir stumbled in the tiny space and clattered to the top of the aide's neat desk.

"Come to attention," Tremmore snapped.

There was a long second—marked only by the sound of Captain Grace's matched desk set and nameplate falling to the floor—before all the soldiers responded.

Tremmore walked past his unruly subordinates toward Dee Ann, who was shivering and crying softly.

"Did anyone touch you, miss?" he asked kindly.

She shook her head. "No."

"I'm Larry Tremmore," he said. He unbuttoned and removed his blouse, draped it over her shoulders and took her hand gently.

"Dee Ann James," she said. "Thank you."

Harlan Veir sat on Grace's desk, holding his nose with steepled fingers. Blood dripped from his chin to his shirtfront.

Tremmore held Dee Ann's hand as he spoke. "I understand you came all the way here from West Virginia to tell me about the last time you saw your friend, Cindy Racze," he said.

"Yes, sir," Dee Ann said, swallowing. She was terribly uncomfortable with everyone standing around like a bunch of statues, staring off into space. But at least they'd stopped yelling.

"Can you tell me when that was, exactly?" Tremmore asked.

Dee Ann looked around. There was a big black man, soaking wet and stone still. Behind him, she recognized the lunatic Bennett, subdued now. Darlington was within a few inches of the general, standing rigidly, staring past the older man as if no one was around. When she looked at Isen, his eyes clicked to meet hers. He nodded slightly, then turned his gaze straight ahead.

"Yes, sir. Me and another girl was down at Jiggles to collect our paychecks. We was in the manager's office, drinking beer, and so didn't hear the commotion. When we came outside we seen Cindy in a red pickup with that one."

She pointed at Veir, who sat on the desk, blood running unchecked from his nose.

Veir pressed two fingers at his cut lip.

"You lying cunt."

Tremmore did not even look at Veir. "Would you happen to know what time that was, by any chance?" he asked Dee Ann.

"I'm not sure," she answered. "But it shouldn't be hard to find out. You could ask the police. There was cop cars all over the place, and an ambulance, too. They came to get that dead boy. The one that shot himself."

Epilogue

Isen, McCall and Darlington sat in the family room of Sue Lynn's house and watched the network news coverage of the President's visit, which had concluded only hours before.

"I swear he looks bigger on TV," McCall said.

On the screen, Major Leonard Foote was standing beside and towering above the President as the Commander in Chief shook hands along a rank of soldiers in full combat gear. Responsibility for briefing the President and the Secretary of Defense had been turned over to Foote by General Tremmore just before dress rehearsal the previous day. Foote, still dripping water in the CG's office, had saluted, delivered a crisp "Airborne," and marched off to take over the battalion.

"I heard it went off without a hitch," Sue Lynn said.

"Foote is a good man," Isen commented around a mouthful of pretzels.

"Now there's a change of heart," McCall said. "I guess it's a good thing you two didn't shoot each other during your first week here."

Isen laughed. "We could say the same thing about you and me," he added.

"Another beer, Terry?" Darlington asked, standing and moving toward the kitchen.

"No thanks," McCall said. "I didn't get much sleep last night and I've got a big day ahead of me tomorrow."

"You stay up questioning Veir?"

"I talked to Bennett," McCall answered, rubbing her eyes with forefinger and thumb. She dropped her hand and blinked widely.

"Or it might be more accurate to say that I *listened* to Bennett. That boy had a lot of conscience to clear."

"So what did happen in the parking lot?" Isen asked.

"According to Bennett, he and Veir had been harassing Hauck about rooming with Savin. They threatened to out him, embarrass his family. It really got vicious after Hauck started seeing Cindy."

"So Veir just wanted Hauck to leave Cindy alone?"

"That was part of it, but it wasn't that simple. Bennett figures Hauck had some dirt on Veir. Maybe Hauck knew Veir was harassing Cindy. If she was on the same road that Barbara Ann Yonders was on—say Veir beat her like he did Dee Ann—maybe Cindy knew she was in trouble. She might have reached out for help from Hauck."

"Who was too vulnerable to help her," Isen said. "Judging from what I know of Hauck, how he always wanted to help people, he probably did see himself as her savior."

"He might have made it," McCall said. "Hauck never paid much attention to Bennett anyway. My guess is that a whole combination of things did Hauck in."

"Bennett?" Sue Lynn asked.

"Bennett was the last straw, I think," McCall said. "According to Bennett, Hauck really cracked when Bennett started telling him how Cindy was using him. How she didn't really care for him, that she just wanted Veir to leave her alone. Bennett thought it was a power trip—'Look how much I can fuck with this guy'—but it probably only confirmed what Hauck suspected about Cindy. I mean, the girl was no Sunday School teacher. Bennett told Hauck that Cindy used to do both of them—Veir and Bennett—at the same time."

Isen let out a long breath.

"Hauck must have felt abandoned by everyone. His battalion commander was out to get him, as was one of his fellow lieutenants. This woman he was trying to help was using him. His own uncle had told him he was fucking up. And all of this was because the kid wanted to belong to an organization that deserved his loyalty."

They sat quietly for a moment, Hauck's last requiescat.

"What'll happen to Bennett?" Isen asked after a moment.

"He could be court-martialed for making false statements to an investigator. He knew more about what happened in that parking lot than he told me initially. Or they might just boot him."

"How about Veir?" Sue Lynn wanted to know.

"We let the colonel stew a little bit last night while we searched his apartment," McCall continued. "Turns out he had a lot of memorabilia from his victims: underwear, shoes, jewelry, Barbara Ann Yonders's driver's license." She ticked the inventory off on her fingers.

"Why would he have all that?" Sue Lynn asked. "Didn't he realize that would be evidence? Did he want to get caught?"

"Didn't look to me like Veir wanted to get caught," Isen said, twisting the cap off another beer. "He led me around Washington, knowing that Cindy was dead, so that I'd think she was still alive and that he was looking for her."

"I think that pattern holds for Veir: he was always after the ultimate rush, the ultimate brush with the law. 'How close can I come to getting caught without getting caught? How can I manipulate the investigators?' And every time he got away with something, the stakes went a little higher, the challenge had to be a little more difficult."

"The games he played in DC had to be way up there on the challenge scale," Isen said. "He knew what we'd suspect he was doing there, and he didn't care. He led us—me— around, probably laughing the whole time."

"So he was the one who jumped you," Sue Lynn said.

"No doubt."

"But even that wasn't the supreme statement of his confidence," McCall said. "Turns out Veir was the one who called in the anonymous tip about where to find Cindy's remains. He felt so in control that he thought he could lead us to her body *and* make us believe that Hauck killed her."

"But you have enough evidence to get him? I mean, with all the stuff you found in his apartment?" Sue Lynn asked.

"Sure. Probably murder one," McCall said. "But I wouldn't be surprised if he confesses. I mean, he sees the case stacked up against him. If the interviewer acknowledges how clever he's been, Veir might talk. That's what he wants—recognition."

"Conspicuous by his absence is Colonel Kent," Darlington said as the television cameras panned the division's VIPs.

"You think it'll go hard on him?" Isen asked.

"I hope so," Sue Lynn said. "It's because of people just like him—people willing to turn away, to ignore wrong-doing—that Veir made it this far."

"It would have been better if Kent had come clean earlier," McCall said. "He and Tremmore spoke about those transfers; he had a chance. But at least if Tremmore ends his career, Kent has enough time in to retire."

"Speaking of retiring, what about Flynn?" Sue Lynn asked. "Do you think he'll hang it up?"

"I don't know," Isen answered. "He's a pretty tough old bird, but I'm sure he'll beat himself up about all this for some time."

"Why did he jerk you around so much?" McCall asked. "Letting you go ahead, then trying to pull you back in so many times. What was he afraid of?"

"Of finding out just what he found out, I think," Isen said. "That his harping on his nephew about rooming with Savin made Hauck vulnerable. More important, it alienated Hauck; he didn't feel like he could go to his family for help with all this other crap."

"When someone gets to be in Flynn's position," Darlington continued, "with that much invested in the Army, well, you want to believe you've dedicated your life to an institution that's fundamentally good. I can see why he wouldn't want to uncover so much that was wrong, so much evil."

"And it is—the Army is still fundamentally good," Isen said. "Because most of the people are good."

McCall stood; Isen looked up to see her watching him, a tiny glint of a smile on her lips.

"I'd best be going," she said. "I'm sure I'll see you around the courtroom, Major Isen."

"Don't you want me to come down here and be your partner?" he asked her as he pulled himself upright.

"Not a chance," McCall answered. "I made just enough points with this case to get me out of the hole I fell into when I linked up with you in the first place."

Isen and McCall shook hands. McCall held out her hand to Sue Lynn, who pulled the smaller woman into an embrace. McCall, relaxed as a two-by-four, mumbled "thanks" when Sue Lynn turned her loose.

Darlington and Isen walked McCall outside, then stood arm in arm and waved until her car disappeared around a corner.

"She'll make a good investigator," Isen said. "A good cop."

"So you're a fan of hers, now, too?" Sue Lynn asked.

"Everything except that wardrobe."

Alone again, they sat on the couch and kicked off their boots. On the screen across from them the President was shaking hands with a soldier who was all of nineteen. The President smiled widely; the soldier had given up all pretense of looking martial and was simply staring wide-eyed in the glow of celebrity.

"I can't help but wonder," Isen said, "if Hauck's family is satisfied. If they're even happy they pushed so hard. I mean, Veir had to be stopped, but finding out the reasons Hauck killed himself doesn't make it any easier to accept. We got an explanation, but their son is still dead."

"At least no one else is going to die because of Harlan Veir," Sue Lynn answered. "And considering that this investigation almost didn't take place, that's quite an accomplishment.

"You did a good job, here. One that needed to be done," she went on. Then, smiling, "Maybe you should take up a new line of work: Mark Isen, Military Private Eye."

"No, I don't think so. All I did was find another line of work that doesn't suit me," Isen said. "Like my job at the Pentagon."

He slouched down on the couch, watching the television screen.

"I just wish I was going to stick around here with the troops. With guys like that."

The young soldier in the picture was now smiling broadly at the President, even mugging for the camera. Isen wondered if the GI would have been so relaxed had Veir been at the helm.

"You've done a lot for those guys, Mark. And not just the ones in Veir's battalion. Don't you think it's a little self-centered to want a bigger role than that? By exposing Harlan Veir you've done something for the *Army.* How many people can say that?"

Isen smiled at her and tucked his hand under her leg.

"Maybe you're right," he said. "It's just that I think of myself as a field soldier, and I've always told myself I'm happiest in that role. I guess I've said that for so long I really believe it, to the exclusion of other things."

"Roles are great," Sue Lynn said. She used the remote to turn down the sound on the TV. "They help us define who we are. But they can be limiting, too."

Isen turned toward her on the couch, reached out and brushed her hair away from her face.

"I got a scare down here," Isen confessed. "For a few days there I thought I'd torpedoed my career. And I realized I didn't have much else."

He picked a beer bottle off the table and took a slow drink.

"I felt like the Army was ready to turn on me," he said.

On the TV screen, the President was happily posing for pictures amid a group of GIs who were clustered around him, some with their helmets off, one brave enough to put his hand on the President's shoulder. The Chief Executive, mobbed by admirers, looked like the winning coach in a team picture.

"So what kept you in the fight?" Sue Lynn asked, taking his hand, lacing her fingers and his.

"Look at that," Isen interrupted, pointing at the screen. A few of Foote's men had pulled cameras from the deep pockets of their uniforms and were snapping pictures like mad tourists. One youngster, standing behind the President's left shoulder, mouthed *Hi Mom* to the television.

Sue Lynn didn't repeat the question. Instead, she studied Isen's eyes, alight and alive, as he watched his precious soldiers.

ED RUGGERO

"Ed Ruggero writes about men in combat like a soldier who's been there."
—John Harrington, *The Oklahoman*

○ **38 NORTH YANKEE**   70022-7/$5.99

○ **THE COMMON DEFENSE**   73009-6/$5.99

○ **FIREFALL**   73011-8/$5.99

○ **BREAKING RANKS**   89172-3/$6.99

Available from Pocket Books